A LABOUR
OF LOVE

Anne Baker

headline

First published in 2007
by HEADLINE PUBLISHING GROUP

First published in paperback in 2008
by HEADLINE PUBLISHING GROUP

8

ISBN 978 0 7553 3339 4

Typeset in Baskerville by Avon DataSet Ltd,
Bidford on Avon, Warwickshire

Printed and bound in Great Britain by
CPI Group (UK) Ltd, Croydon, CR0 4YY

HEADLINE PUBLISHING GROUP
An Hachette Livre UK Company
338 Euston Road
London NW1 3BH

www.headline.co.uk

I'd like to thank those who helped me research the complexities of dyslexia for this novel.

While A LABOUR OF LOVE can be read independently and has a story that stands alone, readers of my earlier novel THE WILD CHILD, which also touches on the subject of dyslexia, will recognise the characters and will find out what happened to them in later life.

Anne Baker

CHAPTER ONE

March 1982

IT WAS RAINING hard as Hilary Snow drove home from Birkenhead. She was well pleased with her shopping spree; she'd found a lovely cream dress and a pair of jeans that really fitted.

She was almost home – the Oak Tree Garden Centre was round the next bend in the road – when her eye was caught by the grey and green uniform of Loxton House School. Her fifteen-year-old son Andy was waiting at the bus stop with his satchel balanced on his head to protect his shoulders from the downpour.

Hilary braked but had passed him before she could stop. What on earth was he hanging about there for? And where was his twin Charlie?

Seconds later, she pulled into the drive of her house and swung the car round to face the garage door. While she was feeling for the gadget to open it, the Birkenhead bus drove past on its way to Chester. Understanding came at that moment and left her struggling with alternate waves of exasperation and sympathy.

She'd garaged the car and got her packages as far as the

front door when Andy and Charlie came running up together. They were non-identical twins and really not very much alike, though both were tall and skinny and had fairish hair. Andy was a little taller and broader than his brother.

'Hello, Mum,' they chorused cheerily.

'Inside, you two,' she said, grimly pushing the door open. 'Andrew, you're soaked. Go and hang your blazer in the airing cupboard.'

As Hilary passed the hall mirror, her frown showed she was harassed, but although she was struggling to control her figure she still managed to look a little less than her forty-four years. In the kitchen, her husband Ben was making a pot of tea. Hilary had asked him to be here when the children came home from school in case she wasn't back in time. Their ten-year-old son Jamie was already at the table tucking into milk and biscuits.

'I see you managed to find what you wanted.' Ben was eyeing her packages.

'Yes, I'm quite pleased . . .' Suddenly, Hilary felt tired and dispirited. 'Twins.' Her voice was severe. 'You're up to something, and if it's what I think it is, I shall be cross with you.' Both faces assumed expressions of innocence. 'Why, Andrew, were you waiting outside in the rain? Charlie, have you played truant from school today?'

A flush ran up Charlie's cheeks, and she could see he was close to tears. 'Sorry, Mum.'

'You promised you wouldn't!' Hilary felt near to tears herself. She knew dyslexia was the root cause of Charlie's problems and that he found it difficult to cope in school, but there seemed no end to the troubles it brought.

Both twins were dyslexic but Charlie was more badly

affected than Andy. In the early years at school they'd struggled with the alphabet and their reading had fallen behind that of the class. They'd been kept down a year, and it had left Charlie with a crippling sense of failure.

Once Hilary had come to understand the scale of the problem, the twins had had special coaching from her sister Isobel, younger by four years, and her husband Sebastian, who were both teachers. Thanks to their help, the twins were both able to read adequately, but Charlie had never thrown off the insecurity and the feeling that he was going to fail again that had been instilled in him in primary school.

'Charlie, you've got to stay in class.' Ben was angry too. 'Last time you were caught truanting, I told you I'd give you one last chance. What is the point of paying school fees for you if you won't stay there and learn? Do this again and you'll be going to the comprehensive next term. I've had enough.'

Charlie's face was scarlet with distress. 'I don't care. I hate school,' he shouted. 'I don't care about next term. I don't want there to be a next term. I want to leave school for good this summer.'

He shrugged the strap of his satchel off his shoulder and let it thump to the kitchen floor, and then ran upstairs.

When the twins had sat the eleven plus, Andy, who was quieter by nature and able to concentrate for longer, had achieved a grammar school place, while Charlie had not. All through primary school, Hilary had opposed any suggestion that the twins be separated. She thought Charlie needed his twin close to him. Andy was his ally and support.

Ben had been of the opinion that Andy should take up his

grammar school place. Isobel and Sebastian had had their reservations about it.

'The course is academic,' Isobel had said. 'I'm worried Andy won't be able to cope with a foreign language and he might be expected to take Latin too.'

'Only the brightest of dyslexics', Sebastian had said, 'will cope with the written work of a foreign language up to O level standard. Though Andy could be all right orally.'

'He's good at maths,' Hilary had said defensively. 'They both are.'

It was Sebastian who'd thought of a fee-paying school where both could go and had suggested Loxton House.

Hilary had asked, 'Won't they have to pass an entrance exam to get in?'

'They'll certainly be given one and probably an IQ test too. The school will want to know what they're dealing with, but they'll take children who can't get into the grammar schools and the more academic fee-paying schools. Loxton House has smaller classes – fifteen or sixteen is usual. It's a gentler place than the local comprehensive. With a bit of luck they'll both settle down and do reasonably well.'

Ben had said, 'The thought of paying school fees on top of two mortgages scares me.' He was paying one on the business and another on the house. 'We can't afford it.'

Hilary had frowned. 'But we must do what's best for the twins.'

'Then there's Jamie to think of. If we pay school fees for the twins, we should be prepared to do it for him too. It could be a spiralling expense. Wouldn't Andy achieve more if he were pushed?'

'I'm worried Andy will be pushed too hard and won't be

able to cope,' Sebastian had replied. 'Isn't that what happened to Charlie in primary school? His teachers didn't understand his difficulties. Andy can take that sort of pressure better than Charlie – he's emotionally more stable now – but there's a limit to what he can take.'

Hilary considered they'd been very fortunate. When Ben's twin aunts, Prudence and Primrose, heard them discussing the problem, they'd undertaken to pay the twins' school fees. They understood the effects of dyslexia only too well. Now she turned on Andrew. 'I do wish you wouldn't cover for him. Is it the first time he's done it this term?'

'Ah, Mum . . .'

It wasn't, then! Hilary's patience deserted her. 'That blazer . . .'

'Yes, all right, Mum, the airing cupboard.' Andy was pouring two glasses of milk. He took a handful of biscuits and was about to stuff them in his blazer pocket when he caught Hilary's glance.

'Use a tray,' she reminded him, rolling her eyes upwards.

He reached for one and emptied twice as many biscuits on it before rushing upstairs after Charlie. A moment later, Jamie took more biscuits and followed him up.

Ben sighed and pushed a cup of tea in front of Hilary. She burst out, 'What are we going to do with them?' It was a cry from the heart.

'We're doing all we can.'

'I do feel for poor Charlie, but . . .'

'He was squashed in his first school, really put down by some of his teachers because he wasn't able to read. Isobel was so certain she could teach him . . .'

'She has, Ben. His reading age is now officially classed as

fifteen, and that's near enough adult standard. Though she says the twins' spelling will always be a problem.'

Ben said, 'There's more to it than just bad spelling. It's left Charlie with on-going emotional problems we haven't been able to solve.'

'I know. Andy says Charlie's a nervous wreck if he's asked questions in class, and he's just said he hates school and can't wait to leave.'

'For all the good it's doing him, he might just as well. I doubt he's learning anything.'

'No! He has to stay on at school,' Hilary protested. 'At least until he's taken his O levels.'

'But exams are what's bothering him,' Ben barked. 'He's afraid of failing and that we and Isobel will be disappointed in him.'

'I'm going to tell him we just want him to try his best. Perhaps that might help.'

Dyslexia had first been described in Britain in 1896 by Dr W. Pringle Morgan, a school doctor, but his findings were neither understood nor taken up. Then, as now, nobody was sure why dyslexics should find it so difficult to learn to read and write.

Ben said he'd never heard the word dyslexia when he'd been growing up. He'd known that his mother couldn't read or write, and he had difficulty learning to read himself. His mother didn't want to talk about her problems and Ben was ashamed to admit to his. He said his school treated him like an idiot, and in time he'd come to believe he wasn't very bright.

When Ben had to do National Service and leave home, it was his mother's twin sisters, Aunt Prudence and Aunt

Primrose, who had replied to his letters on her behalf. They were sick children's nurses and they not only looked after his mother but had taken on the task of teaching Ben. It was thanks to them he'd learned to read by the age of eight, instead of giving up like his mother. Writing had proved even harder to master, but his aunts had kept him at it.

Ben had had the gift of the gab and he'd always been interested in horticulture. He'd worked for several years as a salesman for a seed company, though he'd longed to have a small business of his own. Without further education and qualifications he knew working for himself was the only way he could earn more.

When he was told that his twins were dyslexic, he'd said to Hilary, 'We need to bring up our boys so they can run this business. If nobody else will give them a job, they can always earn their living here.'

From an early age, Ben had shown them how to make themselves useful in the garden centre. It made them feel grown up and they seemed to enjoy it. They began coming over to join him without being asked.

He taught them all he knew about the soil: why it must have drainage and why he mixed sand and fertilisers into his loam. Ben grew a lot of his stock in pots; he took the boys into his potting shed and showed them how to mix the compost and prepare the pots. He taught them the names of the plants and how to propagate seedlings and take cuttings.

While they worked together he talked about what he was hoping to achieve. He took them round his nursery stock at regular intervals to point out which plants were thriving and which not, and what needed to be done next.

As they grew older he found all three of the boys quite a

help in getting the stock ready for sale. He encouraged them to go into the shop and lend a hand there; they knew how to wrap the plants in cellophane and tie them up with ribbon. He showed them how to keep the books and work out how much was earned by each sowing of seed, and how one variety of plant could fare better and earn more than another.

It soon became clear that a big attraction for all three boys was driving the tractor. They fought to do any job that involved using it. He let them plough and rotovate the nursery beds, spread fertiliser, and move the goods-filled trailers round the internal roads of the site. Charlie was so keen, Jamie didn't often get a look in.

Ben also had a small Ford van with the garden centre logo in red and green on both sides, which he used for collecting seeds and materials and for delivering plants and flowers. He had regular orders to provide cut flowers and plants to hotels in both Chester and Birkenhead and was seeking more.

One day, Charlie said, 'Dad, will you show me how the van works? I'd like to learn to drive it.'

'You're only fifteen. You can't drive yet.'

'I can on your private roads. Go on, Dad. I'll be sixteen in July, and by the time I'm seventeen I'll have learned how to do it. I'll be able to drive when all my friends are just starting to learn. I'll be ahead of everybody for once.'

Because Ben knew how much Charlie had suffered by being bottom of the class, and Sebastian had advised them to play down the bad spelling and let the twins concentrate on what they enjoyed and were good at, he said, 'Come on then.'

'Does it work the same as the tractor?'

'In many ways it's simpler. There's only one gear box.'

'What about cars?'

'Only one gear box in cars too.'

Ben was surprised how quickly Charlie picked up the basics of driving. He could steer and change gear smoothly, as though by instinct. When he told him so, Charlie smiled. 'I've been driving the tractor for years, Dad.'

'So you have.' For once, Charlie seemed to have real aptitude.

'Can I drive the van round the garden centre once in a while, to get the feel of it?'

'Only when the shop's closed. Don't forget we have customers' cars coming into the car park.'

'But when it's closed I can?'

'I suppose so.' Ben reflected that the van was getting old. He'd need a new one soon, so it wouldn't hurt to let the twins learn to drive on this one. 'But you'll have to ask me for the key,' he added.

Immediately, the van became more popular than the tractor and Andy was clamouring to learn to drive it too. It pleased the family to watch Charlie reversing and manoeuvring round the painted markings on the empty car park as he taught himself to drive, and they praised his efforts extravagantly. He was developing useful skills.

Occasionally, Ben would take the boys with him when he took the van out on a job, and talk them through every action as he drove. They both enjoyed that. Hilary gave each of them a copy of the Highway Code so they could learn the rules of the road.

Jamie was banned from going near the van until he was fifteen, but he was getting more time to practise on the tractor. Because he'd had extra help with reading and writing from the beginning of his school career, he'd been able to keep up with his class work. He was still having regular tuition from Isobel and had to work twice as hard as the average child, but he hadn't failed in any way and was a normal happy nine year old, with more self-confidence than either Andy or Charlie. The family was pleased with Jamie's progress.

'Sod's law, isn't it?' Ben said to Hilary. 'We'd be sitting pretty now if it wasn't for the boys' dyslexia. We've achieved so much of what we wanted . . .'

'You may have, but not me.' She was a little short with him.

'Sorry . . . your writing. But Hilly, you aren't doing badly. You've had four books published, another's coming out in the autumn and you're working on your sixth.'

'I'm working hard but I'm not earning much, am I?' Hilary was disappointed with the small amount her work earned for her. She was married to a businessman: she knew that all his enterprises were expected to make a profit, otherwise what was the point?

'It takes time for readers to get to know your books,' he said gently.

'I've been at it for six years and that's a long time.'

'You're aiming for the sky. That's your trouble. Look, we have the comfortable house we always wanted, and after you inherited your share of Aunt Mavis's fortune we were able to pay off the dreaded mortgages.'

'And have capital to invest in the garden centre.'

'Yes. Thanks to that, the business is growing fast and providing all the income we need.'

Ben was right, of course. It helped enormously that their money worries were over, and life was even better for him now that he no longer needed to spend most of his time in the shop.

Three years ago, Stella Ingram, one of the part-time women he'd always employed at busy periods, told them she was divorcing her husband and would need a full-time job. Hilary knew Ben had been thinking of employing a manager in the shop so he'd have more time to give to other parts of the business.

'Shall I ask Stella if she'd like the job?' he had asked. 'She knows what's she's doing and she's trustworthy.'

Hilary had frowned. 'Ask her, but she may not want it. It would mean she'd have to work every weekend and take days off in the week. She's got two sons to look after.'

Charlie was friendly with Gary, the younger of the two. He often came to play football on the pitch Ben had laid out for the boys on the site. However, it seemed Stella's mother, a widow, would be moving in to live with her, and Stella would like to manage the garden shop. From then on, they'd had no need to employ part-timers. When the shop was busy, Ben would lend a hand with one of the boys, or if necessary both he and Hilary could help out.

Hilary was glad Ben still felt as full of enthusiasm for his garden centre as when he'd started, and that everything was going well for him, but she felt success was eluding her.

CHAPTER TWO

T HE FOLLOWING day, when Ben had got up from the lunch table to go back to work, Hilary stacked the dishes in the dishwasher, then set about preparing a casserole for their evening meal.

All morning, she'd been working up ideas for her new book, to be called *The Dog Days of Summer*, and as she chopped beef into cubes and peeled onions her mind was still trying to round out its characters. It would be her sixth book.

Back in 1976, her agent Fern Granville had found a very reputable publisher for her first book, *The Night Star*. They published general fiction, both literary and popular, and in addition also had a strong non-fiction list. Hilary had almost burst with pride when she saw her first book in print.

She was told it had sold reasonably well. Her contract had been only for the one book but her publisher had asked to have first refusal of her next one. She understood that was not unreasonable for a beginner and had set about writing another book right away. She'd called it *The Primrose Path*.

When it was finished, Fern had sent it to her editor Elizabeth Jones, who read it and said she would like to publish it. From then on Hilary had had a contract for her books before they were written, but for only one book at a time.

Recently, she'd heard that two-book contracts were becoming quite usual and had asked Fern if she could get her a two-book contract for her sixth and seventh books.

'I don't see why not,' Fern had told her. 'I'll have a word with Elizabeth about it.'

Hilary was frying the ingredients for her casserole when the phone rang. She pulled the frying pan to one side and went out to the hall to answer it. She was not surprised to hear Elizabeth's voice. 'Hello, Hilary.'

'Hello. How are you?' She felt quite sparky. She was expecting to hear that a new contract would soon be on its way to her. Elizabeth always had news about the publishing world and Hilary enjoyed their telephone chats. Today, however, Elizabeth didn't sound her usual cheery self.

She said, 'I'm afraid I have bad news for you.'

'It's not to be a contract for two books?' Hilary could feel her high spirits slipping away.

'I'm sorry, but it's worse than that. You know the book trade has not done so well over recent years? And sales of your last two books have been disappointing.'

Hilary felt the strength drain from her knees.

'Publishing profits are down too, and I'm afraid that it means we aren't able to offer further contracts to four of our writers. I'm sorry to have to tell you that one of them is you.'

Hilary felt for a chair and sat down with a little bump. She was shocked. Elizabeth had said she was concerned about her sales figures but it hadn't prepared her for this.

'I like your books very much, Hilary. It's just that they are a bit on the literary side and nobody can sell books of that sort in large quantities. You should try a more popular style, something lighter. Your style of writing tends to be a bit over-formal, if you know what I mean?'

Hilary was devastated. It had taken her years to get a publisher and now she was being told they didn't want another book from her. She'd tried so hard, given up so much, to get this far. Sacrificed her nursing job to give herself more time, got up at dawn to write, fought with Ben, delegated the care of her children to others, pushed herself to the limit; and now she was back to square one.

She couldn't get off the phone quickly enough. Tears were running down her cheeks. She went to the kitchen table and let her head sink on her hands. What was she to do now?

It was only a matter of minutes before the phone was ringing again. Hilary blew her nose before she picked it up.

'Hello, Hilary.' It was Fern Granville. 'Has Elizabeth spoken to you?'

'Yes.' Her voice seemed to squeak.

'I enjoy your books, Hilary. They're well written, but they don't appeal to everybody. You should forget the long words and make them easier to read. For volume sales, you need to write what will appeal to the average woman. They need more action, more excitement and perhaps a little less intro-spection on the part of your characters. I think you should try writing for a somewhat different market.'

Hilary stifled a snuffle. Her agent and editor were clearly sharing the same hymn sheet. 'I don't know . . .'

'You write short stories for women's magazines, don't you?'

'I used to.' She'd been devoting herself to full-length novels recently.

'There you are then. They must appeal to a wide market.

That's the style to aim for. Keep it light and keep the story moving.'

'Yes.'

Hilary knew she should be taking notice of this. It was good advice, but it was hard to take in when she'd just been dropped by her publisher. Apart from arresting her writing career when she'd thought of it as being in full flood, it felt like rejection. It made her feel that the books she'd striven over were not good enough. It was easy for Fern and Elizabeth to say they'd enjoyed them, but what did that matter if they didn't sell? She'd hoped to earn her living by writing them.

Fern was going on. 'I do feel for my writers when something as bad as this happens. The best advice I can give is to get down to writing another book as soon as possible. If you want to bounce ideas off me, do feel free.'

When Hilary put the phone down she wept a little and then went to the cloakroom to rinse her face. She decided a cup of tea would help to pull her together, but the first thing she saw when she returned to the kitchen was the gas flaring away with her frying pan six inches from the flames. With a sigh, she stirred the congealing contents and pushed the pan back on the heat. She felt thoroughly deflated and out of sorts.

Ben realised something was wrong as soon as he came in. She told him the bare bones but didn't want to talk about it. Once, she'd have been able to weep on his shoulder, pour out all her troubles and be comforted, but those days had gone. He did tell the rest of the family and within two days they were offering sympathy and support, but that didn't ease her searing disappointment.

It was a week before Hilary could bear to look again at the

manuscript of *The Dog Days of Summer*. The characters had stayed in her mind; what she needed to do was make a lot more happen to them. They would have to lead more exciting lives than she'd originally envisaged. She had a first draft of nearly a quarter of the book, but perhaps it *was* a bit slow. She began mapping out a stronger plot and told herself she was lucky she'd had a contract for her fifth book. At least that would be published in the autumn.

She hadn't realised until she took a hard look at it that her writing style was over-formal. She'd always enjoyed playing with words and language – didn't every writer? And the working of the human mind was an abiding interest. To change was not going to be easy.

She read a couple of short stories in a magazine, and pondered on the style. Years ago she'd sold quite a lot of short stories. She should be able to write a full-length book in a similarly light vein.

She started work on the first chapter, but she knew she wasn't getting it right. It didn't please her. For a bit of light relief she wrote a short story and it sold the first time she sent it out. She returned to her novel and had two or three abortive attempts at knocking it into shape. Then, to give herself a break, she laid the book aside and wrote several more stories. It seemed the easier option and she put off working on her novel for the time being.

It was still dark when Hilary's younger sister Isobel was torn from sleep by the sound of her one-year-old daughter crying in the next bedroom. Beside her, she heard Sebastian, her husband, grunt sleepily as he levered himself out of bed. Then came his soft and soothing whisper.

'Daisy love, it's all right. Daddy's here. Shush, shush now, we don't want to wake Mummy, do we? What's the matter, then?'

The crying subsided. Isobel turned over in bed and caught a glimpse of Seb pacing the floor in the gloom cradling Daisy against his shoulder. It was in the early hours of Saturday morning and Seb wouldn't have to get up for work, so she needn't feel guilty about letting him do it.

Seb had promised this sort of help when he'd been trying to persuade her to have another child. Isobel had put it off for years, though she'd known Seb would be an excellent dad. He'd always been good with Sophie though he wasn't her natural father.

He understood children, had infinite patience with them and seemed to enjoy their company. All the same, it surprised her to find him willing to get up in the night to Daisy like this. What Sebastian had wanted, of course, was to father a child of his own.

Isobel didn't feel particularly drawn to children in general, but her reluctance to conceive another was brought about by more than that. She had what she thought of as *a past*.

She'd counted her first years in London as her happiest. She'd been in love with Rupert Broadbent, a married man, whom she'd met years before when she'd had a student holiday job showing visitors around the Walker art gallery in Liverpool. She'd become Rupert's darling, his mistress, and been cosseted by his love. He'd provided her with a luxury flat, bought her a car and showered gifts on her, as well as taking her to West End shows and restaurants.

Isobel felt guilty when she thought of his wife Margaret, but at the same time she wanted to see more of him and play a larger part in his life.

Once he realised she was pregnant, Rupert had told her he'd ask Margaret for a divorce. Isobel thought he must have been telling Margaret about her when he suffered his fatal stroke, but she didn't really know. Other than hearing it from Margaret, there was no way she could find out. He'd promised to come and see her that Sunday morning. She'd waited on tenterhooks all day but he hadn't come and he'd asked her not to ring him at home. The following day she'd tried to contact him at his office and been told of his stroke by his secretary.

Isobel had been devastated by Rupert's sudden death, and even after sixteen years she couldn't think about it rationally. She'd been working as a primary school teacher, but Rupert's generosity meant she'd never needed to consider the cost of anything. His death had left her pregnant with her salary as her only means of support.

She'd been shocked when Sebastian, Rupert's estranged son, had joined the staff of the same school as their remedial teacher. Father and son had had little contact since Sebastian had left home in his teens following a row. Sebastian felt he was being pressurised to make his career the running of the family business. Isobel could empathise with his loss, though he knew nothing of her liaison with his father. It had been their secret. She felt Rupert's death had traumatised her, clouded her judgement and made her do a terrible thing. When Sebastian had fallen in love with her, instead of telling him the truth she'd tried to pass Sophie off as his child, because she hadn't wanted to face her family without a father for her baby and she'd desperately needed his financial support. She'd been weighed down with guilt about that decision ever since, and had never regretted anything more.

Sebastian had known she was lying; he'd been present at Sophie's birth and knew the hospital staff considered her a full-term baby, not one of seven months' gestation as Isobel had been insisting. But it was years before he knew Sophie was his half-sister. It had soured the early years of their marriage and brought them close to divorce. Isobel had left him and come back to her family, but life as a single working mother had not been easy either.

Seb had never given up asking her to try again. He'd kept telling her he loved her and wanted to be with her and Sophie. Over the past decade they'd at last managed to settle down more happily together.

Isobel felt she owed Seb a great deal and had eventually agreed to give him the baby he wanted. Having Daisy had been a very different experience and she was as thrilled as Seb to have her. Looking after her now, with Seb taking more than his fair share of the child-rearing, had proved to be a shared pleasure and had drawn them even closer. He'd persuaded her to give up teaching for a while and stay home to look after their baby.

'When Daisy starts school you can go back to teaching if that's what you want.'

Isobel couldn't make up her mind what she wanted, but she was glad to be back on Merseyside. She loved her cottage, loved having her mother living a few doors along the terrace and her sister Hilary close by.

When Isobel had found her first teaching job on Merseyside, she'd wanted Sophie to attend the same school because it made it easier to look after her. Sophie had turned out to be brighter than average, and as Isobel was to teach Sophie's age group she was put into the class above, as it was thought unwise for her to be in her mother's class. Sophie had achieved good marks at that level, and so had continued up the school as the youngest in her class. She was also a very pretty girl. Sebastian couldn't have been more proud of her if she had been his own child.

All their circumstances had changed since those early days. Aunt Mavis had left enough money to keep all the family in comfort. Sebastian said it was a huge relief not to have to count the pennies and worry about debt. Isobel knew they now had everything to make them happy.

Later that morning, Isobel held her umbrella close as she took the short cut through the garden centre up to her sister's house. The rain was drumming down but she was not displeased. If it was impossible for Charlie to play football, he'd settle down and work with less fuss. Since the twins had started at secondary school, Isobel had cut down the time she spent coaching them to Saturday mornings only, because they had to do their school homework. Sebastian had worked out a syllabus to help with written work and spelling and Isobel did her best to make it as interesting as possible.

By ten o'clock she had four boys round the playroom table. As they wrote in their books, the only sound was Charlie's heavy breathing. Jamie loved to join his older brothers, and in addition Isobel had him round at her house direct from school on two afternoons each week. She was full of praise for him. Andy was sucking his lip as he concentrated, and Gary Ingram, the fourth, was scribbling hard. He felt it was a privilege to be allowed to join their Saturday sessions.

She studied Gary now. He was small for his age and very skinny. He looked forlorn, with his dark straight hair falling over his face. He always seemed worried and there was a beseeching note in his voice when he spoke. He looked younger and less robust than the twins although he was their age. She felt sorry for him. With earlier help he'd have coped better. The combination of being overshadowed by a clever older brother and the break-up of his parents' marriage had not helped his schoolwork.

Gary had been friendly with the twins since their primary school days. He'd followed his older brother Paul to the local comprehensive, where Paul had done well before going on to Sheffield University to study maths and economics. But Gary had told Isobel he hadn't learned to read until he was ten and that it was Paul who'd done most to help him.

Isobel had met Gary's mother Stella several times in Hilary's kitchen as they'd chatted over cups of tea. They had a lot in common and got on well. It had been Hilary's suggestion that Gary should join the Saturday morning sessions while Stella worked in the shop. She was glad Charlie had found a friend.

The twins were not so close as they'd once been. Partly, Isobel thought, because Andrew was holding his own in class, whereas Charlie had virtually given up.

Sophie Broadbent stretched out on the back seat of her father's car and said, 'I can't wait for the holidays.'

Her friend Judith Salter was sitting beside her. 'We'll be breaking up for Easter next Wednesday. Only another few days.'

Judith was in her form at school and lived in a big house almost opposite Aunt Primmy and Aunt Prue in the village. Her mother was a solicitor and worked four days a week in

Chester. On those days she took Judith and Ross, her older brother, to school, but on Fridays, by arrangement, Sebastian took them in with Sophie. Judith and Sophie saw a lot of each other and their parents had become friends too.

On Fridays, Sophie sat on the back seat with Judith and Dad said they did nothing but giggle. Ross sat in front with him and discussed serious matters like politics or the state of the economy.

Sometimes Sophie walked down to Judith's house in the evenings. They went to the local youth club together, and occasionally to the pictures. When they'd been in the fourth form, Sophie had counted Judith her best friend, but now they were older she thought Emily Burke was more her type. But Emily lived the other side of Chester and it wasn't so easy to see her out of school hours.

Sophie studied the back of Ross's head. He was dark like Judith and on him the strong Salter features were handsome enough, but he had a superior air and a very high opinion of his own abilities. That could get up Sophie's nose; she didn't like him much.

She took a small mirror from her school bag. She'd been taking more interest in her looks for the last year. Now, at just turned fifteen, she was encouraging her long corn-coloured hair to curl round her face.

She was pleased with her fair complexion except for the pimple she'd developed near her mouth. This morning she'd helped herself to some of her mother's make-up base to hide it but now that had all worn off, leaving the spot pink and shiny.

Sophie sighed, and let her green eyes wander to Judith. She looked even worse with her rather too large and masculine nose. Sophie thought her rather plain, poor girl.

'Holidays are bliss,' Judith sighed happily.

Sophie couldn't agree more. 'We're going to have a smashing time, aren't we, Dad?'

'I hope so, but I think of them more as a well-earned rest.'

Sebastian Broadbent was a Londoner born and bred, but had come up to live on Merseyside because this was where Isobel came from, and she wanted to stay near her family. He was the headmaster of a primary school in Chester, and since Sophie was ten he'd been taking her back and forth to the Queen's School in the city. Now, Sophie felt they were close. He said it was because the daily drive gave them a chance to talk on their own.

He had his window open an inch at the top and his hair was lifting up and down in the draught. It was a faded brown now in middle age and just a tad thin on top. He had that broad-shouldered confidence that most schoolmasters develop, with a rather high-bridged nose and dark green eyes like hers. Well, they were the same colour as hers, but his were kind eyes, understanding eyes, and eyes that showed love. Her dad was one in a million. At home you'd never even know he was a schoolmaster, and he treated her like an adult.

Easter was a good time, with chocolate eggs in every shop window. If they got fine weather, Dad would take the whole family on trips out. But what Sophie was really looking forward to was going to London with him. She would have him to herself on the long journey and Dad's family always made a fuss of them both. Mum was a bit funny about his family. She said she couldn't get on with them and preferred to stay at home.

CHAPTER THREE

ISOBEL'S MOTHER Flora turned over the brochure Tom had given her and watched him pile logs on to her fire. 'A trip to New York?'

'It would be exciting, wouldn't it?' His dark eyes danced with enthusiasm. 'A treat to wake us out of our lethargy.'

He sat back in the armchair on the other side of the grate, smiling and rubbing his hands in a show of satisfaction. 'It's lovely to have a wood fire crackling in the hearth on these chilly spring evenings.'

Tom kept saying things like that, to show her how much he appreciated sharing her comfortable cottage. She tried to respond in the same vein.

'Lovely to have you to carry the wood in and stoke the fire.'

He often told Flora that he loved her and how happy he'd been since they'd been married. He'd smile at her and say, 'Four years of bliss.'

Flora didn't want to let her misgivings show. She was no longer sure that marrying him had been the right thing to do, though she had proposed to Tom. He'd told her he had no worldly goods to bring to the marriage and he didn't want to sponge off her. At the time, it seemed she'd had to persuade him, but now . . . ?

She frowned. 'New York, though?' The city that never sleeps. It would be exhausting, but she didn't want to say so. It would surely make Tom see her as an ancient relic. She was ten years older than he was, and the passing years didn't seem to show on him. She'd thought those ten years a bit of a turn-off when she was contemplating the marriage, but it hadn't changed her mind.

She had been a little concerned that she seemed to be making all the running. She didn't want him to think her forward.

She'd known Tom was living in somewhat straitened circumstances. He'd never talked much about himself; she'd had to ask. He'd told her he'd been made redundant by a building firm. Hilary had pointed out that there was a lot of building going on these days and if he wanted another job, he shouldn't find it impossible.

Flora was seriously thinking of proposing to him when Tom had told her he'd spent his life running a construction business he'd inherited from his father, but it had crashed with many others in the recession of the early seventies. His comfortable lifestyle had collapsed and his wife of thirty years had become depressed at their situation and had committed suicide. Flora could see that he had been devastated and could quite understand why he hadn't wanted to talk about it.

She'd been very much in love then and had devoted herself to helping him forget the past. In the early heady days of marriage, she'd told him she was glad he was the younger because he'd probably live longer than her and she didn't want to be on her own again.

When she'd said that, Tom had reached across the table to kiss her cheek and said seriously, 'Flora, I don't know how I'd manage without you. I can't even contemplate it. I mean, the thought of having to move out of this lovely cottage and live by myself in rooms or lodgings . . .'

Flora was conscience-stricken. 'Tom! I wouldn't want that to happen.'

'But it's your cottage . . . If anything happened to you, all this would go to your daughters, wouldn't it?'

Tom was right. As her will stood, everything she owned would be divided between Hilary and Isobel.

His voice was gentle. 'I think if you marry, it makes your existing will null and void. That it's usual to make a new one, because your wishes will have changed.'

'Of course, Tom. I must do it. I'm sorry.'

'You shared what your sister Mavis left you with your girls.'

'Yes, they're well provided for.' And Tom was not. Flora felt she wasn't being fair to him. 'I'll make an appointment to see a solicitor.'

'There's Mrs Salter who lives opposite the twin aunts in the village. She's a solicitor with a practice in Chester. Shall I make the appointment for you?'

Flora had made a new will in his favour; at the time it had seemed only common sense. Now she was changing her mind and it was so very painful.

She could see the two of them reflected in the mirror on the opposite wall, sitting one each side of the dancing flames, the picture of domestic harmony. It was hard to admit even to herself that the harmony was fading.

Her hair shone silvery white. She'd stopped trying to

colour it, though she still had it stylishly cut. Flora sighed. She was beginning to feel her age.

Tom had the sort of looks that attracted women. They'd attracted her and still did. He had a pencil moustache and dark wiry hair flecked with grey; olive skin that looked tanned even in winter and crinkled round his dark eyes when he smiled. He hadn't any wrinkles and looked years younger than he was.

His appearance reflected the attention he lavished on himself. He chose his clothes with great care. Today he wore a Jermyn Street shirt and silk cravat, topped with a pullover she'd knitted for him, from wool of his choice. Flora studied his bespoke leather brogues sadly. Did marriage have to be like this?

She remembered that at their wedding breakfast Tom had raised his glass of champagne and said to their guests, 'I want you to drink to my bride, and to the many years of contentment we'll share in our old age.'

But the passing years had shown her that Tom didn't want mere contentment. He didn't want to sit at home in carpet slippers to grow old quietly. He still had plenty of drive, wanting to whirl her away on holidays and trips out shopping, and to share treats of all sorts. At seventy-one, Flora sometimes felt less than eager for his frequent treats, though she wanted Tom to enjoy himself and after she'd been drawn into them she often enjoyed them too.

All the same, the words 'A treat to wake us out of our lethargy' had grated. She didn't feel lethargic.

Her first marriage to Harold had been very different. He'd been generous; he'd shared all he could earn but it hadn't been enough to meet their needs. It had taken thrift and tight budgeting on both their parts to manage. After almost four decades of widowhood, money was undoubtedly easier to come by, especially for Flora who had inherited a fortune from her sister Mavis.

She'd always felt sorry for Mavis, who'd never seemed to have much of a life. She was very much older than Flora and had never married, but worked as an accounts clerk in the investment department of a big insurance company. She'd been a loner, never telling her family about her lifetime hobby of investing on the stock market. Her satisfaction had come from watching her investments increase in value, and she was so miserly that she went without instead of meeting her own needs. Flora had to agree with her daughters that her sister had wasted the chance to have a more comfortable life, and she must be careful not to do the same.

Tom's attitude to money was very different from Mavis's: he was a spender. He believed money was meant to be enjoyed.

'How does he earn his living?' her children had wanted to know. 'What does he do?' She'd had to ask him.

'Very little, I'm afraid. I suppose you'd say I live on the largesse of the state. I'm not much of a catch for you, Flora.'

That had made her want to share her good fortune with him. It was only after they were married that she found Tom was spending some of his time going round demolition sites seeking out old fireplaces, bathroom fittings, doors, door knobs and fancy panelling of any sort: anything that might be used to restore a period house. He bought them for a song, cleaned them up and sold them on for much more.

'From building I moved into household bric-a-brac and furniture,' he'd told her. 'Antiques too if I can pick them up cheap.'

He'd taken Flora to some of the sales he attended, but while Tom was in his element talking to the auction room staff and making notes, she got bored with all the waiting about. She'd been surprised to discover he had a lock-up garage where he stored what he bought until he could sell it on. He also had a trailer to transport his stock.

Once they were married, Flora had wanted to share everything she had with Tom. When he confided that he sometimes had difficulty paying for what he bought, she'd made an appointment to see her bank manager and taken Tom with her. She'd turned her current and deposit accounts into joint accounts. After all, thanks to Mavis, she had more than enough money for their needs.

In the first year of their marriage, she'd been surprised at how much Tom could get through, but she'd told herself it didn't matter. Her inheritance could cover it. She'd gone along with his choice of new clothes, though she'd thought the number of expensive suits he wanted rather excessive. On their first Christmas together, she'd helped him choose a Rolex watch as his present, and for their second Christmas he'd wanted a new Mercedes.

Tom had suggested a bigger house, but Flora loved her cottage. She liked the village atmosphere and she was close to her family.

'I don't want to move, Tom.' She'd had to smile at the very notion.

But gradually Flora had begun to resent the way he was spending her money. She didn't want so many new clothes or such frequent holidays.

She sighed and opened the brochure he'd given her showing the delights of New York. Fly out by Concorde and sail back on the *Queen Mary*. Stay in a top hotel and shop in the glossy stores on Fifth Avenue.

'I don't fancy New York,' she told him. She loved being at home. 'No, New York is not on.'

His face fell. 'Oh! But it would be lovely. We could take the ferry out to Staten Island and—'

'That's not my sort of holiday. I prefer to stay put in an interesting place and relax.'

'Like Paris? Would you like to go there?'

Flora had been thinking of a long ago holiday she'd had in Eastbourne with Hilary. They'd sat in the afternoon sun in the hotel garden with books. She smiled. 'Paris isn't the place to relax.'

'But a holiday, yes?'

'In the summer perhaps, when the weather's better.'

Tom got up and kissed her cheek. 'You've been very good to me. You've been my salvation and I'm very grateful. You rescued me, brought me back from the brink.'

It helped to know Tom appreciated what she'd done for him. He had charm and he really showed his love for her. She ought to feel the luckiest woman in the world to have him.

The schools had broken up for the Easter holidays and Sebastian was planning a visit to see his mother before they reopened. He called her *a creaking gate*, and was concerned about her. She'd been ill on and off since his father's sudden death. He telephoned her every week for a long chat and every school holiday he went down to see her. He'd spent a few days with her at New Year but now that seemed a long time ago.

Isobel had never quite managed to throw off her guilt

about Sebastian's family. In the long ago days when she'd been his father's mistress, she'd been full of curiosity about his family. She used to drive past the house to look at it and imagine what it would be like inside. But since she'd married Sebastian, she'd never liked visiting the Pines, his old home. His mother, Margaret, was the wife they'd cheated.

Now she blamed that history for her lack of ease with his family. Sebastian understood her difficulty and tried to reassure her.

'I don't think she knows, love. She's never breathed a word about it to me. I know what Mother's like. If she knew, I'm sure she'd be furious and let fly. It would all have come out long ago.'

'She's been ill for such a long time,' Isobel said. 'Too ill, d'you think, to talk about things like that?'

'She hasn't been too bad these last few years, and she's never mentioned my father.'

'Also, it could be embarrassing, even humiliating for her.'

'She's never said anything to you, has she?'

'No, it's just that I feel uncomfortable in her presence.'

'It's all in your mind, Izzy. Tell yourself Mother knows nothing. She knows you only as my wife; but if you'd rather not, you don't have to come down to see her every time I go. Mother's fond of Sophie; I'll take her. She'll enjoy a few days in London after Easter.'

For some years his sister Charlotte had been living in the family home with her husband and three small boys, so Margaret did have some of her family round her.

Isobel thought it fortunate they lived in London and she didn't have to meet them often.

*

It was seven o'clock and Isobel was almost ready to dish up the chicken supper she was cooking. The kitchen in the cottage was also the dining room and the family had already collected there. Sophie was playing with Daisy, while Sebastian was reminiscing about a holiday they'd had on Anglesey last summer and suggesting they have a few days there this year. Her family was in a relaxed and happy mood.

The phone rang. Isobel happened to be nearest and picked it up. She recognised the rather haughty voice immediately. 'Charlotte here.'

Isobel was expecting the usual stiff enquiries about her health and Sophie's before Charlotte asked to speak to Seb. She met his gaze across the room, and silently mouthed 'Charlotte' to him.

'Is Sebastian there?' Charlotte asked abruptly with no preliminaries. She sounded upset.

Isobel handed over the phone, and was aware that Sophie too was watching Sebastian's face. He began to look serious.

He said, 'I'm so sorry. Give her our love. Yes, of course. I'll ring you back when we've had time to think about it.'

'What's the matter, Dad?' Sophie asked when he put the phone down. 'Is it Gran?'

'Yes.' He sighed. 'She's not at all well. Aunt Charlotte says she has another chest infection and she's asking for me.'

'You'll be going down after Easter for a few days,' Isobel said. 'I thought you'd arranged that?'

'I have, but Charlotte says the doctor has warned her that Mother could be fading. She's not responding to the antibiotics this time and it could be the end. Charlotte's afraid she may not last through the Easter holiday.'

'You want us to go down straight away?' Sophie asked.

'I think we'll have to.' Seb's eyes were troubled.

Only Daisy was not affected by the news. She was still playing with her toy dog on wheels. 'Wuff, wuff,' she cooed, ramming it against her father's legs and laughing up at him.

He stroked her head. 'Mother's asking to see us all. Including you, Daisy.'

Isobel could feel her stomach churning. She'd planned to stay at home to look after her toddler while Seb and Sophie went down after Easter. Now it seemed she'd have no excuse to stay away.

'We have to eat.' She threw herself into dishing up the meal. 'It'll spoil if we don't.'

'When are we going?' Sophie was lifting Daisy into her high chair. 'Tonight or tomorrow?'

'If we went tonight,' Seb said, 'Daisy would sleep through the journey, but I'm tired . . . I suggest we pack after supper and load the car. Then we'll go to bed early and set the alarm for half five. We can be on our way by six and should be through Birmingham before the roads get busy.' His green eyes turned to Isobel. 'You'll come, won't you, Izzy?'

'If you want me to.' She knew it sounded grudging.

'I think, if it's as serious as Charlotte believes and Mother's asking to see us, we all should go to say goodbye,' he said.

'Poor Granny,' Sophie said, tucking into her supper.

It was lunch time when they reached the Pines. Daisy had been quite fractious for the last couple of hours and Sophie had lost patience with her. Isobel had shared the driving with Sebastian and was tired. He pulled the car up by the front door.

Charlotte came out moments later. She wore her dark hair

drawn back in a sophisticated chignon, but she looked drawn and tired. Her brown eyes fixed themselves on Isobel with great intensity.

'I'm glad you're here. I've been watching for you.'

'How's Mother?' Seb asked, climbing stiffly out. 'Not worse, I hope?'

'No, she's rallied a little.'

Isobel's spirits fell. Wasn't this what always happened?

'That's good,' Seb said, but Charlotte was shaking her head.

'She can't get comfortable. She's restless and irritable – in pain, I think. Come in and say hello. She's pleased you're coming. Lunch is all ready, so we'll eat as soon as we can.'

Sebastian was pulling their suitcases from the boot. Daisy started to whimper, so Isobel lifted her out of her seat and hugged the small body to her. She saw Daisy as a protective shield between her and the Broadbent family. Even when Charlotte led the way upstairs she didn't want to put her down, though the little girl was no lightweight.

'You could hand Daisy over to my nanny,' Charlotte suggested.

Daisy let out a yell of protest. Isobel said, 'She's hungry and tired.'

'Nanny will give her something to eat and put her down for a rest; keep an eye on her.'

Sebastian said, 'Better leave her with us for the moment until she settles.'

Isobel had two minutes alone in the bathroom and splashed cold water on her face to liven herself up. Daisy started to cry every time she put her down. Seb was trying to placate her while Isobel tried to tidy herself in front of the dressing table mirror. She wished she'd had more notice of this visit, her hair needed trimming and the colour had faded from blonde to dun. She wanted to look her best when she came here and today she looked washed out. She could hear Sophie's voice in the passage outside talking to Charlotte.

'Are you ready?' Seb asked, he was trying to comb Daisy's flaxen curls and she didn't like it.

'Yes.' Isobel knew she was as ready as she ever would be. They were following Charlotte to a bedroom at the front of the house. 'It might soothe Mother to see you again. You too Sophie, she often mentions you.' Isobel could hear Margaret moaning even before the door had been opened. Charlotte said, 'Mother, Sebastian's brought his family to see you.'

A nurse in full uniform had been sitting beside the bed, but she got up to leave them with the patient. Charlotte followed her out to the passage and in a stage whisper asked, 'Has there been any change?'

Isobel didn't catch most of the answer, but she heard the word 'agitated'. She took her turn to kiss the flaccid cheek after Sebastian and Sophie. Her mother-in-law was a shadow of her former self. She'd lost weight and seemed to be all skin and bone.

The curtains were half drawn, putting the room in semi-darkness. The air was heavy with the smell of illness and infirmity. Seb held Daisy out to kiss her grandmother but Isobel saw the little body stiffen and jerk back. Seb sat down and cuddled his daughter on his knee.

'How are you, Mother?'

Her voice was faint. 'I think I'm finished.'

'No, you'll go on for ages yet.' Sebastian sounded full of false heartiness. 'Is there anything I can get you? Anything you want?'

'No. Charlotte's very good to me. No daughter could have been better.'

'Sorry I haven't always been a good son.'

'Not your fault. I blame your father. He drove you away when you were young.'

'It wasn't all his fault,' Seb said. 'He thought he was doing his best for me.'

It blew up like a storm from nowhere. His mother's voice, which had been faint, was suddenly strong with venom.

'Rupert humiliated me. I gave him everything I could and did my utmost to keep him happy. I brought up his children and I was a dutiful wife.'

Isobel cringed, trying to shut her mind against what she guessed was coming.

'After thirty-three years of marriage, he asked for a divorce. He was ready to cast me off like an old shoe. He gave me no warning. He'd taken up with some girl and had the nerve to face me with it. Got her pregnant . . . I couldn't believe it.'

Charlotte tried to soothe her. 'Don't fret yourself, Mother.'

'But he got his just deserts, didn't he?' She leered up at them. 'In the nick of time, before he could do anything, he was struck down by a stroke and dead within hours.'

Isobel felt paralysed. She could hardly breathe. For years she'd wondered what exactly had happened, and now she knew. Eyes like incandescent coals were burning up at the group round her bed. Isobel expected them to stop at her. She was about to be revealed to Charlotte as that heartless girl whose affair had over-stressed her father and led to his death. The girl who'd ruined her mother's life. Isobel swallowed and closed her eyes. When she opened them again, those hate-filled eyes had moved on. They had not picked her out!

She was wet with perspiration, but knew with absolute certainty that Rupert had died without revealing her name. Her secret was safe. Margaret didn't know her son had married his father's mistress.

'You must try to forgive.' Seb took hold of his mother's hand. 'Then you'll find peace.'

'I'll never forgive him. He ruined my life. I've been an invalid ever since. I hope he's rotting in hell.'

Isobel heard Sophie's swift intake of breath and was reminded of her presence. She should not be here, listening to these terrible family secrets. Isobel touched her arm, indicated they should leave. Sophie's eyebrows shot up and she shook her head, letting her mother know she had no intention of missing any of this.

It was Charlotte who moved them out. 'You can't rest with us all here, Mother. Sebastian will come back later to sit with you.'

Once out of the room, she said, 'I'm going to ask the doctor to call. He's been giving her light sedatives but they don't seem to work any more. She often gets agitated. I hate to see her all upset like that. I feel so powerless to help her.'

Daisy was falling asleep in Seb's arms. 'Come on, bring that child up to the nursery,' Charlotte said, 'then you can eat your lunch in peace.'

'Our old nursery?' Seb asked.

'Where else?'

Isobel followed them up another flight of stairs to a traditional nursery in the attic with a uniformed nanny in charge. She was bottle-feeding a baby of about six months.

'You remember Graham, Isobel? Rupert our eldest is at school. He'll be five this summer. Where is Nicholas, Nanny?'

'He hasn't woken from his afternoon rest.' She took them into the adjoining night nursery and Isobel looked down on a sleeping three year old.

'Here, Seb.' Charlotte let down the side rail of a cot. 'You can put Daisy down to sleep here.'

Isobel took Daisy's shoes off. 'Do you have a blanket to cover her?'

'Yes, in that cupboard.' The nanny was still nursing Graham.

'She'll be hungry when she wakes up,' Isobel told her. 'She's had nothing since her breakfast.'

'There's some minced lamb stew and mashed potatoes left from the children's lunch. Will that be all right?'

'Excellent,' Isobel said. 'Thank you. She'll like that.'

'You can rely on Mary,' Charlotte said dryly. 'She's Norland trained.' Isobel was surprised at the hostility on Charlotte's face.

It was well after two when they sat down to lunch in the dining room. Sebastian and Sophie greeted Gloria, the maid who served them, like an old friend. She'd apparently worked for the family for most of her life. There was little conversation at table; Isobel knew her own family was tired and Charlotte was worried about her mother. She did not seem sorry to have her meal disturbed by the doctor, who arrived as they finished the first course. 'Do carry on with your lunch,' she said, before taking him upstairs.

When she returned to the table, she reported, 'He's given her an injection to calm her and ease her pain, and he's left more for the nurse to give her later on.'

When the meal was over, Sebastian suggested they all have

a rest to make up for their early start. Isobel was only too glad to agree.

'You see?' Seb said as soon as they were alone in their room. 'You've been worrying unduly all this time. Mother doesn't know you had any contact with my father.'

Isobel nodded. 'So it would seem.' But she still felt uncomfortable here, and Charlotte was less than friendly.

Tired out, she fell asleep in moments. Some time later, she was aware of Seb getting up. He said, 'I'm going to sit with Mother for a while. No need for you to disturb yourself.'

Isobel turned over and went back to sleep. Sebastian woke her again.

'Come on, Izzy, it's gone four o'clock. You won't sleep tonight if you don't get up now. Come downstairs and have a cup of tea.'

Feeling sleep-sodden, Isobel did so. 'How's your mother?'

'Asleep. I don't think she knew I was there.'

Downstairs in the drawing room, the atmosphere was uneasy. Charlotte's husband Esmond had come home. He was wearing a dark formal suit and shot to his feet to kiss Isobel's cheek. She understood he worked in a city bank. Sebastian and Charlotte were telling him in near whispers about their mother's condition.

Isobel was beginning to think she should go to the nursery to see how Daisy was getting on when Sophie brought her down. Her girls brought an air of normality with them and they all began to talk of other things. It surprised Isobel to see how relaxed Sophie was and how quickly she'd settled into the routine of Seb's family. It had always impressed Sophie that they employed a maid, a cook, a gardener and a nanny.

She'd asked, 'Daddy, was it like this when you were small?'

'Yes.'

'Why don't we have a maid and a cook now?'

'I can't afford it on a schoolmaster's salary.'

'What about Uncle Esmond, then? Does he earn more money than you?'

'I think he must do,' he told her. 'I don't really know.' Isobel kept quiet. She was of the opinion that the household ran on the money Rupert had earned in his office furniture business.

'I wish you could earn more,' Sophie told Sebastian. 'Whatever made you take up teaching?'

'I wish I knew,' he said.

CHAPTER FOUR

A FTER TEA, Charlotte went to sit with her mother. Sebastian said, 'Why don't we all go out for a walk?'

Sophie didn't want to but Isobel was glad to go. However, it was miserably cold and they were back within fifteen minutes. She played with Daisy, took her to the nursery to have supper and then got her ready for bed. Sebastian went to relieve Charlotte at his mother's bedside.

By dinner time Isobel was beginning to relax. Margaret had slept since the doctor had given her the injection and the family thought it was the best thing for her. At least she would feel no pain.

For Isobel, it was a treat to sit back and have a drink instead of having to cook. Dinner was beautifully set out and served by Gloria. Esmond had changed out of his formal suit and wore a cashmere pullover with an open-necked shirt and a silk cravat. Even the conversation was what she would expect at any dinner party.

'The night nurse arrives at ten o'clock,' Charlotte told them.

'You have a night nurse and a day nurse?' Sebastian asked.

'Yes. While there are two of them, they settle Mother for the night. She has to be lifted and turned now. It's heavy work.'

Sebastian wanted to see her before he went to bed and Isobel went with him. Margaret looked pathetically old and frail. Her face was grey and expressionless; her mouth was open and she was breathing heavily.

'Has she woken up at all?' Seb asked the nurse.

'No.'

Isobel went to sleep wondering how long this could go on, but shortly after they'd settled down to sleep she was roused by knocking on the bedroom door. It was dark; it seemed like the middle of the night. Charlotte called, 'Sebastian, are you awake?'

'Yes.' He sounded quite befuddled. 'What is it?'

'The nurse has woken me. She's afraid Mother's near the end.'

'I'll come.'

Isobel felt her heart turn over. She wasn't sorry the end was coming. They wouldn't be able to leave until it was all over and she was acutely uncomfortable here. Though of course she couldn't say that even to Seb.

Daisy was in a cot in the corner of the room. She'd been disturbed too and let out a soft whimper. 'She'll probably go off again,' Seb whispered.

Isobel got up too and pulled on her dressing gown. All the adults were congregating in the sickroom. The patient hardly seemed to have moved. She was breathing even more slowly and the breaths were noticeably shallower. Her chest was barely moving.

'Mother, we're here with you.' Charlotte was holding her

hand on one side of the bed and Sebastian on the other. 'Can you hear me?'

Isobel could see no sign that she had. Then she heard Daisy let out a cry of protest from their room. Seb looked up and caught her eye.

'I'll see to Daisy,' she said, glad of an excuse to leave them to their vigil.

Margaret died in the early hours of Good Friday. The nurses laid her out and dressed her in a flattering blue taffeta dinner dress. They cleaned and tidied her room, stripping out every sign of her having been ill. Nothing more could be done until the following day, when Esmond booked a firm of under-takers. Although Sebastian asked for the earliest possible date for the funeral, it couldn't take place until the following Thursday.

Isobel found the wait interminable and there seemed to have been little point in coming down before Margaret died. There had been no last-minute messages for Sebastian or Charlotte. Margaret had gone from being irritable and agitated to being asleep, and had just drifted into oblivion.

'At least I was able to say goodbye to her,' Seb said. 'I did my best, but I doubt I was much comfort to her in her last hours.'

It was a miserable Easter, with the weather too cold and wet to spend much time out of doors. On Sunday, they all went to church. Afterwards, Isobel walked home with Sophie while the vicar discussed the funeral arrangements with the rest of the family.

The afternoon was a time to reminisce. Charlotte and Sebastian talked about their parents.

'Poor Mother. She's been an invalid for years.'

'Ever since Father died.'

'Ever since we were married,' Charlotte said. 'In July 1966.'

Isobel shuddered. Almost from the time she'd discovered she was pregnant with Sophie. She thought about Rupert and listened to his children's memories of him. Here in his house he seemed closer to her than he had for years.

Esmond went to work on Tuesday. He was leaving as Isobel brought Daisy down to breakfast. She heard him say to Sebastian, 'I'm glad you're staying here. You'll be able to help Charlotte finalise the funeral details.'

They were still at the table when Charlotte produced a copy of their mother's will.

'It's quite simple,' she said. 'She's left small bequests to some of the staff. Those who've worked for her for a long time.' She looked across the table to Sophie, who had been late coming down and was still eating egg and bacon. 'There's a bequest for each of the grandchildren, and you too, Sophie.'

A forkful of bacon hovered halfway to her mouth. 'How much?' she asked.

'Five thousand pounds.'

'Wow!'

Isobel was thinking how much she'd needed a bequest like that at the time of Rupert's death when she found Charlotte's gaze on her. It seemed full of hostility. Charlotte went on, 'The residue of the estate is to be divided equally between you and me, Sebastian. And we've both been appointed executors.'

Clearly their mother had been quite wealthy. Sebastian asked, 'Have you any idea how much she'll have left?'

'Yes. I've been managing Mother's affairs for the last few years. What we need to establish is exactly what her estate was worth on the day she died.'

'Of course.'

'Esmond has explained to me what we have to do.'

'Good. I haven't any idea.'

'Or taken much interest in her affairs,' Charlotte said dryly. 'I'd like to have the house, if I may. It's always been my home.'

'Of course you must have it,' Seb assured her. 'But isn't it a bit grand for present-day tastes? It would be a bit big for us, wouldn't it, Izzy?'

'Yes. We're happy in our cottage.'

Charlotte had a way of looking down on her as though she were of inferior social class. She probably was, but Isobel resented Charlotte's attitude. She hoped Sebastian had told his sister that she'd inherited a handsome sum from her Aunt Mavis and that their present prosperity came from her side of the family.

Charlotte said, 'I'll see about getting the house valued for probate. Sebastian, if you'd like to come to the study, we could start adding up her assets as far as we can. We'll have some phone calls to make and some letters to write.'

Isobel knew Seb was grieving for his mother and that he'd find looking through her personal papers unpleasant and embarrassing. It also left Isobel feeling at a loose end. Sophie was still tucking into toast and marmalade. On the night before they'd left home, Isobel had given some thought to the possibility of a funeral, and had packed a suitcase with Seb's funeral suit, black tie and black shoes, and her own black suit and hat. But Sophie had had nothing suitable to bring.

'Would you like to go up to the West End and buy an outfit for Granny's funeral?' she asked.

Her eyes lit up. 'Mum! Yes, please. I'd love to.'

'One stipulation. It must be plain and simple. Nothing too punky.'

'Black . . .'

'No. You're too young for black.'

'What then?'

'Navy blue or grey.'

'I hate navy blue.'

'Grey then, and sober in style.' She could leave Daisy in the nursery with Nanny. 'We might have lunch out. We'll see how things go.'

'Lovely.' Sophie sighed with pleasure.

As they walked up Regent Street and into Oxford Street, Isobel said, 'When I got my first job in Clapham I used to come up to shop for clothes. I knew all the best fashion shops to go to then but I expect everything will have changed.'

Nevertheless they had a successful morning in the shops. Sophie settled on a pearl grey coat which Isobel was sure would meet with Seb's approval and from which she'd get some wear in the future. Isobel bought herself a new cream blouse and indulged them both with new underwear.

She'd meant to go to one of the restaurants Rupert used to take her to, but she failed to find it and Sophie got tired of looking. Lunch turned out to be mediocre, but Isobel suggested making a full day of it and taking in a cinema matinee. They arrived home somewhat later than Esmond.

'I've had a lovely day,' Sophie breathed. 'Can we do it again tomorrow? It'll be boring otherwise.'

Isobel said, 'I wouldn't dare take you away all day again tomorrow. We mustn't upset our hostess.'

Charlotte's attitude was disapproving, especially when Sophie told her they'd been to the cinema. She and Sebastian were busy all day on Wednesday, and Sophie was right, she was bored. For Isobel, time seemed to be standing still.

The funeral was to be held at eleven o'clock on the Thursday morning. Isobel was relieved to hear Sebastian say, 'We'll have something to eat and be away as soon afterwards as we can. You've put up with us long enough, Charlotte. We don't want to overstay our welcome.'

'You'd not do that,' Esmond said politely.

'Charlotte's exhausted and needs a rest,' Isobel said. 'A death in the family is emotionally draining. Especially after a long illness like her mother's.'

'I won't argue with that,' he agreed. 'I'm glad it's over at last.'

Their mourning clothes came out of the suitcase looking crumpled and unsightly. Isobel had to ask Gloria to press them. She brought them back looking quite different.

'You'll look smart,' Isobel told Seb as she hung his suit in the wardrobe, but he shrugged and said, 'Does it matter?'

The morning of the funeral was sunny and spring-like, which should have cheered everybody up after so much rain, but Isobel could see Seb was in a sombre mood. She took his arm to show support but nothing would distract his attention from the oak coffin standing on its bier at the front of the church. She saw him mop his eyes with his handkerchief. 'For me and Charlotte it's the end of an era. I can't believe Mother's gone.'

Charlotte was weeping openly. Isobel was in no doubt that

they'd both miss their mother very much and felt guilty that she didn't feel the same.

Esmond had invited the vicar and some of the congregation back to the house for sherry and refreshments. These were laid out on the dining table, but Charlotte had arranged for a more solid lunch to be served to Isobel's family in a small room off the kitchen.

They changed into more comfortable clothes and sat down to fish pie followed by chocolate sponge pudding, the nursery menu for the day.

When they were ready to leave, Sebastian led them in search of Charlotte and Esmond to say goodbye. The reception was still in progress and only Charlotte came down to the car to see them off. She kissed the children and Seb, but when Isobel went forward to kiss her she stepped back to stay out of reach, while her lips kissed the air an inch from Isobel's cheek. Isobel could not mistake the hostility she saw on her sister-in-law's face.

The last thing she did was hand a large manila envelope through the car window to Sebastian as he was starting the engine.

'Father's personal possessions,' she said. 'I think you ought to have them. I don't know what else to do with them.'

Sebastian passed the envelope to Isobel, who tried to push it unopened into the glove box, but it was too bulky and the box wouldn't close again. She slid it under her seat to get it out of sight. As Seb drove out into the road, she sank back and closed her eyes, relieved to be going home at last.

It was a slow journey, and they hit the early evening rush hour around Birmingham. They had brought a picnic tea for Daisy, and she went to sleep after eating it. The others had intended to stop for a meal, but they couldn't leave Daisy alone and asleep in the car and to wake her up would shatter the peace, so they went straight home. Sebastian carried Daisy upstairs to her cot, where Isobel managed to undress her and tuck her up for the night without fully wakening her. Sebastian and Sophie had carried all the baggage upstairs by then.

Isobel was exhausted. She threw herself on the bed while Seb was unpacking.

'What d'you want for supper?' she asked. 'There's chicken pies in the freezer or I could do something with eggs.'

'I fancy scrambled eggs on toast.' Sebastian was opening the manila envelope.

Isobel watched him tip out Rupert's Rolex watch, gold cufflinks and tiepin on the duvet beside her. She sat up. It felt like a voice from the past. The gold no longer shone; easy to see it had not been worn for many years.

Seb shook the envelope and two signet rings and some documents fell out. Isobel picked up one of the rings. She remembered Rupert wearing it; it was pulling at her heartstrings.

Sebastian was smoothing out the papers. 'There's a letter.' He began to read.

'Who from?' Isobel choked. Unaccountably, her first thought was that Rupert had written it.

'Charlotte.'

Isobel's gaze settled on two airline tickets that had also come out of the manila envelope. Suddenly she couldn't breathe, and her chest felt tight with anguish. Rupert had promised to take her to Florence for a real holiday that fateful summer. Her hand felt for the top ticket. It would enable Miss Isobel Wilcox to fly first class from Heathrow to Pisa on 15 August 1966 and return two weeks later. The other ticket had Rupert's name on it, but he'd been dead by then. They had never had that holiday. Tears were pricking her eyes.

Sebastian's troubled gaze met hers, and he put the letter aside. She put out her hand to take it.

'No,' he said and caught at her hand. 'Better if you don't, love.'

She gave him the air tickets. 'Charlotte knows about me, doesn't she? I want to know what she says.'

'She's known for a long time.' Sebastian was distressed.

Isobel tried to focus on the letter. She felt stricken. Tears danced in front of the page and made it difficult to read.

Dear Sebastian,

For many years now, I have known that Isobel was Father's long-term mistress before you married her. You will understand why I couldn't speak of this to you while Mother was alive.

She didn't know he had a mistress until the day of his death. She told me it came as a huge shock to hear that he'd got some girl pregnant and wanted a divorce so he could marry her.

Poor Mother never really recovered from this plus the shock of Father's sudden death.

After his funeral, Mother started going through his belongings but found she couldn't face it. She was ill and didn't want to think about him. Fortunately, she just locked all his things away. All she wanted to do was forget him. Eventually she asked me to dispose of his belongings. I didn't rush to do it as I had her to look after as well as a new baby. I was shocked to the core when I came across these airline tickets.

I never did show them to her or breathe anything of what I discovered. I was afraid it would make her really ill again to know you had married Father's ex-mistress and was bringing up his child as your own. She was fond of you both, and it would have altered the way she felt about Sophie.

You saw how much she loathed Father when she became agitated on the day you arrived. She thought he'd had too easy a death and ought to be punished for what he'd done. She was always getting worked up and railing against him like that. It shows how much she suffered. Had she known who Isobel was, she'd have taken your marriage to her as the greatest of insults.

I have no way of knowing whether this is news to you or not. If you don't know, then it's certainly time you did. I would rather not see your wife again. This has caused us all much anguish.

Charlotte

'This is awful,' Isobel gulped. 'I can really feel the hate . . .'

'You've got to forget it.'

'At least I know what happened when Rupert told her.'

'Don't worry about it.'

'I couldn't bear it if Sophie started asking questions. Everybody here accepts you are her father.'

'So does she. Put it behind you, Izzy.'

As Sophie unpacked her suitcase in her bedroom, she thought of poor Gran. Her death had overwhelmed the whole family.

Dad had been taking her down to see Gran and Aunt Charlotte three or four times a year. They'd always made a fuss of her. They'd given her little gifts and arranged outings to amuse her as well as themselves.

A trip out might be just a drive round and afternoon tea in

a hotel, which was what Gran liked. But it could be a theatre visit or a concert. Depending on the time of year, it could also mean being taken to see the trooping of the colour on the Queen's birthday, or the boat race. Sophie had looked forward to the visits and enjoyed them immensely.

This time it had been very different. Sophie hung her new clothes in her wardrobe deep in thought. Even at the beginning of the visit, the atmosphere in the house had felt tense and emotional. She'd wondered whether that was because Gran was very ill or because Mum was with them. Somehow she didn't fit in, and Aunt Charlotte didn't seem to like her.

Gran normally lay back passively. Sophie had thought her quiet and accepting until she'd come out with that heart-stopping outburst on her deathbed. Sophie had never seen her so boiling with anger and full of hate. That it was directed at Grandpa made it all the more shocking. It made Sophie wonder what he was supposed to have done.

It had torn the family's nerves apart. Sophie couldn't imagine Gran at the centre of a real story like that. It was like something on the telly – extraordinary.

Of course, it had all happened before she was born which made it ancient history, but her sympathy was with Gran. Married men should not chase other women. Marriage was supposed to bring love and happiness, as it did to Mum and Aunt Hilary and Nana.

Then, of course, Gran had died, which had made them all anguished except possibly Mum, who'd seemed strangely untouched by it.

Sophie made a bundle of her dirty washing and prepared to take it down to the washing machine. The door to her parents' bedroom wasn't properly closed, and as she was passing she heard her father's gentle voice.

'It's all over now. Mother's dead. We don't need to see Charlotte again. Don't worry about it.'

Sophie stopped. She knew her mother was crying. 'Look what I've done to you. I've alienated your family.'

Dad's voice was sympathetic. 'We've never been a close-knit family like yours. I was fond of Charlotte, but . . . What are these airline tickets? Why does she see them as proof?'

'Rupert was planning to take me to Florence for a holiday before he had his stroke. This ticket has my name on it; that one has his. Charlotte's known since she found them.'

'Oh, Lord! You must put it behind you, Izzy.'

Sophie knew she shouldn't be eavesdropping. She pushed the door open and asked, 'What's the matter?'

She knew from their faces and the way they sprang apart that she'd caught them at a raw moment. Dad picked up a letter and tore it into pieces. 'We're a bit upset about Granny.'

Sophie knew her mother wasn't, but she was mopping surreptitiously at her eyes. Dad was looking round for a waste paper basket but there wasn't one in the bedroom.

'It's been rather a difficult time, hasn't it?' he said, pushing the pieces under the glass tray on the dressing table where Mum kept her brush and comb.

Sophie asked, 'What are those rings and things?'

He swept them into a drawer in his bedside table and closed it.

'They belonged to my father. Charlotte thought I might like to have them.'

They'd belonged to the grandfather she'd never known? Sophie was curious. Had Mum and Dad been talking about

Gran being so agitated and railing against her husband? She thought they had.

She said, 'Shall I make some tea?'

'We need more than tea, Sophie,' her mother said. 'I'll come down with you and make us scrambled eggs.'

It was a silent meal. They were all tired after the long drive home. Sophie had always been impressed by the living standards at the Pines. Now there was interesting family history too and she couldn't get it out of her mind. She was intrigued by what had happened.

On her way up to bed, she peeped into her parents' room. The pieces of the letter Dad had torn up were still under the glass tray on the dressing table. She scooped them out and took them to her own room, and like a jigsaw puzzle she pieced them together on her dressing table. She had to read the letter through three times before the awful truth sank in. It made her heart thud and her hands shake.

The sentences leaped off the page: *I never did show them to her or breathe anything of what I discovered. I was afraid it would make her really ill again to know you had married Father's ex-mistress and was bringing up his child as your own.*

Sophie was struggling to get her breath. That child was her? Of course it was. Who else could it be?

She snatched up the pieces of paper, mixed them up again and ran back to her parents' bedroom to replace them under the glass tray where she'd found them. She felt sick. She shouldn't have read another person's letter; she wished now she hadn't done it. She didn't want to know facts like these. It altered everything; she wasn't the person she'd believed she was.

The facts went round and round in her mind for hours.

She heard her parents come upstairs and wanted to get up and talk to them about it. She wanted to be told it wasn't true, but that would have meant admitting she'd read the letter and she was ashamed she had. Dad had high standards when it came to that sort of thing and thought she should have too. Sophie couldn't bring herself to own up and as a result she hardly slept that night.

She couldn't believe Sebastian was not her natural father. He was protective; she could tell he cared about her. He was always there with a guiding hand, and what else would explain the love she felt for him? She wanted him as her dad; he was a fountain of knowledge and always ready to help her in any way he could.

Neither could she see Mum as another man's mistress. She looked quite pretty in old photos, but she was long past that now: she was too staid, too practical and too wrapped up in her home and family. Altogether too motherly.

If it was true, it would make Sebastian her half-brother! She'd have laughed if the whole thing hadn't been so desperate. She couldn't see him as that – he was much too old!

Sophie felt out of kilter for the rest of the Easter holiday, and brooded in her bedroom feeling thoroughly miserable. As the days passed, she forgot the actual words of the letter, but the message lingered. It was so unbelievable, she began to wonder if she'd got it all wrong. She hoped she had.

For Isobel, Margaret Broadbent's death was opening old wounds; it brought back the agony she'd lived through all those years ago after Rupert's death. She couldn't open a book without seeing his face in front of the page. Sebastian had tried to be sympathetic but he was grieving for his mother.

Isobel had burned the letter Seb had torn up, together with those tell-tale airline tickets, but it still rankled that for years Charlotte had known she'd been Rupert's mistress and had kept it to herself. She told herself she should have guessed; Charlotte had made no effort to hide her hostility.

She couldn't put it out of her mind, but she was even more worried about what Sophie was making of all this. Sophie had been fond of her grandmother and had heard what she'd had to say on her deathbed. She'd surely put two and two together; very little got past her. Now she was unusually quiet and seemed to be watching them, her eyes following Seb's every move.

One night when they were getting ready for bed, Isobel said to him, 'I couldn't bear it if Sophie started asking questions. You know what she's like – full of curiosity.'

'What sort of questions?' The bedsprings creaked as he sat on the edge to take off his socks.

'About whether you're her father or not.' She saw Seb wince. Nobody could have been more of a father to Sophie.

'If she asks, will you tell her?'

'I don't know. She has a right to know the truth.'

'No, Seb, please don't. Nothing would ever be the same again. She'd feel we weren't a proper family.'

He got into bed. 'It's better that she hears it from us. I wouldn't want somebody else to tell her.'

'Who could except Charlotte? You've said you won't be going down much now your mother's gone. All my family accept that you're her father. So does she.'

'I'm not so sure now. If she asks . . .'

'Up here, none of them has an inkling of the truth.'

'I want things to stay as they are, of course. I want Sophie to see me as her father and I want us to be seen as a normal family. Heaven knows it took us long enough to get going.'

'That was a painful time for us both.' Isobel winced at the memory. 'How would Sophie feel if she knew the truth? I think it would be better left until she's older.'

He sighed. 'If she asks now, it means she's thinking about it.'

'I don't want you to tell her. It would be like opening Pandora's box.' Isobel felt desperate. 'Sometimes I wonder if there ever will be an end to all this.'

CHAPTER FIVE

O N THE SECOND morning of the summer term, Sophie sat in the passenger seat looking at Sebastian's profile as he drove her to school. He was the best dad in the world, but she was afraid he wasn't her real dad. It made her feel the secure and happy life she'd known was crumbling away. She had to talk to him about it. Nothing else would settle her mind.

She'd put it off until the holidays were over, so she could talk to him while they were on their own in the car. She'd tried to do it yesterday but her nerve had failed. But she had to know what he thought about it. She had to get it out in the open.

The miles were being eaten up, and Sophie forced herself to say, 'Dad, I've got a confession to make.'

'Oh?' He glanced at her with a quick smile. 'A confession, eh? Let me guess. You've finished off Daisy's chocolate eggs?' His tone was teasing; he had no idea what was coming.

'Worse than that. Much worse.' She knew she'd have to admit to reading his letter to make him understand.

'Fire away then. Get it off your chest.'

Her voice dropped to a near whisper. 'That letter Aunt Charlotte wrote to you . . .'

She saw his grip tighten on the steering wheel and the colour ebb from his cheeks. 'You tore it to bits, Dad, but I pieced it together to read. I'm sorry. I know it was very wrong.'

'It was.' She saw him moisten his lips. He knew now what was coming.

She forced herself to go on. 'She wrote that I was Mum's love child and that you weren't my father.'

'She did.' He glanced at her again but this time there was no smile.

He wasn't denying it! Sophie panicked. It was true then, all that stuff Gran had raved about. She burst out, 'Why didn't you tell me?'

'There's nothing to tell.'

'But there must be. Everybody needs to know their roots—'

'You know your roots, Sophie.'

'Yes, but that letter said—'

'Charlotte has a bee in her bonnet. Gran too. If you look on your birth certificate you'll find it gives my name as your father.'

She thought for a moment. 'Oh, yes. I've already seen it.'

'Well then. You probably think it's romantic to be a love child, with deep secrets about your birth. The truth always seems more humdrum. I'm your dad. Ask Nana, or Aunt Hilary, or anyone in the family.'

Sophie felt disorientated. 'But that doesn't explain . . . I mean, Gran was very upset about Grandpa. She thought—'

'Yes, she was an old lady near her end, who was unhappy

59

and confused. What she said had nothing to do with you.'

'Or Mum?'

'No, and better not mention it to her. I mean, you don't want to upset her. Can you see her as another man's mistress? She'd be cross you could even think it.'

Sophie smiled half-heartedly.

'That's better,' he said. 'You're my daughter and I love you very much. I'm certainly not going to be elbowed aside to share you with another father.'

Sophie was comforted. 'I didn't like the idea. I've always thought of you as my dad. I don't want anybody else. It scared me to think it might be true.'

'Don't be scared.' The car was pulling up outside the school gates. 'You must forget all these far-fetched stories, all right?'

She kissed his cheek. 'All right. See you at four.'

'As usual. Nothing's going to change, Sophie.'

She walked into school thinking that if Dad said everything was all right, it must be.

It settled her down and she thought no more about it until she awoke early the next morning, before it was light. Then she wondered again about what Gran had said and Aunt Charlotte had written. There'd been the ring of truth about it. It explained why Mum didn't like going down to see them, and why she wasn't at ease in their company.

Dad hadn't denied it was true. He'd told her not to be scared about it, not to think about it. Nobody in Mum's family knew about it. Really it was a big secret, a skeleton in the closet.

But Sebastian didn't want anything to change; he still wanted to be her father. Sophie decided there was nothing to worry about. She knew she could trust Dad to keep everything as it was. Hadn't he said 'You're my daughter and I love you very much'?

Hilary had been writing all day and felt exhausted. She'd polished an article on growing geraniums for a gardening magazine, having picked Ben's brains to do it, and she'd almost finished another short story.

Ever since she'd been rejected by her book publisher, she'd turned her attention to short pieces. It came as a huge relief to find she could sell this sort of work without difficulty – at least she could still call herself a writer. She immersed herself in journals and magazines, became more interested in the short story market and began to sell her stories regularly.

One had been published this week and the magazine featured it prominently. Ben told her it was excellent and he was proud of her. Both to read and to write, Hilary preferred full-length novels in which she could get deeply involved, but writing short stories and articles had its compensations.

Jamie came home from school, followed shortly afterwards by the twins. She went down to the kitchen to make a pot of tea for them all and the house that had been silent all day was suddenly full of bickering voices.

Having seen to the needs of her children, Hilary poured herself another mug of tea and took it to the sitting room where she could have twenty minutes on her own before she needed to start thinking about supper. She closed her eyes and sank back against the cushions to rest.

Minutes later, she heard the back door slam and recognised Sophie's voice. 'Save a piece of that cake for me,' she told the twins. 'I'll be right back.'

Hilary knew why she'd come. Isobel had called in yesterday and mentioned that she intended to go shopping in Liverpool today. Hilary had asked her to change the school pullover she'd bought for Jamie for a larger size. He was growing fast and she'd thought it was a bit tight for him when he tried it on.

Sophie put her head round the door. 'Hello, Aunt Hilly. Mum asked me to bring up this pullover for Jamie.'

An excited Jamie was at her heels, still nibbling cake. 'Is that my new pullover? I want to see it.'

'Come and try it on.' Hilary took it from the bag.

'Oh, it's just another school pully. I thought it was going to be a different one.'

Hilary said, 'Try it on, Jamie. So I can see how it fits.'

'Ah, not now, Mum.'

'Yes, now.'

He hesitated, and without ceremony Sophie peeled the pullover he was wearing over his head. 'Try it on.'

Reluctantly, Jamie pulled on the new one. It was identical but larger.

Sophie's eye had been caught by a magazine on the coffee table. It was folded open at a story entitled 'Hunter's Moon' by Hilary Snow.

'Is this your new story, Aunt Hilly? Mum and Nana were talking about it last night. They said it was smashing. Can I read it?'

'Of course.' Sophie picked it up eagerly. 'You can take it home to your mother.' But Sophie had already shot back to the kitchen.

'It's too big,' Jamie told her.

'It won't be by next term.'

62

'It's horrible.' He rushed out, leaving the door wide open, and moments later she was surprised to hear Charlie's voice loud and clear and full of irritation.

'I wish Mum wouldn't write that awful stuff. It's about sex. It makes me cringe.'

Sophie's half-suppressed giggle reassured her. 'Don't be daft,' she said. 'It's not about sex at all.'

'It is,' Andy insisted. 'It's about kissing and feeling his hands fondling her hair . . .'

'That's romance, you ass. Grow up, you two.'

Hilary had no idea her boys felt so strongly about what she wrote, although they'd said they didn't like the lovey-dovey bits and why couldn't she write crime or adventure or war stories or something decent? She'd tried to explain that wasn't the sort of story carried by women's magazines.

She knew that at fifteen Sophie considered herself an adult. Her twin boys were actually seven months older, but she'd heard Sophie tell them they were behaving like kids. Perhaps she was right. Hilary would have liked to get up and close the door to cut off the voices from the kitchen, but couldn't summon up the energy.

'It's a lovely story,' Sophie said.

'You wouldn't call it lovely if it was your mother churning them out,' Andy said. 'It's embarrassing.'

'I tell all the girls at school she's my aunt, and they're all very impressed.'

Charlie grunted. 'You should hear what they say about them at our school. It's sloppy, toe-curling stuff.'

'Bollocks,' Sophie said. 'I think Aunt Hilly's clever to write stories like this.'

'They make me cringe, and she's always doing it. Every

week or so she has a story in one magazine or another. It's all so public. People laugh about them and take the mickey.'

'Take no notice,' Sophie advised. 'They're fools and they'll soon get fed up. You rise to it, Charlie.'

'There's always somebody ready to read out the juicy bits,' Andy complained. 'Like this . . .'

'Oh, shut up.'

Hilary knew from the crackle of paper that Sophie had snatched the magazine from him.

'It's all thudding hearts and fluttering eyelashes.'

Charlie said, 'I liked the article in last month's *Garden News* about climbing roses. Why can't she stick to that sort of thing?'

'I wish she'd write another book,' Sophie said dreamily. 'I loved the last one.'

'It was positively pornographic.'

Rattled now, Hilary hauled herself to her feet and strode to the kitchen.

'I couldn't help but hear what you've been saying about my book,' she burst out. Both the twins looked stunned. 'Did you actually read it?'

'No.' Charlie had the grace to look shamefaced. 'Reading's hard for us.'

'No,' Andy admitted.

'Then you don't know what it's like. It's certainly not pornographic.'

'That's what the boys at school said.'

'They probably don't know what the word means. You read it and see for yourselves. Where is it?'

'We burned it,' Andy told her and it was his turn to look shamefaced.

'Burned it?' Hilary couldn't believe her ears.

Sophie was shocked and echoed her words. 'Burned it? Which one?'

'*The Night Star.*'

'How childish can you get? You must know that destroying one copy is pointless. There's plenty more around. I know Nana's got one and we've still got ours at home. You can borrow that.'

'Thanks a bundle,' Charlie said.

'I loved it,' Sophie sighed. 'I wish I could write that sort of thing. Will you teach me how, Aunt Hilly?'

Hilary was mollified and wished her children were more like Sophie.

Then she heard Charlie mutter under his breath, 'Heaven forbid. We don't want another writer in the family.'

Isobel was half awake when their alarm clock went off. She'd been musing about Sophie's GCE results, which were due out today. It was Seb who lifted a sleepy arm to switch the alarm off.

A moment later, Sophie was banging on their bedroom door. 'Dad? Are you up? I want to get to school early this morning.'

'It's school holidays,' he called, teasing her. 'Aren't we having a lie-in?'

'Dad, stop pulling my leg. You promised.'

'I'm already up,' he called. To Isobel he said, 'Sophie can't wait to find out if she's done better than anyone else in the school.'

Isobel stifled a yawn. 'I'm glad you changed your mind about telling her. She needed to work hard for her exams, not fret over something like that.'

'By the time she asked, I'd had time to think it over and I decided you were right, but I didn't want to tell her a deliberate lie.' Sebastian reached for his electric razor. 'I tried to reassure her, but she'd read that letter so she must know.'

'But she's never mentioned it to me.'

'Then she's not bothered about it. Better to say no more.' Sebastian sighed. 'You and I got worked up about it, but she's all right.'

'She's anticipating good marks,' Isobel said.

Yesterday, Hilary had said to her, 'You don't know how lucky you are to have a daughter like Sophie. She's a little angel. Here she is, two years ahead of the twins and you don't have to worry about her exam results. Andy's already a bag of nerves.'

Isobel tried to reassure her sister. 'Andy's got another two years extra tuition. With that, and the twenty-five per cent extra time in exams his dyslexia assessment allows him, he should be all right in English.'

Hilary said, 'Yes, but between him and Charlie I'm not looking forward to their results.'

While Seb got Daisy dressed, Isobel set about making breakfast. Sophie was down before her. 'I'll just have toast,' she said. 'I couldn't eat anything else, not this morning.'

'There are things I need to do at school,' Seb said when he came down. 'Since I'm going into Chester I might as well spend an hour or so there.'

'Come on then, Daddy,' Sophie urged. 'Let's get going.'

'I'm ready.' He was looking for his car keys. 'You'll come back on the bus?'

Isobel said, 'Ring me, Sophie, as soon as you know.'

'Of course, Mum.'

She watched her daughter dance out to the car. It was lovely to see her so sure that she'd done well. Isobel set about the daily chores with Daisy crawling round in her wake. It was more than an hour later when the phone rang. She felt a jolt of anticipation as she picked it up.

'Mum?' Sophie was squealing with excitement. She could hear unmistakable school sounds in the background. 'I've got ten ones.'

Isobel laughed aloud with pleasure. 'That's marvellous, love. Well done.'

'I can't believe it. I thought chemistry might be a bit dicey – I didn't expect better than a three.'

'I'm proud of you, Sophie. Very pleased. How have your friends done?'

'Emily got seven ones and three twos so I've beaten her.'

'What about Judith?'

'She didn't expect to do much. She got four ones, three twos and two threes.'

'That's good, Sophie.'

'She's pleased with it. Don't expect me to come straight home. I'm going to celebrate now.'

Isobel asked cautiously, 'Celebrate? In what way?'

'We're going into town. We'll go round the shops and have lunch out.'

'All right. Does Dad know how well you've done?'

'Yes, I rang him at school. He said he was thrilled.'

'I am too. Congratulations, love.' Isobel put the phone down feeling a bit put out that Sophie had rung Seb before her.

*

Sophie gave a little skip. She was swinging on one of her father's arms and one of her mother's as they strolled three abreast down the lane to Judith's house. It was a warm August evening and she was wearing her new scarlet dress. Even Mum was wearing a sleeveless cotton outfit. They'd all been invited to a barbecue in the Salters' garden.

This was the first grown-up party she'd been invited to, and she'd been looking forward to it ever since Ross had pushed the invitation through their letter box. He'd stopped to talk to a friend in the lane outside their cottage, giving Sophie time to read the card and rush after him.

'It sounds great.' She was enthusiastic. 'I'll definitely be coming. Mum and Dad? Well, I expect so, but Mum'll let you know. Such a lovely idea for the summer hols.'

'It's by way of a celebration,' Ross said. 'As both Judith and I got through our exams.'

'Judith says you've got a place at Oxford.'

'Yes. University College.' His smile broadened. It had clearly been the icing on his cake when he received four As in his A levels.

'Congratulations,' Sophie said.

'Same to you. I gather you did very well too.'

'Not bad.' She deliberately made it a throw-away response before turning back home. Ross Salter had an exceedingly high opinion of his own worth. And boy oh boy, did he let it show.

The Salters had the largest house in the village, a detached one with a big garden. Ben's twin aunts lived almost opposite. As Sophie led the way round the back of the house, she could hear the party music, and once in the back garden they could see the red and orange Chinese lanterns hanging in the surrounding trees. They were meant only as decorations as it was still full daylight. Judith and her mother left the knot of guests that had already arrived and came over to greet them.

Judith said, 'Hello, Sophie. What would you like to drink? It's soft drinks or punch. Try the punch – I sneaked extra wine in when Dad wasn't looking.'

When they both had a glass of punch in their hands, Judith took her out along the terrace past the three tables that had been pushed together.

'We're going to eat here,' she said. Other tables had been set out on the grass and the grown-ups were already occupying them. At the far end of the terrace Ross was barbecuing watched by a circle of friends. Sophie knew most of them because they were local and regulars at the church youth club. Kim Caldwell was there from school, and Dan Cookson with his girlfriend Gemma and younger sister Nancy.

Ross was wearing a very manly striped apron over his fawn slacks and check shirt and expertly flipping hamburgers over with one set of implements and prodding at the charcoal to keep it red hot with another.

He beamed at Sophie, did a little twirl and swung his cooking irons round with all the style of a television cook.

'Show-off,' she mouthed at him.

'A little show makes it taste better,' he said.

'It smells lovely.'

'Looks heavenly,' Nancy said. 'Could I try just one sausage?' She pointed. 'That one.'

'No, I'll never get the job finished if you all start picking. It'll be another half-hour before I've cooked enough for us all.'

Judith nudged Sophie and whispered, 'Ross fancies you, you know.'

Sophie couldn't suppress a giggle. 'Go on. He's never given the slightest sign.'

She'd never thought of him in that way. She watched him now; he was exuding self-confidence. With his dark blue eyes and dark hair falling forward over his face the girls at the youth club had fancied him. But he was the sort of person she couldn't get close to. He thought himself so superior, so much more able than anyone else. Not her cup of tea at all.

On Sophie's other side, young Nancy Cookson said, 'He's quite something. Going up to Oxford too.'

'Why don't we all try our hand at the treasure hunt?' Judith asked. 'Dad and Ross set it up, which means that although I can play Mum said I mustn't win.'

She handed all the guests a piece of paper on which was written the first clue. Sophie studied hers. *Gold is the treasure, gold the prize. To find the second clue, let gold fill your eyes.*

'What does it mean?' Thirteen-year-old Nancy was frowning over her piece of paper. She'd just started coming to the youth club and usually wore her brown hair in pigtails, but tonight it was held back with a red velvet Alice band and was still showing strange kinks where it had been plaited. Sophie thought her brother Dan was the best dancer at the club.

She liked to win competitions like this, but Nancy's brown eyes sparkled up at her; she was obviously keen too and looked touchingly childlike.

Sophie bent closer to whisper. 'If I were you, I'd have a look in that bed of golden rod over there. If there's a piece of paper just read what it says and put it back.'

A few moments later, Nancy was back at Sophie's side. 'Help me, please. I've copied down the next clue but I don't understand what it means.'

'What's it say?'

Nancy pushed a small notebook closer. *Search under the Arbor vitae in the arboretum.*

'It'll be a special tree of some sort in that clump at the bottom of the garden. I'd look for one that's a bit different.'

Sophie went on helping Judith put out bowls of salad and baked potatoes on all the tables. Mrs Salter brought out a brass gong and hammered on it now.

'Ross is ready to serve,' she called. 'Ladies first. Come and get your plates and cutlery.' She and Judith helped Ross dish up the barbecued gammon steak with pineapple, the sausages and hamburgers. The number of guests invited was not great, the service was slick and they were all soon served and sitting down.

The food was delicious. Everybody congratulated Ross on it. Sophie was sitting on the opposite side of the table and watched him preen with satisfaction.

Nancy was up between courses seeking further clues. Some she managed to decode herself but she sought Sophie's assistance several more times while Sophie helped to clear away the used plates. One clue had Sophie guessing but she sought help from her schoolmate Kim. For afters, the Salters carried out big bowls of trifle and fruit salad.

Finally Nancy came back shouting in triumph and holding the treasure aloft. It was a net holding chocolate coins covered in gold paper. Mr Salter announced she was the winner and everybody applauded.

She came to Sophie's side, her cheeks flushed and rosy. 'Thank you,' she whispered. 'You must have half the prize.'

'No, just one coin to taste,' Sophie said.

Supper was over; the temperature was dropping and it was getting dark. Mr Salter changed the tapes to dance music and Judith led them all into the entrance hall. It was imposingly wide and had a parquet floor.

The music blared forth, but everybody seemed to be hanging back, reluctant to start. Sophie found Kim beside her and tried to pull her on the floor to dance, but Kim was shy and refused.

Sophie's feet were tapping. She started to move to the beat and within moments her feet were flying and her scarlet skirt swirling out. She laughed when Dan Cookson joined her on the floor. He was a vigorous and flamboyant dancer and her favourite partner at the youth club monthly dance. She'd danced with him often enough to match her steps to his. She gave herself up to the music and was aware that the other guests were crowding round to watch them.

When the tape ended, a round of applause broke out. Sophie felt spent as she walked off the floor and almost bumped into Ross.

'Who's showing off now?' he asked. Sophie couldn't find the breath to answer. 'How about having a dance with me? This one's slower. More my style.'

'I can believe that,' she puffed. The parents were taking to the floor now. 'It's a bit old hat.' It wasn't the first time she'd danced with him, so she knew what to expect. She said pointedly, 'This is a waltz.'

He took her in his arms, which felt as stiff as poles,

and held her rigidly with a foot of space between them. Sophie stepped backwards, feeling as if she was towing her partner.

'Loosen up,' she said, beginning to giggle. 'You're as stiff as an old goat.'

'Sorry.'

'Don't be, it's fine to find something you aren't good at. Why don't you get Judith to teach you?'

'She's tried. She says I have two left feet.'

Sophie smiled. 'She could be right.' Brilliant Ross, the great all-rounder, couldn't dance.

'I was hoping you'd take me on – that you'd teach me.'

'Ross, you're off to Oxford to learn more important things.'

'Not yet. I've still time to learn to dance.'

Here it was again. He had a head the size of a house. He reckoned he could learn anything in next to no time. It was good for him to know there were some things in this world he wasn't good at.

'OK. Try to relax, and we need to get closer,' she said.

He jerked her forward, his face lungeing towards hers. Sophie turned her head sharply away but he managed to plant a kiss on her cheek. He wasn't much good at kissing either – he had a lot to learn about what would turn a girl on. He really wasn't her type.

CHAPTER SIX

Spring 1983

Sophie had just turned sixteen when their school
caretaker retired. None of the girls took the slightest
interest until they noticed his replacement was a really
handsome young man. Within weeks, half her form, the
lower sixth, was swooning over him. They all loved his pony
tail of dark hair, but they agreed that if he was to have it cut
and grow sideburns he'd look a little like Elvis Presley.

Sophie would walk round school at break time hoping for a
glimpse of him. Her day was made if she came across him
trying to clear a blocked sink in the cloakroom or bleed radi-
ators in the hall. He was always ready to stop and talk to her.

It became almost a competition to chat him up and to find
out all they could about him. It was Emily Burke who told
them his name was Darrell Marchbanks and he was twenty-
seven years old. Interest increased fourfold when they learned
he sang and played lead guitar with a band called Top Flight,
and that the job of caretaker was just to pay his way until he
and the band became famous. They were sure it would
happen soon.

Now the girls wanted to know about the band's gigs, and

those who lived near enough went to hear him. Last month, Top Flight had had a booking at the Gateway Theatre and Sophie and Emily Burke had gone on the Saturday night to hear them.

Darrell was the star of the show. It was obvious he thoroughly enjoyed performing, strutting about centre stage, strumming his guitar and occasionally punching the air. On stage he wore his hair differently. It hung loose, as long as Sophie's, a thick dark brown tangle that he spun round his head as he played.

They thought he had a marvellous gravelly voice, which was strong enough to rise above the three guitars and crashing drum set. The fans adored him. All the band were dressed in costumes loosely based on air crew uniform. Darrell was the pilot and Sophie could see his muscles ripple through the cotton as he gyrated to the beat. They played everything from the pop tunes of the moment to rock and heavy metal.

Sophie and Emily had dared each other to go backstage in the interval and try to talk to him. Darrell recognised them and introduced them to the other members of his band. Bernie played the drums, Roddy played bass guitar and wore a dark wig to cover his bald head, and Kev, who played keyboard or guitar, had split his navigator's trousers and was trying to sew them up.

In the second half of the show, Darrell flung off his shirt, making the audience stamp and cheer. Sophie wanted to swoon as she gazed at his bronzed shoulders and chest glistening under the lights. On his left shoulder he had a tattoo of twisting serpents.

Emily whispered afterwards that the 'crew' of Top Flight

seemed incredibly old, but Sophie saw them as sophisticated and about Darrell's age. She was thrilled; to hear them play, and to meet them, was an experience she would never forget.

It had been arranged that Emily's father would pick them up afterwards, and he went well out of his way to drive Sophie home.

He looked severe. 'Emily,' he said, 'you gave me to understand it was a play you girls were coming to see. I don't approve of loud rock bands. The noise level will damage your hearing.' Emily's father was a doctor and Sophie thought him rather forbidding.

She could hardly believe her good fortune when, in the following week at school, Darrell asked her for a date.

Tonight she was tingling with anticipation as she got ready to go out with him for the first time. She'd spent all her pocket money on stockings with a seam up the back and a satin suspender belt to hold them up. Much more glam than her usual tights.

She'd learned to use a light hand on her make-up, but it took her a long time to achieve the result she wanted. With her fair colouring it was easy to overdo things. She finished off with two applications of pale pink lipstick, well blotted. Darrell was used to seeing her in school with nothing but a bit of foundation over her nose. She meant to knock him out tonight.

That done, she opened her bedroom door and listened. She could hear the clatter of plates and her parents laughing about something down in the kitchen. Now was a good time. She crept the few steps along the landing to their bedroom. It took only a moment to skip across to Mum's chest, open one of the drawers and snatch out her new cashmere jumper.

Back in her own room with the door firmly closed, she pulled it over her head. It was a pastel shade of blue and clung to her body, feeling soft and sensuous. With its deep horseshoe-shaped neckline it was absolutely gorgeous. Sophie had loved it from the day Mum had bought it, and she saw her try it on.

'Could I borrow it once in a while?' she'd wheedled. 'For a special occasion? Please?'

'No.' Mum had folded it away carefully in her middle drawer. 'I paid a lot for this. I'm keeping it for best. My best.'

Now Sophie eyed the result in her mirror. It looked even better than she'd expected. Mum intended to wear it as a pullover with a blouse underneath, but it looked and felt wonderful with nothing but her bra beneath it.

It would look good with her jeans, but she wanted to wear a skirt and look feminine tonight to go out with Darrell. She had one of darker blue corduroy. It was a bit full and girlish but it would have to do. She must get herself a tight straight skirt, something more grown up.

She ran a comb through her blonde hair and put on her best red coat, buttoning it up so Mum wouldn't catch sight of her jumper as she went out. Lastly, she pushed her feet into her shoes. Red to match her coat, with marvellous high heels. She'd saved up her pocket money in the autumn to buy them. Dad hadn't approved; he said the heels were too high and would ruin her feet. Mum said they were the sort of shoes tarts wore. Emily thought they were smashing.

She paused at the living room door. 'I'm going now, Mum,' she called.

'Don't be late home, love. You've got to get up for school tomorrow.' That was the sort of thing Mum always said.

'I might be a bit later than ten, Mum. I'm going to the pictures with Judith. I can't ask her to come out before the end, can I?'

Her father looked up from his newspaper and said, 'I'm going down to Primmy and Prue's in a few minutes. I can give you a lift.'

Sophie hadn't expected that and it threw her. She did her best to hide it. 'Thanks, Dad, but I'm meeting Judith at the corner of Bank Road so we can walk up to catch the bus together.'

'In the dark?' her mother said. 'Which cinema are you going to? Dad could drop—'

'I've got to go, Mum, or I'll keep Judith waiting and we'll miss the bus.'

Sophie whisked out of the door and ran as fast as her high heels allowed. She was meeting Darrell in the car park of the Dog and Gun.

He was waiting for her and flashed his lights when she reached the entrance. He got out of his car to greet her like a gentleman, though she knew her family wouldn't think of him as that. He gave her a welcoming kiss, and she couldn't suppress a soft giggle.

'Sorry,' she said. 'It tasted of cigarettes.'

'Then it's me who should say sorry. I've got some peppermints here – they should do the trick.'

Sophie refused one. There was a blue fug inside his car. 'Sorry about this too.' He smiled at her in the half light and kept his window down until it cleared.

'It doesn't matter.' As far as Sophie was concerned nothing mattered now they were together.

'You don't like cigarettes?'

'I've never tried one.'

'Then you should,' he said.

'Where are you taking me?'

'There's a quiet country pub, the Eagle and Child, in the lanes out the other side of Whitby. It's far enough away to be pretty sure you won't meet people you know and they keep a lovely blazing fire if we can get near it.'

They also had a large dark car park on the opposite side of the road. Darrell pulled into it and drove to the furthest corner before switching off his engine and lights.

He turned to her. 'You're the most beautiful girl I've ever seen,' he whispered. 'Now my breath is fresh, how about a little kiss before we go in?'

Sophie's heart lurched as she put up her mouth to his. For weeks she hadn't been able to get down to any serious study. He'd been in her mind the whole time.

He put an arm round her shoulders and pulled her closer to kiss her. She shivered with delight as his cold fingers crept up her leg until they reached her stocking top. While she'd only been able to imagine his kisses she hadn't dreamed he could make her feel such a wave of passion.

'Shall we move to the back seat for a little while?' he murmured. 'We'd be more comfortable without this gear lever between us.' Sophie agreed; she felt like putty in his hands.

Once there, he undid the buttons on her coat and put his arms inside it. She asked, 'Do you like my new jumper?'

'I can't see it but it feels lovely, all fluffy and downy.' His fingers felt round the low neckline. Sophie could hardly breathe as his hand slipped just inside to stroke her breast.

'You're lovely, absolutely lovely,' he whispered, his lips

moving against her ear. When he bent his head to kiss her breast the thrill was more than she could bear.

Tom Waite was driving home from Liverpool where he'd attended an auction at a large house near Prince's Park. Originally, it had been the home of a wealthy shipowner but decades ago it had been turned into a number of cheap flatlets and bedsits. Since then the building had fallen into disrepair and was about to be demolished. All that was left was some rusting garden furniture and the fixtures and fittings. Many similar articles had been brought in from other sites for the sale. Tom had had an excellent day. He'd picked up some period doors with knobs and finger plates, together with some fine panelling and three Victorian iron grates.

He was almost home when he saw the For Sale notice on the side of the road. He'd passed the two pillars at the end of the drive many times, and had admired the red sandstone house set well back from the road and half hidden in a knot of mature trees. The sale sparked his interest.

Tom had always hoped he'd be able to persuade Flora to buy a really good house. It was what he wanted now above everything else. He thought this one might tempt her because the garden centre was quite close; to live here would not take her far from her family. He decided to go straight on to Chester to visit the agent named on the board and find out more.

He was afraid the house would be too big, but it turned out to have only four main bedrooms, although there were two more in the attic which had once been occupied by servants. It would be easy to shut off the attic floor. The description made his mouth water: the position was magnificent, the lounge was superb and there was a large conservatory. It came with two acres of garden and was truly impressive. It was a house that had everything.

As he drove home, Tom hoped Flora would like it as much as he did. He knew it wouldn't be easy to move her from her cottage because he'd already tried, but for this house it was worth putting in a big effort. He needed to think it through and make careful plans.

Tomorrow morning he'd have to take his trailer over to Liverpool to collect the goods he'd bought, but the next day he'd take Flora into Chester, give her a slap-up lunch with wine at the Grosvenor Hotel, and then walk her past the estate agent's office and point out the photographs of the house in the window. He needed to get her inside and make an appointment to see over it.

He expected to be able to persuade her. He had a well-tried technique that he thought was guaranteed to work for him. He could get Flora to bend to his will; he already had many times.

It was never easy to claw one's way up from the bottom of society, especially after a fall such as he'd had in the early seventies. While he was struggling to get on his feet again he'd really needed to escape from the dire lodgings where he'd been living. He'd often spent time in his local library, which was warmer and brighter than his bedsit, and he'd read up on psychology, which had always interested him.

It had been a stroke of genius to learn to play bridge and join several local clubs. It was a well-known fact that an easy way for a woman to go up in the world was to marry a wealthy man. Why shouldn't he do it the other way round?

He hadn't expected to achieve wealth, but a new partner

with a pension and a comfortable home was a possibility. One who would meet his needs and be happy to wash his socks and cook for him.

Playing bridge catapulted him into the world of middle-class widows and gave him the opportunity to make friends with them. The game represented a common interest, and provided something to do and talk about. His first aim had been to become established amongst the widows and liked by them. His second was to pick out one who would fill the bill, preferably one he could fancy.

For months he'd greeted them all with smiles and warmth and been as charming and attentive as he could. It had taken him a while to find Flora. Once he'd settled on her, he'd done everything he could to develop their friendship and scrape an acquaintance with her family, without making it obvious what he was doing.

In the early days he'd made sure he talked to Flora about what interested her. He'd taken her out for drinks and meals and been as pleasing and witty as he could. He'd read that once a person had invested time and interest in a relationship they would begin to respond.

When she started talking about her dyslexic grandchildren he knew he'd succeeded in forging a bond with her. Once he'd been inside her house to sample her cooking, seen her family photographs and heard about the garden centre, he understood what made her tick. She was more eager than he'd expected, and soon she was issuing invitations and trying to draw him closer. Once he'd succeeded in getting her into bed, he knew he was home and dry.

He let her take all the time she needed. Already his life was much improved. When her sister Mavis died, Flora had told him how she'd earned a fortune and left it to her and Hilary. Tom had hardly noticed Mavis and had thereby missed a fine opportunity. It might just have been possible to inherit some of her wealth himself. Nevertheless, it made Flora doubly attractive to him though it was a pity she'd given so much to Isobel before he'd got wind of it.

All went well with his plan to get Flora to see the house. The estate agent whisked them there in his own car to show them round, because the owners were away. It seemed the vendor's employer was moving him to London. The house was still fully furnished.

'I love it.' Tom couldn't believe how elegant it was. The rooms were large, and everything was spick and span and newly decorated. 'It feels homely too.' He was enthusiastic. He'd taught himself to be sensitive to Flora's moods and he thought this time she was on the same waveband. 'You like it, don't you?'

'Yes, it's lovely. A fine house. Just look at the view across the valley.'

Tom was very hopeful that he'd succeed in moving them to it. He was really very fond of Flora – she was good company. He'd been happy with her. Marrying her had given him an immediate leg up to her more comfortable level, but she could afford better.

Flora watched Tom as he drove home. He was in an exultant mood. 'I can see us living there, can't you?' he said.

She was having second thoughts. 'It's too big. What would we want with six bedrooms? We only use one.'

'The attic floor could easily be shut off. That leaves only four. Wouldn't you like to live there?'

'It's too grand for me, Tom.' She knew she'd have to be firm. She mustn't let him persuade her into this as he had into so many things. 'It's a gorgeous house, but it's not for me.'

'No reason why not. You said you liked it.'

'In the rosy aftermath of a romantic lunch I did. I've come down to earth now.'

'The garden centre's less than a mile up the road.'

'It's too big for us.'

'Don't you feel the cottage is a bit on the small side? A bit cramped?'

'I don't need more work, Tom. It would mean more rooms to clean and I'm not getting any younger.' Age was a sore point, because she was so much older than him, but she had to lay it on thick.

'No problem. I could find you a cleaner.'

'I can't afford that!' She was shocked. 'D'you think I'm made of money?' Usually, she made herself refer to it as their money, so as not to point out he was living on her.

'Flora love, your girls are worried you'll end up saving it all like Mavis.' He shot a glance at her; he looked exasperated.

'Not much danger of that with you around.' Never before had she voiced displeasure at the amount he spent.

'Come on, I'm sure you could sell some of Mavis's investments and pay cash for that house.'

'If I did that, we wouldn't have enough income left to live on.'

When he pulled up outside their cottage she rushed to unlock the door. Once inside she felt more secure.

'I'm very happy here,' she told him. 'I've told you before. I don't want to move.'

She expected him to be as irritable as she was, but instead

84

he took her into his arms and kissed her. He led her upstairs to bed and made love to her, but for once it didn't soothe Flora's anxieties.

Isobel felt everything was going well for her and her family. Daisy was thriving and learning something new every day and Sophie was almost grown up. She and Sebastian had never been happier and she was very thankful he'd persuaded her to try again rather than go for a divorce. It seemed a small miracle that they should be deeply in love after all their early problems, but they were. It had come as a wonderful bonus.

They'd all had a good year, though the summer had flown faster than she'd have liked. She and Seb had continued to tutor Hilary's boys so they'd seen a lot of her and her family. This year, the twins had sat their O levels. Andy had taken seven subjects and Charlie six. Andy had told her he'd found the concession of twenty-five per cent extra time useful. So it had been worth having him professionally assessed as dyslexic, and they were hopeful that he'd do reasonably well.

About Charlie, they were not so confident. He'd said he hadn't needed extra time, that he'd finished every exam before anybody else, long before the time was up.

The results were due out today. Isobel was watching the clock as she waited for Hilary to ring her. Her sister had been anxious and on edge for most of the summer and had worked herself up into a near panic about them. She said the twins were dreading them. It was another half-hour before she rang.

'Izzy, I can't believe . . .' Hilary sounded fraught. 'It's awful.'

'It's not all bad news, surely? How's Andy done?'

'We're trying to take heart from that. He's got four twos and three threes.'

'That's good, Hilary, taking account of his handicap. Andy's done well.'

'Well, at least he can go on and have a go at A levels.'

'What about Charlie?'

Hilary groaned. 'His results are abysmal. Absolutely awful.'

'He said he'd try.'

'That's the last thing he did! As you know, arithmetic is his best subject. He got a four for that, and also for general science, and he got two more fives. That's all.'

'But what about the other subjects? He was sitting six, wasn't he?'

'So we thought. It seems he didn't even go into the exam room for English language and English literature. He truanted on those days.'

'You didn't know?'

'Not till this morning.'

'But didn't the school tell you?'

'Well, you could say they tried. They wrote to us, but gave the letter to Charlie to deliver. We got that this morning too.'

'Hilary! They should have phoned.'

'Well they didn't. They trusted Charlie, that was their mistake.'

'What does he say about it?'

'That he wished he'd bunked off for history and geography too.'

'Oh dear! What are you going to do with him?'

'Ben thinks we need a council of war to decide. If we come round after lunch today, will you be in? We'd value your opinion.'

'Yes. Seb's gone in to school but he said he'd be back for lunch.'

'When I think of Sophie gaining ten ones . . .'

Isobel knew how crushed the twins had been made to feel by a performance like that from their younger cousin.

'You don't know how lucky you are.' Hilary laughed mirthlessly. 'Not a worry in the world about that one. Right, Ben and I will be round about two. See you then.'

When they arrived, Isobel thought Ben looked beaten. She could see he'd taken Charlie's failure hard. She was glad she had a pot of tea to offer them. They nursed their cups sitting side by side on her settee.

'For years we've been trying not to push him, to let him find his own level, to take out as much of the unpleasantness of school as we could,' Ben said. 'And what does he do? He opts out of sitting his exams and then hides from us that he has. I remember asking him how he got on in his English language exam, and he said, "All right, I hope."'

'He didn't even have the courage to tell us what he'd done. He let us go on thinking all was well,' Hilary added.

'You know what Charlie's like.' Sebastian's voice was gentle. 'He's got this chip on his shoulder; thinks he's stupid. He won't attempt things he could do.'

'It's all in his mind,' Isobel agreed. 'It's his own fear, but it's impossible to get him to see that.'

'He wants to leave school now, I suppose?'

'Yes. He's determined to. And they won't let him stay on in the sixth form with fewer than five O levels, anyway.'

'The point is,' Sebastian said, 'what does he want to do now, and how best can he be helped to achieve it?'

'He won't be helped,' Ben said. 'He does exactly the opposite to everything I suggest.'

Hilary said, 'He says he wants to be a long distance lorry driver.'

'Heavens!' Isobel had to smile. 'You can't accuse him of not looking to the future. He's only just seventeen, and he hasn't even learned to drive yet.'

'He wants a motor bike,' his father said. 'He's saved up almost enough to buy one second hand.'

'I'm afraid he'll kill himself,' Hilary sighed. 'But Ben thinks we should agree, or he did until . . .'

'Until what?' Seb asked.

Ben shook his head impatiently. 'Charlie seemed to enjoy working in the potting shed. I really thought he was interested. He helped me work out when we needed to start planting the spring bulbs. We have to have them in flower for the Christmas trade and then plant another lot every two weeks to keep up a steady supply through to the spring. Hyacinths are always popular . . .'

Hilary said, 'When Charlie said he was desperate to leave school, Ben offered him a job in the business to start straight away.'

'I mean, we've brought all the boys up to work there. But for Charlie, I meant it as a backstop if he couldn't find anything else.'

'Ben had it all worked out,' Hilary explained. 'The garden centre was a place where Charlie knew he could cope, where he'd have nobody on his back wanting him to do things he'd find difficult.'

Ben's face was red with exasperation. 'I still find it difficult to believe he turned it down.'

'Turned it down? Why? Even if he's serious about being a long distance lorry driver, he's got a few years to fill before he could get an HGV licence.'

'Exactly.'

Sebastian said slowly, 'So what does he want to do? I take it he has some idea?'

'He wants to take a chef's course at the technical college.'

Isobel frowned. 'I didn't know he wanted to cook.'

'Neither did we,' his father said dryly. 'But his friend Gary Ingram does and Charlie fancies going to technical college with him.'

'Let him go,' Sebastian advised. 'Raise no objections. It won't do him any harm. He might even enjoy a practical job like cooking and settle down.'

'And pigs might fly,' Ben told him.

They laughed and somehow it cheered Ben up to have talked it out. 'It's really not a question of asking your opinion.' He smiled. 'As I said, Charlie doesn't take advice. He makes up his own mind.'

'What about Andy?' Isobel asked. 'Is he going to stay on at school to do A levels?'

'Yes, it's what we all want,' Hilary said.

'Does he have some career in mind?' Sebastian asked.

'He's talking of engineering of some sort, but of course he may change his mind,' Ben replied.

'You are lucky', Hilary said again with even more envy, 'having a clever daughter like Sophie. Andy says she's already decided to go to university to read law.'

'So she says.' Isobel had her reservations about Sophie. She was more than a handful in other ways.

CHAPTER SEVEN

SOPHIE WAS living on the crest of a wave, and having a fantastic summer. She continued to see as much as she could of Darrell. Sometimes he picked her up and they spent most of the evening on the back seat of his car; on other nights he took her to the hall where the band was booked to play.

On those occasions she usually dragged herself away after the interval, because Dad had ruled that she must be home by ten o'clock and would create if she hadn't made it by half past. The show never finished before eleven and after that the band liked to have a beer together to unwind. Darrell booked and paid for a taxi to take her home but Sophie never allowed it to take her right to her front door where her parents might see her getting out.

She was in love. Darrell had taken her in his arms; his dark eyes had looked into hers as he'd whispered, 'I'm head over heels in love with you. Can't get enough of you, Sophie.'

It had given her a delicious feeling of happiness. Just to know she could rely on seeing him several times each week lifted her up. Life promised so much. Sophie had never felt so alive.

Darrell was everything she could ask for in a boyfriend. She saw her future with him, but she knew instinctively that her family wouldn't approve of him. She felt there must be some way she could introduce him that would make them see him as the attractive man he was, but try as she might she couldn't come up with any ideas.

It wasn't Darrell's fault he was eleven years older and his first marriage had failed, but that would be enough to put her family off. Neither would they approve of his music; they were into Beethoven and Mozart. These were not things Darrell could change. If she wanted them to meet, he'd offered to take out the steel ear studs he wore, four of them in one ear, and wear his flowing mane of hair in a tight pony tail as he did at school.

Sophie was afraid Darrell would reveal too much about what they did when they went out, and Dad would forbid her to go on seeing him.

In the meantime, she had to tell fibs about where she was going and who she was with, which made her feel underhand and rather dented her feeling of happiness.

She expected to see less of Darrell in the school holidays, but Dad had arranged with Mrs Salter that she should have work experience with her firm. She'd decided ages ago that she wanted to read law when she went to university next year, and though she was aiming to be a barrister rather than a solicitor everybody thought it would do her no harm to find out how a solicitor's office functioned.

'You'll be there too?' she asked Judith.

'No, but Ross will be for the first week, and Mum will take you both there and back. We're having a family holiday in Nice after that.'

When Sophie told Darrell about her work experience job, he said, 'Couldn't be better. The office is in the centre of Chester so it'll be easy for us to meet at lunch time.'

He was supposed to work at the school as usual and had certain chores to do. 'But I'll stretch my lunch hour a bit and perhaps you'll be able to too. After all, they aren't paying you a proper wage, are they?'

On her first day in the office, Darrell had arranged to meet her outside at twelve thirty. When the time came, Sophie looked down from an upstairs window and saw him on the pavement. She wasn't pleased to see Ross preparing to go out too.

'I'm meeting somebody,' she had to say as he held the front door open for her.

Darrell stepped forward to greet her. Sophie tried to walk away from Ross and take Darrell with her. She planned to keep his existence a secret from her parents and the Salters were too close to them.

Ross put a hand on her arm. 'Aren't you going to introduce us?'

Sophie felt forced to say, 'This is Darrell Marchbanks,' before she hustled him round the corner out of sight as fast as she could. It upset her. 'I wish I'd arranged to meet you somewhere else,' she said.

Darrell took her to a small café for a snack, but it was crowded and noisy. Sophie was distracted because Ross Salter had seen them go off together.

Darrell didn't seem to enjoy it much either. 'I'll rustle up some sandwiches and take you home tomorrow,' he said.

Sophie felt a quickening of interest. He'd talked about his one-bedroom flat. 'I can't wait to see where you live,' she told him.

But when she went back to the office, Ross said in a very superior tone, 'I'd drop that fellow if I were you.'

'You aren't me,' she snapped. It sounded rude even to her own ears.

'Doesn't he play in some heavy metal band? Judith said you'd been to see him perform.'

'It's nothing to do with you, Ross.'

'No, but I wouldn't be happy to see my sister going out with him. What does your father say?'

'Nothing, because he doesn't know, and I'll never speak to you again if you tell him. It's none of your business.'

'Well, that puts me in my place. Come on, don't let's have a row about it. Tomorrow I'll take you to Quaintways for a bite to eat at lunch time.'

'No thank you, I'm already booked for tomorrow.'

Sophie was glad to see the Salter family go off to France for their holiday, although after that she had to rely on the bus to get into the office. She found it interesting to see what went on there and she earned a little extra pocket money. The clerk, Mr Walsh, was a jolly, middle-aged man who teased her a good deal, but taught her a lot too.

Darrell's flat turned out to be in a Victorian two up two down cottage in a back street that had been divided to make two dwellings.

'I have the top flat,' Darrell told her the first time he took her there. 'It's just two small rooms really. My bedroom is at the back and the front room is my living room and kitchen.'

He threw open the door and ushered her in. Sophie looked round. From the way he'd spoken of it, she was expecting to see a sophisticated bachelor pad, but it was cold, comfortless and shabby. Basic kitchen furniture filled one wall, the sink was full of dishes waiting to be washed, the meagre electric cooker showed ample evidence of previous meals and beer cans were overflowing the waste bin.

'Is your bathroom off the bedroom?' she asked.

'Not nearly so handy.' He pulled a rueful face. 'It's in an extension built out in the back yard and I share with the downstairs flat.'

Her curiosity wasn't yet satisfied. 'Could I use your loo?' It was really an excuse to see it all. The only thing wrong with his bathroom was that it could do with a good clean. The atmosphere was heavy with damp but also perfume.

There was a large wooden box on the floor with Darrell's name on it. Sophie lifted the lid and was surprised at the contents: fragrances for men, bath gels ditto, fancy shampoos, mousses for styling his hair, body oils, tanning lotions, and creams in a hundred and one half-used bottles and pots. More cosmetics than she used herself, or had seen in Judith's house. She hadn't known men used such things. Dad certainly didn't.

Sophie went back upstairs and sat down on a lumpy armchair saying nothing. She didn't want to belittle his home or show her lack of experience. Perhaps young sophisticated men lived like this.

Darrell switched on a one-bar electric fire. Two packets of sandwiches from Marks and Spencer stood ready on the table beside her. She watched him fish two mugs out of the sink, rinse them, drop a tea bag in each and pour on hot water.

'Do you like living here?' she asked.

'I'd love to have somewhere better.' He smiled. 'I'll be looking to move up as soon as the finances allow, but I'm happy here. Quite settled. It's very central and it's private.'

'It must be lovely to live alone. No parents demanding to

know where you're going all the time and spoiling for a row if you're five minutes late. You have freedom to do what you want.' Sophie shivered. 'The sandwiches are great.'

'Sorry,' he said. 'It's a bit nippy here. Look, it'll be warmer in the back. Finish your tea and we'll move in there.'

Sophie shivered again but this time it was a shiver of delight. She guessed what was coming. He'd made love to her more than once on the back seat of his car. She knew she was playing with fire, but Darrell was always careful to take precautions and he said it was perfectly safe. The fact that it was strictly forbidden by all adults and Dad would be absolutely horrified made it even more exciting.

His small bedroom was almost filled with a rumpled double bed and there were large mirrors on three of the walls. There were cosmetics spread over every available surface, including some on the floor, pushed into one corner.

'You've got a lovely lot of stuff.' Sophie picked up a pot of mousse. 'Do you use all these things?'

'All the time.' He looked in the mirror and pulled up a few strands of his hair. 'I have to tie it in a pony tail for work but it ruins my style.' It was usually loose about his shoulders when he was away from school.

'It looks lovely when you go on stage.'

'I have to shampoo it first, rub in lots of that mousse and let it dry naturally to get the right look.'

'The just got out of bed look?'

He laughed. 'Right now I'm more interested in getting in.'

He threw off his shirt. He had a marvellous body, she thought. She loved the serpents on his shoulder. He pulled her against him and unfastened her bra.

Soon after she'd met him, he'd told her that if she'd just

relax and let him make love to her he'd teach her to enjoy it, and he had. 'One of life's wonderful experiences,' he'd whispered.

Sophie agreed. Darrell made her feel very grown up and she was very much in love with him.

September came. Hilary hoped Charlie was happy with his chef's course and would settle down. He seemed suddenly keen on cooking and would come home and take over her kitchen to make cakes or perhaps produce a curry for supper. His food was surprisingly good and she and Ben showered him with high praise.

She made a point of calling in the garden centre shop more often than she used to, to chat with Stella Ingram. Stella was tall and willowy with a pert upturned nose. She was friendly to the customers and had an efficient manner. Ben was delighted with the way she ran the shop.

Stella reported that Gary was enjoying the course and thought it a great improvement on school. Hilary wondered if Charlie always attended the lectures, but when she tried to discuss this with Stella it seemed it hadn't occurred to her that the friends might truant.

Ben helped Charlie buy a second-hand motor bike and insisted on lessons to teach him to ride it safely. He passed his test without any trouble. Gary was said to be disappointed that he couldn't have a bike too, but Charlie took him into college on the pillion and often took him out in the evenings or at weekends.

Charlie felt his O level results branded him a failure, and the fact that he'd left school at the earliest possible moment while

Andy was staying on to do his A levels made him feel he was falling behind his twin brother.

But in the following months, Charlie felt he'd gone up a notch in status by possessing a motor bike. There was quite a gang of bikers at the technical college, some of whom he knew slightly. On many evenings, they rode some distance from home and gathered at a pub called the Cheshire Cheese.

Charlie wanted to be one of the group. He saw them as the leaders of the pack, the go-getters. They were out enjoying themselves as free agents while lesser mortals caught the bus or waited to be ferried about by their parents.

The first time Charlie went to the Cheshire Cheese the publican refused to serve him, saying he didn't look eighteen, though Charlie assured him he was.

'I'll need proof before you can come in here. Bring your birth certificate next time. I could get in trouble if I served you.'

Feeling downhearted, Charlie made for the door and was followed outside by one of the bikers. It was a dark cold night.

'I know you, don't I?' the biker said. 'You live at the garden centre. I'm Wally Stevens.'

'Yes, I've seen you in college.'

'Hang on a sec till the landlord turns his back. It's pretty full tonight. We're all together in that conservatory place at the back and he doesn't come in there much. Now . . . Come on, this way.'

Charlie followed him with his head down and was pushed into the corner and surrounded by the bikers. Wally went to get him the pint of lager he asked for. Charlie admired Wally's black leather jacket and trousers and wished he could have a similar outfit. It seemed Wally was accepted as the group's leader.

'What you have to do to be served', he told Charlie, 'is to photocopy your birth certificate, and alter the date of your birth on the copy. Then you make a copy of the copy. That way, you can get it to look unaltered. Show him yours, Buster. Looks pukka, doesn't it?'

'It took a few copies to get it like that.'

Charlie examined the date on it. Nobody would think it wasn't genuine. 'Will he accept a photocopy?'

'He has to, doesn't he? All you need say is you can't carry an important document like your birth certificate round with you. It's not something you can afford to lose.'

Packets of cigarettes were passed round and sometimes something different. Charlie didn't need to ask what it was. Drugs of many sorts were being pushed at the bus stops outside secondary schools and colleges. He and Gary, like many of the boys, had already tried a few of them.

Charlie set to work on his birth certificate and got Gary to do the same, and the landlord of the Cheshire Cheese accepted their evidence at face value. They became regulars on two or three nights each week.

One night, when Gary's mother insisted he stay at home because she had relatives visiting, Charlie turned to his twin.

'Give yourself a night off from your books,' he urged, 'and I'll take you out on my bike.'

It would give him the chance to show off his riding skills as well as his new friends. Now that they were no longer going to school together, Charlie felt they were drifting apart and he didn't like it.

Almost immediately, he realised Andy didn't fit in with the biker crowd. He sat over his first pint looking uncomfortable and wanted to leave when they started passing a joint round.

'Don't do it, Charlie,' he said on the way home. 'You'd be better staying away from that gang. I don't like them.'

'They're good fun.'

'I don't call that fun. You'll get hooked on that stuff.'

'I only had the odd puff, and hashish won't hurt anybody.'

'It will. They had heroin there too, and that's dangerous stuff. You'll become a druggy.'

'No I won't. Wally's been at it for a couple of years and he can handle it. They reckon cigarettes are more addictive.'

'What about Gary? Does he . . . ?' Andy looked shocked.

'Since he was fourteen. Paul – you know, his older brother – lets him have a reefer from time to time. They can handle it too.'

'Does Stella know?'

Now it was Charlie's turn to feel shocked. 'Of course not. Don't you tell her, or Mum.'

'They'll say I should.'

'No!'

'I won't if you stop doing it. It's dangerous.'

'I'm sorry I took you. I wouldn't have done if I'd known you'd be like this.'

'Promise, Charlie.'

'OK, I promise,' he said. It seemed the only way to shut Andy up. He wouldn't take him again so he'd never know whether he kept his word or not.

One thing Charlie did share with his twin was an interest in girls. Going to a boys only school had made finding girlfriends difficult. Just about the only possible place was the church youth club. There were more girls there than lads and once a month they danced to tapes. Then it was possible to choose a partner.

Charlie hankered after red-haired Frankie Oldshaw, who was a great dancer, but she'd turned him down. She gyrated round kicking up her heels so high, Charlie joined the line of fascinated boys waiting to catch a glimpse of her knickers.

Sophie usually came with her friend Judith Salter. Both he and Andy had tried chatting Judith up. Andy had even taken her to the pictures once or twice but said they hadn't hit it off. Sophie would sometimes dance with him if she couldn't get a partner she liked better, which wasn't often. The other lads thought her dishy.

They both fancied Pauline Godfrey who lived next door to Judith and was sometimes to be seen riding in the lanes wearing a hard hat and a smart hacking jacket, but she looked down her nose at them.

For most of that year, Charlie was passionate about his motor bike. Then a customer told Dad and Stella that he'd seen him and Gary with a large gang of bikers in a country pub and that they'd been making a rowdy nuisance of themselves. Dad had confronted him and had a real cob on about it. Charlie had done his best to calm him down. 'We were with some friends from the college. There's a few that have bikes.'

It didn't help. Dad was ready to do his head in. 'If I hear of you doing that again, I shall lock your bike away so you can't use it. You are forbidden to ride round in a large gang or go inside pubs. You're only seventeen, for goodness' sake.'

It was one of those dull dark days in the run-up to Christmas and Hilary was feeling low. It seemed ages since she'd written anything but short pieces. With daily practice her technique was improving and it was taking her less time to write short stories, but they no longer satisfied her. The urge to write full-length books had returned; she wanted to get more deeply involved with her characters. It made her look out the note-books in which she'd drawn up her ideas for *The Dog Days of Summer*.

She read through the whole plot again. She'd added extra scenes of action which she hoped might turn out to be exciting. She had several subplots and what could be a good climax. Surely now she could write it in the light popular style she was using for her stories?

She'd rewritten the first few chapters some months ago but she'd grown dissatisfied and given up on it. It didn't seem quite right now but she couldn't put her finger on the reason. Perhaps she should run her ideas past her agent and get her advice? Fern had offered that sort of help the last time she'd spoken to her.

Hilary spread her notebooks out in front of her and rang Fern Granville's number. A voice machine told her the number had been withdrawn from use. She rang directory enquiries but the girl couldn't give her a new number. She suggested the business was no longer operating.

That made Hilary uneasy but she found it hard to believe. She wrote a letter to Fern and posted it to her office, but it was returned to her with 'Not known at this address' scrawled on the envelope.

As a last resort, Hilary went to the library to consult the latest edition of the yearbook in which Fern used to advertise, but the name of her agency was no longer listed. It seemed directory enquiries was right. Fern was no longer in business.

Hilary felt thoroughly depressed. It seemed she'd lost not only her publisher but also her agent. She was right back where she'd started all those years ago.

She tried to tell Ben she was feeling disenchanted with her lot but Ben was both busy and delighted with the way the garden centre was expanding. He hardly seemed to notice anything she did.

He talked a lot about Stella, and how she was bringing new ideas to the shop. She'd found a company making fancy pots and baskets for houseplants and persuaded him to order some. The shop looked dazzlingly festive with scented gardenias in gold ceramic pots, scented stephanotis in silver ones, and poinsettias in containers made of glass. They were all selling like hot cakes. Christmas 1983 looked as though it was going to be the busiest and most profitable so far.

Hilary was impressed and wrote an article about festive plants for *Horticulture Week*, a magazine to which Ben subscribed. She was afraid it was too late for this Christmas, but next year she'd polish it up and send it off in good time.

Stella was glowing with success and bubbling with enthusiasm. She'd admitted to Hilary that at last she was able to push the horror of her divorce behind her. She looked less stressed, younger and smarter than she used to. She made Hilary feel frumpish, and lazy, because she'd made no preparations for Christmas as yet. She went less often to the shop for a chat. It made her feel disgruntled to see so much bustle and jollity.

To cheer her up, and by way of a reward for the boys, Ben booked a holiday in Spain during the week between Christmas and New Year. It would be their first trip abroad and they were all looking forward to it.

CHAPTER EIGHT

HILARY FELT no better. Ben and the boys were in high spirits and looking forward to the festive season, but Ben had been a bit offhand with her recently. She didn't feel as close to him as she used to. Perhaps it was her fault: she was tied up with her writing and taking less interest in the garden centre. After she'd cleared up after breakfast she couldn't summon the energy either to drive to the supermarket or to sit down and write.

The day was cold and grey, and she decided to walk down to the village shop. She could pay their paper bill and pick up a few groceries there. She found Isobel leaning on the counter gossiping with Mrs Grant, the postmistress.

'Such a jolly time of the year,' the postmistress said. 'I do love Christmas, don't you?' Hilary wished all the jollity could be over and done with.

'I was thinking of stopping in at your place for a cup of coffee on the way home,' she told her sister.

'You're very welcome, but I want to ice my Christmas cake. You can give me a hand.' Isobel beamed at her. 'You're better at cake decoration than I am.'

Hilary didn't feel like it. She'd have liked to call on her mother instead, but she and Tom had gone away for a few days.

'Do come,' Izzy said. 'We can have a heart to heart while we get on with it.'

As they left the shop, Mrs Grant wished them a happy Christmas.

Once outside, Hilary said irritably, 'Everybody's so damned happy. All I see is the extra work Christmas brings.'

'You are in a bad way. What's brought this on?'

Hilary didn't want to talk about Ben. Anyway, what could she say? It was just a gut feeling that she was getting less of his attention than she used to. In any case, Isobel couldn't think straight about Ben. That he'd been her boyfriend to start with still clouded things.

'It's all right for you.' Hilary launched into an account of her other problems.

Isobel didn't seem all that sympathetic. Instead, she asked, 'D'you think Mum's all right?

'All right? Of course. Why shouldn't she be?'

'I've got the feeling all isn't well.'

'With Tom, you mean?'

'Yes.'

'They were up at my place the other day and seemed OK. I mean, he waltzes her round. They're always going out for meals or away for weekends and holidays. I'm quite envious at times. Ben's a stick-in-the-mud by comparison. I can't see Mum has anything to complain about.'

'There's something odd about Tom.'

'Well, he went bankrupt and his first wife committed suicide – that's bound to leave scars. But what do scars matter if Mum's happy with him?'

Isobel looked thoughtful.

'I thought you liked him when he first came on the scene?'

'I did, but then I met him when I went shopping. He sort of latched on to me in the supermarket. I thought he was going to make a pass at me.'

'Oh, Izzy! You do flatter yourself. You had plenty of boyfriends dancing round you when you were young, but by then?'

'I wonder if Mum's worried about money?'

Hilary gave a mirthless laugh. 'She can't be. Didn't Aunt Mavis leave a fortune? Even shared between the three of us, it's a lot of money. It makes me feel rich.'

As soon as they reached her cottage, Isobel took her into the kitchen and made them both a cup of coffee. Then she measured her icing sugar into a bowl. She said, 'I expect you're bored being at home all day by yourself. It doesn't make me bubble over with joy. It was great at first, but long term and when the weather's bad . . . At this time of the year I miss all the nativity plays and end of term parties we had at school.'

'You can always get another job.'

'I might when Daisy's in school.'

'And you don't have the worry with Sophie that I do with the twins.'

'We all worry about our kids, Hilly. Is that somebody at the door?'

'Yes, I heard a knock.'

As Isobel was separating out an egg white, Hilary went to see who it was.

'Hello. Come in.' She raised her voice. 'It's Primmy and Prue, Izzy.'

They crowded into the kitchen. Primmy said, 'Oh, goodness, you're cooking? We were going to ask a favour of you.'

'More cooking, I'm afraid,' Prue said ruefully. 'You know the curate's taking a group of youngsters out carolling tomorrow night?'

'Yes, to sing to the parish invalids. Sophie's going.'

'Is she? They were practising last night, but we didn't see her there when we went over to have a word with the curate, did we, Prue? Anyway, there's the carol concert in church afterwards and the curate says he'd like to offer the youngsters tea and mince pies in the church hall.'

'We offered to make the mince pies but he wanted so many that Flora said she'd do half.'

'But now it seems Tom has taken her over to France for a couple of days on a Christmas shopping trip.'

'Of course we'll do them,' Isobel said quickly. 'How many do you want?'

Primmy unpacked frozen pastry and jars of mincemeat from her bag. 'As many as you can get from this. Small ones, please – they go further. It's the old people's Christmas lunch the next day and if there are any left over they'll come in for that.'

'Are you sure you don't mind?' Prue asked. 'You don't think we're battening on you?'

'No. Hilly will help me. In fact, Hilly, you could start rolling out the pastry now.'

When the aunts had gone, Isobel said, 'Mother may have her problems with Tom, but she never complains of being depressed or bored.'

'Lucky Mum.'

'I don't know about that, but keeping busy helps,' Isobel told her firmly. 'Stay and have a bit of lunch with me for a change. I'll ring Ben and tell him he'll have to shift for himself today. Then we'll sit down and try to list what we need to prepare for Christmas.'

Hilary was still there when Seb and Sophie came home from school. Sophie seemed in a lively mood and made a cup of tea for them all. As she handed a cup to her mother, Hilary heard Isobel say, 'Didn't you tell us you were going to carol practice last night?'

Hilary noticed Sophie's momentary freeze. 'Yes,' she said, and looked up smiling.

'Aunt Primmy said she went in to talk to the curate and she didn't see you there.'

'I saw her though,' Sophie said quickly, but something in her manner made Hilary wonder if she had. She was reminded of Charlie when he was trying to skate over something.

Were Seb and Izzy having problems with Sophie that she didn't know about?

Over recent months, Flora's doubts about Tom had niggled at the back of her mind. She'd learned that she only had to question something and he'd put his arms round her and explain it all away. He had a gift that seemed almost magical of dispelling all her worries. He could convince her that her doubts were groundless, making her think that her nature must be overly suspicious.

She knew Tom hadn't given up the idea of moving to a bigger house. He would pause in front of any estate agent's window they happened to pass to check the display. He'd got into the habit of bringing in the local paper from the doormat and turning straight away to the houses advertised for sale. Often he folded the pages to point one out to Flora.

'You're no longer satisfied with this cottage?' she asked once. 'You're not happy here?'

He looked abashed. 'Flora, of course I am. You must forgive me. I've always been interested in houses. I get carried away sometimes.'

She frowned. 'I get the feeling you're tired of being here and you're edging me towards a move.'

'Oh, no! I must try to stop, then. It's just that building houses was once my life and their design fascinates me.'

That put her in the wrong and left her wavering and uncertain.

His arms came round her in a hug. 'There's nowhere nicer than your cottage. I love living here.'

Flora would have liked to talk her worries over with her daughters but it seemed disloyal to Tom to discuss such personal concerns with them.

Hilary had always invited all her family to spend Christmas Day in her house. 'I don't know whether I'll bother this year,' she told Ben over supper that night.

'Why not? You love family get-togethers.'

'It's a lot of work and the twin aunts are almost eighty. They can't help with the Christmas cakes and puddings as they used to.'

'What about Flora?' Ben buttered a slice of bread. 'She'll do her bit.'

Her mother usually cooked the turkey lunch. Hilary said, 'She's getting on a bit too, and cooking for eight adults and five children is a lot to ask. Especially when three of the children are teenagers with appetites like horses.'

'What will they all do if we don't have them here?' Ben wanted to know. 'We've set a precedent. I think we must.'

It was Charlie who stepped in and did much of the cooking. The turkey lunch with all the trimmings was excellent. Hilary was pleased to hear Flora sing his praises.

Charlie seemed to be blossoming. He might have been nervous and lacking in confidence at school but he certainly had plenty of confidence when it came to cooking. His Yule log, mince pies and small fancy cakes were absolutely delicious.

He had had a spurt of growth and broadened out across the shoulders. He was now taller and heavier than Andy and looked suddenly more mature. His fair hair had darkened to light brown and always seemed to be falling across his face. Suddenly, he seemed a handsome young man, while Andy was still a schoolboy.

Despite everything, Hilary enjoyed Christmas Day with all her family around her. She'd always loved seeing her house decorated with holly and all the presents round the tree. Ben persuaded his aunts to play carols on their mandolins and the rest of the family sang along. There was a party atmosphere.

As soon as Christmas was over they flew to Spain for their holiday, and she found it soothing to lie on the sand in the warm Spanish sun. The twins had promised to keep an eye on Jamie and they were playing football with some other boys further along the beach.

Hilary closed her eyes and pondered on why she was unhappy with her writing career. Her ambition had not been to write for magazines and newspapers; she wanted to write books. Right, she told herself, then she'd better get on with it.

This time, though, she wouldn't stop writing stories and articles. She'd devote her mornings to the book and her afternoons to the shorter stuff.

It was no good moaning that she hadn't got a publisher or an agent. She didn't have a book ready to send out. Her first step must obviously be to write one. It was silly to think she was back where she'd started. She had experience now, and what could be more valuable than that?

This holiday was providing a rest, and clearing her head. She'd go home and make a new start.

Ben was dozing in the deck chair beside her. She tried to talk to him about his future plans for the business, but he was not very forthcoming. Last night, after they'd enjoyed wine with a good dinner, he'd made Hilary cross.

He knew she was worried about Charlie. Since getting the motor bike, he'd stayed out late almost every night. She'd tried to reason with him, to set boundaries for him, but to no effect. She'd done her best to persuade Ben to back her up and be stricter with him.

'Tell him you'll confiscate his bike for a week if he doesn't come home on time.'

'He wouldn't care if I did. He says it's too cold for biking now and he wishes he had a car.'

Hilary had heard Charlie wheedle, 'Will you give me driving lessons for my eighteenth birthday?' Last night, without so much as a word to her first, Ben had promised him he could have them.

'Thanks, Dad.' Charlie had beamed at them both. 'That's marvellous. The perfect present for me.'

'It's a long time off yet,' Hilary had said, and was

comforted by the thought. She would have liked to make the lessons conditional on Charlie's coming home earlier and having fewer late nights.

Ben had been thinking about buying a new smarter van for his business for a long time. In the first week of 1984, he ordered it, and the twins helped him design a new simpler logo to have painted on the sides. For Hilary the festive season had gone better than she'd expected but she was glad it was over and the schools and technical college were reopening their doors.

On the first day back, Charlie learned that one of his biker friends had skidded on an icy road and broken his leg. Another had had a worse accident and gone over the top of a car that had stopped suddenly in front of him. He was in hospital with head injuries.

Charlie told himself he was too good a rider to have accidents like that, but on icy mornings, or when there was a covering of snow on the roads, he took the bus to college. He was tired of his motor bike; a car would be both warmer and safer.

A week later, Stella asked if she might have a day off work in order to take Gary's older brother Paul back to Sheffield University at the start of the new term there.

'He has so much luggage, it's difficult for him to go by train,' she explained.

Ben agreed immediately, saying he would stand in at the shop for her on that day. But two days before, he went down with what he thought was a bad cold, and the next day he was running a temperature and took to his bed.

'I think he's got flu,' Hilary told Stella. 'But I can run the shop tomorrow – no need to alter your plans.'

'You'll have Ben to look after,' Stella fretted. 'I feel awful taking time off.'

'Don't worry. It's the first day off you've asked for in ages. We can't complain about that.'

Most mornings, Charlie rode down the road to call for Gary and take him to college. Everything had fallen flat since their holiday; the fun was over and they were back to the daily grind. Charlie was bored with his lectures. He thought the instructors treated them like idiots, going slowly over and over the same few points instead of getting on with things.

Gary lived quite close, in a smart new semi-detached on a housing estate only a few hundred yards from the garden centre. On the day Stella was taking Paul back to Sheffield, Charlie could see their garage doors wide open and all the Ingram family milling round the family car. It was an old one and Gary referred to it as a shed. Charlie knew Stella had planned an early start this morning, in order to get home in daylight.

'What's the matter?' he asked as he joined them.

'Mum can't start the car,' Paul told him. He looked fraught.

'Why not?'

'The battery's flat.'

Charlie reckoned he knew more about cars than any of the Ingram family. He had plenty of confidence in his driving skills and was interested in how engines worked. He'd been given books for Christmas on cars and driving and had studied them.

'Can I try?' he asked. Stella was more than ready to let him. He thought she knew little about what went on under the bonnet. Paul wasn't that interested in cars either; he'd had a few driving lessons but he hadn't taken his test yet.

Charlie sat in the sagging driving seat. When he failed to start the engine too, he was able to tell Stella, 'Paul's right: the battery's flat. I can start it if you have a battery charger.'

'I don't have one.'

'Who do you know who has?'

The Ingrams were shaking their heads. Knowing his father was ill and his mother would need to open the shop, Charlie said, 'I could telephone Nana. I think Tom might have one.'

Stella ushered him into the hall and sat him in front of her phone. It was Tom who answered, and Charlie asked him if he'd mind coming round to start Stella's car for her. 'Bring jump leads or a battery charger,' he told him.

Tom arrived within ten minutes. He was knowledgeable about cars and soon had the jump leads attached and the power running in from his own engine. He diagnosed the problem.

'Your dynamo seems to have packed up,' he told Stella. 'It isn't charging the battery.' He tried to start the car again. 'It's a garage job, I'm afraid. It'll have to be towed in. You need a new dynamo.'

'Oh no!' Stella was upset. 'That settles it, Paul, I won't be able to take you back today. You'll have to go by train after all.'

Tom said to Stella, 'What about you? Can I run you round to the garage so you can arrange it? It'll probably take twenty-four hours to order the part.'

'Yes, please. I usually take it to Eddie's garage in the village. After that, if you could drop me off at the garden centre, I might as well go to work. It'll save Hilary running the shop. She'll have enough to do looking after Ben. Paul, get your things out of the boot and stack them in the hall.'

'Mum, I'll need money for the train.'

'So you will.' She opened her purse. 'Here, this should cover it. Ring up first to check the times.' She turned to Tom. 'I'll just tell my mother what's happened. I won't be a minute.' She ran into the house, and when she came back she saw Gary and Charlie were still there.

'Off you go, you two. What are you hanging about for? You're going to be late.' Without waiting for a reply, she got into the passenger seat of the Mercedes.

Charlie had had an absolutely spiffing idea. As Tom drove off, he grinned at Paul and said, 'I could take you. All I need is a car.'

'You can't drive.' Paul was four years older than Gary and Charlie, and his attitude was dismissive.

'Of course I can. I could drive you to Sheffield.' Charlie had never been there. If he had misgivings, they were about finding the way. 'Do you know how to get to Sheffield?'

'Yes, I think so, but Mum has maps in the car.'

'Get them.' Charlie found maps confusing. He hoped Paul was better than he was at reading them. 'Come on, Gary. Where can I hide my bike?'

'Behind the garage? Nobody will see it there and it'll be safe.' Charlie wheeled it round. 'Where will you get a car from? You're joking, aren't you?'

'My mother's got a car she doesn't use very much. Just to go shopping and that sort of thing. She wouldn't miss it.'

'Can you drive it?'

Charlie had never been allowed to try. 'Yes, I think so.'

He was sorry Dad had bought a new van; having learned

to drive on the old one he felt more comfortable with that. The new one was the same make and Dad had allowed him to try it round the site; he'd managed all right but the gears were a bit stiff. The trouble was, Dad was much fussier about the new one and not nearly so ready to let him play about with it, as he called it.

Charlie made up his mind. 'I'll borrow the van.'

Gary looked a bit shocked. 'Are you sure it'll be all right?'

'Course I am.'

Charlie had fantasies about driving his friends around – not in his father's van, of course, but in some much fancier James Bond type car. They were always full of admiration that he could do it, especially older boys like Paul, who'd had plenty of time to learn to drive but hadn't got round to it.

'I need to fetch the van now,' he said, 'while Mum's in the shop.'

'Shall I come with you?' Gary asked. 'I could keep look-out.'

Charlie didn't want Gary with him; he'd attract less attention on his own. He didn't want Mum or Dad to know he was taking the van. They definitely wouldn't allow it, but it would be such a lark. Much better than going to tech, and he'd be doing Paul a good turn.

'You two stay here,' he said. 'I'll bring it round so Paul can load his things in. Ten minutes at the most.'

His heart was thumping when he got home and let himself into the empty kitchen, where the scent of the breakfast bacon still hung in the air. Dad was sick in bed upstairs and wouldn't be able to see or hear what he was doing from there, but he needed to get away before Stella relieved Mum and she came home. He found the keys to the van and the gadget that opened the garage door and slid them in his pocket. He listened: the house was absolutely silent. For a moment Charlie hesitated. Sheffield was a long way and he'd only ever driven the van round the garden centre, but now he'd got this far he wasn't going to bottle out. He crept to the back door and shut it as quietly as he could behind him.

The garage door creaked up. He slid into the van's driving seat and pulled on the door until it clicked softly shut. It smelled dauntingly new, but the layout was pretty much like the old one. With his heart in his mouth, he started the engine. Mum would have a fit if she saw him leave. He wanted to hurry, get away as quickly as he could, but knew he must be careful.

He backed out slowly. So far so good. He brought the garage door down again and headed for the gate and the main road. There wasn't too much traffic, and he felt he could cope with it. He was used to driving his bike, after all. Dad had said he had real aptitude for driving, hadn't he?

The shortest way would be to turn left and go past the garden centre, but he didn't want to meet Tom and Stella about to turn in, or have Mum catch sight of him as he drove past. It meant a bit of a detour, but it was the safest thing to do. Moments later he was drawing up outside Gary's house. He felt buoyed up. He could drive, all right – he really could do it. Going to Sheffield was going to be fun.

Paul and Gary were watching from the bay window and came rushing out with bags and parcels when they saw him. Charlie got out and opened the rear doors of the van. Suitcases thudded in, Doc Martens, coats, rolled-up sleeping bags tied with string, plastic bags full of books. They kept running back to collect more of Paul's belongings.

'I've been in halls of res up till now,' he explained, 'but I'm going to share a flat with three other blokes this term. That's why I need all this clobber.'

'Have you brought the maps?' Charlie asked. He was worried about not being able to find the way.

'Yes,' Paul hissed. 'And the picnic lunch Mum made for us. Oh, Lord! Grandma's come out. I'll have to say goodbye to her.'

Charlie watched him kiss her. He knew her from visiting the house, and waved to her.

'Get in, let's get going,' he said.

'Where shall I sit?' Paul asked.

For the first time, Charlie realised he had two passengers and only one passenger seat. He thought he'd read that it wasn't safe to ride in the back of a van. Would that be the Highway Code?

'Gary can sit next to me.' Gary was his friend. 'Paul, you'd better go in the back. Can you sit on a suitcase or something? I want you to tell me which way to go.'

'Hang on while I look at the map.'

In Charlie's experience maps didn't always help. In the summer, he'd taken Gary to Wrexham on his bike to visit a friend, and although he'd consulted Dad's book of maps and written down the route and the road numbers, he'd written down A438 instead of A483. He'd failed to find the road he was looking for and got horribly lost.

Gary was even worse with road numbers, and when they set out for a day in Blackpool the same thing had happened. Blackpool had defeated them; they'd driven twice round Preston, had lunch in a roadside café, then gone back home. Of course, it would be easier in the van: they could take the whole book of maps with them and Paul wasn't dyslexic anyway.

'I think I know the way – Mum's taken me several times. Head for the motorway. It's the M53 then the M56.'

Charlie felt he was being adventurous enough without that. He said, 'There must be another way? On ordinary roads?'

'Well, that's the most direct route,' Paul said. 'We need the motorway to get us off the Wirral and south of Manchester. Anything else and you'd be driving miles out of the way. After that it has to be ordinary roads. It's the A57.'

'Right, the motorway it is. Tell me when I need to come off.'

Once on the motorway, Charlie put his foot down. He felt exhilarated. He could do this; it was easy-peasy and a lot of fun. The Ingram boys were laughing and joking, their spirits soaring. Before long they opened up the picnic lunch saying they were hungry although it was barely eleven o'clock.

'That's not fair,' Charlie said. 'I'm hungry too.'

The packet was put away temporarily until Charlie pulled into a motorway service station. They shared out the sandwiches which had been intended for Paul and his mother and then walked over to the shop where Paul bought a large packet of jam doughnuts to fill up on.

'I think I might need more diesel to get us back home.' Charlie had been watching the gauge for some miles. 'It could be touch and go.'

'Then let's get it now,' Paul said. 'It would be on my conscience if you ran out of juice. My train fare can pay for that.'

Charlie felt they reached Sheffield quite quickly, but driving round the town he had a couple of sticky moments. He had to turn right and he didn't at first notice the silver car coming towards him at speed. He got across all right even though the driver hooted violently at him. There was another bad moment on a roundabout, when they were lost and Paul didn't know which road to take. He drove round it three times while Gary and Paul read the signs, but they got it right eventually.

They wasted a lot of time looking for the flat. It turned out to be in a high rise council block of the type becoming hard to rent to families.

Paul said, 'It's a bit of a comedown after living in halls.'

The other three students he was to share with were already there. They were all a bit upset at the poor condition of the furniture and equipment. Paul introduced them. Roger looked quite old; he must be thirty at least and was beginning to go bald. Frank wore gold-rimmed spectacles and looked studious, though they said he wasn't. Jim was a redhead with a Yorkshire accent.

Charlie basked in their admiration that he was able to drive the family van halfway across England, and that his parents allowed him to, especially when he told them it was almost brand new. Nobody mentioned that not only had he not passed his driving test yet, but he hadn't even had a driving lesson. Charlie was on a high, though he was a bit nervous of leaving the new van outside in a district like this. He followed the others round the flat on a tour of inspection. There were two bedrooms, each with two beds, a living room and very run-down bathroom and kitchen.

Paul made mugs of tea, but he and Gary were feeling

hungry again and he suggested something more substantial than the cake and biscuits the other lads' mothers had sent back with them. Roger had stocked the larder with several tins of baked beans and a carton of eggs. Paul decided on both with plenty of toast, and Gary and Charlie cooked for them all.

The flat was equipped for four people, so there weren't enough chairs to go round. Charlie perched on the arm of the settee to eat his share and found it much more fun than a meal at home.

Afterwards, Frank passed his packet of Embassy cigarettes round the table. Charlie had been smoking since he was twelve but had managed to hide it from his parents until last year. When his mother said she could smell smoke on his clothes, he'd managed to convince her it was because his friends smoked, until that is he put out a bomber jacket to be washed and overlooked the cigarette packet still containing three fags in the pocket.

His conscience pricked when he thought of his mother cooking a meal and expecting him home to eat it. Suddenly he noticed the navy blue sky and the myriad twinkling lights in the distance. It was already dark!

It made him uneasy. Would he be able to find his way home at night? He'd never tried driving anything but his motor bike in the dark. He'd never even turned the van lights on and wondered if he'd be able to. Of course he would. There was a book of instructions telling him how to do everything. Paul would help him if he couldn't make them out. And he'd got here, hadn't he? He'd get home all right, he was sure he would. He had a good memory for a road once he'd driven along it, but perhaps they should start soon.

'Why don't we make a night of it?' Frank suggested. 'What about going out for a drink?'

'To the students' union?' Paul asked. 'It seems an age since we were there.'

'Or we could have a bit of a pub crawl. It's our first night back. We could use a last fling before settling down to work, couldn't we?'

'We haven't any money.' Charlie was fingering the small change in his pocket.

'We've all got our allowances for the term.' Paul grinned at him. 'And there's a bit left over from my train fare.'

'Shall we share a joint first?' Roger fetched some cigarette papers and a plastic bag from his bedroom. 'To put us in the mood.'

'Good idea,' Frank said enthusiastically. 'Have you boys tried grass?'

Charlie felt lit up with excitement. It would be a great night out. He'd taken Gary on a few pub crawls with the bikers in the summer when they could get their hands on a few of the readies, and there was no shortage of pushers trying to sell them drugs outside the gates of the tech, but usually it was a question of either buying grass or saving his cash for the pub. To have both and to be with this group of older men made him feel he'd left boyhood behind.

'We should have a rare old time,' Paul said. 'Charlie, you can drive us round, and we'll all chip in to treat the driver.'

CHAPTER NINE

January 1984

THAT MORNING, Hilary made a large pan of chicken and pea soup and was relieved to hear Ben say that he felt better and would come downstairs to have lunch in the kitchen with her. They'd just sat down to eat when there was a frantic knocking on their back door. Hilary went to see who it was and found a worried Stella Ingram on the step.

'Come in and have a seat.' She led her into the kitchen and pulled out a chair at the table.

'Sorry, you're eating . . .' Stella was breathless.

'Don't worry. Is something the matter?'

'My mother's just rung the shop. She told me Charlie brought your new van round and loaded Paul's belongings into it. He's apparently driving him to Sheffield.'

'What?' Hilary felt a dart of fear. 'Surely not?' But she knew it was just the sort of lark he would get up to.

'Gary's gone with them too.'

Ben, his face like thunder, was already on his feet studying the key board inside one of the kitchen cupboards. 'The keys to the new van have gone, and the gadget that opens the garage door.' He sounded horrified.

'I'll get the spare.' Hilary shot upstairs to their study. She wouldn't believe the van was gone until she saw the empty space with her own eyes. It took only moments to run out to the garage; she came back more slowly. Two pairs of eyes watched her sit down in front of her hardly touched bowl of soup. 'It's not there.'

'I'm awfully sorry,' Stella choked out. 'If only my car hadn't broken down.'

Ben's face had gone grey. 'What if he has an accident? The insurance company won't pay out. Charlie doesn't have a licence.'

'Oh, my God!'

Hilary dropped her head on her hands. She had a vision of the front of the van smashed in with Charlie cut and bleeding over the steering wheel and the other two boys unconscious. He could cause a big pile-up with other people hurt too. She groaned. 'Charlie hasn't even had one driving lesson yet. He'll never get to Sheffield and back.' Her tone was accusing. 'You've let him drive it round the site?'

Ben nodded grimly. 'Only once, to try it.'

'Enough to make him feel he can.'

'I'm sorry,' Stella said again. 'I'm afraid Paul might have asked him.'

'How long does it take to get to Sheffield?' Ben asked.

'About three hours.'

'Well, it's now nearly half one. If he started around nine, he could even be there.'

'It could have been after nine when they started.'

'Is there any way you can find out?' Hilary sucked on her lip. 'Could you get Paul on the phone?'

Stella shook her head. 'Last term I could when he was

living in halls, but he's moved out into a flat. I don't know if there's a phone there.'

'So there's no way we can find out? Except wait to hear?'

Stella was frowning, 'Well, he wrote down his new address for me. I don't remember whether he left a phone number too. I could ring my mother and ask her to look.'

Hilary shivered again. 'I suppose we'd hear if Charlie had an accident. The police . . .'

'What a mess,' Ben said.

'I'd better go and open the shop,' Stella pulled herself to her feet.

'Try phoning when you have a quiet moment,' Ben told her.

When Stella went, Hilary turned again to her bowl of soup. It had gone cold, but she couldn't have eaten it anyway.

Ben stood up. 'I'm going back to bed. I don't feel all that well after all. You'll let me know if Stella makes contact?'

Hilary tried to settle down and work on the short story she'd started yesterday but there was no way she could stop worrying about Charlie. She put on her coat and ran down to tell her mother what Charlie had done. Tom was about to go out. Hilary asked, 'Did you have any inkling he intended to take Paul to Sheffield?'

'Heavens, no. It didn't cross my mind that he might. I don't think it crossed Stella's either. She was fraught.'

'What was Charlie thinking of?' Flora said. 'He must have known he was breaking the law.'

'If he stopped to think at all.'

'You can't ask the police to help,' Tom pointed out. 'He must be committing half a dozen offences. They'd charge him.'

Hilary was trembling. 'There's nothing we can do but wait. Either Charlie and Gary will come back unscathed, or we'll hear from the police that he's had an accident.'

'And in that case,' Tom said, 'he'll find he's in very hot water.'

'I do hope he doesn't write off Ben's new van,' Flora fretted.

Hilary didn't stay. If any news broke it would be at home, but she did call in at the shop to have a word with Stella. She was equally worried, and blaming her boys.

When Andy came home from school, Hilary couldn't stop herself from questioning him closely, although she'd already worked out that it must have been a spur of the moment decision of Charlie's. It was only after Tom had pronounced it was impossible to start Stella's car that Charlie would have thought of it. She satisfied herself that Andy could tell her nothing and thought sadly that Andy and Charlie were no longer the friends they'd once been.

To Hilary, it seemed an impossibly long drawn out day. Every hour or so she went up to see Ben and commiserate with him. By evening, she knew that Charlie had had more than enough time to drive both ways. Even allowing for stops to eat and rest, he could be back any time now. Until it grew dark, she kept going to the window to look at the front gate, hoping to see him turn into the drive.

The phone kept ringing and each time it did Hilary flew to it, her heart pounding, expecting it to be the police with devastating news.

This time it was Isobel. 'Mum's told me that Charlie's disappeared and so has your van. Is there any news?'

Isobel was clearly worried too, although she tried to

comfort Hilary. Then it was Stella, wanting to know if they'd heard anything. Hilary promised to ring her the moment they did. Then it was Mum again. Each time, Hilary was relieved it wasn't the police.

A white-faced Ben came downstairs in his dressing gown, coughing and sneezing. Suppertime came and went, and although Hilary cooked, only Andy and Jamie managed to eat anything.

'Where can he be?' She felt on tenterhooks. Ordinary life was over. Until they knew Charlie was all right, it was impossible to watch television or read.

'We've been too soft with him,' Ben said when they were alone again. 'Too concerned with his lack of confidence because of his dyslexia. We've tried far too hard to find something he could do and enjoy, and then praised him too highly. To take my new van shows massive over-confidence about his driving. I'll give him what-for when he comes back.'

Hilary agreed with every word Ben said, but whispered, 'I just wish he'd come home.'

Ben sighed, 'There wasn't much diesel in the van. Charlie might have let it run out without noticing. Even if he did notice, I don't suppose he'd have much money with him.'

'He wouldn't just sit in a lay-by if that happened. He'd do something.'

'Such as what?'

'Ring us, ask us to take him a can of diesel or something—'

The phone rang at that moment. Hilary's mouth went dry. Ben was nearest and picked it up. She stopped breathing to listen.

She saw Ben relax. 'No, Aunt Primmy, I'm afraid no news, we're still waiting and hoping.' He went on in that vein, repeating very much what Hilary and Isobel had said to each other. Hilary put the kettle on to make a cup of tea.

When Ben finally put the phone down, she said, 'He's endangering his own life and the Ingram boys'.'

She went through her usual evening chores, glad of something to keep her busy. She saw Jamie into bed and still there was no sign of Charlie. Andy turned off the television and went upstairs, and then Hilary's own bedtime came.

'Come on,' Ben said. 'Let's go up.'

'I won't be able to sleep.' Hilary felt near the end of her tether. 'I wish he'd come.'

'There's nothing we can do about it.' Ben climbed into bed, humped over to face the wall, and took most of the bedclothes with him. 'You must try to sleep.'

'Absolutely no chance.' Hilary felt restless. She heard the church clock strike at midnight, and again at one. She was convinced by then that the van had come off the road in some isolated spot and the boys were lying injured and unconscious.

Charlie watched Roger roll the joints, mixing the dried fibrous weed with the tobacco.

'There's enough to make three,' he said. 'We'll be able to get some more while we're out.'

Gary picked up the first and lit it, dragging on it heavily before handing it on to Charlie. He took a couple of light puffs, having read that marijuana could have the same effect on driving as alcohol. In fact, he'd felt light-headed several times as he'd driven his motor bike. That had been great fun as he'd had no worries about controlling his bike. He was very aware that the others were watching him.

'To get the most out of the weed', Roger said, 'you have to draw the smoke into your lungs and hold it there for as long as you can.'

Charlie had heard that advice before. He thought himself an experienced smoker whether of cannabis or tobacco. Within minutes he could feel a sense of calm, contentment and well-being creeping through him.

He let Gary have the end bit, which was prized because of its greater potency. Paul produced pins so the roaches could be smoked to the very tip. By then, they had all developed an acute sense of the absurd and were laughing hilariously.

Charlie giggled with them. He felt torn in two as he pulled on his bomber jacket to go out. He knew the others expected him to chauffeur them to the students' union. He wanted to shine, show off his skills, earn their admiration, but he was a stranger in town and hadn't found driving here easy. Now when they got outside, and the van loomed up in the darkness, he felt a shaft of fear.

The others paused to admire it, giggling helplessly and asking questions about the garden centre. It was cold and beginning to rain. Charlie shivered, half afraid he'd be persuaded against his better judgement. His father would have a fit if he could see him now.

'I can't drive tonight,' he told them with as much firmness as he could muster. 'Not if I'm going to have a drink. I don't want to be picked up for driving under the influence, do I?'

Not that it seemed much safer to leave the van on this car park amongst the collection of old bangers. It was not the best end of town. They didn't quibble about his decision and decided not to go far. The King's Head was on the next corner.

'We might as well start here.' Paul ushered him inside. It was shabby and full of blue smoke. At least, now, he didn't have to stay sober enough to drive. Paul had already said he and Gary could bed down for the night in the flat. Charlie thought that his best option.

He swigged down his first pint and began to think he might have enjoyed going to university after all. The evening got better as it went on. They became more rowdy and bawdy as they moved from pub to pub.

Roger managed to buy six tablets of LSD. As the barman brought them another round of beers, he put a tablet beside each glass.

Charlie didn't want to take his. He knew it would make him feel good, more alert and more in empathy with his companions, but he'd tried LSD before and the comedown had made him feel like the pits for the following twenty-four hours. His jaw had felt tight and his mouth dry, and Wally had had hallucinations. He left his on the table. Jim got up to talk to a girl at the bar and shortly afterwards disappeared with her.

'Whose is this?' Roger asked, pointing to the LSD tablet.

Charlie grinned up at him. 'Is it the one you bought for Jim?' Roger stowed it safely in his wallet amidst paroxysms of laughter.

By closing time the remaining five were all more than merry. They stayed until the landlord put them out and closed the doors behind them. It was raining. Charlie reckoned the cold, wet walk home sobered him up. He noted as they crossed the car park that his van had not been disturbed. Frank had brought some cans of beer home and they settled down to carry on drinking.

Jim came home at three in the morning and announced he

was going straight to bed. That broke the party up. Two sleeping bags were found for Charlie and Gary. There was only one settee and that had several broken springs, so Charlie elected to have a few cushions on the floor. He got into his bag and settled down to sleep.

Some time after that the noise of someone being sick woke him up. He crawled out of his bag and found the light switch, then ran to the kitchen to fetch Gary a bowl, but it was already too late. There was vomit all over Gary's sleeping bag and the settee.

Charlie went to wake Paul. An elder brother seemed the right person to deal with this emergency, but he found Paul retching in the bathroom. By then all six of them were awake. It was Jim who loaned Gary a clean T-shirt and Frank who mopped inadequately at the settee.

Charlie tried to open a window because the place stank of vomit, but the metal frames had distorted and none of them would budge. Gary called for water and they made him drink a whole glassful.

It was five thirty when they tried to settle down again. Charlie felt awful. He had a blinding headache and wished he hadn't come. Dad was going to give him hell when he found out what he'd done.

The next thing he was aware of was people walking round him, and he was surprised to find it was full daylight and gone eleven o'clock. Gary was still hunched up on the settee. Frank woke him and told him to get dressed. Charlie began to pull on his trousers. He didn't feel too good, but he didn't want to stay here either. He needed to get the van home and have a bath. There was no hot water here and he had no clean clothes.

Roger made some tea, but there was no milk left. Charlie was offered a slice of Victoria sponge or a biscuit to go with it. He accepted a digestive. Gary looked grey-faced; he drank some tea but was sick again. Paul didn't look any better.

The older boys were sorting out books and talking of lectures. The air of goodwill and generous hospitality had faded. Even Paul was short with his brother.

'Time to go,' Charlie told him. He was reassured to find the van had not been touched. He pushed Gary on to the passenger seat and climbed in himself.

Hilary was jerked back to life by her alarm clock. It was morning.

Beside her Ben stirred. 'Has Charlie come home?' he asked. 'Did you hear him?' He slid out of bed and padded in bare feet to the twins' bedroom. Hilary listened for Charlie's voice, but all she heard was Ben telling Andy it was time to get up and then calling Jamie.

For Hilary, it was a shock to find Charlie had been out all night. Was he lost? She knew he had a problem reading signposts and road numbers. Was he capable of finding his way to Sheffield and back? She had to get up to make breakfast and see Jamie and Andy off to school.

'I'll get up too,' Ben said, starting to dress.

'Are you well enough?'

'I can't lie here any longer.'

Hilary felt drained and went about her tasks like a zombie. When the boys had gone and she'd cleared breakfast away, she said to Ben, 'I'll take the car and go out and look for him.'

'No,' he said. 'What good will that do? Charlie knows his way round here. You could pass him on the road and never see him. I couldn't stand it if you disappeared too. The sensible thing is to stay here. Either Charlie will come back safely, or we'll hear from the police that he's had an accident.'

Ben went to the study, got out his ledgers and tried to occupy his mind with business matters. Hilary pottered through household tasks with her mind on Charlie. The phone kept ringing, and each time she picked it up in a sweat of nervous trepidation, but it was always a member of the family asking if there was news. They ate a late lunch and sat over cups of tea for a long time.

By three o'clock Hilary felt as though she couldn't stand another minute of idle waiting.

'I wish there was something we could do,' she was saying when she heard the van pull on to the drive. She jumped to her feet and from the window saw it turn slowly to face the garage door. Charlie was at the wheel.

She was so overwhelmed to see him back in one piece that she was slow to move. Ben was outside before her and running to wrench open the driver's door. Charlie almost fell out. He looked confused and weary.

Hilary snapped, 'Come indoors and explain where you've been.'

She left Ben walking slowly round the van examining every inch. It no longer looked spanking new. A lot of road dirt had been thrown up on it.

On the way into the kitchen, Charlie grunted, 'I've been to Sheffield.' She could hear the triumph in his voice that he'd managed it. 'Took Paul back to university. Somebody had to.'

'Nonsense. He could have gone on the train. Where's Gary?'

'I dropped him off at home.'

132

Hilary pointed to the phone. 'Ring the shop and tell his mother that he's back.'

'No, Mum. He wants to go to bed. She'll find him when she goes home.'

Hilary was shocked to find he'd given no thought to their anxiety. 'Ring now,' she ordered, in no mood to stand any messing. 'This minute. Don't you realise we've all been worried stiff?' Reluctantly Charlie lifted the handset. She listened to Stella's distorted voice and almost felt her relief.

Ben came in, his face black with anger. 'I do hope you aren't proud of yourself? Taking my van without permission. Stealing it.'

'I only borrowed it, Dad. You knew I'd bring it back.'

'If the police had found out, you'd have been charged with stealing it. I couldn't say I'd given you permission to drive it, could I? You don't have a licence. If I'd given my permission I'd be breaking the law.'

'You disappeared for thirty hours', Hilary put in, 'without letting us know where you'd gone. We've been sick with anxiety.'

'Gary's granny was in their house. She knew I was taking Paul back. He said she'd tell his mother.'

Hilary could see Ben was taken aback. 'And did you think your mother and I would derive any comfort from that? You saying you were going to drive all that way when you haven't had even one driving lesson?'

'Where have you been?' Hilary demanded. 'You can't have taken all this time to drive there and back.'

'Paul put us up in his flat.'

'You mean you stayed the night with him?' Hilary wondered why that possibility hadn't occurred to her.

'Yes. They loaned us sleeping bags.'

'Why didn't you ring to let us know? Stella's been out of her mind too.'

'There wasn't a phone. Anyway, it wouldn't have helped, would it? You'd have been just as worried about me driving back.'

Ben said severely, 'It's time you grew up, Charlie. Did you go on the motorway?'

'Yes. Paul said it was the only reasonable way.'

'Learner drivers aren't allowed on motorways. That's another law you've broken. You can't go on like this, with no thought for the consequences of what you do.'

'I'm sorry.'

'You endangered your own life, and that of Paul and Gary.'

'Rubbish, Dad. You know I can drive.'

'No, you can't. Don't be so silly. You only have a motor bike licence. If you'd had a crash, the insurance company wouldn't have paid up. It's also the law that you have to be insured against hurting other people, but you were driving without insurance of any kind.'

'That means', Hilary put in, 'you could have written off the van and we wouldn't have had a penny in recompense.'

Charlie's smile disappeared. He was no longer treating it as a jolly escapade.

'Even worse,' Ben added, 'if you'd injured somebody else you'd have been liable to pay damages. I don't know whether I'd have been held responsible for that, but if so, it could have amounted to more money than we have as a family. It could have ruined us.'

Charlie looked hang-dog now. 'Sorry, Dad.'

'You'd have been in big trouble too. You'd have been sent to some young offenders' institution. You were breaking half a dozen different laws.'

Charlie sighed. 'I've said I'm sorry. I won't do it again, I promise.' He went to the biscuit tin, but it was empty. 'I'm very hungry. Can I make some toast?'

'Did you have any lunch?' Hilary asked.

'No, and there was nothing for breakfast but a cup of tea.'

'It won't hurt you to go hungry,' Ben said crossly. 'You could have killed somebody.'

'But I didn't.'

'No, thank God. It's a miracle you didn't have an accident.'

While Ben went off to the shop to fill Stella in with the details, Hilary poached two eggs on toast for Charlie.

'Why didn't you come home last night?' she demanded. If he had, it would have put their minds at rest much sooner.

'It seemed to get dark almost as soon as we got there and I've never driven a car in the dark. I was tired, too. Paul thought it would be safer to wait until this morning.'

Hilary wasn't going to say that was wise. Charlie rarely seemed to use his head.

'He's sharing this flat with three other blokes. Gary and I cooked tea for us all. It was good fun.'

'What's the flat like?'

'Pretty awful. You wouldn't want to live there.'

As soon as Hilary had put the food in front of him, she went to the shop to see Stella too. There were no customers. Ben was rearranging the plants and Stella was talking on the telephone in the room behind. She came out a moment later.

'You don't know how thankful I was to hear they were back safely,' she said. 'That was my mother ringing to let me know Gary was back. She came home from the shops to find his anorak and trainers on the kitchen floor and him asleep on his bed.'

Stella had a lot of brown hair, which for work she piled on top of her head in a large bun. Hilary admired her simple style of dressing: crisp open-necked shirts and longish skirts. She looked elegant. Her face was pretty but today she had blue shadows under her eyes and looked tired. Hilary guessed she'd had a sleepless night too.

A customer came in, and while Stella served her Ben moved Hilary into the room behind, which was used as both an office and a rest room. He filled the kettle and plugged it in.

'I've been telling Stella how Charlie stymied me. I almost told him there'd be no driving lessons for his birthday as a punishment. But then I thought you and I might rest more easily if he did have a licence. What do you think?'

'Oh, heavens! I want him to pass his test as soon as possible so that I know he's competent.'

'Well, it's still six months away, but I'm glad I didn't say anything.'

'Has he damaged the van?'

'No. I'm amazed – there isn't a scratch on it. But it's filthy, so I'll make him clean and polish it.'

'So, no ill effects after all?'

'Hilly, it's put years on me.'

Charlie went upstairs, eased off his shoes and lay down on his bed. He felt shattered but also triumphant. Not only had he driven to Sheffield and back, but the expected row had not been as bad as he'd thought it would be. Mum had given him a bad moment but he'd managed to gloss over how they'd spent the evening. She would have hysterics if she knew they'd had drugs in that flat. Parents had no idea of how life was lived these days.

He felt uneasy about Gary. He'd stopped on the motorway and bought coffee and teacakes for them, but Gary had had to rush off to be sick again. Charlie had drunk both cups of coffee and felt better. He'd buttered Gary's teacake and wrapped it in a paper napkin, but he'd not wanted it before they got home.

'You overdid it,' Charlie had told him.

'I had too much beer.'

'Too much of everything, if you ask me. You've got to learn when to slow down.'

'It was the grass,' Gary groaned.

'Don't tell your mother you've been sick,' Charlie had said half a dozen times on the way home. 'She'll want to know why.'

'It'll be Gran I have to face first.'

'Don't forget. No mention of beer or drugs or going to any pub. We drank nothing but tea. Better admit to the odd ciggy if you're pressed but don't say anything about drugs. Paul will kill you if you do.'

CHAPTER TEN

HILARY HAD been so worried and upset by Charlie's taking the van to Sheffield that she'd not written anything for a month. All the good intentions she'd had while on holiday had produced nothing. She felt lazy and frustrated. Ben called it 'a touch of writer's block'.

The morning post brought a cheque for one of her short stories. With it came a letter from the editor of the magazine, suggesting she try a serial for them.

Hilary sat down at her desk and gave it some thought. A serial of five episodes would be short compared to a full-length novel, but it would allow her to write a story with more detail. It might be a good move for her.

She made herself a cup of coffee and let her mind sift through ideas for a plot. Ten minutes later she had her outline, but it was for another short story. She pulled her typewriter closer and got down to it. It was a relief to be writing again and she kept at it all day.

When the phone rang, she only half recognised the quavering voice. 'Is that you, Aunt Primmy?'

'Yes, it's me, dear.'

'How are you?'

'Feeling a bit flustered, I'm afraid. A bit out of kilter.'

'Is something the matter? Do you need a hand with something?'

'Would you ask Ben if he could come down?'

'Ben's in a bit of a panic at the moment. The heating unit for the glasshouses is playing up and there's a heavy frost expected tonight. He's got an engineer here trying to fix it.'

'It'll do later – it's not urgent.'

'Can I be of help? What's the problem?'

'The electric light bulb in our bathroom has burned out. Prue tried to climb on a chair to change it but she fell. She said there was nothing to hold on to and she felt dizzy.'

'Primmy! You two shouldn't be climbing like that at your age. Is she hurt?'

'Yes. She banged her head on the bath and she's twisted her ankle.'

Hilary was alarmed. If it wasn't one thing it was another. 'Oh dear. I'd better come down and see her.'

'No, it's all right. Mrs Wright from the upstairs flat heard the bump and came down.'

'The policeman's wife?'

'Yes. She's a nurse too. She's taken Prue to casualty at Clatterbridge.'

Hilary sighed with relief. That was one job she wouldn't have to do.

'The thing is,' Primmy went on, 'Mrs Wright tried to change the bulb too, but our ceilings are high and she couldn't twist the glass shade off. She thinks it might have rusted in, with the steam, you know. It'll need a strong wrist.'

'Ben will come down, Primmy, but he's got to be in Chester by seven tonight. He wants us to have supper early.'

'There's no need for him to come tonight. Tomorrow will be all right.'

'But it's already getting dark, and you'll need a light in your bathroom.'

'I've stood the table lamp from the sitting room on a chair near the bathroom door. We can manage.'

'Right.' Hilary wondered if that meant there were trailing leads they might trip over. 'I'll tell Ben. I hope Prue hasn't broken any bones.'

She rang off, wanting to go back to her typewriter, but Andy and Jamie were sparring noisily in the playroom, and she needed to go and break that up. She felt she had more on her plate than she could cope with. She'd be able to write so much more if she didn't have all these interruptions in her day.

But the worry about the twin aunts niggled. She felt she should do something about their light bulb before they had another accident. She went back to the phone to dial her mother's number. It was Tom who answered. He said, 'Flora's out at the hairdresser's.'

'Tom, it's you I want to speak to. Are you busy at the moment?'

'No, I'm waiting for her to come home. We're going to the ballet tonight, to celebrate her birthday.'

'Of course! Would you have time to go down to Primmy and Prue's place?' She told him about the dead bulb in their bathroom and Prue's fall.

'Yes,' he said. 'It's only half five or so. I'll pop down and do it now. I'll be glad to.'

*

Tom put the phone down. When he'd said he'd be glad to go round to Ben's aunts' flat, he'd meant it. He'd been there with Flora many times. Primmy and Prue had brought their furnishings from their mother's house, and their goods and chattels intrigued him. Everything they had was very old.

He welcomed a chance to look round without Flora's eye on him. He was particularly interested in some jugs he'd seen on the Welsh dresser in their dining room. He thought they might be Liverpool pottery, and if so, they could be worth a bob or two. Quite possibly, the old dears would know nothing of their value and he might be able to get them for a pound or two.

He took a light bulb with him in case they didn't have one and put a torch in his pocket. As an afterthought he added a magnifying glass. Flora had taken the car but they only lived a quarter of a mile or so away. Although it was a raw March evening, he'd walk down rather than wait. He didn't want Flora to opt to come with him.

Ben's aunts' flat was on the ground floor of a large Edwardian house. The front door was substantial. He rang the doorbell and waited, but Primmy didn't come. Through the fanlight he could see a light on in their hall. The curtains hadn't been drawn in their sitting room and he could see there was nobody in there. Surely Primmy wouldn't have gone out? He rang the bell again and listened. All was silent inside.

He began to think he might have had a wasted journey. He got his torch out to light his way round to the back door and knocked but it opened to his touch. Tom stepped inside and shone his torch round.

'Anyone at home?' he called. 'Primmy, are you there?' He went through into the hall. The grandfather clock was chiming six. It was quite a handsome piece, but Tom knew nothing about clocks. He called out again, and as there was no response decided this was a heaven-sent opportunity to have a good look at their bits and pieces.

He went to the dining room, shone his torch round and then switched on the electric light. On the Welsh dresser were the jugs he was interested in. Six of them, all about ten inches high, all pot-bellied with a good lip for pouring. Each was decorated with a different transfer print and none of them was handsome. He lifted down the first and got out his magnifying glass to look more closely. It was a scene of the American civil war, as were all the others. He felt a surge of excitement. It did look like Liverpool creamware. No chips or cracks, but the transfer print was wearing thin in parts.

Tom put it back and was getting another down when he heard a movement behind him; then an ear-splitting yell shattered the silence, making him jump. He almost dropped the jug and only just managed to fumble it back on its shelf. A distraught Primmy was standing in the doorway screaming in terror.

He shouted, 'Primmy, it's all right. Nothing to worry about. It's me, Tom.'

She stopped only to gulp air, then her shrill cry pierced the air again. Her fear cut into him like a razor, panicking him. He tried to put his arms round her in a comforting hug as he did with Flora, but she fought like a wild thing to free herself.

'Primmy,' he screamed. 'Listen to me. It's Tom. There's nothing to be afraid of.'

Slowly she took her hands from her face and looked at him. 'Tom?'

'Yes. Hilary sent me to change the light bulb in your bathroom.'

'Oh dear!' She was shaking with shock. He pulled a chair out from the table and made her sit down. 'Sorry,' she whimpered. 'I've come over all queer.'

He tried to smile. 'Did I frighten you? I'm sorry. I was just admiring your jugs.' She looked confused, even ill, as though she was going to faint. He asked, 'Can I get you something? Brandy?'

'Water.' Her voice was muted. He ran to the kitchen to get it. She sat back on the chair with her eyes closed as she sipped it.

'I was looking for you,' he said. 'I called for you. Didn't you hear me?'

'The bathroom, yes. I thought Ben would come tomorrow. I went to rest on my bed – I must have fallen asleep.' Her eyes were swimming. 'Did Hilary tell you Prue had a fall?'

'Yes. That's why she wanted me round here now to change it, before you tried.'

'I couldn't. I don't feel up to it. I've been a bit off colour today. What a fright you gave me, Tom. A man in our dining room. I thought you were a thief,' she gulped, 'come to steal our jugs.'

'No, of course not. They caught my eye, and I paused to admire them, that's all. They're very handsome.'

'D'you think so? We think they're quite ugly.'

Tom knew this wasn't the moment to ask if she wanted to sell them. She'd caught him in the act. What he ought to do was calm her down and placate her; make her think there was nothing strange about finding him in her house fingering her belongings. But at the same time she was talking about them, and she was so flustered he thought she'd agree to anything. No harm in dropping a hint.

'If you don't like them, I do. I'll buy them off you. Flora would like them.'

She shook her head. 'No. She'd be scared to have them set out in her cottage. The grandchildren, you know.'

'They're growing up. Getting past the age when they might break them.'

'Not Daisy. They were our mother's, and before that her mother's. They go back in our family a long time. There're some very similar jugs in the Williamson Museum in Birkenhead.'

'Really? I didn't realise . . .' In the museum? It was as well he hadn't mentioned a price. He'd hoped to get them for next to nothing. He should have kept his mouth shut.

'Ben had them valued a few years ago. They're worth a bit. We've been worried about having them stolen. That's why . . .'

Tom sighed and said awkwardly, 'I'd better get on and change that bulb.'

He had to take two chairs to the bathroom. Primmy sat on one and shone the torch upwards while he stood on the other. One hard twist of the fancy glass bowl that covered the bulb and it was off. It took only a moment to change the bulb itself. He tipped the dead flies from the bowl down the lavatory.

'I'll wash that,' Primmy said.

'You nurses are too hygienic.' He smiled, wiping the dust of ages away with toilet paper. 'It's a good rule not to put water near electrics. There you are, the bathroom light restored.'

'Thank you.'

Tom carried the chairs back to the dining room.

'Sorry I made a fool of myself,' she said. 'It's being here on my own, I'm not used to it. And I'm worried about Prue.'

'She should be back from the hospital before much longer.' He patted her shoulder. 'You'd better lock your back door behind me so you don't get any more strange men coming in.'

She gave him a wavering smile.

'You go and lie down again. After a fright like that another little rest won't do you any harm. We won't tell Hilary about it, will we?'

Tom stepped out briskly as he walked home. He was disappointed he hadn't been able to get those jugs, but it had been a long shot anyway. If they were museum quality they wouldn't be that easy to sell. Instead, he looked forward to having a good night out tonight with no expense spared.

Under the restaurant lights, Flora could see more silver in Tom's dark hair than there had been at the time of their wedding. Nevertheless, despite the hard times he'd had, he still looked younger than his years. He was a handsome man. Sophisticated too; he knew how things should be done.

He took the champagne from the wine cooler beside their table to refill their glasses, then raised his to her. 'Happy birthday, Flora.'

She would be seventy-three tomorrow. She fingered his gift, the antique diamond brooch pinned to her dark red dress.

'I love it, but it's very extravagant of you.' It felt underhand to think of it as her money he was spending.

'Nonsense. It was a bargain – I bought it in an auction. I want you to have nice things. You deserve it.'

'Dear Tom, you know how to put on a celebration. You make me feel very special.'

They'd been to see *Swan Lake* at the Liverpool Empire. Tchaikovsky's beautiful music still echoed in Flora's head. Now they were finishing the evening with a supper dance at the Glass Slipper.

'And it isn't even my birthday until tomorrow.'

He smiled at her. 'I thought we ought to start early as you were born at five minutes past midnight.'

'That's true.'

'And tomorrow we've been invited to a birthday tea party at Isobel's.'

'For the family.' Flora had always been close to her family, but being with Tom had somehow moved them further away. 'Do you feel swamped by them, Tom?'

'No. I feel they welcomed me into their circle.'

Perhaps they had to start with, but recently Flora had had the feeling they were cooling towards him.

'I love them all,' he said. The strength of his emotion surprised her. She was afraid her girls wouldn't say they loved Tom. Isobel in particular could be rather cool towards him.

'Love them all? Even the wilful Sophie, and Charlie who never listens to reason?'

'They're young and finding their feet, Flora. The family does what it can to help and support them.'

That Tom thought like that seemed to show his loving nature.

Flora said, 'It's Hilary I feel sorry for. After losing her publisher, she's been trying so hard to write a really good book and get it published. I'm afraid she's disheartened and she's had a lot to put up with from Charlie.'

A LABOUR OF LOVE

*

Isobel felt she had to put on some sort of party to mark her mother's birthday. She'd come close to quarrelling with Hilary about it last week. It seemed Hilly could no longer be bothered doing anything, though last year she'd put on a big family dinner at her house.

'Shall we take her out, book a table somewhere?' Isobel had suggested. 'What about Grange Manor?'

'Tom always takes her out the night before, and you know Mum. She won't be able to stand eating late on consecutive nights.'

Isobel thought Hilly had become very inward-looking , too wrapped up in her writing and her boys to think of anyone else. Mum had always been sympathetic, saying Hilly was worried that dyslexia would blight Charlie's future. Isobel had done her best to help. She'd tutored the boys for years; was still working with Jamie and Andy.

She'd said, 'It could be some other flaw in Charlie's character. After all, Andy and Jamie are turning out all right.'

Hilary had flared up at her then. 'You don't understand. Why should you? Sophie's never given you a moment's worry. She's a star and never needed special tutoring; she can come top of her class without it. You expect her to get three or four A levels this summer and sail on to study law at university. The twins don't have life chances like that. Charlie's had a hard time. Don't talk to me about flaws in his character.'

'I'm sorry, I shouldn't have said that.' Isobel made an effort to change the subject. 'So what d'you suggest we do for Mum's birthday then?'

Hilly was quite rude. 'Isn't it time you did something

instead of leaving it to me? I have the oldies round to my place for Sunday lunch every week.'

That irritated Isobel. She couldn't stop herself saying, 'Mum does the cooking for you and you have the only house big enough to take us all in comfort.' She'd sensed her sister found it too much, and for the last eighteen months she hadn't taken her family there for meals except on special occasions. 'But if you feel like that I'll have a little celebration for Mum here.'

Isobel knew that inviting all the family to her cottage at once would result in a squash. There wasn't enough space to provide a sit-down meal. She would have liked to make it afternoon tea, but as some of the family worked they wouldn't be able to come until the evening and by then they'd be looking for something more substantial to eat. She decided to make savoury finger food and set it out buffet style, so her guests could help themselves.

'I'm sorry,' Hilary said. 'I'll help, of course. I'll bake some cheese tarts and a quiche lorraine. What about the birthday cake? Foster's do handsome celebration cakes. Shall we order one?'

'You know what Mum thinks of shop cakes. Lovely to look at but disappointing to eat. We'll have to make it.'

'I'll ask Charlie, then. He reckons he's good at celebration cakes.'

Sophie ran across the school grounds and cut down to the main gates, where every afternoon at four o'clock her father picked her up. Usually, she came out in a stream of other girls and the road outside was busy. Today the bustle had died down. She was late and knew she'd kept her father waiting.

His car was parked by itself. He was reading something propped against the steering wheel.

'Sorry, Dad.' Sophie tossed her satchel on the back seat and got in hurriedly. She was hot and knew her face was flushed. She was puffed too, but she tried to control her breathing so he wouldn't notice.

'Hello, Sophie. What kept you?'

She'd had most of the afternoon to get her excuse ready.

'My form mistress kept me talking. She wants me to enter an essay competition.'

'That sounds interesting. What competition is this?'

She had it all off pat. 'We heard about it at assembly this morning. One of the governors has set a competition on Canada for the whole of the senior school.'

Sebastian said, 'It's just that Mum wants us to be home on time today. She's having a tea party for Nana's birthday.'

'Oh yes.' Sophie suppressed a groan. She'd forgotten about that. 'Sorry.'

She'd had a ghastly afternoon but she'd had to do it. She'd been turning it over in her mind for the last few weeks. It had taken her time to screw up enough courage. She'd eaten her school dinner then told everybody she didn't feel well. The gym mistress was in charge of the first aid cupboard and the camp-bed sick bay, and took responsibility for dealing with pupils who became unwell.

Sophie asked if she might go home because she was starting her monthlies and had dragging pains and a headache. Permission had been given but only after she'd received painkillers and a lot of advice.

Darrell had driven her to a family planning clinic where

she'd had to wait her turn. She'd asked the doctor for the pill. She'd eventually prescribed it for her but she'd kept her talking for ages pointing out all sorts of moral problems. Then Sophie had had to see a nurse who explained in words of one syllable and at length exactly how it must be taken though full instructions were printed on the packet.

It was that that had made her late – well, that and the fact that she'd had to change out of school uniform in Darrell's car, and then back into it again before she met Dad. It had also made her jumpy and very much on edge.

But she was relieved she'd done it and got what she wanted. Darrell was pleased; he said they'd have much more fun now. Sophie had been a bit worried that he was being less careful with his condoms than he had been at first, and it would solve that. The doctor had told her she'd be better not having sex until she was older and given her a lecture about telling her parents. Sophie had felt she had to get the pill whatever it cost her.

It would have been more convenient to go to evening surgery and see her normal doctor to get the pill, but he knew her and was quite chatty with both Mum and Dad. She'd wanted to go where she wasn't known, but even so it had been a dreadful experience.

'Sophie.' She saw her father glance at her. 'Mum thinks we should have a little talk – you and me.'

Her heart dropped; she knew what that meant. She could do without a pep talk today. 'What have I done?'

His voice was calm, gentle even. 'You rush about too much. You're always going out in the evenings. Wouldn't it be better if you limited your jaunts to the weekends? For the rest of this school year, I mean, while you're studying for A levels.'

'Dad! I'm working hard. I've got to have a bit of time off to enjoy myself.'

'But it isn't just a bit of time. I'm worried you're overdoing things. Also, you don't always tell Mum and me where you're going, or who you're going with.'

Sophie opened the car window a little so the draught would cool her burning cheeks. 'I do,' she protested.

'Well, we've been hearing rumours and we feel you're sometimes a bit sparing with the truth. Sophie love, it makes us uneasy if we don't know what you're getting up to.'

She gripped the seat. How could she tell him where she'd been this afternoon? He'd have a fit. She caught him glancing at her again.

'Have you got a boyfriend?'

Sophie was caught unawares. Oh, my God! What was she to say to that? She pulled herself together, forced herself to say lightly, 'Lots of them, Dad. There's a whole gang of nice lads go to the church youth club.'

'Yes, but a little bird told me . . . Well, you've been seen getting into a car behind the Dog and Gun with a lad, and he wasn't local.'

Sophie felt the blood rush into her cheeks again, and she snapped, 'What little bird is this?' Today of all days to be faced with this!

'I don't know whether I should tell you.'

'Why not? You're telling me everything else.'

'Well, it was the postmistress, Mrs Grant.'

'The nosy old biddy . . . Why can't she mind her own business?'

'Is it true?'

Sophie felt she had to deny it. 'No. I generally go round

with Judith and Ross or Danny Cookson. The problem with the village is that everybody thinks they know everybody else.'

'Mrs Grant does know everybody. If you do have a boyfriend I'd like you to bring him home to meet us.'

Sophie swallowed. Once she'd thought she might take Darrell home, but now? If Dad guessed they were having regular sex, he'd be horrified. He'd kill her.

'We want to share your life, Sophie, not be shut away from it. So you do that. If – or when – you have a boyfriend, bring him home or give him the push, eh?'

Sophie closed her eyes and tried to calm her jangling nerves.

CHAPTER ELEVEN

EARLY THAT afternoon, Isobel was setting up for her party when Hilary came in with what she'd baked that morning. The table looked great with the birthday cake as a centre piece. Charlie had brought it down last night, all beautifully iced and decorated.

'He reckons he knows what the elderly like.' His mother couldn't suppress a giggle. 'He insisted on making a large Victoria sponge, saying Nana and the twin aunts would find rich fruit cake bad for their digestion.'

Before anybody else arrived, Hilary went to pick up Ben's aunts in her car. They were eighty now, and though keen to be out and about they tired easily. Aunt Prudence's ankle was strapped up after her fall yesterday and she was limping slightly.

'How are you?' Isobel asked as she took her coat. 'It looks painful.'

'Not too bad. I've had it X-rayed – it's only a sprain.'

'Good. I'm glad to see you've brought your mandolins and you're well enough to play. We'll have your party piece after tea.' They could play rousing duets. 'The Camptown Races' was Isobel's favourite.

As children, the twin aunts had always been dressed exactly alike, and on becoming adult they had agreed that that must stop. But even if they went shopping separately, they seemed to end up with very similar clothes, mostly long-sleeved dresses that came high at the neck.

They came warmly clad in the wool dresses they'd worn all winter for Sunday lunch at Hilary's, one maroon and one dark green. They wore the usual thick woolly-looking tights much like those Isobel bought for Daisy, but Daisy liked red or white while the twin aunts always chose beige.

'Primmy hasn't been feeling too well either,' Prue told them.

Isobel thought she looked a bit grey-faced. 'I'm sorry. What's the matter?'

'I don't really know. I haven't been sleeping well, and it leaves me feeling a bit light-headed and dizzy.'

'She'll feel better now she's here with other people,' Prue said. 'The party will take her out of herself.'

To Isobel, it didn't seem much of a party, just her and Hilary trying to entertain the twin aunts. Then through the living room window she saw her mother and Tom walking down from their cottage and ran to open the door. The fun could start now they were here.

'Happy birthday, Mum.' Flora was wearing a new cream and brown dress. 'You look very smart. That suits you.' Isobel kissed her. 'Is that a new brooch too? Diamonds?'

'Yes, it's my present from Tom.'

'It's gorgeous.'

'It's old jewellery. I bought it at auction,' Tom said.

'Antique diamonds,' Flora added.

'It's lovely,' the twin aunts said as one. They were sitting side by side on the settee.

Isobel was glad to hear the chorus of happy birthdays and see her mother open up a jar of bath salts from Prue and a box of handkerchiefs from Primmy. She'd bought her three pairs of expensive tights that acted as support stockings and were said to ease tired legs. Isobel had seen Flora studying an advertisement for them in a monthly magazine and she seemed delighted with them.

Daisy was careering round excitedly in her frilly white party dress. They all made a fuss of her. Isobel poured sherry for them all and hoped Seb and Sophie would be home soon to help.

Ben brought Jamie and Andy down as soon as they came home from school and they presented Flora with two pots, one containing a lemon tree and the other an orange tree. Isobel wondered where Mum would find space in her cottage for them as they'd have to be kept indoors over the winter.

She wished they'd all loosen up. They were sipping their sherry too slowly and the party wasn't taking off. She was glad to see Sebastian's car pulling up outside. He was later than usual, but he and Sophie would soon jolly things up.

The pastries were warming in the oven. Isobel went to take them out; it was time to start eating. Back in the living room, she looked round for Sophie to help her hand them round, but she wasn't there. Jamie scrambled to his feet to help.

Sebastian had a grim face and was helping himself to a stiff whisky, which wasn't something he usually did at this time of day.

'Did Sophie go upstairs?' she asked him.

'She wants to change her clothes.'

'Of course.' Sophie would want to get out of her school uniform, but Isobel had the feeling that something was wrong.

When she hadn't come down after twenty minutes, she went to fetch her. Her bedroom door was firmly closed.

'Sophie,' she called. 'Are you coming? The food's disappearing. You'll go hungry if you don't come soon.'

The door burst open. 'Just coming.' Sophie was wearing her stylish red party dress.

'You look lovely,' Isobel told her. 'Very grown up.' Sophie ran downstairs ahead of her but not before Isobel realised she'd been putting on make-up. Sophie knew exactly how to enhance her already beautiful face; she used lipstick, eye shadow, foundation and a little rouge to make the most of the planes of her face, all applied with a light and practised touch.

She went across the room to kiss her grandmother. 'Happy birthday, Nana.'

'Darling, you look stunning. Like a model. Another present? Lovely. I've been given some gorgeous things this year. I am lucky.'

'I don't suppose you'll think this gorgeous.' Flora was untying the ribbon on Sophie's gift. 'It's only the lavender soap you like.'

'The scent is beautiful and you know it's my favourite. Thank you. I shall think of you every time I wash with it.'

Isobel watched Sophie take a plate and pile it high with food. She seemed a greedy child again.

'Pass me another of those cheese tarts,' Seb said to her. 'They're really good.'

She said rather rudely, 'Dad, if you stood up, you could reach them yourself.' She did as he asked, then flounced off to the other side of the room to perch on the arm of Hilary's chair and eat.

Isobel could see she was tetchy with Seb and wondered why. They were usually on such good terms that she could feel excluded. Was it casting a bit of an atmosphere? It was not festive at all. Isobel was afraid this would be remembered as the most boring party ever.

Charlie arrived on his motor bike, the last to come. After kissing his nana he accepted orange juice instead of sherry because Ben was watching. He squeezed in to sit next to Sophie and helped himself to food from her plate.

Flora had Daisy on her knee and Tom was playing some game with her. Isobel sent Andy over to them with plates of food, since they didn't seem to be eating much. Seb was chatting quietly to Ben instead of livening things up. Conversation was not general and seemed stilted. Isobel picked up the sherry bottle and went round refilling glasses, hoping alcohol would help.

'Had I better put the kettle on for tea?' Hilary whispered as she refilled her glass.

'It is on. Mum will want tea, but I thought I'd get her to cut the cake and we could sing happy birthday first.'

Isobel wished she'd asked Prue and Primmy to jolly things up with a tune earlier, but they were eating now. Aunt Primmy's glass was still on the table under the arm of the settee. It had not been touched. Next to her, Prue held out her empty glass.

'Primmy's gone to sleep. I thought it better to leave her. She'll feel better when she wakes up.'

Isobel glanced at Primmy and went suddenly cold. She straightened upright with a jerk, spilling sherry on Prue's dress. 'Oh, no!'

Primmy was slumped back against the cushions. A plate

with a half-eaten chicken sandwich was balanced on her knee. Her face had droplets of sweat on it and seemed lopsided; her left eye was almost closed but the right was dragged down and the pupil stared out unseeingly from under a distorted lid.

Prue leaped to her feet wailing with distress and Tom, who was also sitting on the settee, got up too.

'Hilly, come quickly,' Isobel shrieked, but she was already beside her.

'I think she's had a stroke,' Hilary gasped. She lifted Primmy's legs and turned her to lie on the settee. Her mouth was pulled down on one side and saliva dribbled out on her chin. Her breathing was shallow and slow.

'Primmy, talk to me.' Prue bent over her and shook her arm. 'You're all right, aren't you?'

Ben said, 'Had we better ask the doctor to come? Shall I ring?'

'No,' Hilary said. 'I'll dial 999 and ask for an ambulance. Better if she goes to hospital.'

Isobel listened appalled as Hilary said, 'Yes, urgent. She seems to have lost consciousness.'

Sophie fetched the duvet from her bed and spread it over Primmy. Daisy pushed in close and gave a little squeal of distress when she saw her face.

Flora said, 'I'll take the children away. There's too many of us here now Primmy's been taken bad.'

'Thanks, Mum,' Isobel said. She was right.

'I've got homework to do,' Andy said quickly. 'I'll go home and take Jamie with me. We'll be in the way here.'

'Me too.' Charlie got up.

'You come with us, Sophie,' Flora invited.

'No, I'm not a child any more. I'm staying here.'

'Just Daisy then.' There was a sense of rising panic in the house and the child was beginning to cry. Flora lifted her on her knee for a cuddle. 'Where's her coat?'

'No,' Daisy screamed, struggling free to wrap her arms round Isobel's legs. 'Want Mummy.'

'Don't worry about Daisy,' Isobel said. 'She'll be all right here.'

Prudence wailed, 'Why didn't Primmy say she was feeling worse? Why didn't she tell me? What's the matter with her?' Isobel shuddered and wished the ambulance would come.

It was at the door before anybody had time to leave. Paramedics came rushing in and within seconds were giving Primrose oxygen and getting the history from Hilary. A light folding stretcher was brought in and pushed under Primrose.

'Where are they taking her?' Prue demanded, her face ravaged with tears.

'To hospital.' Ben put his arms round her and gave her a hug.

Hilary was holding her coat. 'Come on, you'd better come too.'

'I'll follow with the car,' Ben said. 'So we can get home again.'

The cottage emptied in moments. Only Isobel's own family were left. She sank down on the settee, shocked and exhausted. Daisy clambered up on her knee and she hugged her close, burying her face in her freshly shampooed hair.

Sophie looked horrified. 'What is a stroke?' she asked. 'Will Aunt Primmy die?'

'No necessarily.' Isobel sighed. 'But she's likely to be left with some paralysis. I do hope Prue will be able to cope. She'll have to do much more . . .'

'What a terrible thing to happen,' Seb said. 'We were all round her and didn't even notice.'

Isobel said, 'None of us will forget this in a hurry – the most awful party ever.'

When they started off Ben was able to keep the ambulance well in sight, but once it was on the main road it switched on its alarm and roared past the other traffic. Ben was glad Hilary had been there when it happened. She was the only one who knew what to do. He felt sick. This reminded him of going to the hospital with his mother when she'd been taken ill. She'd died the same night and he was very much afraid Primrose might do the same.

By the time he reached Clatterbridge there was no sign of the ambulance. It was a rambling site with buildings built all over it, more like a small town than a hospital. It was getting dark as he drove round looking for somewhere to park, and he wondered in which of these buildings he'd find them.

It was only when he got out that he saw the neon sign A & E. That would be it: Accident and Emergency. He went in and asked the receptionist about his family and was told to sit down and wait. It seemed a long time before a nurse led him across the department and behind some screens to where his aunt was lying on a trolley. Hilary was sitting beside her holding her hand.

For a moment, he thought he was looking at Primmy, who seemed much recovered. He almost said so.

'They're going to keep Prue in for observation overnight,' Hilary said. 'They're trying to find her a bed on a ward.'

It was Prue, not Primmy. She smiled up at him. His head swam as he felt his way on to a chair. 'Why?' Ben was confused. Apart from her ankle, Aunt Prue had seemed fine when she'd got into the ambulance.

Hilary gently disengaged her hand, got up and led him further away. 'They're identical twins. Prue's blood pressure is sky high too. The same thing could happen to her.'

'She could have a stroke too?'

Hilary nodded.

'Oh, my God!'

'They've given her something for it and a sedative to calm her down. She was getting upset.'

'How is Primmy?'

'Not good. There're two doctors working on her now; they'll come and let us know when they have news. Come and sit down near Prue. It may comfort her to see us here.'

It was an anxious vigil. Prue seemed to be dozing; Hilary looked drained. Ben felt restless and uneasy; it seemed a very alien place. Twenty minutes later, a nurse put her head round the screens and indicated he should follow her. Hilly's eyes leaped nervously to his as he left her.

He was taken to a cell-like room with chairs round the wall. 'How is my aunt?' he asked.

'Dr Stanley will come and have a word with you in a moment,' she said.

Ben was lowering himself on to a chair, but straightened up immediately as the door opened and Dr Stanley came in.

'Mr Snow, isn't it? Primrose Foster was your aunt?'

He noted the past tense and couldn't suppress a shiver. He gasped, 'Has she died?'

'I'm very sorry, Mr Snow. We did our best but we couldn't save her. She had another even bigger stroke after she arrived.'

It was something Hilary had said that made him ask, 'Would she . . . Would she have been able to recover from the first?'

The doctor thought for a moment. 'Her age was against her. I think a complete recovery would have been unlikely. She'd probably have been left with some paralysis. She might prefer it to happen this way.'

Ben let his pent-up breath out slowly. He knew Prue wouldn't see it like that.

The doctor went on, 'We are concerned about her sister; sometimes the same problem can be mirrored in identical twins. But not always, you understand. We'll monitor her condition closely over the next few hours.'

The interview was over. The doctor was going. 'Thank you,' Ben said. The future looked bleak. Prue would be inconsolable. He hoped against hope nothing was going to happen to her.

When he found his way back to the cubicle, a porter had come and was about to wheel Prue's trolley to a ward. He and Hilly went with her to see her settled, but she was very drowsy.

Ben kissed her cheek. 'We'll say good night, Prue. You'll feel better if you can get some sleep.'

Her lips moved, he knew she was asking about Primmy. He kissed the other cheek.

'Come on,' he whispered to Hilary. 'She hardly knows we're here. Better if we leave her now.'

Outside in the deserted corridor, Ben felt he could take no more of this horror. He paused by a window and rested his forehead against the cold glass.

'Are you all right?' Hilly took his arm. 'What did the doctor tell you about Primmy? Shall we go back to A & E to see her?'

Ben put an arm round her shoulders and pulled her close. 'She died,' he choked. 'She had another stroke.'

'You didn't tell Prue. She was asking.'

'I know. I just couldn't. It wouldn't help her to know, would it? Not now. She might be stronger in the morning.'

'Ben love, it's probably better for Primmy this way. She could have been left very disabled.'

'But Prue would have wanted to look after her.'

'Prue's getting on in years too. Would she have had the strength to manage her? If Primmy needed lifting, it would be too much for Prue. That would have meant a nursing home.'

'You're right, of course,' Ben said. 'Primmy was very good to me when I was growing up. They both were.'

'Let's go back and ask to see her,' Hilary said. 'Before we go home.'

Isobel was still in a deep reverie about Primmy when Sophie got up and helped herself to a sausage roll from the table.

'There's a lot of food left.' Seb was piling more on his plate.

Isobel lifted the dozing Daisy from her knee to the corner of the settee, then pulled herself to her feet. She'd hardly eaten anything yet, and she felt empty. She took a generous slice of quiche.

'We didn't even cut Nana's birthday cake.' Sophie was back for more.

'Perhaps I'll take it to her. It'll go stale if it isn't eaten.'

'Cut it in half,' Seb advised. 'She and Tom won't want to eat it all.'

Isobel picked up the carving knife and sliced it into three.

'Some for Hilly's family too. Come on, we might as well eat ours now.'

'Some party,' Sophie said.

'You didn't help,' Isobel pointed out. She turned to Sebastian. 'What were you two at loggerheads about?'

He sighed. 'It seems insignificant after what's happened to Primmy. Sophie's had a piece of my mind about a boyfriend. I've told her what I think she should do, so let's leave it at that.'

Sophie sulked silently, biting into a slice of birthday cake.

Sebastian said slowly, 'With one thing and another, it's been the very bitch of a day.'

Isobel lay back against the cushions of the settee feeling spent. Daisy was asleep with her thumb in her mouth.

Sophie had gone up to her room, saying, 'I might as well take off my glad rags. There's not going to be a party tonight.'

Sebastian said, 'It's past Daisy's bedtime. Hadn't you better put her to bed?' He was on his feet and pottering round.

Isobel asked, 'What are you doing?'

'Clearing the table and putting the food away.'

'Let's divide it up and take some to Mum's. Hilary won't go home without calling in to tell us how Primmy is.'

Seb said, 'I don't like Sophie sulking up there by herself. I'll ask her if she wants to come to Nana's with us.'

Isobel hadn't moved when she heard him coming down again. 'She doesn't want to do anything, but I've persuaded her to listen out for Daisy. Put her to bed, love.'

By the time Isobel had done that, Sebastian had put

together two packages of food, one for Hilary and a smaller one for her mother. Together they walked up the terrace of cottages.

Tom opened the door to them. 'Come in. The waiting's terrible, isn't it? You haven't heard anything?'

Isobel shook her head.

'I'm glad you've come, it gives us something to do. Your mother hasn't been able to sit still.'

Flora set her piece of birthday cake out on a plate straight away. 'I'll put the kettle on for a cup of tea.' She was quite agitated. 'I've made our spare bed up for Prue. She'll be out of her mind with worry about Primmy. I don't think she should go back to an empty house on her own tonight.'

The tea was brewing when Ben's car was heard drawing up outside. Flora rushed to let them in and found only Hilary and Ben.

She said, 'Prue's decided to stay with Primmy, then? I hope it won't be too much for her. She's really quite frail too.'

Isobel could see from Hilary's face she had bad news.

'Prue's being kept in,' she said. They were all shocked to hear it.

Ben looked quite emotional. 'Primmy died, you see.'

'Primmy's dead?' Flora covered her face with her hands. 'How will Prue manage without her?'

Flora couldn't understand how Primmy had died so suddenly. 'She seemed so well,' she said, and the rest of the family agreed with her. They were all shocked.

Prue was kept in hospital for two days. Ben went to see her each evening.

'How is she?' Flora asked him.

'Very distressed and dreading going home without her twin. Hilary thinks she should stay with us for while, till she's more used to being alone.'

'Ask her if she'll come and stay with us,' Flora said gently. 'We have more time to give her and I've already got our spare room ready.'

The next day Ben rang Flora to say, 'Prue's very low. I don't think she minds where she goes as long as she isn't alone. Hilly and I are very grateful for your offer.'

Isobel and Flora went to Prue's flat to tidy up and remove any food that might go off. The aunts had always shared one bedroom. They made one twin bed up with clean bedding and collapsed the other and got Tom over to help carry it up to the attic where she wouldn't see it. When Prue was due to be discharged, Flora and Tom went to fetch her and take her to their cottage.

'You're welcome to stay as long as you like,' Flora told her, 'and certainly until after the funeral.'

She insisted Prue had a rest on her bed every day after lunch, and usually went to wake her with a cup of tea about four o'clock. Prue was weepy and talked of Primmy the whole time.

'I was so unprepared for this. I was the one with the cricked ankle, though Primmy did say she was a bit off colour. "Just a little dizzy," she told me. "Nothing to worry about, I'll be better tomorrow." Of course, the day before, Tom had scared the living daylights out of her. That shook her up. When I got back from the hospital she was still quaking. I don't suppose that did her any good.'

Flora was surprised that Tom hadn't mentioned it. Later, when they were alone, she said to him, 'What's all this about you giving Primmy the fright of her life? Why didn't you tell me?'

'Oh, it was nothing. When Hilary sent me down to change her light bulb, she'd fallen asleep and didn't answer the bell. I went in through the back door and it frightened her to see me there.'

'Prue thought it upset her,' Flora said. 'She was afraid it might have caused . . .'

'No. Primmy seemed quite confused then. Looking back, I think she was failing, but none of us realised at the time. Poor Primmy.'

Flora took Prue back to her flat to get more clothes. She was inconsolable. 'I feel I can't live without Primmy. All our lives we've been together. I've never been lonely. Always, Primmy was there, a marvellous friend and companion. We shared everything. Being a twin has been lovely, but now . . . I've always hated to be parted from her. At work, of course, we had to be, though we were both at the children's hospital. We each had a ward to manage, but we discussed all our problems. We've been so close. More like one person with two bodies than ordinary sisters.' Prue gulped. 'Many years ago, when we were young, I fell in love and married. I wanted a husband and children of my own and I knew Primmy wanted the same things. We thought it was just a matter of time.'

Flora was stunned. She had never heard any of this. She broke the silence to ask, 'Was Primmy jealous?'

'I didn't think so at the time, but afterwards she said she was, but had tried not to show it for my sake.'

'What went wrong?'

'My son caught diphtheria. I wanted to nurse him at home

but in those days infection . . . Well, he had to go to the fever hospital, but he recovered from that and came home.'

'Good.'

Prue was shaking her head. 'Somehow he never picked up. He lingered for months. Primmy spent most of her off duty with me, trying to help. We were so sure we could nurse him back to health, but no. Derek died before he was two.'

'I'm so sorry.'

'My husband was a good man, but I couldn't bear living with him and not having Primmy in the same house. He was certainly jealous of her. I left him because I couldn't live without her.' She sighed. 'But now I have to, don't I?'

'You feel low at the moment,' Flora sympathised. 'But you have to go on, and time may ease it.'

'I wish I'd had a heart attack and died at the same time.'

Prue was weepy throughout the funeral and the reception Hilary provided. Flora took her home and put her to bed, afraid she'd make herself ill. She now had medication for her high blood pressure but didn't want to take it. 'I'd rather be dead,' she told Flora.

It was spring and the days were lengthening and becoming warmer. Flora tried to keep Prue occupied. On Sundays, there was the family lunch at Hilary's house, and she persuaded Prue to attend two bridge sessions each week. She and Tom took her out on other days, and eventually she began to accept her loss.

'It's just that I relied on Primmy for so much,' she tried to explain. 'I'm scared of living alone, but I feel I can't stay in your house for ever.'

'You can stay as long as you want to,' Flora assured her.

'Really, I'd like to go home now, but I'll find it hard to be on my own. I know there's the family in the flat upstairs and Mrs Wright is very good, but downstairs there'll be just me. I don't know what I do want, except to have Primmy back.'

'We all want that,' Flora said sadly. 'But we can't have it.'

The family discussed Prue's difficulties and decided between them that it might help if she had someone to live with her.

'What about Sophie?' Hilary suggested. 'Would she like to? She's always got on well with the twin aunts.'

Flora wasn't so sure. She said, 'Sophie can be a bit of a handful. She likes her own way and knows how to get it.'

CHAPTER TWELVE

ISOBEL HAD agreed to talk to Sophie about living with Prue, but Sebastian said, 'I'm against it. She'll have too much freedom if she leaves home.'

'Isn't it time she thought of others?'

'Prue will give her a front door key and she won't ask questions. She's a little deaf and probably goes to bed at ten o'clock. I think Sophie might have a boyfriend. She could stay out half the night with him and no one would be any the wiser.'

'Sophie's quite responsible.' Isobel frowned. 'And she's working hard for her A levels. She wouldn't stay out half the night.'

'She believes in having a bit of fun too,' Seb pointed out. 'I'd feel happier if she lived here with us, where we can keep an eye on her.'

'Sophie's growing up, Seb, and I'll be over to see Prue on most days. I think we should trust her.'

Over breakfast the following morning, Isobel said to Sophie, 'Nana and Hilary think it would be nice for Prue if you moved in with her for a few weeks.'

Sophie lifted her gaze from her bowl of cornflakes. 'Move

in? Live with her, you mean? Why would Aunt Prue want me hanging about her place?'

Isobel was taken aback at her vehemence, but kept trying. 'She's frail now and grieving for Primmy. You could take her a cup of tea in bed in the mornings. Be company for her.'

'Sounds like one of Nana's ideas.'

'And Aunt Hilary's too.'

Sophie was pulling a distasteful face. 'Not Aunt Prue's, that's my point.'

'Well, will you?'

'No. I don't want to.'

'Why not?' Isobel demanded. 'Don't you want to help her?'

'I need to study for my A levels, Mum, not chat to Aunt Prue and do her washing up. Sorry. I really don't feel I'll have the time.'

Isobel saw Sebastian lift his eyebrows and, knowing how he felt, she didn't press Sophie further.

When she went upstairs to get ready for school, Seb said softly, 'I didn't think she'd want to.'

'Selfish little minx.'

'Prue will be better off with Andy. Ben's sounded him out and he seemed happy to do it. He's got more of the milk of human kindness.'

Isobel let out her pent-up breath. 'You're right. He does have more sympathy for others.'

'He's had hard times and remembers what that feels like. Sophie's always had it easy.'

Charlie knew evenings spent with the gang at the Cheshire Cheese placed certain obligations on him and Gary. One afternoon in class, he said, 'We've got to get grass or something to pay our whack.'

When lectures were over for the day, they tagged on to the rush to the bus stop, although Charlie's bike was in the car park. They didn't know the name of the plump lad who used the going-home-time crush to do a bit of pushing. He didn't attend the college but he was well known to them all as Tubsy. Charlie had seen him there several times and occasionally he'd bought.

'Shall I get grass too?' Gary asked. 'Or something different?'

'That's up to you.'

They stood back for a moment. Tubsy was selling uppers and downers to another customer. Amphetamines to keep him alert and downers to help him sleep, so he could turn night into day. Tubsy also had heroin and LSD.

They each bought a screw of cannabis. When they reached Gary's house, Charlie went up to his bedroom with him to open up the packages to see how much was inside.

'Not a lot of it for a tenner.' Charlie sniffed at it. 'And doesn't look much different from the dried grass up on our football field.'

'Pity you can't grow it.'

Charlie slapped his thigh and laughed aloud. 'Gary! What a good idea. The very tops. I can see a couple of seeds here.'

'Tubsy will get you a whole packet of seeds if that's what you want.'

'I do.' Charlie prodded at the dried bits. 'There's only five seeds between us, but I might as well start with these. Pass me one of those fag papers to fold them in.'

'Will it grow outside?'

'Yes, almost any plant will grow leaves and stalks. I've heard this is a weed that'll grow anywhere. We might already have some growing in the garden centre, on the bits of ground that aren't planted up. Like round the football pitch.'

'D'you know what it looks like while it's growing?'

'I think Wally said it was like a tomato plant. Let's take a recce.'

They packed up their purchases again and Gary hid both under the corner of his carpet. He said, 'Your dad does a lot of pot-grown plants, doesn't he, and stands the pots out in rows? You could plant up your own pots and push them between his and they'd all get watered. Who'd notice them there?'

'Gavin and Rory might know what it was.'

'Would your dad?'

Charlie shook his head. 'I don't know. He'd know it wasn't daffodil bulbs though, and he'd tip my plants out and start again. I don't want that, do I? These seeds don't come cheap.'

When they rode round to the garden centre they found Jamie and three friends kicking a football round on the pitch.

'Join in,' Charlie said to Gary. 'Don't give Jamie any clues about what we're up to.'

They spent half an hour playing three a side, then retired to the kitchen for a cup of tea. There was a plate of Nana's scones on the table, and between them they cleared it.

Charlie had to wait until after supper before the garden centre closed and he could have a scout round on his own. He started by taking a good look at the tomato plants growing in the nursery, but there was nothing remotely like that growing wild on the untilled ground.

Everybody knew it was illegal to grow cannabis, and should he ever be unlucky enough to be suspected of it, Charlie wanted it to be impossible to prove it had been planted. He wanted to make it look as though it was growing wild, and searched around for a good place to sow his five seeds. He needed to keep them well away from Jamie's football-playing friends. He'd seen how they fought over their ball and didn't want his growing plants to be kicked down accidentally.

On the edge of the coppice, the roots of the trees were near the surface and he could see bare soil through the grass, just the sort of place where weeds might grow. It was the perfect site for several small seed beds. In fact, he'd plant his seeds far enough apart to make it unnecessary for them to be moved. The ground here was south-facing which meant his plants would get the maximum amount of sun and it sloped slightly which meant it would be well drained. Dad had taught him well.

He kicked away the top turf and found there was nothing but subsoil underneath. Not that that mattered. Adjacent to the potting shed Dad had a huge mound of compost he mixed up himself with everything seeds needed for growth.

No, Charlie told himself, not that. A scientist would be able to tell where it had originated, and thus prove the seeds had been deliberately planted. Dad always had at least one bed being rotovated ready to be planted up. Charlie would simply take a bucketful of native soil and just move it a hundred yards or so to put it between the tree roots.

He started preparing his beds. He'd hide them by scattering a few dead leaves and grasses over them, not that anybody would be looking for them at this stage. Dad was a nutcase to slave away planting hyacinths and daffodils. By comparison, cannabis would be a real money-spinner.

Not that Charlie intended to deal. No, he could get caught

doing that and the rozzers came down heavily on dealers. This crop would be for his own consumption and he'd treat the gang once in a while. It would be safer than buying it and save him a mint of money. If he got a bumper crop, he could always ask the gang to pay him back in pints and ciggies, but they would anyway. It was the best way of providing for himself and his friends.

A week later he had a packet of seeds labelled *Cannabis sativa* and spent a late evening planting them. For the first few weeks he kept them well watered, and was rewarded by seeing strong green shoots pushing through the soil.

Charlie took a little stroll every two or three days to see how his plants were faring. He was pleased with them. They were soon growing taller and sprouting leaves. He took Gary to see them.

'Let's try smoking a couple of leaves,' Gary suggested.

'The problem is they're fresh and full of sap. I expect they need to be dried before you put them in a joint. But let's try it and see.'

Charlie picked a few leaves, cut them up and mixed them with tobacco. They tried it out in Gary's bedroom while his mother was at work. The joint didn't burn properly, and it didn't taste the same, but when the familiar sense of calm and contentment flooded through him Charlie was triumphant.

'We do need to dry it first, though. It's hard to keep the joint burning when it's like this.'

'Get too much of it together and the fag goes out. It smells funny too.' Gary threw open his bedroom window.

'I could try putting a few leaves in the airing cupboard,' Charlie said, 'and see how that turns out. I'll have a recce to see if it's possible.' The last thing he wanted was questions from his mother about what he'd put in her airing cupboard.

'It's pretty dark inside,' he reported to Gary, 'and the top shelf is well above eye level.'

He took an old handkerchief out of the washing, folded it in half and stitched the edges to make a bag. Then he put a handful of leaves inside and sewed them in.

The next time he found himself alone in the house, he put a chair in front of the airing cupboard and taped his package to the wall above the top shelf, as near to the back wall as he could reach. Nobody would be able to see it if they were standing on the floor and it couldn't be dragged out with the clothes.

They had a spell of warm dry weather. Charlie was on his way to see if his plants needed watering when he caught sight of Sophie in her red anorak coming through the garden centre to the house.

'Hello, Charlie,' she called.

He stopped. This was not the moment to go near his plants. She'd more than likely follow him and start asking questions.

'You coming up to our place?' he called.

'Yep.' She quickened her step. 'I had to get out. Dad's having a go at me. I went to see Judith but she's gone out.'

'You're in the dog house?'

'Yep. What are you doing tonight?'

'I'm at a loose end too. I thought I might go out for a run on my bike.'

'Where's Gary tonight?'

'He's grounded. His mum found stuff she shouldn't have in his coat pocket.'

'What?'

176

He pulled a face but said nothing.

'Well, it can't have been chocolate. How about taking me with you? I've got to do something different or I'll go barking mad.'

'OK.' He wondered if he dare take Sophie to the Cheshire Cheese to meet the lads. Why not? 'You game for having a drink?'

'A pub? You bet.'

'Don't tell your mum, you know what she's like. It'll be round the family in ten minutes and I'll be in trouble for taking you.'

'As if I would.'

He hurried her round the house to the garage where he'd parked his bike. 'You can borrow Gary's helmet. He won't mind.'

He viewed her skimpy skirt as he kicked over the engine. 'You'd be better wearing trousers.'

She grinned. 'I'll manage.'

'Get on then. Put your arms round my waist and hold on tight.'

He let his bike cruise down to the gate and took off along the road.

'Wow, this is great.' Sophie had to repeat what she said, her words being snatched away by the wind. Charlie thought, for a girl, she was all right.

The gang at the Cheshire Cheese rated her much higher after she'd been to the Ladies and combed out her wind-tossed hair.

'She's a real stunner,' Wally said. 'You jammy thing.'

'She's just my cousin,' Charlie told him. 'When she was a kid she was a real pain in the neck, but she's not so bad now.'

'So she's free?' He sounded amazed.

'Can't answer for her, mate, but free as far as I'm concerned.'

'Wow.' Wally's eyes went to her again. 'She's a real looker. Where does she work?'

'She's still at school.'

'Oh!'

Charlie smiled. He thought that took away some of her attraction for Wally.

Sophie was worried. Her body wasn't behaving as it usually did. She'd felt sick before she'd eaten breakfast this morning and was terrified she might be pregnant.

For months, a possible pregnancy had been her worst nightmare. She thought she'd scotched it by getting the pill. She'd started taking it, but had something gone wrong? Had she left it too late? Sophie felt petrified. She spent ages with a calendar and a pencil, counting the weeks both forward and backward, but kept the worry to herself, hoping and praying she was wrong. As the days went on, she knew she wasn't. The Easter holidays came and she wasn't able to see as much of Darrell. That and her growing certainty about being pregnant ruined them for her.

April came and the first days back at school. She'd managed to have a word with Darrell behind the gym yesterday but there were far too many eyes watching them there for her to talk about what she suspected. He'd been playing with his band in Warrington last night and tonight he'd be in Liverpool.

Her breasts began to feel sore and that convinced her that her fears were well founded. The thought of having to tell her dad was paralysing. She couldn't!

As it was Saturday, she'd arranged to meet Darrell this morning. She caught the bus into Chester, having told her mother she was going shopping with her school friend Emily, and that they'd have something to eat and then go to a matinee in the afternoon. There'd be more questions if she didn't get home by early evening, but she'd face that problem if it came.

Darrell had suggested they meet on Bridge Street, and she studied a display of engagement rings in a jeweller's shop window while she waited for him. He hadn't asked her to marry him but he surely would now.

Her eye was caught by a magnificent solitaire diamond sparkling on its black velvet stand. She'd love a ring like that, though she didn't think Darrell would be able to afford it until he had a big hit. But money wasn't important. It was his love and support that mattered now.

Here he was, striding along the pavement towards her with a wide welcoming smile. His long hair was loose and flying round his shoulders. He looked so marvellously handsome it made her heart turn over.

'Hi.' He took both her hands in his and kissed her full on the lips.

'I've got to talk to you,' she said. It was almost a sob. She felt desperate.

'There's a good pub round the corner.' He took her arm. 'Let's have a drink while we chat.'

Sophie felt tears start to her eyes. Chat! What she wanted was a serious talk, a profoundly serious and important talk. Minutes later, she was blinking in a dark interior that smelled of beer.

'What will you have?'

She'd always found that something of a problem. Dad had forbidden her to go into any pub while she was under eighteen. She didn't much like alcohol and preferred orange juice, but that was a juvenile drink and she wanted to appear grown up to Darrell. She said, as she usually did, 'A glass of white wine would be nice.'

She didn't take her eyes off him as he stood at the bar. She wanted him to take this seriously; she needed his help and support.

He came and sat beside her. 'Right then,' he said. 'What was it you wanted to talk about?'

She took a gulp of her wine and blurted out, 'I'm afraid I'm pregnant.'

'Oh!' His eyes searched into hers. 'That's a bit of a shock. I thought now you were on the pill . . .'

'It must have happened before I started it. What am I going to do?' she wailed.

'Are you sure?'

'Of course I'm sure.'

'I need time to think . . . When will it be due? Have you worked that out?'

'Mid-November.'

His dazzling smile lit up his face. 'Wouldn't you like a baby? Wouldn't that be rather nice? I quite fancy having a son.'

Sophie was astounded. She'd expected him to be as horrified as she was. 'I want an abortion. I want to have it taken away. I want the whole business over and done with.'

'Don't be hasty. Think about it, Sophie.'

'I'm taking my A levels this term.'

'Yes, soon now. They'll be well behind you by the time the baby's due.'

'I need a clear mind to work for exams, not be worried like this.'

He took both her hands in his. 'I'll look after you. I don't want you to worry.'

'But what am I to do?'

'Move in with me. Live with me. I'd love that. I want to take care of you.'

Sophie let herself think about it for a moment. She would love it too. 'But I can't! My father would go spare. Couldn't we be married?'

He didn't answer immediately. He was biting his lip.

'Don't you want that?' She was shocked. The bottom was falling out of her world.

'Yes, I'd love it, but I'm afraid I'm already married.'

That took Sophie's breath away. She felt wet with perspiration. 'You didn't say.'

'I did. I told you I had a failed marriage behind me.'

'Yes, behind you. I thought you meant divorced! I thought . . .' Hadn't he said so?

'You didn't ask me. I'd have spelled it out if you had.'

Sophie could feel tears welling up. What had she been thinking of ? This made everything twice as bad.

'We never did get round to divorce. I suppose I could ask Lucy if she will. If you're keen?'

'My family will be.' They'd see it as the only respectable way out. 'Please ask her.'

'Lots of people don't bother these days,' he said easily.

'My dad would have a fit. All my family . . .'

'Sophie, just move in with me and let's get on with our lives.'

In one way that sounded like heaven. Darrell would take all

the responsibility off her shoulders. But she wasn't eighteen yet. What if Dad and Mum refused to let her go? Sophie had been back to his flat many times now. It had seemed a romantic love nest at first, but now she wasn't too keen.

She said, 'It's too small for the two of us and a baby.'

'We can find something bigger. Something you'd like. We'll start looking now.' He put a comforting arm round her shoulders and pulled her closer. 'We'll sort it out, honest. I want us to be together, bring up this baby between us. I do love you. You know that.'

Sophie could see herself living with Darrell in an old cottage like the one her parents had. She'd have a lovely time buying furniture and curtains and fixing it up to their liking; she'd spend her time keeping it swept and polished and cooking lovely meals. She'd give Darrell the son he wanted and the three of them would be very happy. No more school, no more examinations and having to worry about the rules Mum laid down. It would be grown-up bliss.

'Well, Sophie!' A hand slapped her playfully on her shoulder. 'Fancy seeing you here. Naughty girl! What would Aunt Izzy say if she could see you now?'

Sophie jerked away from Darrell to look up into Charlie's grinning face and felt the heat run up her cheeks.

She gasped, 'Don't say anything, Charlie, please.'

'Course not.' He chortled. 'I just can't get over it. Sophie, the clever one of the family. You're always being held up to me as an example I must follow. Mum keeps saying, "Why can't you be more like Sophie?" She thinks you're a star.' He laughed again and said to Darrell, 'She's kept quiet about you, too.'

'This is Darrell,' she choked.

'Hi, Sophie.'

For the first time, she noticed Gary Ingram was standing two steps behind Charlie. She'd never been more embarrassed. Had they heard enough of what she and Darrell were talking about to get the gist? She hoped not, but surely it must have shown on her face? She felt all churned up.

She'd thought she could keep Darrell a secret from her family, but already she'd had to take Judith and Emily into her confidence because she'd used them to cover her dates with him. It had long been an open secret at school. The whole form knew and most were envious.

'Can I buy you both a drink?' Charlie asked.

'No.' Sophie leaped to her feet and pulled Darrell up after her. 'We were just going. Please don't tell them at home. It would get me into awful trouble.'

'Don't worry,' Charlie said. 'We don't say anything about going to pubs, do we, Gary?'

Sophie was glad to get Darrell on his own. Her worries spilled out as they walked to his flat. 'I'll have to have an abortion,' she said. 'How do I go about getting one? Do I have to go to my family doctor or can I do it through the family planning clinic?' She knew he was unlikely to know, but whom could she ask who did?

He smiled. 'I rather like the idea of a baby.'

'What?'

'And even better, I like the idea of having you with me all the time. I love you. We'd be very happy, wouldn't we?'

Once inside his flat she looked round, wondering why she'd thought it was a romantic nest. Mum would say it was dirty and needed a thorough spring clean.

'Please don't get rid of this baby,' Darrell begged. 'I can

really see myself as a father. Sit your exams, you ought to do that, then move in with me.'

Sophie wanted to say yes. How could she not love Darrell, when he was offering such a marvellous solution? To leave home and live with him . . . She could present her plans cut and dried to her parents when she told them about the baby, but her gaze went round the room again. Should she?

'This is just a bachelor pad,' he said quickly. 'We'll start looking for a proper home right away. Let's see if there's anything in the local paper.'

She went to sit beside him while he fluttered the paper looking for the right page. 'Here, what about this? Three bedroom semi-detached . . .'

'Could we afford that? I'd like a bit of garden for the baby.'

'I'd have to get a mortgage, but so does everybody else. We'd be a real family, you, me and baby. If the band goes over big, then we'll move up a notch. There're some smashing houses here.'

'A small one would do,' she said.

'You shall choose it, I promise.'

Sophie was reassured. 'It would be heaven.'

It meant she needn't tell her parents for a few weeks, but she'd have to shut her mind to the plans she'd been making for next year. She'd expected to go to university. Mum and Dad were ambitious for her. All they wanted to talk about were the merits of trying for a place at Oxford or staying home and applying to Liverpool. But it was her life, and being with Darrell seemed vastly more important now.

CHAPTER THIRTEEN

CHARLIE WAS boasting he could pass his examinations at the technical college without bothering to go to many of the lectures. When the staff got wise to him, Charlie was told he wouldn't be allowed in the examination room unless he'd attended at least 80 per cent of the lectures first, and a letter saying as much was sent to his parents.

When Ben tried to tell him off, he blustered, 'The tutors make such a song and dance about their lectures and they're dull as dishwater. Everybody knows cooking is just practice and common sense.'

He left the college before the end of the course. So did Gary, for the same reason. Hilary was afraid Charlie had led him astray. Nevertheless, they both found jobs as commis chefs in local restaurants. They'd wanted to work in the same one, but that turned out to be impossible.

Charlie was pleased to be taken on at the Barley Mow: a restaurant in a small hamlet four miles from home along the Chester high road. He was able to use his motor bike to get there and back, but his mother was worried that he was regularly coming home after midnight.

'I'm afraid it's my job to help clean the kitchen,' he said. 'So it's late before I'm allowed to leave.' But he'd also got into the habit of having a glass of beer with George the barman before they locked up.

He told everybody he was looking forward to his birthday so he could start taking driving lessons. When he started he was full of enthusiasm for driving and roadcraft, but after a couple of weeks he said to his father, 'You're wasting your money, Dad. All I do is drive the instructor round.'

His father wasn't pleased. 'You need to learn from him. Concentrate on doing what he tells you.'

'I do, but Mum's just as good at telling me.'

Ben was exasperated. He said afterwards to Hilary, 'He's got a big head now, thinks there's nothing the instructor can tell him about driving. Unbelievable when he was so lacking in confidence over his reading.'

After very few lessons, Charlie was put in for his driving test and passed at the first attempt. Now his motor bike no longer satisfied him. He was saving for a car of his own. In the meantime, he nagged to be allowed to borrow either the van or his mother's car. Within a month, he was caught speeding in the car and fined. It happened again six weeks later.

Six months after starting his job, he announced, 'I'm fed up with the restaurant trade. I hate split shifts. What good is a couple of hours off in the afternoon to me? By the time I get home it's almost time to go back and I hate working every evening. I want to go out, especially on Saturday nights, but that's our busiest night and we all have to jump to it. We close on Monday nights, but everything else is closed too. There's nowhere to go then.'

His parents were horrified when he told them he'd handed in his notice. But within a week, Charlie found a job as a cook in the care home where his mother had once worked.

'You liked working there, didn't you?' he said. 'I think I might like the hours better.'

Hilary asked him about the staff, but it seemed the nurses she'd known had moved on in the intervening years.

'I'll still have to work what they call unsociable hours,' he said, 'so I won't get every weekend free. But the oldies like to have their main meal in the middle of the day, and we serve their tea at five o'clock which means I get my evenings free.'

'Don't they get anything to eat after five o'clock?' Jamie asked, appalled.

'Yes, a milky drink and a biscuit, but they don't keep a cook on for that.'

Sophie felt in a flat spin. She couldn't settle to her studies. Did she really want a baby to bring up? Did Darrell? He kept saying he did, but she couldn't see a baby fitting into his lifestyle. He liked to go out every night and was always burning the midnight oil.

She couldn't talk about it to anyone but Darrell, and the thought of telling her parents gave her the shivers. Still, they'd have to know sooner or later.

Should she tell Mum? Usually, she confided her problems to Dad, but it would be difficult to explain when so recently she'd said categorically she didn't have a boyfriend. She'd have to admit to lying too.

Or she could tell Aunt Hilly and ask her for her help? The rest of the family all did that because she knew about medical matters. Sophie walked up to the garden centre with her mother one evening, and was not sorry to find all the boys had gone out. She hung about waiting for a chance to take Hilary aside, but in the end she bottled out.

She no longer felt well; she knew her problem was pulling her down. She caught a cold and had a bout of earache in her left ear. Her mother kept her off school and made an appointment for her to see the family doctor.

Sophie saw it as her chance. She'd tell him she was pregnant at the same time. She very rarely needed to go to see the doctor. Her last visit had been a long time ago and Mum had taken her.

'I'm old enough to go alone now,' she told her and Mum didn't quibble. Sophie could feel her heart pounding as she sat in the waiting room; she was sweating and her ear was really painful. When it was her turn to sit facing Dr Tanner across his desk, she could feel herself shaking.

'Hello, Sophie.' He smiled. 'What can I do for you?'

She told him about her earache and he examined both ears. 'I'll give you some antibiotics and you can take the rest of the week off school and rest. How are you getting on there? Is it this year you take your A levels?'

Sophie had prepared the words she'd need to bring up her pregnancy. She'd say, *There's something else . . .*

He was being friendly and asking about the rest of her family. She found it off-putting. Then the phone on his desk rang. He excused himself, picked it up and started to speak, then covered the receiver with his hand.

'Sophie,' he said, 'one last thing. Remind your mother that Daisy's due for another vaccination, would you?'

Sophie said, 'There's something else . . .' But he'd turned back to the phone again and seemed not to hear. She felt she'd been dismissed and got to her feet. She could hardly stay here listening while he was talking to someone else, could she? She went slowly out, knowing she'd let the chance slip away.

It comforted her when Darrell suggested they start looking for a house. Sophie was eager. She expected house-hunting to be fun, but there was little available for rent and everything she thought hopeful Darrell dismissed as too expensive. She lowered her sights to a flat but that market was no easier.

She felt horribly insecure. Life as she knew it was going to change for ever. Her London grandmother had left her some money she could use to buy a house for them, but not until she was twenty-one. The baby would be born in November and she wouldn't even be eighteen until the following February.

Aunt Hilary had another of her family get-togethers and Sophie felt quite shy about coming face to face with Charlie, in case he'd overheard her and Darrell talking in the pub. But he gave her a theatrical wink as she went in with her parents and whisked her off to the empty playroom to say, 'We keep our mouths shut, agreed? We see no evil, hear no evil, and speak no evil.'

She smiled at him. 'Much the best thing. It would only upset the family, wouldn't it?'

Sophie allowed herself one or two nights away from her books each week depending on when Darrell was free to take her out. She was quick to see a way in which Charlie could help her.

'We could say we were going to the pictures together, and you could collect me and give me a lift.'

Mostly Charlie was able to borrow his mother's car, but if

not there was still his motor bike. She couldn't say she was going out with Judith too often, because if Mum met her mother in the village they always stopped for a chat.

The last time she'd seen Darrell, she'd suggested they go to the Odeon to see the rerun of *Gandhi*, but he'd argued that a Shirley MacLaine film called *Terms of Endearment* showing at the ABC Cinema was more to his taste. Sophie had heard in school that both were exceptionally good films and had decided she'd be happy with either.

Tonight Charlie was giving her a lift as far as the Eagle and Child pub, to which he and his biker friends had transferred their custom. It was near Mollington and easier for Darrell than collecting her from the car park of the Dog and Gun.

He was waiting in the bar with an empty pint glass in front of him. Standing up to greet them, he said, 'Charlie, let me buy you a pint.'

'Good idea.' Charlie grinned. 'It looks as though my friends aren't here yet.'

'A glass of white wine?' Darrell asked Sophie.

'I thought we were going to the pictures,' she said.

'Let's give that a miss tonight. I've got something to tell you. Really exciting news.' His dark eyes danced. He whispered, 'Tell you when we're on our own.'

Sophie was intrigued and thought he might have seen a solicitor about getting a divorce. They'd talked about that; it was the one thing that might make Dad see him in a better light.

Darrell returned carrying three drinks. He pushed a tankard in front of Charlie. 'How you doing?' he asked.

'Not very well. I'm quite depressed.'

'You'd never know it.' Darrell smiled.

Sophie said, 'That's Charlie's way. A real bundle of laughs.'

'I'm in the dog kennel at home because I've been caught speeding yet again. Got another summons this morning.'

'When d'you go to court?'

'Not for a few weeks but Dad thinks I'll be banned from driving.'

Shortly afterwards, Gary arrived with three other lads, and as there were not enough seats near by, Charlie went to join them on the other side of the bar.

'What is it you want to tell me?' Sophie asked eagerly.

'Wait till I get us another drink.'

He came back, spilling a little of his pint, and slid a packet of crisps and another of peanuts across the small table.

Sophie was on the edge of her seat. 'Come on, what's your exciting news?'

'We're putting together a tour round Europe for the band. We've got two firm bookings in Frankfurt and another in Hamburg, and we've got an agent trying to fix up more.'

Sophie felt a sudden cold spasm. Did Darrell mean to desert her?

'A tour of Europe! I don't call that exciting, not for me anyway. I'll miss you. When is it to be?'

'We'll play in Frankfurt on September the fourth and fifth. Hamburg is on the eighth.'

'Darrell! I thought you'd asked me to live with you?' She was scared. 'I don't want you to leave me on my own.'

'You can come with us,' he said, his brown eyes smiling into hers. 'It needn't cost you anything because we'll have to buy a van to get there.'

'Buy a van?'

Darrell often complained about being short of money but he spent it like water. He was always paying out for new clothes or another round of drinks. He'd promised to buy her an engagement ring as soon as he could put his hand on enough readies.

'Yes,' he said. 'It's the only way to get us all there and take all the lighting equipment, the loudspeakers and the drum kit and stuff.'

'But a van will cost a lot, won't it?' Even Uncle Ben and Dad considered a motor vehicle to be a major purchase.

'We'll all put in.' He smiled at her. 'We're saving up for it. We have to have it to go to Germany.'

'But what about me? The baby will be born in mid-November.'

'We'll be back before then.'

'But I'll look very pregnant; I'm bound to.' Sophie was shocked. Her eyes were prickling with tears, and it was an effort to hold them in check. She could feel her belly expanding now. 'I might not feel up to it.'

'You will, you'll see. Have you been to your doctor?'

'No, not about the baby.'

'No hurry. It's obvious everything's going well. Your exams are almost over, aren't they?'

What Sophie found so painful was that he was thinking of himself and not her and the baby.

'Don't you see, Soph, this is a big chance for the band? We can't pass it up. The Beatles made it big in Hamburg.'

Sophie had never worried about exams before. She was competitive. She'd always aimed to come top of her form and mostly she'd managed it, but even if she came second or third her marks had always been good. This time, she felt she hadn't quite got on top of her A level revision, and that she hadn't acquitted herself as well as she usually did.

But the exams were over now. It had been history this afternoon, her weakest subject, but the last one, and now she could relax. Her wrist had ached when the papers were being collected and she'd done nothing but talk about the exam since. When they'd been released from the hall, she'd joined in the post-mortem as her form mates compared the answers they'd given. She was not too pleased with what she'd done.

Sophie climbed into her father's car, sank back in the seat and closed her eyes. She was exhausted.

He started the engine. 'How did it go? Did you like the paper?'

'Not bad.'

Dad went on asking about the questions she'd had and wanting to know the answers she'd given. Sophie felt she hardly had the energy to think.

On the whole she was feeling better; the awful morning sickness she'd had to hide had passed off at last. But nearer now, imminent in fact, was the moment when she'd have to tell him about Darrell. Not today, though. She was spent.

Instead she said, 'Guess what? There's a rumour going round school that we're being burgled or robbed or something. Small amounts of cash have been stolen from the office, but there's said to be a serious shortfall in food ordered for school meals. Helpings of dinner do seem to have been getting smaller, but who would want to steal yukky food like that?'

'It isn't yukky just because it's served in school.' Dad had put on his headmaster's voice. 'You say food is being stolen?'

'Well, it was rumoured last term that dry goods were being ordered and checked in, but later the cooks couldn't find them in the store room. Now the fresh food is walking too. We've had detectives in today – quite exciting.'

Sophie found it easier to think of that than her own problems.

As she pulled herself out of her bath that night she assessed the size of her abdomen and was appalled to find she looked positively pregnant. She certainly couldn't wear a bikini without its being noticed. Time was going on; she had to get focused and do something about it. It was turning her into a nervous wreck.

In the car today, Dad had been trying to persuade her to try for a place at Oxford. It had been an opportunity to tell him she wouldn't be able to go to university in the autumn and why, but she hadn't been able to get the words out. She wasn't ready. Instead, she'd got quite tetchy with him. With a baby to look after, would she ever be able to go to university? She couldn't see her future beyond November.

She was upset because Darrell wanted to tour round Europe, and though he'd said he wanted the baby he was giving no thought to it now, or to her welfare.

That evening, Charlie called round with Aunt Hilly's car and drove her to a hall in Ellesmere Port where Top Flight were playing. There were no seats; the audience stood around with their drinks. Sophie got tired and eventually had to sit on the floor with her back against the wall. Charlie was happy to sit beside her.

'Darrell's pretty good.' He was enthusiastic. Sophie thought he looked wonderful as he strutted his stuff on stage. 'Look at the crowd. They couldn't get many more in here.' The audience were noisy in their appreciation, clapping and shouting and cheering. 'They love the band, don't they?'

In the interval, Darrell showed them the new van the band had just bought, a large Ford Transit. Charlie examined it with great interest but Sophie had a lump in her throat and wasn't prepared to like it. Darrell could find the money for the things he wanted, but he should be looking for a better flat and thinking of her and his coming child. It seemed she was the one making all the sacrifices and she hadn't wanted the baby in the first place. Still didn't, come to that.

'Touring Europe should be marvellous fun.' Charlie sounded keen on that too. Sophie wondered if it was practical for her to even think of going, and if when the time came she'd be able to enjoy it.

'You'll love it,' Charlie assured her. 'I wouldn't miss it if I were you.'

Sophie reflected that it might be her last chance of a bit of fun for ages. She must have shown her feelings to Darrell, because the next day he told her he'd buy her a ring.

'Can't afford the earth for it,' he apologised. 'But I want you to have one so you can see I'm serious.'

To hear him say that calmed Sophie's fears. If Darrell loved her and meant to provide a home they could share, all would be well. An engagement ring would make his intention official.

At lunch time the next day they went to a Chester jeweller's shop. 'I came here earlier,' he said, 'and picked out several rings for you to choose from.'

With a little frisson of excitement she accepted the salesman's invitation to sit at the counter, and he brought out several trays. Sophie was dazzled. They were beautiful rings,

rings she'd be proud to wear. Darrell was being very generous. He slipped a sapphire on her finger.

'No,' he said, 'perhaps not. Which would you like?'

She settled on a large opal with a small diamond on each side of it, in an old-fashioned gold setting.

'You've got good taste,' the salesman told her.

'I like it.' Darrell kissed her fingers. 'I promise I'll buy you the largest diamond in the shop if we go over big in Germany.'

'This ring is really pretty. I'm very happy with it.' She smiled. He'd slipped it on her engagement finger and she felt reassured to see it glinting there.

'Shall I wrap it for you?' the salesman asked.

'No,' Darrell said. 'My fiancée would prefer to wear it.'

Instead, the little box of tooled leather was wrapped up empty. Sophie put it in her pocket. She linked her arm through Darrell's but kept her hand where they could both admire her ring.

'I won't be able to wear it at school,' she said sadly. 'The girls would notice and ask a thousand questions. I won't be able to wear it at home either. Mum would want to know who gave it to me, and I haven't told her about you yet.'

At the school gates she placed her ring in the little box and kept it in her blazer pocket. Every time her fingers touched it that afternoon, she remembered Darrell and was warmed by the thought of his love.

For Sophie, leaving school was the end of an era and now it seemed too close. Too much was changing in her life. People were coming into school to give talks about further education and careers, but she felt excluded from all that.

Her form mistress assumed Sophie's plans were

unchanged. 'I do hope you get a place at Oxford,' she said. 'You are lucky. You've always known you wanted to read law.' It brought Sophie to the brink of tears.

Her peers were making their choices. Emily Burke was hoping to go to Guy's Hospital to do medicine and Judith Salter had applied for a place in Liverpool to read law.

'I was hoping you'd apply there too,' she said to Sophie. 'Then we could go together.'

Sophie longed for that with all her heart. She felt on the brink of tears again and almost told Judith why it couldn't be.

'But marvellous if you get into Oxford . . .'

Sophie tried to focus on the summer holidays instead. She'd get a job to earn a bit of cash. She had no need to bother about useful experience this year; she'd go for whatever paid most. She'd need it if she were to go touring on the Continent. Darrell and the band were full of plans. They now had nine gigs booked, and to Sophie's relief it meant the tour would have to start a little earlier, at the end of August.

She knew she couldn't put off telling her parents any longer. Mum would surely notice her changing shape. She'd have to make herself tell Dad tomorrow. If she broke it to him on the way to school, it would give him all day to get used to the idea. If she did it on the way back, the row would carry on for hours after they got home. It probably would anyway, but like this she could escape into school and he could ring Mum, and they would be over their first shock by the time she had to face them.

She was half afraid her parents would throw her out when they knew, and it was a comfort to have Darrell's flat to go to, but she didn't want to live there by herself. It would be better to go on tour with the band.

*

Isobel took the tray into the living room. Every day she made a pot of tea to have with Seb and Sophie when they came home from school. Her timing was spot on. Through the window, she watched Seb's car pull up in front of the cottage.

Today, Sophie leaped out, looking red-faced and rebellious. Sebastian looked fierce and came banging into the house. Isobel knew he was angry. Seb and Sophie had not been on such good terms recently – she'd heard them arguing – but then since Primmy's death everything had seemed a bit fraught. Sophie was heading for the stairs.

'In here,' Sebastian ordered, holding the living-room door open.

'What's the matter?' Isobel asked as Sophie flounced in and threw herself on the settee.

'Come on, Sophie, tell your mother,' Seb said. Instead she jumped up again and helped herself to a buttered scone. 'She's got a boyfriend. I told her a month ago it wasn't on.'

'What isn't?' Isobel started to pour the tea.

'The boyfriend. She's changed her mind about going to university next year.'

'What? Why?'

Sophie munched sulkily.

'She's going to take a year off to go round Europe with this lad.'

'Why shouldn't I take a year out?' she flared suddenly, speaking with her mouth full. 'I'm a year younger than anyone else in my form. It'll do no harm.'

'You know that isn't what I'm quibbling about,' Sebastian said gently. 'It's you leaving home, going off with that fellow.'

'His name's Darrell Marchbanks.'

Isobel was shocked. 'Just the two of you?' she asked. 'You and this Darrell something or other?'

'Marchbanks. No, Mum. There'll be three others.'

'All men,' Sebastian said.

'No,' Isobel said forcefully. 'We absolutely forbid it. You're too young. It isn't safe.'

'Safer with them than anyone else. Darrell's been to Germany before, and so has Bernie. They know their way round.'

Sebastian said, 'Tell your mother the facts, Sophie, go on.' She said nothing, biting into another scone, giving that her full attention.

He went on himself. 'Darrell is eleven years older than Sophie. He's got a job as the caretaker of her school, but he's about to throw that up.'

'He sings with a band, Mum. It's called Top Flight, and they're planning a European tour. They've got a van and they're booked to play in Frankfurt and Hamburg . . .'

Isobel was shocked. 'No, Sophie, definitely not.' She'd got used to hearing from Hilary how lucky she was that Sophie was sailing through her education without causing her any problems. But now this!

'He's lovely, Mum.'

'No,' Isobel said firmly. 'Much better if you go straight to university next year. You can take a year off when you've got your degree.'

Sophie tossed her head. 'It's my life. I'm going with Darrell whatever you say.'

'Are you thinking of marrying this man?'

'No.'

Isobel didn't know whether to be relieved by that or not.

She couldn't believe it. He'd be older, more experienced, more demanding, and probably more able to persuade Sophie to do what he wanted. And there'd be three other men. What would they expect of Sophie?

For once, Sebastian looked every inch the strict headmaster. 'And who do you expect to support you through this year abroad?'

'I've got the money Granny left me.'

'Under the terms of her will, you won't be able to draw on the capital until you're twenty-one, and the interest won't get you far. You're only seventeen, Sophie. We're your legal guardians and we say no. You must stay here with us.'

'He'll ruin your life,' Isobel warned her. 'You'll throw away everything you've worked for.'

'Course I won't.' Sophie's pout increased.

Isobel took a deep breath. She couldn't stomach the thought of her beautiful daughter, so full of promise, trailing round Germany in the back of a van with four men.

'I suppose they're all much older than you?'

'Of course they are,' Seb grunted.

'They're all very nice. It's a smashing band.'

'They expect to be famous and rivalling the Beatles before too much longer,' Seb said. 'And it goes without saying they'll be multimillionaires as well.'

Isobel burst out, 'Sex is what he wants from you, Sophie. He'll get you pregnant. If that happens you'll never get your degree or have a proper career. You'll end up without qualifications and have to work behind the counter in Woolworths.'

Sophie slammed out of the room and raced upstairs.

CHAPTER FOURTEEN

SOPHIE THREW herself across her bed and fumed. Dad had lost his rag this morning when she'd tried to talk to him. He'd kept on and on. She'd not seen him so angry for a long time. Giving him all day to think about it had been a big mistake. He'd had time to harden his resolve and organise his objections and on the way home he'd nagged at her again.

The trouble was, she'd managed to get out only half her confession. She still hadn't told them she was already pregnant or that Darrell was married. The worst was yet to come. It would alter everything and they'd have much more to object to.

Sophie could hear them below, heatedly discussing what they thought was the problem. She had to straighten them out before it went any further. She waited until she thought Charlie would have had time to get home, then she went across to the bathroom and washed her face. Tiptoeing downstairs to the hall, she lifted the phone to ring him. It was Jamie who answered and he had Charlie on the other end within moments.

'I'm in terrible trouble, Charlie,' she said. 'There's a huge row boiling up and I want to get out of here fast. Could you come and pick me up asap?'

'I haven't eaten yet and Mum's got pork chops on the go.'

'You can't be hungry, Charlie? You work in a kitchen. You told me you nibbled all day.'

'So I do, but—'

'We'll have a meal out, you and I. If there's pork chops on the menu, you shall have them. Please come and rescue me. I'm a coward – I can't face this.'

'All right. I'll be there in ten to fifteen minutes.'

'Thanks, Charlie. You won't let me down, will you?'

'As if I would. See you.'

Sophie raced back to her room to run a comb through her long hair and dab a bit of foundation on her face. Then she went down again. There was silence now from the living room, and she went through to the kitchen. Mum was basting some chicken pieces, and the scent of roasting filled the air. Dad was sitting down with a strong whisky and water in his hand. They both had long faces. Sophie felt a stab of guilt that she'd upset them.

'I'm sorry,' she said. Both pairs of eyes shot up to look at her. She could see they expected her to apologise and agree to stay at home.

'Dad, you didn't get the full story. You went off at half cock before I could get it out. The fact is I'm pregnant. The baby is due in November so there's no question of my going to university next term. I've known Darrell for over a year and we love each other. And before you start talking about marriage, he can't. He's already married to someone else.'

They looked absolutely stunned. Daisy came out from

behind her father's chair to stare at her. Sophie ignored everything.

'I know I've made a mess of things but it's no good going off the deep end. What's done is done. Darrell has a flat in Chester. I intend to move in with him and I'm also going to Germany with him.'

She heard Charlie hoot outside. She retreated to the hall and grabbed for her coat. She was putting it on when Mum snatched open the door.

'I heard a car. Is that the man out there now? Get him to come in and meet us.'

'No, it's Charlie. He's taking me out. Don't keep supper for me. I'm giving you time to argue this out before I come back. Sorry, Mum, but there's nothing you or I can do about it. You must see the plans we were making have to change.'

She let herself out. She hadn't meant to slam the door but the wind caught it and it crashed shut. She ran to the passenger door of the garden centre van, glad that at last she'd got her problems out in the open, but she felt guilty and ashamed that she'd let her parents down when they were thinking only of her well-being. Her eyes prickled with tears, but she wasn't going to cry on Charlie's shoulder.

He was slouched over the steering wheel looking the picture of misery himself. He started the engine.

'So you've joined me in the dog house? Let me guess, they've found out about your boyfriend?'

'I told them.'

'Then it's self-inflicted trouble. What made you do that?'

Sophie sighed. 'I've put it off for months, but I can't any longer. You might as well know – the whole family will soon. I'm expecting a baby.'

203

'Christ!' The van jerked towards the gutter, and Charlie fought to get it back on course. 'That's bad. What are you going to do? Marry Darrell?'

Sophie let it all pour out then and had a silent weep, wiping away her tears surreptitiously. Charlie had to keep his eyes on the road so he was unlikely to notice.

She'd had a reputation for being clever because she often achieved the top mark in end of term exams, but she'd done some very stupid things.

She knew where she'd gone wrong. If she'd gone to the family planning clinic as soon as she'd met Darrell, she might have avoided this pregnancy. Instead, she'd let Darrell take responsibility for contraception. He had said he'd see to it. It must surely be easier for the man?

Why had she not confided in her parents sooner? She should have clamoured for an abortion as soon as she'd realised she was pregnant, not allowed herself to be persuaded to do otherwise. That she'd done nothing when she'd had the chance was crass stupidity.

She'd loved and trusted Darrell. She'd relied on him to help her find the best way to cope. She'd agreed to his plans; followed his wishes instead of thinking for herself. There could be no bigger fool anywhere.

She was fond of Charlie. She didn't have to put on a front for him. She didn't have to hide anything from him, or strive for effect. It was a comfort to be with him. He couldn't protect her from the avalanche of parental wrath she could see coming, but he'd help shut it out of her mind for an hour or so. He understood what trouble was – he'd been through enough himself.

'Did you say you were in trouble too?' she asked.

'Yes, but I ought to be used to it by now. My trouble pales into insignificance compared with yours.' He turned to smile at her. 'That cheers me up in a way, but tomorrow I've got to go to court again.'

Isobel went back to the kitchen, flopped down at the table and let her head sink on her hands.

'Sophie having a baby? I can't get over it. It's like history repeating itself.' She felt tears well into her eyes. 'I know what she must be going through. She didn't even give me a chance to sympathise.'

'She didn't seem to want sympathy.'

'No, but she must feel awful. Didn't she say, "I know I've made a mess of things but there's nothing you or I can do about it"?' Isobel groaned. 'She's only seventeen, Seb.'

'I know. It's a dreadful mess.'

'Have you met this boyfriend?'

He shook his head. 'She doesn't expect us to like him, otherwise she'd have brought him home, but now . . . We'd better invite him here for a meal and see what he's like.'

'But she says he can't marry her. He's married to somebody else.'

'He's a lot older. He should have had more sense. He sounds the worst sort of bounder.'

'Tying herself to a man like that!' Isobel felt indignant.

'If they aren't going to be married, she won't be tied and neither will he. What sort of future is that for her and the baby? I don't like the sound of it.'

'Personally, I'd rather see her have an abortion and get back on track.'

'Izzy, she's left it too late for an abortion. She says the

baby's due in November. Anyway, it has to be her choice.'

'If they love each other . . .'

'I've no doubt he swept Sophie off her feet,' Seb said dryly. 'Probably she's besotted with him, but will he stand by her and the baby?'

'I feel as though I'm to blame too,' Isobel wept. 'What she must have gone through all these months.'

'She must have known when she was sitting her A levels.' Sebastian shook his head. 'Hardly conducive to doing her best work.'

'When I think of what happened to me. Didn't I get into the same trouble? I was young but she's years younger.'

Seb got up to put an arm round his wife's shoulders. 'She's decided to have the baby and go to live with him. I think all we can do is to let her know we'll support her in any way we can.'

'Mum will be upset. She'll say Sophie's ruining her life chances. This was absolutely not the thing to do in her day.'

'Like us, she'll have to accept it. We'll tell her this is the modern way.'

Charlie counted his day in court to face yet another charge of breaking the speed limit in a built-up area as one of his worst.

He'd now been found guilty of speeding not only when he was driving Mum's car and the van, but also when he was on his motor bike. This time, he was banned from driving for six months and he had to surrender his licence.

'Good job I came with you,' his mother told him. 'Otherwise you'd have had to take the bus home.'

That didn't amuse him. By the time they got back, Jamie

was due home from school and Dad was in the kitchen brewing up.

He pushed a cup of tea in front of Charlie and said, 'A bit late to have a long face. It's what you expected, after all.'

'That doesn't make it any easier to bear.'

'It's going to give you another problem,' Ben predicted, sounding like the wise old man. 'You won't be able to use your motor bike to get to work and back.'

Charlie grunted, 'That's what's bothering me.'

'You can either get your old push bike out or go on the bus,' Hilary told him. 'If you break the law you deserve to be punished.'

Charlie was appalled at the thought. 'I have to be there by half seven in the morning and be ready to serve breakfast by eight.'

'You could sell your motor bike and buy a moped,' Ben said.

'A moped?'

'Yes. You don't need a licence for a bike with an engine of less than fifty ccs.'

'Sissy stuff.' Charlie was indignant. He'd talked of getting a big Harley-Davidson before he'd had his car licence. 'I'm sick of work anyway. It's all I do, day in and day out.'

'It's what everybody does, my love,' Hilary told him. 'You'll get used to it. You might even enjoy it eventually.'

'Never.' Charlie was vehement. 'There has to be some other way round this.'

'Yes.' Dad's eyes seemed to look into his soul. 'You could come and work for me in the garden centre. The offer's still open if you want it.'

Charlie didn't. It would keep him right under Dad's thumb

the whole time; there'd be no escaping him. But after a long pause he made himself say, 'Thanks, Dad. I'll think about it.' Things looked so damned dire, he might have to.

The following morning Charlie went to work on the bus. Later he told Gary, 'It was absolute hell. I was late, breakfast was late, and everybody blamed me. They were mad at me all day.'

'I'm fed up too. Sick to death of working those split shifts.'

Charlie had heard the plans his biker friends were making for their holidays. 'Why don't we take a backpacking trip? Get away from here for a few months?'

'I'd love that.' Gary grinned at him. 'Why don't we?'

Andy had started his driving lessons at the same time as Charlie, but he lacked his confidence and had needed many more lessons. On the day he sat his driving test, he was very nervous. His mother went with him, since he was using her car.

'Better if you drive down to the test centre,' she said. 'Then when you start your test you'll feel loosened up and ready for it.'

Andy didn't think he'd ever feel ready, and having to wait five minutes for the examiner in a bleak little room put him more on edge. That and the knowledge that Charlie was brilliant at driving, while he was not.

'When you get your licence', his mother had been full of encouragement, 'you can borrow the car at weekends. Perhaps take Aunt Prue out for little drives.'

Andy started his test doing all the right things, though he was quaking inside, but when the examiner told him to make a right turn he turned left by mistake. He was perennially confused between left and right and knew what he'd done before the examiner told him. It made him more nerve-racked than ever. He and Charlie were both affected by dyslexia but in quite different ways.

Andy was determined not to make the same mistake again. The next time he was told to make a turn, he thought about it so long before putting on the indicator that it seemed he meant to ignore the instruction. From that moment he went to bits and made other mistakes, and he knew he'd failed before he was told.

'I'm sorry,' Hilary told him. 'It means you'll have to go through it again. More lessons, too.'

After that, she took him out many times to practise in her car and he solved one problem himself. He inked a letter L on the left hand side of the steering wheel and an R on the right using a felt pen, and hoped they wouldn't be noticeable to anyone but himself.

Andy had moved into the spare bedroom in Prue's flat some time ago and it made him feel more grown up to be away from home, though it gave him a longer journey to school. Sometimes he cycled all the way, but on wet mornings he cycled up to the garden centre, left his bike there and caught the usual bus. Coming back in the afternoons, he'd call in to see his mother, eat her cake and give her an update on Prue's state of health before cycling back through the village to the flat.

He felt at ease with Prue and found it easy to settle in with her. The twin aunts had looked after him and Charlie when they were children, escorting them to nursery school and back. Later on, they used to tutor them when Isobel and Seb went away.

Nowadays, Prue was much given to reminiscing. Mostly she talked about Primmy, but she also told him about their sister Ethel, Ben's mother and Andy's grandmother. He was totally captivated when he heard she was unable to read and write as an adult. Dyslexia was in his genes: it wasn't his fault.

'How are you getting on at school?' Prue asked Andy one evening, when he was getting out his homework.

'Not bad, I suppose, considering . . . I know my handwriting's difficult to read. All the teachers complain about it, but it takes me a long time to get anything down on paper. Aunt Izzy gave me lessons on how to form my letters, but however hard I try my work always looks messy with crossings-out, blots and smudges.'

'Didn't Isobel tell you not to worry about your writing and spelling, but concentrate instead on taking in what the lesson was about and absorbing the meaning of what you read?'

'Yes, but all writing is difficult for me.' He groaned. 'I've seen Sophie do her homework. She can dash off an essay with incredible speed. Her pen moves across the paper like lightning and it's all neat and correct when she's finished. I have to write an essay tonight. I started it in school, just a draft to get my ideas down. I now need to pad it out and go through it with a dictionary to correct my spelling. Then when it's right, I'll copy it out in my best handwriting.'

'That sounds like hard work,' Prue said. 'Could I check your spelling and punctuation for you? Is that allowed?'

'Would you? That would be great. Sometimes Mum did that for me. The teachers don't know I work that way. I think most of the boys dash their essays off like Sophie. They probably assume I do too.'

When he passed the draft to Aunt Prue, and had found her

spectacles for her, she said, 'You're right about the bad handwriting, and you've got capital letters sprinkled everywhere and no punctuation whatsoever.'

'I put the full stops and commas in last. I have to concentrate on one thing at a time.'

'But your ideas are good, Andy. It's an interesting essay.'

'Really?'

'Yes. Doesn't your English master tell you?'

'He gives me high marks, but says I'm the worst at spelling in the form.'

'Your Uncle Sebastian thinks you might improve as you get older.'

He said dryly, 'I wish I could improve now.'

Prue was screwing up her face in thought. 'You should learn to type and use a typewriter. That would solve your handwriting problem. Would you like to?'

'It would be marvellous if I didn't have to write things out twice.'

'Perhaps in your summer holidays. Give you something to do. That assessment you had when you were ten, did that help?'

'Yes. I was glad to be officially diagnosed as dyslexic because then everybody knew there was a real reason Charlie and I couldn't read, and the masters could understand too.'

The day before Andy was to resit his driving test, he was putting Hilary's car back into the garage after a practice session when she said, 'I'm thinking of getting a new one. If you pass your test tomorrow, you'll be able to take this one over.'

He felt a burst of joy. 'Wow, that would be marvellous.'

'Dad thinks you deserve it, for trying so hard.'

'But what about Charlie?'

'You'll have to share it with him, but he's got himself banned, hasn't he? Anyway, all he wants to do is to get away on a backpacking trip, goodness knows why.'

The following day, Andy was determined to stay calm and pass his test and was delighted when the examiner told him he had.

He felt six inches taller. Mum would let him have her car and it would feel marvellous to be able to take it out by himself. He'd even enjoy taking Aunt Prue out on Sunday afternoons.

CHAPTER FIFTEEN

BEN HAD always liked Stella, and knew he was in the habit of going in and out of the shop more often than was really necessary. That Charlie had pinched the van to drive her lads to Sheffield had seemed to draw them closer.

Stella was a good-looking woman and a good worker. She'd been managing the garden centre shop for five years now and he'd built up a rapport with her. She took more interest in it than Hilary did and he was able to bounce ideas off her. She was an outgoing chatty person and they had long discussions when the shop was quiet.

She'd even talked about her marriage breakdown. Ben had been sympathetic.

'What happened?' he'd asked.

'My husband couldn't keep his hands off beautiful women,' she'd said flatly. 'I couldn't stand any more of his playing round.'

'Beautiful women?' Ben said. 'I can't see why he bothered, when he had a good-looking wife like you.'

She'd laughed at that; she had an infectious giggle. Stella had always dressed well; recently, Hilary had remarked that she was wearing very smart outfits to work in the garden shop. Her dainty feet were always shod in high-heeled shoes.

More and more Ben found his eyes following her. Stella was even-tempered, good-humoured and always ready for a gossip or a laugh. Ben found himself thinking about her a lot, comparing her slim svelte figure with Hilary's.

Poor Hilary liked both cooking and eating, and inevitably was putting on more weight than she should. Her shape had grown decidedly middle-aged. She had been a bit low recently, always more deeply involved in her writing than in real life. When he took her out these days she rarely bothered to put her contact lenses in. She said it was too much trouble.

He couldn't help comparing Hilary's blue eyes behind her thick glasses with Stella's wide-awake look. Ben knew Stella was only six years younger, but she seemed to belong to a different age group. She dressed to look attractive and took great pains with her appearance. Stella spent more time and energy looking after herself than Hilary did.

It was months before he accepted that it was her wide-set pale eyes that attracted him. They gazed into his and seemed to respond to every word when he spoke. Even then he resisted the idea, denied to himself that he felt an urge to touch her. He couldn't, wouldn't, ever do anything like that. It would be betrayal. Hilary was the mother of his sons and it was thanks to her money that the garden centre had been able to expand so quickly and could now support the family.

It was a long time before he'd admit even to himself that he found Stella sexy, and that she was on his mind even when he wasn't with her. It made it more difficult that she was friendly with Hilly. He'd gone into the shop today to find them laughing together.

'I'm glad Gary's made a friend of Charlie,' he heard Stella say.

'Even though they're talking of throwing up their jobs and going to France for the summer?' Hilary asked. 'I hoped Charlie would settle down.'

'Gary's never looked as though he'd settle. I've always felt uneasy about him. He didn't find things easy at school.'

'Nobody could have found school harder than Charlie.'

'Our Paul did so well. I was proud of him. He always got good marks. Gary tried hard, but he can't compete. It knocked him back, sapped his confidence. Paul wants to be a journalist. It worries me that he'll get a good job and earn a good salary, while poor Gary . . . I can't see him holding down a job.'

'We're all ambitious for our children,' Hilary said. 'But in the end it's up to them. Charlie's got no sense.'

'As long as they're happy,' Stella said. 'We have to look at it that way.'

Sophie got out of her father's car and walked slowly into school, feeling bemused. It was her last day here and it had crept up on her without her noticing. Teachers and pupils were relaxed; they'd be breaking up for the long summer holiday this morning.

In the cloakroom she ran a comb through her hair. In the mirror she could see it had lost its bounce and hung lankly about her shoulders. She looked a ghost of her normal self, her face pale and drawn, purple shadows under her eyes.

The other girls were chattering excitedly. She heard Majorca mentioned and Tuscany, and then Polly Adams was describing her new bikini. It made Sophie cringe. Her uniform dress was already tight across her belly. The only way she could disguise her bump was by wearing her blazer over it. On hot days like today, that was a trial.

It was just the same in the form room. Some girls were saying they were glad their schooldays were over and others that they were sorry. Sophie felt she'd outgrown all this, but she felt safe here and the future loomed ominously.

Emily said to her, 'Let's go to Quaintways for a bite of lunch when we get out of here. You don't have to go straight home, do you? Shall we ask some of the others, like Becky and Avril? Get up a party?'

Sophie agreed half-heartedly, feeling she'd heard all she could stand about their further education, proposed careers and ambitions for the future. Things were going to be very different for her.

She'd never cared much for Becky, who said, 'Sorry, I won't be able to. My mother's meeting me, and we're going shopping for my holiday clothes.' She had a rather gloating smile as she asked, 'Is it true what they're saying, Sophie? That the police came into school yesterday and arrested Darrell Marchbanks?'

'What?' Sophie was instantly stricken.

'They're saying he stole that food.'

A burst of panic was making her feel weak at the knees. 'I don't know.' She felt breathless. 'Who's saying that? I've heard nothing.'

Darrell had had a gig in Manchester last night; she hadn't seen him since lunchtime yesterday. She looked at her watch. They had a standing arrangement to meet behind the gym every morning during break.

Her friends were agog with amazement at the latest twist

to the theft. There was much chortling and chatting about Darrell. Sophie trailed after them when they took the last of their text books to the library to sell to next year's upper sixth. Sophie unloaded hers but she felt shivery and desperately worried.

The girls' spirits were high on this last morning; they were laughing and joking together. It made Sophie feel very much in the dumps. Her form knew she'd been out with Darrell a few times, but none of them knew how deeply she was involved with him.

Nothing was as usual today, not even the morning break. They were packing up their belongings and exchanging addresses when their form mistress called for their attention. They were all to be in the hall for assembly in ten minutes.

Sophie shot out of the classroom and ran to the spot behind the gym where she usually met Darrell. He wasn't there, but perhaps he didn't know the timetable would be different today. She saw a groundsman tidying up the flower borders and went to have a word with him.

He confirmed what Becky had told her. Darrell had been driven off to the police station just before the end of afternoon school yesterday and hadn't come to work this morning.

'Just him?' she asked. 'Why?'

'To help with their inquiries, we were told.'

Sophie tried to take comfort from that, but why wasn't he here now? She was just in time to file into the school hall with her form.

She was frightened; because the whole school had been curious about the theft, she'd talked to Darrell about it more than once. He'd been a mine of information, but then he would be, wouldn't he? They'd all seen him checking in goods from vans pulled in at the kitchen entrance. One thing she had noticed was that his sympathy was not with the school for its loss but rather with the thieves.

Today assembly was very much extended. As well as the usual prayers, the choir sang and there were several soloists. Prizes were then presented to the girls, amongst them one for the essay on Canada. Sophie had never completed her entry, and the prize was won by Avril Thomas. If things had been different Sophie was sure she could have beaten her.

Before they broke up there was also a presentation to their retiring geography mistress, a few words from a visiting governor and a farewell speech from the headmistress.

Sophie took in very little. Her hymn book, when she opened it to sing, shook in her hand. Could Darrell really be a thief? She found it hard to believe, but he'd bought that van for the band, though beforehand he'd said he was skint, and he was a big spender considering his job. Her mind was spinning with horror. If he was innocent all well and good, but if he wasn't, it threw an entirely different light on what she was proposing to do.

Then there was an awful round of last goodbyes and promises to keep in touch. The last thing Sophie wanted was to go to Quaintways with Emily and the others for lunch. She felt sick but also a little light-headed. She knew she ought to eat something, so she walked with them almost as far as the café.

But no, she couldn't face it. Hurriedly she made her excuses and escaped. It was more important that she see Darrell and find out whether these stories were true or not. She'd go round to his flat before she caught the bus home.

Now, at midday, the sun was blazing down from a cloudless sky and it was hot. She took her engagement ring out of its little box and slid it on her finger. That made her feel better. Then she took off her blazer, folded it across her arm and held it in front of her stomach. Her school bag was heavy on her shoulder. It was quite a walk to his flat and she felt weary before she got there. She hadn't been sleeping well.

Parking was notoriously tight here, and as she turned into his street she could see his car parked some distance from his house. It told her she'd find Darrell there and she breathed a sigh of relief.

She pushed at the front door to the building. It was usually left unlocked and now it gave to her touch. As she climbed the stairs, she could hear angry voices and knew he wasn't alone. She tapped on his living-room door but the voices continued. They hadn't heard her. She tried to go in but couldn't; both his doors were fitted with Yale locks to provide security.

'Darrell?' she called and hammered on his door as hard as she could. The voices stopped abruptly. Seconds later, the door was snatched open and Darrell, hot, angry and dishevelled, stared down at her.

'Sophie?' He was surprised to see her. She was equally surprised to see him looking so unkempt. Darrell was fussy about his appearance.

'Who is it?' a voice asked behind him. She knew it belonged to Bernie, who played the drums in his band.

'I was worried,' she said, stepping forward. 'I heard you'd been taken to the police station yesterday.' The rest of the band were there, staring at her, equally angry and dishevelled.

'Yes, well . . .' Darrell said. Sophie knew she'd come at a bad moment. Through a haze of cigarette smoke, she could see the room was a chaotic mess of dirty dishes and strewn belongings.

'Get rid of your girlfriend,' Kev the keyboard player burst out. 'We've got important things to decide.'

Sophie lost her patience. 'What's happened? I want to know.'

'He's been charged with theft and fraudulently altering receipts for goods he's checked in at your school,' Bernie said harshly. 'He's in a bloody mess, and that goes for the band too.'

Sophie felt the room eddy round her. Her knees were giving way. She heard Bernie say from a distance, 'For God's sake, she's going to faint.'

Everything was going black. She knew Bernie was right.

Pain jabbed through her as she came round. She thought she must have twisted her back as she fell. She closed her eyes and lay still for a moment until it went, aware of the heated voices carrying on above her.

'A rich kid from that fancy school where you work.'

'Where I used to work. They'll sack me now.'

There was general sniggering. 'I suppose you thought her dad would set you both up for life?'

'Is that why you put a bun in the oven?' There was more sniggering.

'A good fall-back position in case we have to wait a bit longer for the band to go over big?'

'Why not? It was good fun while it lasted.'

That was Darrell's voice, his giggle! It knocked Sophie's breath away and made her sink back for another moment. It was hard to believe that Darrell felt like that.

'Poor bugger.' It was Kev's voice. 'She's just a kid; doesn't know what's good for her. Carting her round Germany was never on, was it? Is she all right?'

Sophie could feel tears coursing down her face as she tried to get up. She was horrified at what she'd heard. It was Kev who helped her to her feet and steered her backwards into a chair.

'Are you all right?' Darrell asked. Her left elbow hurt. When she twisted it round, she saw it was bleeding. Bernie dampened a corner of a grubby tea towel at the sink and wiped the blood away. More blood flooded out and dripped down her school uniform as well as on to the upholstery of the chair. Bernie rubbed at it then folded the tea towel over the mark.

'D'you want a drink, Sophie?' Darrell held a mug of tepid water to her lips. She gulped at it, feeling utterly betrayed. They were talking about her as though she wasn't here.

'What are we going to do with her?'

'You'd better run her home, Darrell. Go on, before she does that again. Gave me quite a turn.'

'Come on then.' Darrell and Kev yanked her to her feet. They helped her downstairs and out into the bright sunlight. Darrell was trying to get her into his car.

Sophie straightened up against it. 'My blazer and satchel,' she gasped. Kev was dispatched back to get them.

Once he'd thrown them on the back seat they set off. She assessed Darrell while he kept his eyes on the road. He was not in a good mood and not at all the sort of person she'd thought he was.

They came to a stop in heavy traffic. 'Did you do it?' she asked. 'Did you break into the school stores to steal food?'

'I'm going to plead not guilty.'

Sophie had learned a little about the legal process. 'But did you do it?'

He grimaced in her direction and said plaintively, 'Everything's blowing up in my face. All at once. My life's disintegrating round me.'

'You did it then.' He didn't deny it. Sophie felt sick at the thought. 'The band's breaking up?'

'You heard them: you know it is. The band, the job, everything.' He hesitated. 'All I've got left is you.'

Sophie pulled herself up in the sagging seat. 'You can count me out,' she said coldly. She'd heard enough today to put her off him for life. She didn't want Kev's sympathy. *Poor bugger . . . just a kid . . . doesn't know what's good for her.*

'Come on. I'll meet you at the Dog and Gun tomorrow and we'll go out for a drink.'

'No thanks.'

'Tonight then? D'you want to make it tonight?'

'No.' How stupid she'd been! 'I never want to see you again.'

'I need you, Sophie.'

'I've had all I can take of you.' She was dragging her engagement ring over her knuckle. 'You can have this back.' She put it on the console between them.

'No. I've given it you.' He put it in her lap where it sparkled up at her against the navy blue serge. 'I want you to keep it.'

'I wouldn't wear it now if you paid me,' she said, and flung the ring to the back of his car.

'Don't be like that.' He clicked his tongue with impatience as his car was able to roll forward only a few yards. 'This traffic's dreadful. I'll never get you home at this rate.'

'You don't have to. Take the next turn right. You can drop me off outside Dad's school. It's only half a mile from here.' They didn't break up there for another two days.

He gave her an anxious sideways glance. 'Are you sure?'

'Quite sure.' She wanted to be with somebody she could trust. Somebody reliable. She wanted her dad.

Sophie could hear the children playing in the school yard before she was out of the car. Their piping voices, little screams and shouts.

'Goodbye,' Darrell said. He moved as though to touch her but she grabbed her belongings from the back seat and got out as fast as she could. She was too choked even to say goodbye. She ran up the path and in through the swing doors. Inside, the noise volume was less, though there was a clatter of plates from the dining room. The corridors were empty.

Dad's office was to the right somewhere here. She went through his secretary's office. Her desk was piled with papers but she wasn't here. Sophie crossed to Dad's door. Habit made her knock before throwing it open.

He was writing at his desk and looked up in surprise. He just managed to get to his feet before she launched herself at him, shedding her blazer and satchel as she went. His arms came round her, holding her in a tight hug.

'Sophie love? What is it?'

She put her head down on his shoulder and wept. Nothing could hold back the torrent of tears. She felt as though she'd fallen into an abyss and was touching bottom.

By the time she had let all her troubles come out and was able to quieten her sobs the bell was ringing to signal the start of afternoon school. Dad patted her back and put her to sit in the visitor's chair in front of his desk, saying, 'Don't worry, we'll sort this.'

Dad was convinced it was possible to sort everything and that it was his job to do so. Sophie was afraid it would be beyond his power this time, but she was grateful that he was willing to try. Even so, she was overwhelmed by misery.

'What am I going to do now?' she whispered.

'I need to think about that and so do you. Let's give ourselves time. Have you had lunch?'

She shook her head.

'You have to, love. You can't skip meals now. Look, let me show you where you can bathe your eyes and comb your hair. Make yourself feel better, while I see if I can get you some food, then I'll take you home.'

When she went back to his office, he said, 'I've tried to ring Mum to say we'll be home early, but she's gone out.'

Sophie felt better when she'd eaten the sandwich he brought her. 'Is it all right for you to go home in the middle of afternoon school?' she asked.

'Yes, for once. It's the end of term and I've not made a habit of it.'

The house was still empty when they got there. 'Go and have a rest on your bed,' he advised. 'We'll have a talk when Mum gets back.'

Isobel had worried about Sophie ever since she'd told them she was pregnant. She'd made an appointment for her to see Dr Tanner, who'd assured Sophie all was well. He'd referred her to the antenatal clinic to make arrangements for delivery in hospital.

Teenagers were traditionally difficult and at the moment

Sophie was worse than most. She'd been moody and rebellious all summer and told them lies. They'd known she was hiding her problems from them and probably from herself as well. Isobel did her best to offer sympathy and help and to remain calm, and was careful to take no offence when Sophie was rude.

That afternoon she had taken Daisy shopping at the supermarket, and when she returned home she was surprised to find Sebastian's car parked outside. She gave Daisy the cereal packets to carry in and lifted the numerous plastic bags of groceries herself. Seb met her at the door and took some from her.

'Has something happened?' she asked. 'You're home early.'

'Yes. I wanted to bring Sophie. She's reached crisis point, broken off with the boyfriend, finally decided he's no good for her. I can't say I'm sorry.'

Isobel stood still for a moment. 'Oh, Lord! Her world's collapsed, then. She must feel terrible.'

'I know, but it was always built on hope and what might be. Pie in the sky. There are loads of singers and bands doing the rounds but very few make it big.'

Isobel felt sick. 'She was sure Darrell would. She believed in him. She loved him.'

'If only she'd told us sooner, she'd have had a choice. He persuaded her to keep the baby.'

'Perhaps she wanted to keep it too.'

'I don't think so.' Seb screwed up his face in agony. 'From her outpourings today, I think she'd have chosen to have an abortion. It was Darrell who wanted it otherwise. She'd certainly opt for it now if it was possible.'

Isobel said, 'Still, I'm glad she won't be trailing round Europe after him whilst she's seven months pregnant. That would have given me nightmares. And it seems she wants our help at last?'

'Yes, but what do we advise? I can't see Sophie devoting her life to bringing up a baby. I'd want her to go to university and have a career.'

Isobel said with feeling, 'So would I.'

'These days hardly any girls have their babies adopted, but she says she will and it might be best for her.'

'That would solve her problem.'

She heard Seb's agonised sigh. 'I was wondering . . . if she wanted to keep it whether we should look after it.'

Isobel was taken aback. 'You mean me? Take on another child to bring up? You know I've never been that fond of children. I've never yearned for babies, or billed and cooed over them.'

He said gently, 'You love Daisy and she'll only be four years older. A new baby would fit into our family quite well.'

Isobel was stunned. 'Of course I love Daisy, but she'll be going to school in September and a new baby will tie me down for another four years.'

All the same, she ached with sympathy for Sophie. Sophie was having to shoulder all the responsibilities of an adult when she was barely out of childhood. It would ruin her life chances if they weren't careful. Like Seb, she should do all she could to help her.

'Anyway,' he said, 'we don't have to make any promises about that yet. She'll have to take a year out to have the baby, but I think she should apply for a university place now for next year. It will lay down a definite plan for her. Not Oxford.

If she went to Liverpool, she could live at home and have time to spend with the baby.'

Isobel sighed. 'I don't think she'll want to leave home after this. She craves security now and this is the only place she'll find it.'

'I told her we'd talk about her future when you got home. It would be as well for us to give it some thought before we do.'

Sophie lay on her bed dozing for most of that afternoon, feeling dispirited and listless. When Dad called her down first for tea and then for supper she went, but she had to force herself to eat. She felt awful. Mum and Dad were trying to be all sweetness and light but it grated. She'd made up her mind to have the baby adopted but Dad was trying to persuade her to keep it. She wasn't having any of that. She did her best to resist discussing her future.

She spent most of the next three days lying on her bed. Dad's school broke up and he made her go for walks with him. Mum tried to inveigle her on a trip to PYO strawberries and gooseberries, but she didn't want to do anything.

Dad talked about taking them all to Anglesey for a few days' sailing, but when he tried to book a hotel they were all full. He'd left it too late.

Charlie came round to see her one evening. Mum sent him up to her bedroom where she was lying on her bed reading.

'Aunt Izzy says you aren't very well.' He sat on her feet. She had to sit up to pull them out of his way.

'I'm all right, just fed up to the back teeth.'

'You wanted me to ask at the care home if you could have a holiday job. Well I did, and they said yes.'

Sophie groaned. All her plans had changed. 'I wanted money to go away with Darrell. Now that's off I won't bother.'

'Won't bother?' Charlie was indignant. 'A lad I know from tech came round asking for holiday work today. If I hadn't said my cousin wanted it, they'd have given the job to him.'

Sophie felt guilty. She gave Charlie an edited version of her rift with Darrell and tried not to sound too sorry for herself.

'You might as well take the job as lie here feeling fed up. You could buy yourself some new clothes. That would make you feel better, wouldn't it?'

Sophie wanted to cry. How could she get through to Charlie that new clothes wouldn't help in her present state?

'You are in the dumps.' His eyes were full of sympathy. 'Come on, I'll take you out for a drink.'

'I'm not supposed to drink now. Anyway, I don't like alcohol and I don't like pubs.'

'Oh dear, you are in a bad way. OK, it's youth club night at the church hall. Do you still go there?'

'Haven't been for ages.'

'Nor me, but they show films on a Friday night. It's that or the Dog and Gun. Come on, you need to go out.'

'I'll have to change.'

'Not for me you won't. Just get your shoes on and come along.'

They went to the youth club. The film had started before they arrived and all the seats were taken. Charlie found two chairs in the vestry and carried them just inside the hall door. Sophie tried to make sense of what she was watching but it wasn't easy. After a few minutes Charlie began to whisper.

'I'm pretty fed up, too. Not being able to drive is maddening. And it's doing my head in working day in and day out for a pittance. Gary and I are thinking of going backpacking for the rest of the summer.'

'Where to?'

'We'd love to go to Thailand, but cash is short so we thought we'd take the ferry over to France and hitch down to Spain.'

'Sounds good. Quite an adventure.' Sophie felt envious, but it wasn't possible for her. 'Have you told Aunt Hilly?'

'Yes. She isn't pleased. Dad tried to talk me out of it too, but we're going. We've had our noses to the grindstone for too long – we need a holiday. I've given in my notice at work. If you start on Monday, I'll have a week to show you the ropes.'

'But I can't take over from you. I don't know anything about cooking.'

'You won't need to. There'll be a cook on with you most of the time, so it'll be just like helping out at home. You'll find it's all right to start with, but you'll get bored. I did after a few weeks, but as holiday relief that's all they'll want you for.'

When the film came to an end, Charlie said, 'They're a load of kids here. We've outgrown them, haven't we? I'm hungry.'

'So am I.'

'I'd suggest a bar meal at the Dog and Gun but I'm saving every penny I can for my trip. Why don't you come home with me? I'll cook us something. Mum and Dad were going out and I promised to be home early because Jamie's by himself.'

'Does that scare him?'

'No. It bothers Mum more than Jamie.'

Sophie had missed supper at home and was glad to go with him. Jamie came rushing down as soon as he heard them in the kitchen.

Charlie opened the fridge and said, 'There was a whole pound of sausages here before. I thought we'd have them.'

Jamie piped up, 'Mum cooked them for me.'

'You haven't eaten them all?'

'Josh and Des were here.'

Charlie cooked them double egg and chips with frozen peas. Jamie ate another supper.

CHAPTER SIXTEEN

SINCE AUNT Prue had first suggested to Andy that he should take typing lessons, he'd been keen. A number of holiday courses were being run at a local school that summer, one of which was typing. Aunt Prue had offered to pay for the course and his mother had reserved a place for him.

Some years ago, the Dryden Street secondary modern school had been enlarged and improved into the biggest and most up-to-date comprehensive school in the district. It was officially renamed Barwood Comprehensive, but was still referred to locally as Dryden Street School. Gary and his older brother Paul had received their secondary schooling there. It taught a full range of commercial subjects.

To Andy, it seemed strange to be going into a school again at the beginning of the summer holidays. It was a vast place, and when he went in there weren't many people about. In the corridor, he stopped a girl who was about to overtake him to ask the way.

'I'm going there too.' She had dark straight hair cut short round her small head. 'It's this way.'

Now Andy could hear a babble of girlish chatter from the

typing room. It died away as they went in. There were typewriters set out at intervals on long tables. Suddenly he realised he was the only male student and the gaggle of girls had stopped talking to assess him. He felt a hot flush run up his cheeks. An officious-looking woman had entered behind them and now took over.

She raised her voice. 'All of you, please sit down in front of a typewriter.'

Andy noticed the typewriter keys were all covered so they'd have to read the letters from a diagram of the keyboard laid out beside each machine.

'I'm Mrs Bell, your tutor on this course. I want you to stand up one by one and introduce yourselves. Tell us why you want to learn to type. We'll start here on the front row.'

The girl she indicated stood up. She seemed confident and had a strong clear voice. Andy felt panic-stricken as he counted up. There were fourteen girls plus him in the class. How could he admit, in front of them all, that he was near illiterate? To say he was dyslexic sounded as though he was making excuses and he didn't want to be asked to explain what it was. It was his turn before he'd decided how best to handle it.

He scrambled to his feet and blurted out his name. Then, finding no way round it, he said, 'I'm dyslexic and my writing is rubbish.'

The silence was profound. The girls were so quiet, he could hear the traffic on the road outside. Andy felt a telltale flush run up his cheeks and corrected himself.

'I mean my writing is hard to read. If I can learn to type, it'll make things easier, for both me and my teachers.' He sat down again with a little bump.

Now the girls were all turning to smile at him. Plain girls, pretty girls, tall and small girls, they all seemed more friendly. He tried to relax and listen to what the rest of the class had to say about themselves.

It was the turn of the girl he'd met in the corridor. 'My name is Amy Wright. I left school last week, but I didn't go to one where I could have learned shorthand typing. My dad's found me a job in the ironmonger's shop where he works and he wants me to start after the holidays. But I'd like to work in an office and might be able to, if I learn to type.'

Andy heard the catch in her voice and felt sorry for her. He rather liked her shy elfin looks. He was embarrassed to find himself amongst so many girls, but to get to know them would have its compensations. Charlie might be envious . . . But no, he wouldn't; it was the other way round. He wished he could go to France with Charlie. His twin could talk of little else.

Charlie had said, 'We don't have to hang around worrying about A level results. We're going to see a bit of the world and have a holiday.'

'Dad said you'll have to work.' Andy had let all his envy show. 'That you'll have to come home if you run out of money.'

'We won't. We'll be able to work in bars and cafés – it'll be fun. We're going to have a good time for a change. Roll on next Wednesday.'

That was the day Charlie and Gary meant to set out, but it was also the day Mum was taking delivery of a new Triumph 2000. Andy was really looking forward to that, because it meant he'd have her old car and he could call it his own.

*

For Sophie, the summer was passing too quickly. Charlie had taken her to the care home and he'd been right: she quite enjoyed working in the kitchen and soon learned the ropes. He'd been right about its being better than lying on her bed at home, too.

But she wasn't used to being on her feet all day, or any sort of physical work. She felt tired and had no energy. Nothing would be normal again until she'd had the baby. She was dreading the birth but at the same time longing to get it over and done with. Longing too to get her figure back.

She was also dreading the results of her A level exams. She knew she hadn't done herself justice. The day on which they were due was creeping closer. It was now obvious that she was pregnant, so she had no intention of going back to school to get them.

Anyway, she didn't want to watch any more back-slapping and congratulating and talk of future careers. She'd left that life behind. She sent a stamped addressed envelope instead, which was what those who planned to be away on holiday had been told to do. It meant she'd probably have to wait longer than her friends to find out how she'd done.

Her family talked of little else. She felt restless and on edge, afraid she'd made a dreadful mess of her exams too.

It happened that her day off for the week coincided with the day the A level results came out. That morning, Mum roped her into helping her make chutney. Sophie was chopping up tomatoes when the phone rang. Her mother went to answer it, and she heard her say, 'Hello, Judith.'

Sophie's mouth opened in horror. She signalled to her mother that she didn't want to speak to Judith. Just couldn't right now.

'No, I'm afraid not. No, we haven't heard yet. How have you done?'

A longish pause while Sophie silently studied her mother's face for clues.

'Congratulations, Judith. I'm sure you're well pleased with that.'

Another pause, then, 'Give my regards to your mother, won't you?'

As soon as she put the phone down, Sophie demanded, 'What did she get?'

'An A and two Bs.'

'That's what she expected.'

'It's good, Sophie.'

Her mother went to the back door to relay the news to Seb, who was digging in the garden. He came in, leaving his shoes on the step.

'I wonder how you got on, Sophie,' he said. 'Why don't I ring your school to see if I can find out?'

By now, Sophie was desperate to know, but she felt nervous. 'What if they ask why?'

'Leave it to me,' he said. 'If they want to speak to you, just say Sophie here, I'm dying to know how I've done.' A few minutes later, he handed her the receiver. 'It's the school secretary,' he told her. 'Go ahead.'

Mum was pushing a biro into her hand and moving the jotter closer. Sophie had sat four subjects.

'Congratulations,' she was told. 'Two As and two Bs.'

She wrote down the details though tears were blurring her eyes. Before all this had blown up she'd expected to get four As. If Ross Salter could do it, she felt she could. She tried to swallow back her disappointment, but everything was going wrong for her. Dad was reading what she'd written over her shoulder.

'It's awful,' she choked.

'No, it isn't,' he insisted. 'It's good.'

'You've done very well,' Mum told her. 'They'll be delighted to have you at Liverpool.'

Dad said, 'Come and sit down for a moment. That's what you want, isn't it?'

Sophie fished out her hanky to blow her nose.

'How d'you see your future? What do you want to do?'

'It's what can I do, isn't it?' Sophie was struggling to hold back her tears.

'You wanted a legal career. If you still do, you can get back on track.'

'Dad, the baby,' she wailed. 'How can I?' She gave a sob and ran upstairs to the privacy of her room. She no longer knew what she wanted.

September came. The summer holidays were coming to an end and Sophie expected that her job would too. However, the kitchen supervisor asked her if she'd like to work on for another week or so as one of the staff had given notice and they'd need to find a replacement for her.

Sophie said yes. Time dragged at home. Also, the heavy aprons she had to wear hid her pregnancy better than anything else. Now Dad was back at work, he went in early and made a detour to drop her at the care home to spare her the slow bus journey.

She was saving money because she didn't have the energy to go out when she'd finished work. She felt she no longer had anything in common with her old friends and was sorry

Charlie had gone away. She felt abandoned and a little lonely.

The family were going on at her, and it was getting her down. Dad kept saying, 'I don't think you should work on any longer. It can't be good for your health.'

Mum would shake her head. 'Do stay home and rest. You won't need to buy much. We've lots of things left over from Daisy. Her pram and cot are up in the loft and I put away quite a lot of her baby clothes.'

One evening over the supper table, Sophie could stand no more and burst out, 'How many times do I have to tell you? I'm going to have it adopted. I don't want anything to remind me of Darrell Marchbanks.'

Her outburst stopped Dad in mid-sentence. Her mother's mouth fell open. 'Sophie . . .' she began.

'I'm doing my best to forget him and my troubles but how can I when you talk about nothing else? My mind's made up. The baby's going to be adopted.'

'Sophie.' Her father put his hand on her arm. 'Forgive us for jumping to conclusions, but we thought you'd changed your mind. When I suggested you apply for a university place for next year you seemed concerned that with the baby you wouldn't have time to study.'

'Did I? I just wanted to shut you up. Can't you see I don't know what I want?'

She put her knife and fork down quietly and left the table with as much dignity as she could. Life was pure hell.

She lay on her bed, but couldn't stop her mind going over and over what had happened. To think about Darrell made her weep. With hindsight, she could see he wasn't the person she'd believed him to be. She'd been taken in. He'd used her.

She knew her parents were trying to help her. The trouble

was, she felt completely mixed up. She couldn't think straight. She knew she wouldn't get back to normal until the baby was born.

On the last evening she worked, Sophie was walking home from the bus stop feeling weary when she came face to face with Judith Salter.

'Hello, Sophie. How are you?'

What could she say to that but 'Fine, fine, and you?'

Judith's eyes went immediately to Sophie's abdomen. She'd noticed other people doing that recently, and hated it. It made her feel gross.

Sophie had worked all day and felt a mess, while Judith, with freshly washed hair curling on her shoulders, looked much smarter than she had at school. She said she was going to meet the new friends she'd made on the law course at Liverpool.

That made Sophie cringe. She could have been on the same course if she hadn't got pregnant. She forced herself to put on a brave face. 'How are you enjoying university? Is it very different from school?'

'I love it. Yes, it's different. We aren't treated like children any more.' She smiled. 'Ross was asking about you at breakfast.'

Sophie felt herself curl up. Judith couldn't have said anything worse. So Ross Salter knew she was a fallen woman.

She said as calmly as she could, 'He's back at Oxford now, isn't he?'

'Yes, but he's come home for a long weekend. I'm half expecting him to catch me up.' She turned to look back the way she'd come. 'He said he'd run me into Liverpool, but he and Dad were held up, so I thought I'd better come for the bus while I still had time.'

Sophie wanted to escape before he came. Judith said, 'I hear Darrell's case is coming up in October.'

That seemed to drum home that she and Darrell were the talk of the village. 'Is it? I haven't heard.' Sophie tried to edge round her.

'We never hear anything of his band any more. Emily thinks it's broken up.'

'I gather they didn't go to Germany.' Sophie made an effort to get away. 'Lovely to see you and hear your news, but I must rush.'

The Salters' smart car was pulling into the kerb beside them. 'Oh, good, here's Ross now. I won't have to bother with the bus.'

Sophie froze. Ross looked suntanned and more handsome than she remembered.

'Hello, Sophie.' Oxford had added a veneer of sophistication to him. She was quaking.

Judith's eyes oozed sympathy. She asked, 'Why don't we get together while Ross is home? There's a good play on at the Liverpool Playhouse. We were talking of going. Would you like to make up a foursome, Sophie? How about tomorrow evening?'

'Hang on,' Ross said. 'I've fixed up to go out with Tim Davies tomorrow.'

Sophie squirmed. She couldn't get the words out quickly enough. 'Sorry, I'm booked too. I wouldn't be able to make that either.'

Judith groaned. 'It's short notice, isn't it? Are you going somewhere nice?'

Sophie hastened to add, 'Yes, there's a new restaurant in Chester.' She'd read about it in the paper. Then she had second thoughts. Who would be likely to take her out in her present state? 'Just a family treat, but I said I'd go.'

'Of course,' Ross said easily. 'The next night our parents are taking us out for a meal, and I go back to Oxford the following morning. Next time I come home then?'

'Yes, I'll look forward to that.'

With burning cheeks, Sophie pounded along the pavement at twice her previous pace. She hadn't mentioned her temporary kitchen job. The Salters would think she'd fallen even further if they knew she was washing up in a care home. Sophie knew some people pitied her and others thought her a disgrace and that she'd made a stupid mess of everything.

Her nana certainly did. Yesterday, Mum had sent her up to Flora's cottage with some embroidery silk she'd matched for her in town. Sophie found her sitting by the fire knitting a matinee coat. She held it up. 'For your baby,' she'd said.

Sophie had rounded on her harshly. 'You needn't bother. Things have changed since your day.' She knew she'd upset Nana but went on defensively, 'It's no longer a mortal sin to have a baby without being married. Lots of girls do.'

'I know, but does it make them happy? You don't seem happy, and what of the child? If you'd waited until you were older, more mature and married . . .'

'I'm having it adopted,' Sophie flared. 'It'll get a mature married couple as parents and be perfectly all right.'

'Ah, but these days I understand not many girls have their babies adopted,' Nana said softly. 'Even girls as young as you, Sophie. You must think about it carefully and be quite sure. The family will rally round and help you. If you give your baby away, I'm afraid you'll fret for it. I know I would.'

'My mind's made up,' Sophie said bitterly.

The coming baby was making her thoroughly depressed. If it hadn't been for that, she'd have been able to turn her back on Darrell and go to university as planned. She wished Darrell in hell for what he'd done to her.

With no job to go to, Sophie found the following days dragged. Mum kept sending her on little errands to get her out and about. Today she wanted her to get a loaf from the shop. Sophie always wore the same loose mac swinging round her. It was no longer a case of hiding her pregnancy but of minimising her bump. The shop was empty when she got there. Mrs Grant was reading a newspaper spread out on her counter.

'Hello, Sophie. How are you?'

'Fine, thanks. A large brown loaf, please.' She let her eye linger over the display of chocolate bars and picked one out.

Mrs Grant rang up the prices on her till. 'Have you seen today's local paper? Your friend's been to court. He's been given a prison sentence.'

Sophie gasped and felt the tears start to her eyes. 'I haven't heard . . . haven't seen anything.'

'Here.' Mrs Grant folded up the paper and pushed it on her. 'Read about it when you get home, love.' Sophie saw the concern on her face and fled.

Girls who went to the Queen's School did not become unmarried mothers in their teens. Especially not girls who flattered themselves they were clever. Hadn't Mum predicted as soon as she'd heard about him that Darrell was after sex? It had shocked Sophie to hear her say it quite so bluntly, but to know she'd been right made matters worse.

She left the loaf on the living-room table and went up to

her room. Kicking off her shoes, she lay down on her bed and opened the newspaper. It was some time before her tears cleared and she was able to read.

Yesterday at the Quarter Sessions, Darrell Marchbanks, aged 29, of Union Street, Chester, was found guilty of misappropriating goods and equipment from his place of work, the Queen's School. Prosecuting, Mr Jeremy Holdsworth said quantities of food intended for school meals had been delivered by suppliers and checked in by the accused, but when required for use the goods could not be found. The receipts were subsequently discovered to have been altered. Marchbanks was also found guilty of stealing a sum of £47 from the bursar's office. It was also alleged he obtained employment by using false references.

Marchbanks has two previous convictions for fraud and three for theft. He was sentenced to 6 months' imprisonment.

Sophie was shocked to find he had a criminal record; that he was dishonest had never crossed her mind. She knew she'd been well and truly taken in. It wasn't money she'd lost, but he'd changed her life. Darrell had got what he deserved but that wasn't going to help her now.

She tried to imagine him in prison. She doubted he'd be able to shampoo his hair daily and use his many bath gels and body oils. He'd hate being deprived of those. Sophie felt she had no need to think of revenge. The law had done that for her, and she wasn't going to glory in his come-uppance. It simply settled the score and would allow her to forget him. He was out of her life. Knowing what she did now, she doubted his promises would ever have been kept.

*

Isobel was concerned about Sophie. She was really down in the dumps and nothing she and Seb suggested seemed to lift her out of it. Sophie had isolated herself from her friends and become lethargic. Isobel had wanted her to stop working but now all she did was lie on her bed and stare at the ceiling.

Isobel wished she could do more to help her. Like Sophie, she was counting the days until the baby arrived. Only another two weeks before it was due, but time was crawling now.

On Sunday night, Isobel and Sebastian stayed up late. They satiated themselves with television and then sat up discussing Sophie's predicament yet again. She was hell bent on having the baby adopted. What would that do for her future peace of mind? And if she kept it, how would she be able to study for a career? Isobel was weary when she climbed into bed, and she fell into a heavy sleep immediately. She was woken up by an almost hysterical Sophie.

'Mum, wake up. I think it's happening.' Isobel pulled herself up the bed, still fuzzy with sleep.

Sebastian was out of bed in a moment. 'What exactly is happening, love?'

'Pains. I'm having pains. I think the baby's coming.'

He said, 'I'll ring the hospital and tell them.' He'd taped the hospital number to the phone for just this moment. Isobel started pulling on her clothes.

Seb returned to announce, 'They said Sophie should be brought in right away.'

'What time is it?' Isobel asked.

'Ten past two.'

It had been decided that should Sophie's pains start during the night, Isobel would take her to hospital and stay with her.

Sebastian would stay at home with Daisy. He'd need to go to work in the morning, and the arrangement was that if necessary he'd take Daisy up to Flora. The little girl had started full-time school at the beginning of the term and Flora had offered to take her and meet her coming out while they were busy with Sophie.

Isobel was full of trepidation. Seb had knotted Sophie's dressing gown cord round her and wrapped a blanket round her shoulders. He'd got her case as far as the front door by the time Isobel was ready.

On the journey she fought to stay calm while Sophie gasped and sobbed. It was a fine moonlit night and the roads were empty. Isobel drove as fast as she dared and was greatly relieved when she reached the Clatterbridge maternity block and was able to hand Sophie over to the midwives.

Isobel was shown to a waiting room, where she collapsed on a chair and closed her eyes. Although there were magazines on the table she felt unable to read in the middle of the night. All round her she could hear the sounds of the newborn, the snuffles, the little grunts and cries. A nurse brought her a cup of tea and the midwife returned.

'Your daughter is well on in the first stage of labour,' she told Isobel. 'I've given her painkillers; everything's going according to plan. She's in the labour ward, but it could be another couple of hours before she delivers. Come and sit with her. Bring your tea, Mrs Broadbent, and I'll take you through.'

Isobel followed her. The smell of antiseptic reminded her of the time when she'd been here having Daisy. Or was it when she was having Sophie? All hospitals smelled the same.

She sat holding Sophie's hand, trying to talk her through her pains.

Sophie wept. 'Oh, Mum, I'm sorry. What a mess I'm in. I meant to keep a stiff upper lip . . . Oh!'

Seeing her beautiful young daughter in this situation tore Isobel in two. 'Nothing to be sorry about, you make as much noise as you like. It won't be long now until it's all over.'

'I didn't mean sorry for screaming, I meant sorry for having this baby and all the trouble I've brought on you. You and Dad had such big plans for me. You must be disappointed.'

Memories of her own youth crowded in on Isobel. If, when Sophie had asked about the circumstances of her birth two years ago, she'd told her the truth, would it have prevented this? She thought it might. At least, Sophie would have been warned that such things could happen.

Isobel felt an urge to talk about it now; to bring it all out in the open. 'I made a bigger mess than you have,' she said softly.

Sophie's grip on her hand tightened. Her face was glazed with sweat as she stared numbly up at her. 'Another pain's coming.' She screwed up her face and cried out.

Isobel knew it wasn't the right moment. Sophie couldn't put her mind to her own origins now when her body was racked with pain.

When the birth came, Isobel was not prepared for the emotional impact. Her eyes were swimming with tears. It was a most moving experience to see her grandchild come into the world.

'A beautiful little girl,' the midwife announced. 'Seven pounds exactly.' She wrapped her in a towel and put her in Sophie's arms.

Isobel wondered whether she should have stopped her doing that. She knew that if the baby was going for adoption, it would be kinder if Sophie wasn't encouraged to bond with her first. But already Sophie was hugging the bundle to her and looking down on the child as if she'd produced a miracle.

'What are you going to call her?' The midwife had a pen poised over a wrist band.

'Melissa,' Sophie said proudly. 'What d'you think, Mum? Melissa?'

Isobel nodded her agreement. It was the first time she'd heard any name mentioned, but Melissa was pretty. 'She's beautiful.'

The baby did not have the usual podgy face of the newborn; her features were clear cut and well balanced. Sophie moved the towel back to see more of her. The tiny body was perfect too.

'She's lovely,' Sophie said, with awe in her voice.

CHAPTER SEVENTEEN

T HE NEXT day at visiting time, Isobel and Sebastian
both went to see Sophie, who was sitting up and looking
more alert than she had for weeks. Seb's eyes went straight to
the baby swinging in a plastic cot at the end of the bed. He
said, 'She's lovely. Just like you when you were born.'

Her mother kissed her. 'You're looking better.'

Sophie's big green eyes were beseeching. 'I've changed my
mind, Mum.'

'About . . . ?' Isobel hardly dared to put it into words.

'I want to bring her home. I don't want to part with her –
I don't think I could.'

'Of course you must bring her home,' they chorused.

'I hoped you'd change your mind.' Seb's eyes shone with
relief.

'We both did,' Isobel added, feeling as pleased as Punch.

They were laughing like a pair of kids in the car going
home and immediately set about bringing down Daisy's cot,
pram and baby clothes from the loft. All evening, they busied
themselves airing mattresses and napkins and getting
everything ready.

The following day, Isobel brought her daughter and granddaughter home from hospital. She was delighted to find that suddenly Sophie was her old self again, bursting with energy. She was breastfeeding the baby and wanted to do everything for her. It seemed she couldn't bear to let Melissa out of her sight.

'I'm so glad,' Sebastian said to Isobel as they were going to bed. 'It looks as though she might just take the baby in her stride. Everything could turn out all right after all.'

'I blame myself,' Isobel whispered. 'I never seemed to have enough time and energy to play with Sophie when she was growing up. I wasn't much of a mother.'

'You've no reason to feel like that. Sophie is a person in her own right. She was always full of mischief but she was happy enough as a child. Now she's level-headed and confident and she makes her own choices.'

'Perhaps. I want us to talk to her, tell her about her natural father. It's something she ought to know. Now she has a daughter of her own it's wrong to keep it from her.'

Sebastian pulled a face. 'We will, but I think she already understands. We must wait for the right moment.'

It came more quickly than either had expected. The next night Isobel made cocoa for them all to drink while Sophie gave Melissa her ten o'clock feed. Sebastian was stretched out sleepily on his armchair and commented again on how closely the baby resembled Sophie at that age.

'It takes me back,' he said.

'To happier times, before I messed everything up?' Sophie asked softly.

'They weren't happier for me.' Isobel seized what she saw as her chance. 'I messed everything up too.'

Sophie's gaze shot to her face. 'Mum?'

She said in a little rush, 'It's been on my conscience. I want you to know I made mistakes too. Like you, I found myself pregnant without a husband.'

Isobel couldn't look at Sophie as she explained how she and Sebastian had come to be married and the problems they'd had in the early days.

Sebastian said slowly, 'I almost lied to you about being your natural father.'

Sophie lifted her head and smiled from one to the other. 'I know that. You thought I was too young to take on board that my mum had a romantic history. But Gran had already let the cat out of the bag, hadn't she? And then when I read what Aunt Charlotte wrote to you, I knew exactly what had happened.'

'How did you feel about it?' Isobel asked.

'Upset and worried. I was that unwanted baby, wasn't I?'

Isobel shivered. This was what she'd feared.

Sophie gave Seb a wider smile. 'You made that all right. You said you were my father and you weren't going to be elbowed aside by anybody else.' She gave a little sniff. 'Mum, when I first realised I was having Melissa, I wanted an abortion. I'd have given anything to have one once Darrell . . . when it was too late. I didn't want her.'

Isobel felt a tear roll down her cheek. 'I felt the same, but abortions were illegal when I was having you.'

Sophie said, 'Now I can hold this tiny body in my arms, it seems a dreadful thing to have wanted. I'm glad I didn't.'

'I'm very glad it was impossible for me,' Isobel said.

Sophie smiled. 'I didn't know motherhood would give me this sort of thrill. I can't get enough of it. Caring for Melissa is suddenly the most important thing in my life. It hurts to give her up to you or Nana. As for thinking of having her adopted, I must have been mad.'

Isobel said, 'I want you to know that bringing you up gave Seb and me great pleasure. We wouldn't have missed it for worlds.'

She could see Seb's eyes were filled with tears. He said, 'You turned us into a little family. I tried to soothe your fears, convince you that's what we were. Just an ordinary family.'

'You did soothe me. You told me that you loved me, and nothing was going to change that,' Sophie said. 'That's really what I wanted to know.'

'I think of you as my daughter,' Sebastian told her. 'I always have and so do the rest of the family, so this is our secret.' He stumbled to his feet to put his arms round both Sophie and the baby. 'You burrowed your way into my affections from the very first,' he said. 'Just as Melissa has into yours. I'll always love you.'

Sophie gave another little sniff and wiped away a tear. 'I want you to know I'm ashamed I fell for Darrell's patter. I should have had more sense. I knew you wouldn't like him. But I'm not sorry about having Melissa.'

'As I said, we all make mistakes,' Isobel said slowly. 'It's how we handle them and go on to recover that counts. A year out won't matter for you.'

Sophie nodded. 'A lovely long rest from studying. A real change.'

'No choice now about which university you'll go to,' Sebastian said. 'It'll have to be Liverpool so you can live at home and stay close to Melissa. You'll have to have a car and learn to drive, but there should be plenty of time for that in the coming months.'

Her mother was nodding her agreement. 'You'll be able to go back to studying feeling really refreshed.'

'And ready to get my teeth into books again.'

Isobel said, 'It won't be easy, but you know we'll help in any way we can.' She noticed Sophie didn't ask who was going to look after the baby while she went to university. Clearly, both she and Seb expected her to do that.

She still wasn't sure she felt ready, but she'd thought it through again. If Sophie did three years at law school and then the necessary year of pupillage before she could practise, Melissa would be old enough for school before she'd finished. It might not be too bad after all.

At the end of November Sophie was invited with the rest of the family to Aunt Hilary's house for Sunday lunch. She fed the baby before setting out and dressed her in a new outfit. Melissa was still awake when they arrived, so Sebastian took her out of her pram to show her off to her relatives.

Aunt Prue said, 'How that child is growing! I can't get over how much difference a week makes.'

Isobel recounted how many ounces she'd gained and how good she was at night.

Flora took her over. 'My first great-grandchild.' She walked round the sitting room with Melissa in her arms. 'She's lovely. I'm thrilled with her.'

It was Sebastian who said, 'But I'm afraid we're going to need a bigger house now.'

'Izzy!' Flora swung on her. 'You're thinking of moving?'

'Perhaps . . . I'm happy where we are, but it's getting cramped.'

Seb nodded. 'We had to move Daisy out of our room some

time ago. We got her a half-sized bed but there isn't a proper bedroom for her.' When the extension was built, the way to the new bathroom was through the small third bedroom. 'The passage broadens out to provide space for her bed, and a small chest of drawers, but there's no way of shutting it off. It's all right for now, while she's still young enough to sleep like a log, but not for ever. And of course, now Sophie has Melissa's cot in her room.'

Sophie had heard this several times already. She was keen to move to a bigger house somewhere new, and was visualising something grand, but Mum had yet to be persuaded.

She turned to Hilary. 'How's Charlie getting on? Have you heard from him recently?'

'Yes. He's on his way home. He hopes to be here by Wednesday or Thursday. He's had enough now the weather's turning cold.'

His father said, 'We had to send him money for his fare home.'

'I'm glad he's coming back.' Sophie had always been fond of Charlie and needed a companion now.

The day after Charlie came home, Sophie pushed the pram up to see him. He opened the back door to her and his face broke into a smile.

'Hi,' she said. 'Welcome home.'

'Hi, Sophie. Come on in and cheer me up.'

'You need cheering up?'

'Mum and Dad are nagging. I've got to get a job.'

'Well, why not? Help me lift the pram into your utility.'

'Right. This is your baby?'

'Course it is, Charlie, this is Lissa.'

'Lissa? What sort of name is that?'

'You sound like Nana. It's short for Melissa. I think it's a lovely name.'

'I'd have called her Polly or something plainer.'

'I'm glad it wasn't up to you. She's asleep. I think I'll just leave her here.'

Charlie peered into the blankets. 'I thought you were going to have her adopted?'

'Changed my mind when I saw her. She's drop dead gorgeous.'

Charlie prodded her. 'I bet she's a load of work.'

'She is. How was the trip?'

'All right, I suppose.'

'Only all right? Didn't you have a good time?' Sophie led the way into the adjoining kitchen and filled the kettle. She was quite at home here.

'Well, not bad I suppose, but it was nerve-racking at first. We took the coach to Nice.'

'Yes, Aunt Hilly said.'

'We thought we might as well get straight down to the Med rather than just crossing the Channel. It was nine o'clock at night when we got there and we felt fuzzy and unwashed after a day and a night bouncing round on the coach.'

'Didn't it stop in Paris?'

'It took us round to see the sights, but only from the bus. It stopped on the motorway so we could get something to eat. We were worried because we didn't know where we could spend the night, and we didn't have enough money to stay in hotels.'

Sophie didn't think she'd enjoy that. 'What did you do?'

'There were two other lads on the bus on the same sort of trip. They said there was a youth hostel and we should all go there, but they had no idea where it was.'

'And no money for a taxi?'

'No, but we got there eventually, and they had room for us so it was all right then.'

'Nice must be a good place.'

'Smashing. Lovely and hot. We stayed about six weeks, but everything was dear and money was always short.'

'Couldn't you get work?'

'Not proper jobs, but the woman who ran the youth hostel let us help out about the place instead of paying our dues. We painted all the ground floor rooms. The other people staying there left their empty wine bottles lying about so we took them back and collected a few francs on them. We did our own cooking, mostly eggs and bread, that made the cheapest meal.'

Sophie said, 'It sounds fun.' It sounded like something she'd never be able to do now. Not with a baby.

'Then we hitchhiked along the coast into Spain because we'd heard it was easier to get casual work there. We got as far as Benidorm and I got a job in a bar. Gary was cooking in a caff.'

'Did you like Benidorm?'

'Loved it. Until Gary was offered a job as cook on a posh yacht sailing to the Caribbean. Lucky devil. I asked if they wanted a deck hand or another cook, but no. Once he'd gone I got a bit lonely and decided to come home.'

'A great adventure, Charlie.' Whichever way Sophie looked at it, it had to be more fun than being pregnant. And giving birth had been the pits. 'What are you going to do now?'

'I've got to look for another job, haven't I? There's one advertised in the local paper. I was just going to ring up and ask about it.'

'Cooking?'

'Yes. It's either that or working for Dad.'

Charlie made them mugs of tea and found some biscuits.

'Now I'm back, it seems a bit dismal here. I'm still thinking of Gary, the lucky sod. He'll be sailing round the Caribbean for three months.'

'Charlie, you'll get a job and settle down again.'

'Well, that's it, isn't it? I'm bored with cooking and I can't get anything else that's going to pay me more than peanuts.'

'You could train for something different, something that interests you and pays more. Then you'd be all right.'

'A bit late for that now.'

'No. I'm taking this year off, but then I'll have to get down to studying again.'

'It's easy for you. I'd never get accepted, not to be trained for a halfway decent career. I only have four O levels, and I can't write and spell properly.'

'Charlie, you opted out. You didn't even bother to sit some of the exams.'

'It wouldn't have made any difference if I had. I'd have got rubbish marks.'

'If you'd got down and tried, you'd have passed your exams. Andy did.'

'Don't bring up what Andy did. I'm sick of hearing about his success. I'm jealous, aren't I?'

'Jealous? If he could do it, why couldn't you?'

Charlie was frowning. 'He was always better at school than I was.'

'He tried harder. He wasn't so worried about failing. I believe anybody can do anything if they really want to.'

'I know.' Charlie pulled a face.

'You've got to focus on what you want to achieve and work at it. What is it you want to do?'

'Resit some of my O levels, I suppose. English language anyway. I want to be trained for a career.'

'What sort of career?'

Charlie shrugged. 'I don't know . . .'

'There you are then. You'll just drift on unless you know. Think about it, Charlie. What are you good at?'

Charlie sniffed.

'Cooking interests you, doesn't it? And you're already trained in that.'

'Half trained. I left college before the end of the course.'

'Whose fault was that? And you need bits of paper to say you're qualified. You'll never be paid as much as those who have them. You didn't try.'

'Sophie, believe me, I tried and tried. Didn't I do special lessons with Aunt Izzy for years? And with your dad too.'

'They tried to teach you, Charlie, but how much effort did you put in? You were always ducking out of school. Nobody can learn if they don't stay in class. I don't think you tried. You went backpacking round Europe to forget your problems. You put them out of your mind to have a good time. Go on, admit it.'

'Perhaps I did. Actually, you're right. I did and I'm sorry now. Would you help me? Teach me, I mean.'

'I think my mum and dad would do a better job.'

'You bang it home better. I could take it from you. We're sort of on a par, aren't we? Except you're cleverer.'

'There's nothing the matter with your brain. You just need

to use it. Stop running away every time somebody opens a book. To be happy at work, Charlie, you need a job that uses your brain to the full, a job that interests you and stretches you. If you're working beneath your capabilities, you become bored. That's true for everyone, but for some dyslexics it's a double whammy. If they can't pass basic exams to prove they have the ability, they can't get on to courses that would lead to more interesting work.'

Charlie looked hang-dog. 'Don't I know it. You know, when we were backpacking we didn't always have a good time. Sometimes we didn't know where the next meal was coming from and some nights we had to sleep on the beach.'

'I bet that made you focus on getting work.'

Charlie gave a gusty sigh. 'You're right, of course. I'm brassed off because Andy's doing well. If I'd tried harder I might still be with him.'

'If that's what you want, it's not too late.'

'D'you think so? D'you think I could?' He looked suddenly eager.

'Of course. I'm going back to it. We're all entitled to a second chance.'

'A second chance, yes, but I wouldn't know where to start now.'

'Dad will know. Come down when he's home and we'll ask him.'

Charlie was biting his fingernails. 'Would he know I didn't try very hard? Would Aunt Izzy?'

'I expect so. They know all about kids and school work, but they believe in second chances too.'

'It's asking a lot. They gave me their time, and I threw it all up.'

'Well, I could keep your nose on the grindstone – for the next few months anyway. I'd know whether you were trying or not and I'd stop right away if you weren't. Dad would love to draw up a syllabus for you and he'd provide the books. It's the sort of thing he likes doing and he's good at it.'

'I'll come down to see him tonight,' Charlie said. 'What time would be best?'

Sophie could see how pleased her father was that Charlie was asking for help.

'Very sensible of you,' he said.

'Sophie says it's the only way.'

She said, 'Without reasonable O levels Charlie can't go on to further education, can he?'

'No. Is that what you want, to resit some of your O levels?'

'What I really want is to read more easily and spell better.'

'Isobel says you can read adequately. Do you ever read a book for pleasure?'

'No.'

'You start doing that and it will get easier. All you need is practice.'

'I do read Dad's gardening magazines sometimes.'

'That's good. Good if you resit your exams too. What sort of further education did you have in mind?'

'I'd like a decent job, one that pays better than cooking and with no unsociable hours.'

'Such as? You must have some idea.'

Charlie was shaking his head. 'Perhaps become a professional engineer like Andy. But it seems, you know, like pie in the sky for me.'

'Charlie, your intelligence was assessed as being in the top one per cent of the population.'

'But blighted by dyslexia.'

'You could do it if you really tried.'

'That's what Sophie said.'

'Dad, what's new in the way you help people with dyslexia? There's always new stuff, isn't there?'

'Well, there's a special reading scheme, called the fuzzbuzz books.'

Charlie groaned. 'Not more Jack and Jill books? I've outgrown all those infant readers.'

Seb smiled. 'I know, Charlie. These do go laboriously over and over basic skills. You already have those under your belt, but Sophie could run through them with you, just so you realise you know them. Refresh your mind, so to speak. Then we could prepare you for O levels in English and Maths. That should be enough for one year.'

Charlie's eyebrows lifted. 'I don't want to bite off more than I can chew.'

'You won't,' Sophie assured him. 'You've been through it all several times already. For you, it's more a question of not getting bored with it.'

'Sophie's right,' Seb told him. 'Have a look in the bookcase over there, and choose something you think you'll enjoy reading. You need books meant for adults from which you'll get pleasure.'

Sophie was beside Charlie. 'Do you know what Agatha Christie's like? You've seen her stuff on the telly, haven't you?'

'Yes.' He lifted out a gardening book on how to grow roses. 'This looks interesting.'

'Your dad must have lots of books like that.'

'He has, but this one's full of coloured photographs. Just look at these gorgeous roses with deep pink and white stripes. *Rosa mundi.* I bet plants like that would sell like hot cakes in Dad's shop.'

'That's a sort of text book, Charlie,' Seb said. 'A book to dip into. I meant a novel. Something to absorb your interest and keep you reading.'

Sophie said, 'How about this Dick Francis? I've read it and it's smashing. I think you'd like it.'

'Take them both,' Sebastian said.

Sophie felt she did little these days but look after her baby and jolly Charlie along. She loved Melissa to bits but she needed more going on in her life. Most days, she pushed her pram round the village, often going to the shop on errands for her mother.

Today, she had a loaf and some onions balanced on the pram cover when she came face to face with Ross Salter as he was heading towards the shop.

She'd seen him drive through the village in a very smart sports car, a birthday gift so she'd heard, from his parents, but she hadn't spoken to him since her baby had been born. She felt the heat run up into her face. Hadn't he warned her off Darrell that time she'd done work experience at his mother's office?

'Hello, Sophie. How are you?' Was he looking down his nose at her?

'Fine,' she said.

'Is this your baby?'

'Yes.' Who else could she belong to? Sophie would have gone straight on if he hadn't been standing in the way. She stiffened, afraid he was going to mention Darrell, or say, 'I told you so. I tried to warn you off but you took no notice.'

He looked equally uncomfortable, but what he actually said was, 'Can I see her?'

Why would Ross want to see her baby? It made Sophie cringe, but it was only what everybody else asked.

She pulled the pram blankets down and said, 'Her name's Melissa. I call her Lissa.' She was awake. Dark green eyes stared up at them.

'She's beautiful.' Ross seemed really interested. He put a hand near her, and she grasped his finger. He smiled.

Sophie relaxed and smiled too. 'She's great, and looking after her is lovely.'

'But . . . ? You'll be going on to university, won't you?'

'Yes, but this is a smashing way to spend a year out.'

She walked on with her nose in the air. With no Judith present, he'd made no effort to invite her out. She didn't know whether to be sorry or relieved.

CHAPTER EIGHTEEN

THE NEXT time Sophie went up to see Charlie she found a suntanned Gary Ingram sitting at the playroom table with him.

'Gary's back from sailing round the Caribbean,' Charlie said. 'He was just telling me about it.'

'I'd love to go,' Sophie said. She'd brought Melissa in to sit on her knee, and the baby was yawning sleepily.

'I heard you'd had a little girl.' Gary had beseeching brown eyes under a heavy lock of dark hair that he combed back until it stood up in a tall tuft.

Charlie said, 'Go on, Gary. Tell us what it was like.'

'Did you know that on one side of the Caribbean all the islands have steep hills and on the other side they're as flat as pancakes?'

Charlie shook his head.

'The hilly islands are extinct volcanoes on the sea bed and only the tops stick out of the water. The flat ones on the other side are coral islands.'

'No!'

'And some of the islands don't have a water supply

although there are people living on them. It all has to be shipped in.'

'I bet that's expensive.'

Gary had a cheeky grin. 'Everything's expensive there.'

Sophie drew herself up. 'Fascinating though this is,' she said firmly, 'I'm here to make sure Charlie studies. Dad's set you some geometry problems to work out.' The text book she'd brought had been flagged. She opened it and pushed it in front of him.

'I'll do it later,' Charlie said. 'I can do geometry.'

'Now is the time you've set aside to do it. So come on.'

'You're a hard taskmaster.' He pulled a face. 'I won't be able to put my mind to it.'

'Try, Charlie, try,' Sophie told him. 'I'll take Gary into the sitting room for a chat. Aunt Hilly won't mind, will she? You can talk to him later.'

As Sophie sank with the baby into the comfortable cushions on the settee, Gary said, 'I've got the same problem. Would you help me as well?'

'You're dyslexic too?'

'Didn't you know?'

'Well . . . I've never thought about it, but now you mention it, I remember Mum saying you came to her Saturday morning sessions with Charlie.'

He nodded.

'So what's your reading like? Why don't you read something to me now?'

'No. I dread reading aloud. I'd need to psych myself up for that.'

'You don't have to worry about me,' she said, but he shook his head. He seemed agitated and that touched Sophie's

263

sympathy. 'You must have had a worse time at school than Charlie.'

'It was a waste of time going. I didn't learn anything.' He grimaced. 'I hated the place and was quite envious of Charlie going to Loxton House.'

'You went to the comprehensive?'

'Yep, Dryden Street. They put me in the remedial stream. The clever ones picked on us, called us thickies and dunces. The teachers called us slow learners. I suppose we were.'

'What about your writing?'

'They used to laugh at it so I don't write anything down now. Nobody but me can read it anyway.'

'Were you the only dyslexic in the class?'

'I don't know.' He sighed and wouldn't meet her gaze. 'The top end of the class took the mickey the whole time. It pissed me off.'

Sophie studied him. He was small and slight compared with Charlie. Not even as tall as she was.

'So what exams did you sit?'

'None.'

'None at all? No CSEs?'

'No. The teachers said it would be a waste of time for me to go in for them. I hated the teachers, especially Mrs Thomas, who took us for English. She used to teach our Paul. He was clever and she kept saying why couldn't I be more like him. I told her Paul wasn't dyslexic and I was. I don't think she'd ever heard of it.'

Sophie sat silent. This was not school as she'd known it.

'I used to sit at the back of the class and keep quiet, but when Mrs Thomas discovered I couldn't read properly she started picking on me. She said in front of the whole class that

I was the worst reader for my age she'd ever come across. She'd make me read aloud so they could all jeer at my efforts. She said I was lazy and cheeky.'

'Sounds as if you might have messed her about. Aimed paper darts round the room and that sort of thing,' Sophie said.

'I did worse than that. I let her car tyres down to get my own back.'

Sophie giggled.

'And another time, I helped the other boys block up the staff toilets, all of them. You know, stuff like that.'

'What did she do then?'

He shrugged his thin shoulders. 'Made me sit at her desk at the front and watched me copy things from the board. "You can do it," she'd say. "Just copy what you see." But I couldn't. She used to hit me over the knuckles with a ruler and tell me to hurry up. She said I was hopeless, and I'd never learn anything.'

'Oh, gosh, Gary!' Sophie could see the depth of his misery in his face. 'That's awful.'

'It wasn't always that bad. If I didn't trouble them, mostly the teachers left me alone at the back of the class doing nothing. I think they forgot about me. Sometimes when the rest of the class did history or geometry or something they thought I wouldn't understand, they'd give me a silly book to read. You know, one of those infant readers. I was bored out of my mind. I started bunking off school after that. I couldn't stand it. In the mornings I used to tell Mum I was too sick to go but she always made me. I hated the place. All the teachers were horrible.'

Sophie said, 'But your school has a legal duty to provide

suitable teaching for you.' She'd heard her parents say that.

'I know. Mum was always coming down to see the headmaster to ask for special lessons for me.'

Sophie thought of Stella trying to do her best for him. 'She didn't succeed?'

'Oh, yes. She was over the moon when he agreed to send me to Bangor for assessment. There they said I was definitely dyslexic and that I needed specialist teaching, but I was still left in the remedial class. Mum kept at the headmaster about specially qualified teachers and stuff, and he kept saying he was making arrangements. But it took ages and then eventually they said I'd have to go to a special school. The thought of a new school scared me. I was nearly sixteen and all I wanted to do was leave school for good.'

'How did you get on with my mum on those Saturday morning sessions?'

'She was always kind. She didn't try to rub my nose in it.'

'I should hope not, but did you learn to read?'

He said warily, 'I improved, I think.'

'Would you mind if I asked her how she thinks you did?'

Gary shook his head. 'I expect she thinks I gave up too easily.'

Sophie went home to find her mother almost ready to put their supper of chicken and chips on the table. Melissa was still asleep so she left her in her pram.

'Guess what?' she said. 'Gary Ingram was there. He says the Caribbean's a marvellous place, and the beaches are out of this world. I'd love a holiday there.'

'Wouldn't we all?' her father said, lifting Daisy on to her chair at the table.

'Dad, you wouldn't believe what a bad time Gary had at school.'

'Many dyslexics do.'

'If Mum helped him, why can't he read now?'

Isobel asked, 'Did he tell you that? He can read.' Sophie helped carry the plates to the table. Her mother went on, 'Gary had a reading age of fourteen last year, so he's almost reached adult standard.'

'So he wouldn't need much more help?'

'I wouldn't go that far,' her father said as he cut Daisy's chicken into small pieces. 'Gary will have worked very hard to achieve what he has.'

'He asked me to help him. I said I would.'

'I'm glad,' Isobel said. 'It'll be good for both of you, but if he hasn't opened a book since my Saturday sessions, don't expect miracles.'

'I don't think he has. Dad, I remember reading in the paper some time ago that they'd found a cure. That if a dyslexic pupil reads through a sheet of pink plastic everything is all right.'

'If only it were that easy.' He sighed. 'I understand it does help some people, though I haven't found it helped much at my school. Large print well spaced out helps too, but most books aren't like that and they want to read ordinary books.'

'There have been other so-called cures,' Isobel said. 'Once it was suggested that certain physical exercises before reading would help, and that a wheat-free diet would as well.'

'I'm afraid it's grasping at straws,' Sebastian told her.

'Why?'

'Some of these children seem to be so bright in other ways,

it's hard for us teachers to grasp the difficulties they have with words.'

'Gary seems shy, sort of as if he's ashamed he can't read better.'

'Gary was unlucky not to be recognised as dyslexic until he was fifteen,' her mother said. 'Look how normal Jamie is. He got extra tuition from the time he started school. Gary didn't.'

'Charlie didn't either.'

'Many children, like Charlie and Gary, experience failure before they get any help.' Sebastian sighed. 'That's what's really sad. What we need is an early screening programme to pick out likely dyslexics when they're starting school. Gary must have known for years that when it came to reading and writing he couldn't do what other children found easy, yet his teachers expected him to be able to do it. He probably had no idea what it was he couldn't do, and thought it was his own fault.'

'Yes, he said one teacher told him he was hopeless, and too stupid to learn anything.'

'It disgusts me that any teacher would say things like that to a child,' her father burst out. 'How hurtful that must have been. But even worse, it shows a lack of understanding, and that alienates the child and leads to truanting and behaviour problems. Did you know that over half our prison population is dyslexic? Some say more than sixty per cent?'

Sophie smiled, 'I don't think either Gary or Charlie will be going to prison.'

'I very much hope not, but literacy is very important in the modern world, and not to have it is a terrible handicap. And dyslexia leaves emotional scars, Sophie. These children are told so many times that they're failures that they begin to believe it. That's one of Charlie's problems and bound to be one of Gary's too. They lack confidence in their own ability.'

'So what do I do?'

'Exactly what you're doing for Charlie. Run through the basics – he'll have heard it a thousand times before so move on fast, it's just to refresh his mind. But what he needs is practice, so get him to read.'

'He doesn't want to read aloud.'

'To himself then, and make sure he understands what he's reading.'

'What do I have to look out for, Mum?' Sophie asked. 'How do I handle this?'

'Never show any impatience. Praise where you can, but you have to make clear what you expect of him. Make sure your expectations are within his reach and show him that you care about what he achieves.' Isobel helped herself to more mayonnaise and added, 'Both you and he may find it frustrating, but that's something else you shouldn't show. And like Charlie, you must aim to get Gary reading for his own enjoyment.'

Sophie nodded. 'But spelling?'

'That's likely to be a lifelong problem, I'm afraid, and without specialist teaching nearly all dyslexics underachieve.'

Over the winter months, Sophie enjoyed helping Charlie and Gary. She needed their companionship and it gave her something to fill her days, apart from learning to drive and tending her baby daughter.

Each week it seemed Melissa learned to do something new, while at the same time Gary and Charlie grew more confident.

*

'Another new car?' Flora was shocked that Tom would even suggest it. 'Another Mercedes?' It was a warm evening in early summer; they were eating supper with the windows and door wide open.

Tom was serious. 'We've had this one for over three years. It's hardly new.'

'But there's nothing wrong with it,' Flora protested. Everything was getting more expensive. She was beginning to worry that they might run out of money if they carried on spending at this rate.

'It makes economic sense not to let a car get too old.' Tom forked up the homemade chicken and mushroom pie. 'If we trade it in now we'll get a good price for it, and be selling it on before we have to face the cost of repairs and replacements.'

In her years of widowhood, Flora had always bought her cars second hand and kept them running for years. 'Would there be many repairs? A car like that is built to last.'

'There always are. You like the Mercedes, don't you?'

Flora did. When she'd retired from teaching, she'd sold her car and had almost given up driving, but when she'd married Tom he'd persuaded her to take it up again.

She'd been afraid she'd lost her skill. 'I'd be nervous of driving such a big expensive car. It's been years . . .'

'It'll come back to you just like that.' He'd smiled at her and snapped his fingers. 'Drive round a bit and you'll be fine.'

Flora wasn't convinced.

'A couple of lessons then, that'll be all you need. Just to give you confidence.'

She'd quite enjoyed the lessons and being able to drive again had given her a new lease of life. She loved being able to go into Birkenhead or Chester to buy clothes and it gave her freedom to get the weekly shop on her own.

But even so, 'I don't know . . .'

Their present car still looked new: it was parked outside in the road, and the new one would have to be too. 'I mean, how much will it cost?'

Tom got up from the table to fetch the brochure from his coat pocket in the lobby. 'Here, look at this. The same model we have now, though it has been updated a bit. It looks very nice in pearl grey, doesn't it?'

'But how much?'

'I'll work it out for you when we've eaten.'

When Flora told Isobel about it the next morning, she said, 'Go for it, Mum. No point in saving your money, is there?'

'It's more a question of making the money last than saving it,' Flora told her, but Isobel only laughed. Flora held her peace. It seemed disloyal to Tom to tell her daughter he was spending money like water.

When Tom took her to the garage to look at the latest model, she agreed it was lovely. She sold a few more of the shares Mavis had left her to pay for it, and a day or two later Tom drove it home. It did feel marvellous to be bowling along in such an elegant car.

Tom's eyes shone. 'I love it,' he told her, and spent ages poring over the handbook.

They'd had it only a week and he was still putting it through its paces. He'd taken her to Liverpool to help him choose a new mackintosh and they'd had a good lunch at the Adelphi Hotel. Driving back along the New Chester Road, once they'd left the urban sprawl behind, Tom put his foot down. The speed limit changed frequently from unrestricted to thirty miles an hour as the road wound through various hamlets, and at one point Tom rounded a corner to find two police officers operating a radar gun. One of the men stepped into the road and waved him down.

Flora could feel her heart pounding as he approached their car. Tom swore under his breath as he opened the window. He'd been caught in a speed trap.

'Pull in to the side, sir, if you please. Do you know at what speed you were travelling?'

Tom didn't. He looked disconcerted. His fingers on the steering wheel were showing a slight tremor. He'd been taken by surprise.

'You were doing forty-four miles an hour in a thirty mile an hour area.'

Flora relaxed a little. It wasn't as bad as she'd feared. Moments earlier Tom had been pointing out how effortlessly the car travelled at seventy-five miles at hour. She thought him a safe driver.

'I'm sorry,' Tom said. 'I was slowing down.'

'The law demands that you get your speed down before passing the restriction sign.'

He was asked to show his driving licence and brought out his wallet. A pound note fluttered to the floor of the car as he drew it out. Flora picked it up and pushed it back to him while the police officer studied the document. Then she remembered they'd had wine with their lunch. That might prove an added problem for Tom. She could see beads of sweat appearing across the bridge of his nose. The officer was asking questions and noting down his details.

'Will I be charged with speeding?' Tom asked.

'That will be decided later, sir. You will be notified by post.'

They were free to go. Tom started the engine and with exaggerated caution pulled out into the road. Another driver was already being waved over.

'Damn damn damn,' Tom swore as he drove away. 'That's churned me up.'

Flora sighed. 'Caught speeding fair and square. That's what a new car does for you.'

'Usually, when you're stopped like that,' Tom said, 'the police go round your car looking for faults, but he could see this one was brand new. That helped. At least there's nothing else I could be charged with.'

Flora pulled a face. 'It's put a damper on what was a good day out.' It took a pot of tea and an hour's rest before Flora felt herself again. Tom was in a bad mood for the rest of the day.

The following morning, Flora needed to go to the supermarket and set out early with her list. As she was adjusting the driving seat to her shorter legs, she saw a driving licence on the car floor. She knew it was Tom's. He was usually careful with his documents, but being caught speeding had thrown him out of kilter. She opened it and glanced down the details before slipping it in her handbag to keep it safe.

As she drove, there was a niggle at the back of her mind. She thought she'd seen something on his licence that didn't add up. Or had she misread it? After she'd drawn into the supermarket car park she got Tom's licence out again. What she saw made her catch her breath. His birth date was given as 31 January 1932. That would make him fifty-three! He'd told Flora he was ten years younger than her, but according to this he was twenty-one years younger. Twenty-one years!

Surely he couldn't be? She was beginning to feel her age and was always marvelling at how young he looked and that he had so much energy. He was always wanting to do things, go away for holidays and weekends. He was on the go all the time. Had he deliberately lied to her about his age? She looked again at his date of birth. He must have done. But why? It didn't make sense, unless . . .

She felt the heat rush into her cheeks. Of course she knew why. She'd found it hard enough to accept that a man ten years younger could be in love with her. Would she have married him if she'd known he was twenty-one years younger? She clutched the steering wheel and put her head down on her arms while doubts stormed through her mind. Had Tom really been in love with her at all?

She could feel herself shaking with outrage. Surely he hadn't picked her out as an easy meal ticket right from the beginning? The thought made her feel sick. Compared with him, she was an old woman in her dotage. She must have been blind not to doubt the evidence of her own eyes, not to have the slightest suspicion.

Had he wanted to share her pretty cottage, her pension and the comfortable life she'd scrimped and saved for? He must have felt he'd hit the jackpot when Mavis left her so much money. He was certainly very interested in what it could buy him.

But she'd proposed! Had he schemed to marry her but managed to con her into asking him? He'd made her believe he didn't want to take advantage of her. She'd even had to persuade him, but had that been part of his plan? She felt flustered and befuddled. She couldn't think straight any more. How could Tom have done this to her?

Another wave of anger washed over her. Her shopping forgotten, she started the engine again and went straight back home to have it out with him. As she drove, her worries crowded in on her.

It had surprised her that Tom appeared to have few friends and had never introduced her to even one relative. Isobel had never taken to him and Sophie sometimes showed her dislike of him. Flora had known these things but discounted them, more fool her. His greed for spending had begun to upset her. She'd let him run through almost half of the capital Mavis had left her and that was reducing the income she derived from it. He was bleeding her dry.

When she rushed indoors, Tom looked up in surprise. 'You haven't been long. I thought you were going to do a big shop?'

He'd joined a fishing club and was making colourful flies on their dining table. She flung his open driving licence at him. It skidded through the feathers, sending some on to his lap.

'How old are you, Tom?'

She watched a flush ran up his neck and into his cheeks. He looked acutely uncomfortable. She knew she'd caught him out. 'Born in 1932? That makes you fifty-three, not sixty-four as you told me.'

He leaped to his feet and tried to throw his arms round her. 'I'm sorry. I can explain, Flora.'

She stepped away from him. 'Go on then, explain.'

'It started as a misunderstanding, though I didn't intend to mislead you.' He looked and sounded sincere, but Flora found it hard to believe.

'Right at the start you said—'

He interrupted. 'Age doesn't really matter, does it? Not if we're happy. I know I've been very happy and I think you have too.'

'It does matter, Tom.'

'I loved you very much and wanted to marry you. That's why I didn't correct the misunderstanding. I was afraid you'd be put off by the difference in our ages.'

He'd come close enough to put his hands on her shoulders; she could see he was about to kiss her. She pushed him away and raised her voice.

'Age matters because you want to be out doing things all the time while I'm content to stay quietly at home.'

'That's not true, love. Not true at all. I'm very happy here with you.'

'And telling lies to me matters too.'

'But surely . . . a white lie that started as a misunderstanding? Is it that important when we've had seven happy years? I want us to go on and live happily ever after, don't you?'

Flora did: she wanted to be convinced they could, but there was one more thing. 'I'm worried about how much . . .' she almost said how much *you're* spending, but managed to correct it to, 'how much we're spending. We won't have enough to last if we go on at this rate.'

'Darling Flora, you're always so careful with money. I thought you wanted me to point out all the things that would help you enjoy life? That you didn't want to be like Mavis and let everything pass you by?'

Flora had said as much to him more than once. She'd willingly given him access to her money and altered her will in his favour. Was she being silly, changing her mind now?

Tom said, 'We've just bought a new car, I know, but that will be an investment for the next three years. Perhaps I should leave the spending to you in future? You decide what we have and what we don't. Would that make you feel better?'

That calmed Flora a little. 'Yes it would. All the expensive holidays . . .'

His fingers were tilting her face so she had to look into his eyes. 'We only go away when you agree,' he pointed out gently. 'We've put off all the big trips: New York, the cruise up the Amazon and the trans-Siberian railway journey. We've only done what pleases you.'

It left Flora feeling mollified. Perhaps she was being unreasonable.

CHAPTER NINETEEN

FLORA HAD spent restless hours that night thinking about Tom's lies. Hearing his soft rhythmic breathing close beside her made her shrink away from him. In the morning, she felt drained and exhausted but she got up to cook his breakfast of egg and bacon. He intended to go to Liverpool.

She couldn't face food and told him it was too early for her. While he ate, his dark eyes seemed to be watching her from the other side of the table and his manner seemed somehow different. She was glad to see him go, and submitted to his usual kiss.

With the house to herself, she poured herself another cup of tea and tried to relax before starting her morning chores.

She felt haunted by worries that wouldn't go away. If she questioned anything, Tom always had an explanation that sounded feasible. But this time, Flora was sure he'd deliberately lied about his age. She had clear memories of her own of that time.

She'd first met Tom at a bridge session at the church, shortly after he'd taken lodgings in the village. Nobody seemed to know much about him and he'd given out few facts about himself. Had he told all of them that he was fifty-seven and a widower? Or was she the only one to be told his age?

Flora had thought him a bit of a mystery, but he seemed to like her and invited her out. Then, like a fool, she'd lost her head and fallen in love with him. She'd had to confess to him that she was ten years older, and she'd held back on that for some time because she was afraid it would put him off.

Now Flora thought about it clearly, he'd always had the energy and interests of a man in his forties. There had been no misunderstanding about his age and no white lie.

The more Flora thought about Tom, the more easily she could see other lies he'd told. He'd been reluctant to tell her anything about his first wife Grace, but when she asked he'd said she'd died of pneumonia. At the time she'd thought that strange because in this day and age antibiotics would cure pneumonia.

Flora finished making their bed and started to dust round the bedroom. Tom had said he'd been made redundant from a building firm, but she could see from his immaculate white and manicured hands that he'd never worked physically on a building site.

Then he'd actually changed his whole life story and she'd still believed him. All the facts seemed to fit. He'd told her he'd inherited a building company from his father: that after many years it had failed and he'd gone bankrupt, that his wife couldn't cope with their changed circumstances and had committed suicide.

She'd been so charged with emotion and so sorry for him that night, she'd brought him up here to this bedroom and they'd made love in her bed for the first time.

But was it just a sob story he'd thought up to get her here?

Had it all been a tissue of lies? She was beginning to think the unthinkable: that it was.

And if he'd told her whopping lies like that, could she trust the other things he'd told her? She shivered. When she'd first met him, Tom had told her he had a son of twenty-six called Eric, who had been thrown on the labour market at the age of nineteen when the family business went bankrupt, and had had to emigrate to Australia to find work.

He'd also said he had a married daughter of twenty-eight called Carol. Both she and her husband worked for a merchant bank in London but had landed better jobs in America. That put both children conveniently far away. Flora couldn't remember Tom writing letters to either of them and she'd never seen any mail addressed to him from either continent.

Neither did he have friends he'd known for any length of time. Rather, Tom had infiltrated her family and their circle of friends and acquaintances. She was afraid now that Tom had been playing her as a fisherman plays a fish.

She was an old fool. He'd married her for her money, and for the more comfortable life she could provide. She cooked and cleaned for him and provided companionship and sex.

Flora trembled. Thinking like this scared her but it was all adding up now. Tom was too ready to placate her and offer explanations if she questioned what he said or did. It was almost a reflex for him to leap up and throw his arms round her. And it always worked. He was a clever man, sensitive to her feelings and with a firm grasp on psychology. He must also have iron self-control and was no doubt a competent actor.

She was appalled at what she'd done. His honeyed tongue

had persuaded her to alter her will and give him access to her bank accounts. It had taken her all this time to see through him, and it was bringing her out in a cold sweat. The trust she'd had in him had gone, but what could she do about it now?

Isobel had had their cottage on the market for four months when Gavin, who worked at the garden centre for Ben, brought his widowed mother and brother to see it. They immediately said they liked it. They came again the following morning, and that afternoon the agent telephoned to say they'd made an offer of a thousand pounds below the asking price.

Isobel accepted it straight off. Sophie was excited and hugged her. When Sebastian came home, he said, 'We couldn't get a better offer than that. Now we have to make up our minds what we're going to buy.' They'd been looking round quite hard. 'I quite fancy that Victorian house in the road where Prue lives. Let's go back and have another look tomorrow.'

'I liked it too.'

'I'm coming too,' Sophie said. 'I haven't seen it yet.'

The following afternoon, they walked down, pushing Melissa in her pram. It was a large semi-detached house of the same design as that of the twin aunts. It had been empty for some weeks and the estate agent came to show them round.

Sebastian lifted the baby on to his shoulder before they went in. 'I think this is what we're looking for,' he told Sophie. 'We don't want to go far. Your mum wants to stay near her family.'

'So do I,' she told him.

'We'll have room to spread ourselves here,' Isobel said,

going from room to room. 'Such a lovely sitting room. I've always admired Prue's.'

'It would have been known as the drawing room in the house's heyday,' Sebastian said.

'It is in the brochure.'

'The place needs a lot doing to it,' he said cautiously.

'That's going to be fun.'

It was very similar to Prue's house and like hers had been turned into two flats. Both were empty and they intended turning it back into one house.

On the walk home, they found they were all in agreement. This would be their new home. Sebastian telephoned his offer to the estate agent as soon as they reached their cottage.

Later, when Sophie had gone to see Charlie, Seb said, 'Would we be better to keep it as two flats and let Sophie have the upstairs one? She's told us many times she isn't going to get married.'

Her mother sighed. 'Things have changed since my day. Then marriage was every girl's ambition. If Sophie doesn't want to . . .'

'Probably better if we each have a place of our own,' Seb said. 'She'll want to take over the baby as soon as she comes home, but we'll be close enough to keep an eye on them both. Shall we ask her?'

They put it to Sophie when she came home for supper. She was delighted. 'I'd love that, thank you, thank you. A home of my own? Who wouldn't jump at the chance?'

'We can both be independent,' Isobel said, 'but if you're late coming home from the university, or you want to go out at night, Melissa needn't be on her own. You won't have to worry on that score.'

'We could even fit up a small bedroom she could use occasionally, in our flat.' Seb was drawing a plan of the downstairs rooms, which were familiar because of the twin aunts' home. 'Look, sitting room, dining room, lovely big kitchen, then two big bedrooms, one for us and one for Daisy. Then there's a little room here, big enough for a single bed. I bet Melissa would be happy to sleep here once in a while.'

'That would be taking advantage of you,' Sophie said. 'I shouldn't . . .'

'Of course you should. She's used to being with us and Daisy,' Isobel said. 'You know your dad, he'll want to see as much of her as possible.'

'Sophie, we want you to have a life of your own.' Seb smiled. 'You'll have to spend a lot of time studying, and we don't want you to feel burdened by other responsibilities.'

Sophie was thrilled to have her own flat but found moving in very hard work. She didn't have much time to go shopping for furniture and fittings, but once the essentials were there she knew she could take her time.

Two or three times a year, Maureen Salter invited Sophie's parents to dinner, and they would return the invitation a couple of months later. This time, Sophie had been included in the invitation. At first she'd been reluctant to go. She was afraid the Salters disapproved of her for having a baby out of wedlock.

'I've lost touch with Judith,' she said, 'and I never did get on with Ross.'

'You all got on very well together when you were children,' her mother reminded her. 'You liked Ross then.'

'He fancies himself. Thinks he's better at everything than

the rest of us.' Sophie had heard their neighbours speak of Ross as a young man likely to go far.

'Maureen wants you to come. She says Ross has come home unexpectedly.'

'Why?'

'I don't know. No doubt he'll tell you tonight.'

'I think he rather looks down on me for having Melissa.'

'Nonsense,' Isobel said in a hearty voice, but she thought it more than likely. The Salters had status: they were professionals with the largest house in the village.

Sophie took great pains with her appearance. She'd got her figure back and she'd bought herself a new dress in green and white stripes. She meant to look smarter and prettier than Judith in order to show her and Ross that her problems were behind her.

When they rang the front doorbell, Judith came into the hall with her parents to greet them, but there was no sign of Ross even when they sat down in the sitting room. Sophie hadn't seen much of Judith recently. She had almost completed her first year at Liverpool University and chatted on about how much she'd enjoyed it. Sophie was determined not to feel envious. Her turn for that would come. She thought the pre-dinner conversation rather dull; the older generation touched on their health, the weather and the garden, and enquired after her baby.

Sophie said, 'I understood Ross had come home. Isn't he here?'

'Yes.' His mother seemed to falter. 'He hasn't been too well. Judith dear, run up and tell him our guests are here.'

Sophie was surprised. It sounded as though he was skulking upstairs. 'He's been ill?' she asked.

'Yes,' his father said. 'We thought it better if he came home early.'

'But not before he sat his finals?'

'No, no, those are in the bag. He had an accident in his car. He wasn't hurt but it's left him a bit low. He's down in the dumps.'

Sophie was intrigued. Down in the dumps? Surely not? Ross was always bouncy and full of his own importance. When he came into the room, she was shocked to see how listless and grey he looked. They were led into the dining room and a four-course dinner was served in style, but Ross hardly spoke.

Afterwards, Judith got up to make some coffee and started to clear the table. As she often had here, Sophie helped, and Ross went with her into the utility room to stack the dishwasher.

'Was it very bad?' she asked.

'What?'

'The accident you had.'

'Yes, very bad. Difficult to get over something like that.'

'Ross, you've got to get over it,' she told him. 'Get over it and move on.'

'I can't,' he choked out.

Sophie found herself flooding with sympathy. She hadn't expected to feel like this for Ross, but his look of absolute anguish touched a chord. She'd seen Charlie and Gary like this, and she'd felt something like it herself.

'If I can get over my trouble,' she said gently, 'you can get over yours.'

'You don't understand.'

'No, but I might if you told me about it.' Both his hands

were rubbing at his face. She went on, 'Is this accident you've had bothering you?'

'My car was a write-off.' He took Sophie's arm and led her out to the garden to sit on a bench under the trees. It was a warm early summer's evening, and dusk was beginning to thicken. 'I feel so guilty,' he said.

'So did I, when I had my problem,' Sophie told him.

'I've been charged with dangerous driving.' His face was set in hard lines. 'And two of my passengers – my friends – were hurt.'

She gulped. 'How are they?'

'Michael is still in hospital with head injuries. He was unconscious for days and unable to sit his finals. Bob broke several ribs and his arm – fortunately his left so he was still able to write. He was badly cut and bruised, but I walked away with minor grazes.'

'When did this happen?' Sophie felt sick with horror.

'Two days before the exams started. It was to be our last fling before we got down to work.'

'Last fling? Does that mean you were out on a jolly?'

'Yes.'

'Oh, Lord, Ross, that makes it worse.'

'I know. I was breathalysed but found to be just on the sober side. They took me to the police station and took a blood sample, but that was all right too.'

'You'd been drinking?' Sophie could feel his horror as plainly as heat radiating from a hot plate.

'Yes. We'd been to a pub for a meal. Luckily I'd gone easy on the beer. The other two had had plenty to drink and we were all in high spirits.'

'What happened?'

'It was about eleven at night, dark and raining. I was trying to turn right at a crossroads. A heavy goods truck was coming towards me, wanting to turn the opposite way in front of me. Somehow I misjudged the distance and I ran into the truck. I think I was going too fast.'

'Oh my goodness!'

'It ripped the side off my car. It was a six-vehicle pile-up.'

She felt for his hand. 'Ross, I am sorry. It sounds truly awful.'

'Bob sat his final exams but he was in pain and not well. We both think we've made a mess of them.'

Sophie sighed. 'You don't know that yet, not for sure.'

'I'm pretty sure.'

'You'd both be shaken up. I know it's hard to concentrate on normal work when you're knocked off course by something like that.'

'I was shaking in my shoes, still am. Reduced to a dithering idiot. I can't get over what I did, and Michael – not able to sit his exams at all.'

'How is he?'

'Better, thank goodness. He's come round and is able to talk.'

'Well, that's something.'

'Yes, his mother came down to stay near him. I cringe when I think of all the trouble I've caused, and to louse up our finals . . .'

Sophie said, 'I didn't do as well in my A levels as I'd hoped. Disappointed my dad I'm sure, but I did well enough to go on to uni. You'll have passed. You'll be able to go on to Inns of Court.'

'That was the plan and I have applied . . . but I've been

having second thoughts for some time ... Mum thinks I might be happier going for articles, being a solicitor I mean. She's looking round for a firm to take me. Bit of a comedown all round, isn't it? Now you see why I'm in such dire straits.'

Sophie put a hand on his wrist. 'I felt in dire straits when I found I was expecting Melissa. But I learned one thing, Ross. Feeling sorry for myself did me no good. I had to pick myself up and get on with my life, make the best of my changed circumstances. Why don't you try that?'

He didn't answer.

'Don't forget,' Sophie said, 'I was aiming to be a barrister too.'

His dark blue eyes looked into hers. 'You're still going to do that?'

'No, I've changed my mind. I'm going to follow in the family footsteps and become a teacher.'

'Why?'

'I've been trying to teach Charlie and Gary and I've enjoyed it. Charlie resat two of his O levels and thinks he's done better, and ... well, my trouble has made me grow up in a hurry. I've got responsibilities – a daughter to bring up. I'll need to be with her when she has school holidays, won't I?'

'You're not thinking just of yourself any more.' Ross was frowning.

'No, Melissa has to rely on me,' she told him. 'You think this accident has pulled you down, but you're still in a very enviable position. You can have a career you'll enjoy. The very worst scenario is that you might have to resit some of your exams.'

He wouldn't look at her now. 'You think I'm making too much fuss about this accident?'

Sophie shivered. It was dark now; she'd grown cold as night fell. 'We're all affected differently by what happens to us,' she said gently. 'We all make mistakes. The trouble is, when you think you've made a bad one, it sets you back on your heels and you're likely to make another.'

When she stood up to go in, he said, 'Can I see you again? You seem very wise when it comes to facing up to trouble.'

CHAPTER TWENTY

BECAUSE ROSS had asked, Sophie popped in to see him. The first time it was a sunny day and she suggested he came with her and Melissa on their usual walk round the lanes. Then they had a spell of bad weather and she got him to push the pram to the village shop or collect Daisy from school. He seemed glad to have someone to talk to, and they ended up still talking back at his house or hers.

The following week, Mrs Salter invited her to have a salad with them at lunch time, and told her the walks were cheering Ross up and lifting him out of his depression. With the rest of the family out all day at work or college, she asked if Sophie would keep him company more often. She didn't think it was good for him to be on his own all day.

After that, Sophie took her baby down several times each week and Ross made sandwiches for them. In order to satisfy Melissa's appetite, she was supplementing her own milk with bottles. To start with, Ross had watched as she set the bottle to warm in hot water while she changed her nappy.

'Hold her for me, while I get rid of this.' Sophie had placed the baby in his arms, and her green eyes had studied the new face bending over her. Then a baby fist had reached up and grasped at the lock of hair that fell forward over his forehead. That made him laugh.

'Want to try your hand at feeding her?' Sophie asked, indicating the bottle. He did, but handed her back when she paused to take a breath. However, it had broken his reserve. Soon he was as fascinated with Melissa as everybody else.

When Ross's exam results came out, he was disappointed to find he'd been given a 2:2.

'What about your friend Bob? Have you heard how he did?'

'The same, a 2:2, but it's what he expected. Everybody was expecting better things of me,' he said mournfully.

'You're a graduate,' Sophie told him firmly. 'Lots of people would be glad to be in your shoes. Get your head together and get on with your career.'

He was frowning. 'It sounds as if you think I'm a wimp.'

'You don't know when you're well off. Charlie's over the moon. He got a two in O level maths and a three in English language. The whole family's thrilled to bits at what he's achieved, particularly me. I know how he's had to struggle to get this far and he's planning to take more O levels next year. Meanwhile, he's got a really good job at the Dog and Gun. He's going to be in charge of the kitchen some nights.' She took a deep breath. 'Your problem is, you've had it too easy up to now. It's made you expect everything the world has to offer will drop at your feet. I've had to toughen up, reset my sights, and you must too. Forget the past and concentrate on the future. We've all got to go forward.'

'No doubt you're very good for me,' he said dryly.

She smiled. 'Your mother thinks so.'

A few weeks later, Mrs Salter told Isobel they were all delighted to see Ross more like his old self. Sophie felt she was getting to know him better. He was opening up and could make her laugh.

'I'm very grateful to you, Sophie. I'd like to do something you'd enjoy for a change. How about us going out for a meal?'

'Lovely.'

'Is the Dog and Gun all right for you?'

'Yes, fine.'

'It's the easiest now I've no car.'

Sophie pulled a face. 'I'm taking driving lessons. Dad thought I should learn but I'm not finding it easy.'

'You'll be all right.'

'That's what Charlie says. He's taking me out to practise now he's got his licence back.'

Sophie was besotted with Melissa and often played with her for hours. Bathing her had become a game. The baby was laughing and kicking in the water as though trying to swim, but tonight Sophie had no time to play. She was going out with Ross.

It was the first real date she'd had since the break-up with Darrell. She still didn't want to get close to another man, but she'd made a friend of Ross.

Melissa chortled up at her as she dressed her in her night clothes. She was nine months old now, and Sophie was enjoying her even more now she was more responsive.

She took the baby downstairs to her mother, then as quickly as she could she changed into her best green and white striped dress and ran down to the Dog and Gun to meet Ross. She paused in the doorway, looking round for him.

He came striding across the bar towards her, looking eager and relaxed, his deep blue eyes probing hers.

'I've been watching for you,' he said. 'I've got a table out on the patio. Come on through. It's nice out there tonight.'

He was pulling out a chair for her when his hand brushed her bare arm. It made her jerk away; the thrill she felt was unexpected.

The patio was in the full evening sunshine. At the next table, Sophie noticed two girls appraising Ross. She could see they approved of him.

The pub garden was surrounded by high hedges, and there were tubs of flowers everywhere. At the far end, swings were provided for children to play on.

Sophie studied the menu. 'Charlie's working tonight, so we'll be sampling his cooking – his professional cooking, I mean. He's jolly good in the kitchen at home. He said he'd pop out and say hello.'

She thought Ross much changed. The bad accident he'd had had humbled him. He no longer acted like a superior being who could walk on water while the rest of humanity floundered against the current and got into trouble.

He smiled at her. 'I've had two lots of good news today. The best thing was a note from Michael's mother to say she's expecting him to be discharged from hospital next week and they think he'll make a complete recovery.'

'That's excellent news. How's Bob?'

'He's doing fine. The other good news is my father has asked one of his colleagues to defend me when the case goes to court and he tells me things are not so bad as I'd supposed. He's had the charge reduced from dangerous driving to driving without due care and attention. It carries a lesser penalty.'

'Good for you.'

'There had been an earlier accident in the same place when a tanker had spilled oil on the road. It hadn't been properly cleared up and all the vehicles skidded in it. That and the fact that I was breathalysed and found within the legal limit . . . well, it no longer feels as though it was all my fault.'

'Mitigating circumstances.' Sophie smiled.

'And it isn't just me. Some of the other drivers in the pile-up were also charged with dangerous driving.'

'There you are then,' Sophie said. 'It isn't the end of the world for you, after all. No need to worry about it.'

'I feel a lot easier.'

'Good. Did I tell you I've got a place at Liverpool in September to read English?'

'No. So you've changed your mind about studying law?'

'Yes, I think so. Helping Charlie and Gary made me feel . . . well, it would be more me. Dad still loves teaching, so it must be all right.'

He smiled. 'In this life it helps if you know what you do want. I don't think many of us do when we leave school.'

'But you always wanted to follow in *your* family footsteps and do law.'

'And so I am, though I've lowered my sights somewhat. I'm going to stay at home. I'm going to be a solicitor like Mum. She's found me a place. I'm to be articled to a firm in Birkenhead. When I'm qualified, I'll probably join her practice.'

Charlie was weaving his way through the tables to speak to

them. Sophie had never seen him wear his tall white hat and full chef's uniform before. He grinned at her. 'How did I do?'

'Great. We've both enjoyed it.'

'What did you have?'

Ross said. 'I had baked ham slice with pineapple. It was good.'

'I had steak and mushroom pie with chips. Couldn't fault it, Charlie. You've mastered cheffing. The angel cake was pure heaven.'

'You're very kind.'

They finished their coffee and Ross paid the bill. Sophie felt sleepy and satisfied. He took her arm as they strolled through the village. The lights were going out in most of the cottages.

They were passing his house. 'I'll see you home,' he said. It was less than a hundred yards further up the road. She'd left a light burning on her stairs, and could see the glow in the landing window. Her parents' bedroom lights were on behind closed curtains.

'Thank you, Ross,' she said as they approached the front gate. 'I've really enjoyed tonight.'

'So have I.' Suddenly, he flung an arm round her shoulders to pull her closer, and bent to kiss her lips.

Sophie felt the warmth of his kiss spreading through her. She was melting into his embrace when the spark of his passion touched her. She jerked herself away from him.

'I don't think I'm ready for this,' she said shakily.

'What's the matter?'

Sophie couldn't tell him. She'd sworn she'd never let another man touch her. Love wasn't worth the sort of risk she'd taken with Darrell. He'd really messed her up. She hadn't been able to make a decision about anything, hadn't known what she wanted. Her brain had gone to pot.

She was just beginning to feel she was getting over all that and was in charge of her life again. From now on, she was going to stay independent. Never again was she going to need a man as she'd needed Darrell.

Ross whispered, 'You can trust me, Sophie.'

She was looking for friendship but she knew he wanted more than that. She couldn't give it to him; she daren't.

It took him a moment to ask, 'You're not over that Darrell fellow yet?'

'Oh yes.' It came out in a burst. 'I could kick him to kingdom come and back.'

'Oh, Sophie!' He was laughing down at her. 'You know I've always had a soft spot for you.'

'I know.' Sophie sighed. She'd started to think she might have a soft spot for him. 'But . . .'

'You'll come to have a sandwich with me at lunch time tomorrow?'

'No, Ross, I can't.'

'I haven't ruined everything? I didn't mean to rush you.'

'No, of course not. It's just that I've told Charlie I'll go up to his place tomorrow.'

'You're in love with him?'

'No, no, I'm not in love with anyone. Charlie's a good friend as well as my cousin. In my darkest hour, he was the only friend I had.'

Ross stared down at her for a long moment. 'You've been that to me. A friend and a prop when I really needed one.'

Sophie nodded, then reached up and planted a kiss on his cheek, the sort his mother would give him. 'I want us to go on being friends,' she said, 'but I'm turned off somehow. I can't move on to anything more.'

He shook his head. 'After all you've said about striding into the future and forgetting past mistakes?'

'I know.' She let out her pent-up breath. 'How about if I come down with Melissa the day after tomorrow? Thursday?'

'Right. I'll see you then.'

Sophie let herself in and double-locked the door behind her. She couldn't think of falling in love with Ross or anybody else. She couldn't face another affair like the one she'd had with Darrell Marchbanks.

Hilary was feeling a bit low again. She'd suggested to Ben that they go out for a meal but he'd seemed less than keen and put her off. He seemed more involved with his flowers and his shop than he was with her and the family. Perhaps it was just that they were settling into middle age. Her boys were growing up and becoming independent; even little Jamie was thirteen now and hardly seemed to need her.

She told herself to snap out of it, she had plenty to be thankful for. Andy had achieved respectable A levels this summer and a place at Liverpool university in the autumn to study engineering. He even had a girlfriend. He'd met Amy at the typing class and she seemed a nice girl.

Charlie seemed to be knuckling down to his job at the Dog and Gun, though he still had to work split shifts, cooking both at lunch time and in the evening. He said he hated that and really wanted a nine to five, but he'd got his driving licence back and could be home in minutes on his motor bike.

Charlie had come home to find Andy driving round in her old car. She'd been afraid he might be jealous, but Andy understood it must be shared and Charlie drove it on his days off. For his part, Charlie seemed to accept that Andy's need was greater; he was not earning yet and soon he'd have to get from Prue's flat into Liverpool for his course.

Even Sophie seemed more settled. On a couple of afternoons each week, she came up to spend an hour or so helping Charlie and Gary with their studies, either on the patio in the sun or at the playroom table.

Charlie told his mother, 'Sophie's on our wavelength. She really keeps us at it. I think she's good at teaching.'

'That doesn't surprise me when both her parents are teachers,' Hilary said. 'Uncle Seb's school has a strong remedial class as well as a department for teaching dyslexics.'

Hilary was back in her stride writing short stories and decided she'd try her hand at a serial. She'd had to learn another technique, as each instalment had to finish on a climax, leaving the reader wanting to know what happened next and eager to buy the next issue.

It sold straight off, which made her ask herself why, if she could write a serial, she was finding it so hard to write a full-length book. She decided the problem was in her own mind. She'd grown lazy and let herself become bogged down in the housekeeping, worry about the boys, and the writing of short stories and articles.

She needed to pull herself together and really focus on *The Dog Days of Summer*. It was half finished, but with no publisher and no agent she'd lost the drive to carry on. It could all be a waste of her time.

On the spur of the moment she took out the manuscript and started to read it through. It engrossed her and kept her reading. She mustn't give up on it; it was too good for that.

She made up her mind to work through it and make sure it was the best she could do. Then she'd try sending it round publishers again. She felt it would put her back on the right track and give her the push she needed. Short stories and articles were put on the back burner, and she immersed herself in her book.

Sophie passed her driving test at the first attempt. Taking it, she'd been screwing up with tension, but somehow she'd managed to get through it without making any mistakes. She was ecstatic. Driving home afterwards, she said to her mother, 'I bet you're glad you don't have to take me out on practice runs any more.'

'I didn't mind, and anyway, Charlie did most of that.' Mum was almost as thrilled as she was. 'Dad and I have decided I should treat myself to a new car. This one's beginning to look ancient, but I've just bought it new tyres and a new battery, so it should do you for another year or so. You can have it as soon as I get my new one.'

'Oh, Mum! That's marvellous. Thank you, thank you.'

'If Hilly can do it for the twins, then I feel I should for you.'

'What sort of new car will you get?'

'Another Mini, I think. It's big enough for me. Let's call at Oak Tree House and tell them the good news.'

'Charlie will probably be there. It's his day off.' Sophie felt like singing as she pulled into the drive. She reached the door first and kept her finger on the bell. Charlie came running to pull it open.

'I've passed, I've passed, Charlie,' she screamed before he could ask. He hauled her inside and whirled her round in a victory hug. 'Thank you, Charlie, for your help.'

Andy had come up behind him. 'Congratulations,' he said sedately.

Aunt Hilly kissed her. 'Good for you,' she said. 'Well done. We're having tea out on the patio today. Amy's here and she's got something to celebrate too.'

Amy was a small, gamine-faced girl with a soft voice. She said with a shy smile, 'I've landed a new job as a shorthand typist.'

Sophie knew she'd been taking shorthand lessons at night school.

'I'll be doing secretarial work from now on. I start on the first of next month.'

'It's congratulations all round then.' Sophie smiled.

'It's what I've always wanted.' Amy was all smiles too. 'I hated working in that ironmonger's shop.'

'You've got to work towards what you want,' Andy said. 'Otherwise you achieve nothing.'

Sophie squinted into the sun and giggled. 'You sound like a self-righteous old man.'

Andy ignored that. 'I hear we'll both be starting at university in September.'

'Yes. Mum's going to give me her car so I can get there and back.'

Isobel said, 'I'm going to look after Melissa while Sophie's studying, but she'll want to spend as much time as she can with her. We thought it would be easier if she had her own car.'

'Judith has managed without one for her first year,' Sophie told them. 'But Ross says she's dying to be able to drive.'

The next time Sophie saw Judith, she asked her how she went into Liverpool.

'Mostly by train. I can get a lift to Hooton Station. There's a big car park there where you can leave it all day.'

'Perhaps you and me and Andy could go in together, use one car?' Sophie suggested.

Judith smiled. 'It would be difficult. Our timetables will be quite different, so we'll want to go and return at different times. And the students' car park is always overflowing. Even if you get there early enough to get a parking space you can still have problems. Students come in for lectures later on and block other people in by wedging their cars in wherever they can. My friends are always getting trapped. You might find the train easier.'

Sophie took a deep breath. It all sounded very different from anything else she'd done. She felt apprehensive and half wished she'd elected to stay at home looking after Melissa.

The start of Sophie's university course was on her before she felt ready. She was up earlier than she'd been for months, but it was still a rush to dress Melissa and get herself ready. On her first morning, Andrew had promised to call for her, drive her over to Liverpool and point her in the right direction, though his course was held in a different building.

Sophie took Melissa downstairs and put her in Isobel's arms. Walking away from her for the first time was like tearing herself in two.

'Don't worry about her,' her mother said. 'I'll take good care of her. Don't even think of her today.'

Sophie found that easier said than done. It seemed ages before she could concentrate properly, and get down to studying. She didn't have enough time for all she needed to do. The months that followed were not easy, but she hadn't expected them to be. She felt she coped only because her parents helped wherever they could.

She knew she relied on her friends for support; Charlie and Judith provided exactly what she wanted, but she continued to feel uneasy with Ross.

He made his affection for her very obvious. He often came to her flat and continued to invite her out for walks and meals. 'I love you,' he told her. 'I think I always have.'

To have him close could disturb her, and sometimes his touch made sparks thrill through her. To see him walking down the road to meet her, a tall slim young man in his prime, smiling at her, could make her stomach muscles contract.

When she'd first met Darrell Marchbanks he'd promised he'd teach her to enjoy his lovemaking. The problem now was she'd learned too well. Yes, all right, she'd missed it and still was missing it, but she was scared of it too.

She knew her affair with Darrell still cast a shadow over her. He'd used her and then rejected her. Never again was she going to risk that happening.

It was being at university with people of her own age, hearing them talk of their own problems, that made her realise she wasn't, after all, totally beyond the pale. What really helped was being on good terms with Marina Douglas, who'd had a termination, and now said she bitterly regretted it and wished she'd kept her baby.

In the Christmas holidays, Sophie felt able to catch up with her learning and her chores for the first time. She was getting used to being away from Melissa for much of the day.

Every day, Ross came to the flat to play with the baby and talk to Sophie. He kept trying to kiss her, and often she let him succeed. He could melt ice with his kisses nowadays. On

Boxing night he asked if he could make love to her. Sophie jerked out of his arms.

'I'm not going down that road again,' she said. 'If you want a girlfriend who'll let you do that, you'll have to find someone else.'

He held on to her hands. 'Don't think I haven't tried,' he told her. 'But nobody else will do. It's you I want.'

'It's no good trying to pressurise me.'

'That's the last thing I want to do. It wouldn't be any good if you didn't want it too.'

She said nothing, didn't move. Of course she wanted it, but . . .

'You can't get over it, can you? You were badly hurt and it wasn't just the baby you were left with. It's time you forgot Darrell and the wounds he inflicted.'

'I have.'

'No, Sophie, you haven't. You talked me into putting my problems behind me and moving on, but you don't do it yourself.'

'You got a small fine and a few points on your driving licence. I've got Melissa.'

'I do love you, Sophie.' She heard his gusty sigh but couldn't look at him. 'And I think you love me too. Would you like to get married? I would. Would that help you?'

As the emotional impact of his words struck Sophie, she felt a tear trickle down her cheek. The next moment his arms went round her and pulled her close. She had a little weep on his shoulder.

She asked, 'You're serious about that? Getting married?'

'Very serious. Do you want to? Will you?'

Sophie had to think about it. 'I don't want to hurt you . . .'

He straightened up. 'That sounds as though you're going to say no.'

'I'm going to say I'm not ready yet. My life seems so full. I feel as though I'm on a helter-skelter, always rushing to get the next thing done. I'd like to have more time to savour the idea of being married. To think of you and our future.'

'You can take all the time you want.'

'And then there's Melissa . . .'

'Melissa isn't a problem. I'm very fond of her, and I'd like to be a father to her. If you'd marry me, I'd adopt her legally.'

'Oh, Ross, you're bending over backwards. Don't think I'm not grateful, but . . .' She found it hard to explain. 'I feel because I got pregnant and had Melissa, the fun of being a teenager passed me by. I had to grow up in a hurry. I feel I've missed being young. I think I do want to marry you, but not yet.' Her body was telling her she needed him, but her head said no. She settled back in his arms. 'Here I am with a daughter and a flat of my own, yet I don't feel fully adult. I mean, I'm still a student. I've done everything the wrong way round. From now on, I'd like to do things in the right order. Could we leave getting married for a while? Perhaps until I've got my degree and got myself organised with a job. Would that be too long to wait?'

'It's a very long time, but if it's what you want . . .'

She smiled. 'But I am ready to love you. I haven't been thinking straight, wanting to put that off for ever.'

He smiled. 'I put it down to an emotional hang-up. Something you didn't realise Darrell had given you.'

She nodded. 'But not tonight.' There were precautions she needed to take first. She was going to get everything right this time.

Ross kissed her cheek gently. 'I want you to know that I'd never let you down.'

When they became lovers, Sophie thought she'd sorted herself out. She had a boyfriend she loved very much, and a gorgeous baby daughter. She was content with her life the way it was. She didn't want big changes. She felt safe this way, with Dad and Mum downstairs ready and willing to help.

CHAPTER TWENTY-ONE

HILARY SPENT all winter rewriting *The Dog Days of Summer*, keeping all the best scenes. She developed the characters and strengthened the tensions and renamed it *A Cliff to Climb*. She'd lengthened it and turned it from the literary novel she'd first envisaged into a full-length saga. She was pleased with what she'd done. The problem now was where should she send it to give it its best chance?

She drove into Birkenhead to go shopping and whilst she was there she popped into Waterstone's bookshop and bought a copy of *The Writers' and Artists' Yearbook*. As soon as she returned to her car she looked through the list of publishers. Many seemed to say 'Unsolicited submissions not accepted', or something similar.

She tossed it on to the seat beside her and set off for home. Right. She'd need another agent and must find one. She'd start at the beginning of the long list given in the *Yearbook* and go through them all choosing the ones who sounded most likely to take her on.

Once back home, Hilary sorted out a list of eight agents she thought might be interested in placing the sort of book she wrote. She gave as much care to the composition of the letter she meant to send to them as she had to any story or article she'd written for publication.

She told them a little about the book she had ready to send and asked if they'd read it. She listed all the work she'd already had published, her five novels and the short stories and articles. She would have liked to send a copy of the letter to each of the eight agents at the same time, but there were warnings in the yearbook that writers should deal with only one at a time. So she sent her letter off to the one at the top of her list.

While she waited to hear, she'd start retyping the first three chapters of *A Cliff to Climb* and prepare a summary of the rest of the story. It would all be ready to send as soon as she found an agent willing to read it.

Hilary decided a sensible next step would be to start planning another novel. For the next week, she went up to her study whenever she had a free moment and was pleased at the progress she made. Already the characters were coming to life and she was absorbed in the story.

Today, she suddenly realised she had only ten more minutes before Ben would be back for his lunch. She rushed down to the kitchen wondering what they could eat that wouldn't take long to prepare. Eggs? Long before she was ready, she heard Ben come in.

'Hi, Hilly.' He went on up the hall to wash his hands and brought back the morning post from the front door mat. 'There's one for you.'

'What?' She was stirring the pan of scrambled eggs mechanically, her mind still on her heroine's valiant efforts to shoot down an enemy plane in 1940.

'There's a letter for you.' Ben had already opened his new copy of *Horticulture Week*.

Hilary recognised instantly the print of her own typewriter. It was the self-addressed envelope she'd sent with her letter to the agent asking if he'd read her book. She ripped it open eagerly. It contained a printed slip regretting that his list was full and he was unable to take on more writers at the moment.

She swallowed hard and turned back to her saucepan. She wouldn't be discouraged. That afternoon she sent off a copy of the letter to the next agent on her list. Four days later, she received a reply with pretty much the same message. Stoically, she worked down her list.

It was March. The days were longer now and not so cold. It was late on Saturday afternoon, the day before Mothering Sunday, and the garden centre shop had been busy all day. The stock was being sold quickly, making the shelves look bare.

At lunchtime, Ben organised Andy and Jamie to help Stella in the shop. He was collecting together the next batch of plants to go on sale and with Rory's help was wiping both pots and plants clean and wrapping them in cellophane before stacking them on the low trolley beside him.

At this time of year the spring flowers always sold well. Primulas were cheap and made an ideal gift for children to give on Mother's Day, and this year the tulips and white narcissi were lovely. Ben was preparing some of the old favourites from the hothouse too, the roses, carnations and scented jasmine.

When the trolley was full, Ben asked Rory to take it to the shop while he went to see if he had any more plants about to burst into flower. He went outside, and saw that in the driving rain his pot-grown daffodils and tulips looked mud-splattered and messy. He should have brought them under cover earlier. They'd only be able to wrap from the glasshouses for the rest of the day.

'Dad.' He heard Jamie shouting to him. 'Dad, come quickly. Stella's had a fall.'

Ben felt his heart jerk. 'Is she hurt?'

'Yes, I think so.'

He followed Jamie to the shop at the double. Stella was lying on the floor.

Andy said in horrified tones, 'I told her to lie still for a moment. She's knocked the breath out of her body.'

The trolley full of plants had been pulled against a bank of shelves, its wheels covered with mud and dead leaves from the outside paths. Stella was struggling into a sitting position, and Ben saw that the sole of one elegant shoe was coated with the same mud. He tried to help her to her feet. She moaned, her lovely eyes hazed with agony.

He said, 'Jamie, run and fetch Mum. Rory, clean that mess from the floor before somebody else has a fall. Andy, you serve.'

With the help of a waiting customer, Ben lifted Stella to her feet and moved her into the rest room behind the shop. To have his arms round her like this, to be aware of her light but heady perfume, was a delicious experience. He was tingling all over.

They lowered her to a chair and almost immediately Stella's eyes closed and she would have slumped sideways and fallen again if Ben hadn't thrown his arms round her and held her in place.

'She's fainting,' Hilary said behind him. Seconds later,

she'd pushed him out of the way and was forcing Stella's head between her knees. 'What happened?'

'Mud on the floor and she slipped on it.' Ben's mouth was dry. Could Hilly know what he'd been thinking? He needed to keep his wits about him in future. He tore off a piece of paper towel and wiped the sole of Stella's shoe clean.

'Such dainty narrow slippers,' Hilary said. 'You'd be safer in strong walking shoes here, Stella.'

Ben asked nervously, 'Is she all right?'

'I don't know yet. The shop's full of customers. You go and help the boys. I'll look after Stella.'

Ben couldn't get out quickly enough. His heart was pounding in his chest. Within ten minutes he had the shop cleared of customers. The plants were a sparkling array on the shelves and the floor was clean.

He went back to the rest room. 'How are you?' Stella was able to sit unaided but her face was grey with pain.

Hilary said, 'I'm afraid it's a hospital job. She'll need to go to A & E. When she fell, she put her hand out to save herself. I think she's got a Colles' fracture in her left wrist here. She's hurt her back too.'

'Oh, dear. I am sorry.' Ben wondered if he dare offer to take her.

'Will you take her, Ben, or shall I?' Hilary's eyes met his.

'I'll take her. Had we better go right away?'

'Yes,' Hilary said.

'Sorry to be such a nuisance.' Stella's face was riven with pain. 'My mother will wonder . . .'

'I'll ring her and let her know what's happened, don't worry about that. I'll stay here till closing time, Ben, and cash up.'

He said, 'Let Andy do it. It's good practice for him.'

*

Ben and Hilary helped Stella into the passenger seat of the van. It still smelled new inside, but soon he became aware of her perfume. She sat supporting her left arm with her right, and saying little. He had to park some distance away from the entrance to A & E. He heard her swift intake of breath as she got out and knew she was in pain.

He was full of guilt that it had happened on his premises. She was moving slowly, and he put an arm round her waist to help her along. To have her this close made his senses swim. Stella seemed so much more fragile than Hilary, so much more exciting.

She had to wait to see a doctor and was given painkillers; wait again to be X-rayed. Yes, Hilary had been right: Stella had a Colles' fracture. So there was yet another wait until her wrist could be put in plaster.

Ben sat close and talked softly about his business, trying to distract her during the endless wait. Her pale eyes watched him, alert now. She said her pain had gone, and she certainly seemed more her usual self. Ben felt a tide of energy rush through him. His excitement was rising. He was thrilled to be sitting this close, feeling the warmth of her body. Feeling desire.

Her hair was usually well controlled in a big bun on the top of her head, but today one strand hung loose down the side of he face, making her look young and vulnerable.

She was led away at last to have her plaster put on. Afterwards she was given an appointment to return to outpatients a few weeks hence, and then they were free to go. She sat silently in the passenger seat nursing her arm.

'Shall I take you to my place?' he suggested. 'Hilly will be making supper. Would you like a bite to eat?'

'Thank you, but I'd rather go straight home,' she said. 'I feel a bit shaken up.'

'Of course. Does it hurt?'

'Yes. I'll take the pills they gave me and go straight to bed.'

Ben went home to relate the outcome to Hilary but he couldn't get Stella out of his mind.

A few days later, Charlie went over to see Gary and found his brother Paul had come home for the weekend. Paul was taller and stronger than Gary; he stood up straighter and looked fit and confident.

'Won't you be finishing at university soon?' Charlie asked.

'Just another few months, but we've got to sit our finals first. We're all slogging our guts out now.'

'But then they'll hold their university rag day.' Gary's eyes were shining. 'Paul's asking if we want to go over for that.'

'Me too?'

'Yes. Can you bring Gary?'

'You bet.' Charlie was up for anything that lifted him out of his everyday rut. 'If I can get time off. What's rag day?'

Paul grinned. 'It's great fun. We go round town collecting for charity. Everybody dresses up so you'll need to bring fancy dress. It's on a Saturday, but why don't you come on Friday night and spend a couple of nights in the flat with us?'

'I'd love to.' Charlie grinned. 'This time I'll do it right. I've got my driving licence and I'll ask Andy if I can borrow Mum's old car for the weekend.'

He began asking round family and friends for ideas on fancy dress. His mother offered him an old nurse's uniform and suggested he bandage Gary up as a patient. That was the best he could come up with until Wally offered to lend him a cat costume.

'It was used in a Dick Whittington pantomime back in about 1970, but it's none the worse for being old,' he said. 'I've worn it as fancy dress a few times.' When Charlie brought it home and tried it on, he was very impressed.

'What about the costume for Dick Whittington?' Gary asked the next time they saw Wally, but he shook his head.

'I've no idea what happened to that.'

'So what can I go as?' Gary demanded.

'Why don't you dress up as a schoolgirl?' Wally suggested. 'I've seen that done and it goes down well. And you're smallish and quite slight.'

'I hope you aren't saying I look girlish?'

Wally grinned. 'I wouldn't dare. The good thing is, it's easy to borrow bits of school uniform.'

Gary tried several girls he knew and managed to borrow an old-fashioned navy gymslip. Aunt Prue changed the ribbon round Sophie's old panama and embroidered a badge with the name St Trinian's on it. Sophie also promised to lend him her hockey stick and some make-up.

Charlie was looking forward to his second trip to Sheffield and made other preparations. He picked a generous supply of cannabis and dried it off in the airing cupboard in good time to take with him.

Sophie came home early on Thursday afternoons, and today she had taken Melissa up to her flat. Isobel set out alone to meet Daisy coming out of school. She was looking forward to the evening. Maureen Salter had invited her and Seb to dinner.

'Ross said he'd already arranged to spend the evening with Sophie, and Judith's going out, so it's to be adults only this time.'

Isobel had bought herself quite a dressy new outfit in the spring, a dress and jacket in mauve, and she hadn't yet worn it to Maureen's house. Usually, she took Maureen a small gift: a bottle of wine or a box of after dinner mints. It was some time since she had taken flowers or a pot plant, so she decided she'd walk up to the garden centre with Daisy and see what they had, and then call and see her sister. She knew Hilary wasn't all that keen on visitors earlier in the day because they interrupted her writing.

It was a pleasant sunny afternoon. Daisy came out of school bursting with energy and skipped happily along beside her. They entered the site by the back gate Ben had built in his fence to make a short cut for the twins when they'd started primary school.

They walked past endless rows of plant pots, each showing vigorous green growth. Isobel had to read the labels to find out what they were.

Rory and Gavin were busy weeding the neat beds of nursery plants. She stopped to chat to them, marvelling at how Rory had matured over the years he'd worked here.

'I want to do that,' Daisy told him. 'I want to help you weed.'

Isobel said, 'We don't have a lot of time. Wouldn't you rather come to the shop and choose a plant?'

'No, we often do that. Please, Mummy, can I weed?'

'Just for five minutes then.' Isobel knew she'd be quicker on her own. 'I'll come back for you.'

Rory was good with children and gave Daisy a small fork. Isobel heard him say, 'You must be careful to take out only the weeds and not hurt these big plants that we want to sell.'

Isobel carried on swiftly, taking the back way through the buildings into the shop. It was silent and deserted. She filled her lungs with the heady scent of freesias and the sharp scent all fresh flowers had. Everything was spick and span: the leaves glistened and the flowers were a riot of colour. Should she have the freesias, or one of those pink cyclamen plants? They were really lovely.

The room behind the shop where they made the tea was a little gloomy and she'd assumed it to be empty until she heard a sound. The door was open. She turned round, and saw the couple inside in a close and loving embrace.

Isobel froze in horror, but something alerted them to her presence and they burst apart. It was Ben! His face flushed vividly with guilt. Shock made Isobel feel weak at the knees. She supported herself against the door jamb and struggled for breath.

She'd had to accept Ben Snow as her brother-in-law, but she'd never felt at ease with him. Her heart went out to her sister.

Stella looked paralysed, and her face too was scarlet. She'd been caught in a lover's embrace!

Both Hilary and Mum lauded Ben as an excellent husband and father, but she knew better. He'd been her boyfriend until she'd introduced him to Hilary.

Isobel had never dared tell anyone that as a young girl she'd lost her virginity to him, and she was ready to bet that Ben had kept it a secret too. She'd loved him once but he'd dropped her like a hot pan to marry her sister. He'd betrayed her, so it shouldn't come as a great surprise that he'd betray Hilary too.

The shop doorbell jangled and Stella swept out to serve the customer. Ben moved too.

'Hang on, Ben, I want a word with you. You're two-timing—'

He pushed past her and went striding off in the direction of the potting shed. Isobel was left gasping. She set off more slowly to collect Daisy; then, remembering why she was there, she turned back to pick up a cyclamen plant. She paid a frosty-faced Stella for it without saying a word.

She didn't feel like talking to Hilary now. Her head was reeling. She didn't know whether Hilary knew or suspected what was going on in the shop.

Daisy had tired of weeding, and was clutching a bunch of mixed flowers.

'For Aunt Hilly,' she said. 'Rory helped me pick them.'

'Odd blooms that needed taking off,' he explained.

Isobel took one of Daisy's soil-covered hands in hers and knew she'd have to go to see Hilary as she'd planned. She found her sister making a pot of tea when she arrived and Jamie was home from school. He teased Daisy noisily.

Isobel wouldn't have been able to talk to Hilary about Ben even if she'd wanted to. Not in front of the children. She studied her and wondered if she knew already. Compared to the glamorous Stella, she was looking distinctly unattractive in a washed-out cardigan.

All evening, while they were out to dinner, Isobel felt haunted by Ben's betrayal of her sister. She had every intention of telling Seb what she'd seen but had no chance to talk to him until they were going to bed that night. By then it was getting late and they were both tired.

'Are you sure?' Seb yawned. 'I mean, if the room

was rather dark, did you really see him give her a lover's kiss?'

'I'm sure.'

She'd never told Seb about losing her virginity to Ben, so he wouldn't see him in the same light. Some secrets were better kept for ever.

He said, 'I don't think you should tell Hilly. I mean, if she doesn't know, wouldn't it be unkind?'

'I boil when I think of what he's doing to her.'

'You don't know, Izzy.'

'I saw—'

'You don't know how far the affair's gone. Or even if it is an affair. I think you'd be better saying nothing to either of them.'

Ben watched Isobel go over to the house from the safety of the potting shed. He could feel himself trembling. Life would never be the same if she told Hilary and it looked as though she was going to do that right now.

He should have had it out with her there and then. It had been his nerves that had made him take to his heels. What had she said? *Hang on, Ben, I want a word with you. You're two-timing . . .*

What was he going to do?

He'd always seen Izzy as a volcano that could erupt at any moment and thought it unfortunate she was Hilly's sister. In the first years of marriage he'd been afraid she'd tell Hilly they'd been lovers, but had eventually concluded that she wouldn't. To be on the safe side, he'd talked down his affair with Isobel to make it seem little more than friendship.

But this was very different. Stella was here and now, not an affair in his past. Ben went outside to the adjoining yard where he mixed his potting compost and sat down on the low wall that contained the loads of sand he bought in.

He ached with love for Stella. He thought about her all the time, except when his conscience was troubling him about betraying his wife.

If Hilary knew what was going on, she'd force him to choose between her and Stella. He groaned. It wasn't exactly that he was bored with Hilly, just that Stella was so much more exciting. She laughed more and sparkled with wit. She was very good company.

But Hilly was the mother of his sons and he didn't want to give up his family life. Besides, it was Hilly's money that had helped buy this business and he couldn't possibly give that up. He couldn't envisage life without his business, his home, or his wife and family come to that.

Ben sat there until he felt stiff and cold. He went to one of the hothouses to get warm. The plants had been watered and the skylights closed for the night. Eventually, he went to the shop, knowing that Stella would have gone home by now. She'd cashed up and locked up as usual. He could see the gate had been closed and locked.

Nothing remained for him to do except go home and face Hilly. He had to do that. He'd know right away whether Isobel had told her.

His heart was pounding as he let himself in through the back door. Hilary was in the kitchen stirring a pan on the stove, and he could smell curry. Relief flooded through him as he sank on to a chair at the table.

'Hi. You're late tonight. Have you been busy? You didn't come over for tea.'

318

'No, just got bogged down with chores.' He pulled himself to his feet again, knowing Isobel had kept her mouth shut. 'I'm shattered. I could do with a drink. How about you?'

The next morning, Stella was unlocking the shop doors when Ben went over to see her. With the morning sun on her face she looked drawn and stressed.

'What are we going to do?' she asked. 'Isobel saw us, didn't she?'

'Yes, but she hasn't told Hilly.'

'She did realise? She must have done.'

'She went to see Hilly but she said nothing.'

'I feel awful. Hilary's been so nice to me. Perhaps Isobel's waiting for the right moment?'

'Perhaps she won't tell her. Perhaps we needn't do anything.'

'Ben! She could drop us in it at any time. I feel as though I'm dithering on a knife edge.'

'I know.' Ben's face crumpled with anguish. He knew it was dangerous to let things drift on but he needed Stella in the shop. It had been her ideas and her energy that had made it so profitable. She'd given it sparkle and turned it into an Aladdin's cave of delights. Nobody else would run it so well or be so trustworthy. Besides, he wanted her here with him. What was he to do?

Isobel intended to do a big shop at the supermarket, but first she drove her new yellow Mini a couple of hundred yards to the village garage to fill up with petrol. She couldn't help but notice Ben's new van with the garden centre logo pulled forward in front of the little shop. She could see him inside paying for his fuel.

Isobel jumped out of her car and went to lean against the driver's door of Ben's vehicle. He came briskly out of the shop, but his step slowed the moment he saw her.

'Hello, Ben,' she said.

'Let me get in.'

'Not until you've heard what I have to say. I don't want you running away again.' She took a deep breath. 'I know you're having an affair with Stella Ingram. I want you to finish with her. Sack her, get her out of your shop.'

'Don't be daft. I need her to run it.'

'Find somebody else. All the time Stella's there, it's bound to go on. I know what you're like and I don't want Hilly hurt.'

'Get out of my way.'

'If you don't sack Stella, I'll tell Hilly what's going on under her nose.'

Ben tugged at her arm.

'OK, I'll go,' she said. 'I'll give you a fortnight and by then I want everybody to know she's been given notice.'

'I can't do that!' She could see a tide of anger running up his cheeks.

'You'll manage it, Ben. Otherwise Hilly will hear you've got a bit on the side.'

CHAPTER TWENTY-TWO

I T WAS SATURDAY morning. Tom was in a good mood, pleased the police hadn't charged him with speeding. Flora wasn't sorry to hear him say he'd be going out to a sale straight after breakfast. He gave everybody to understand he made money from the period staircases and fireplaces he bought and sold, but if he did, he didn't tell her how much or what he spent it on.

Flora hadn't made up her mind whether she should confront Tom about telling her a tissue of lies ever since they'd met, or whether it would be better to say nothing. After all, she had no proof. Some days she told herself it was just a groundless gut feeling on her part; on others, she was brimming with suspicion and distrust.

As a result she'd done nothing and they carried on in the way they always had, but it was a worry that wouldn't go away. Things had changed, though. She'd let Tom see she didn't believe everything he told her and he was asking for fewer luxuries. However, it didn't stop him drawing money from their bank accounts. Sometimes he told her what it was for but often he didn't. It made her examine the monthly bank statements more thoroughly than ever to keep an eye on his withdrawals.

Tom carried on just as he always had too, and together they preserved the daily routine. Life was still a round of bridge games, meals out, shopping trips and frequent visits to her daughters' homes.

Tom returned home today with the usual armful of parcels. 'Some little treats for you,' he said, laying his offerings on the table before her. Then he sat down smiling to watch her open them. He'd brought a bottle of expensive sherry, a box of chocolates and a couple of pieces of best fillet steak.

At one time such things had pleased her, but it no longer seemed a token of his love when she couldn't forget it was her money that was paying for these gifts.

She'd bought finnan haddock to have with poached eggs for their lunch, but she hadn't started to cook it until he was home.

'You know I'm not keen on finnan haddock.' He wrinkled his nose up.

'I'd forgotten. It looked nice in the shop.'

'It smells the house out.'

'It does rather. I'll open the window.'

'I tried to get a lobster. It's ages since we had one.'

'It's not that long since you brought one home,' Flora said. She thought them expensive and overrated; they never seemed to have much flavour. 'I thought you were going to a sale of old fireplaces, not round the shops.'

'I did both,' he said stiffly, pushing his haddock away half finished. Flora thought he had less patience with her these days when they were alone together, and he wasn't as quick to hide his distaste.

She washed up quickly and, wanting to get away from him for a while, she walked down to Isobel's flat for a chat. Isobel and Seb were clearing up after their lunch.

'Have a seat,' Seb said.

Flora sank into the cushions on the settee. 'It's so peaceful here.'

'Daisy's upstairs playing with Melissa. Sophie said she'd take them out for a walk later, to give us a restful afternoon.'

It was a cool damp day and neither Seb nor Isobel wanted to go out. Between the three of them, they put the world to rights and passed on the latest snippets of family news. Several hours later, Seb suggested they have afternoon tea.

'That would be nice,' Flora said, 'but I'd better go home and make a cup for Tom.'

'Why not ask him to come here?' Seb suggested. 'Izzy's been baking this morning. Shall I give him a ring? He can drive down while the kettle's boiling.'

Isobel set out the cakes she'd made on the tea trolley and Flora helped her take it into her drawing room. Tom arrived and Flora thought he seemed more relaxed. Almost immediately, he noticed the holiday brochures piled on a side table.

'Are you going away?' he asked Sebastian, picking them up and flicking through them.

'Yes. We have to book early to go during the school holidays. Sophie's suggested we go by ourselves for once and she'll stay home and look after Daisy and Melissa.'

'That's generous of her.'

'Sophie needs a break too,' Isobel said. 'She's worked hard this year. If we go away as a family we can all help with the little ones.'

'We're trying to decide between Spain and Greece,' Seb said.

Flora saw Tom wince, and knew he thought both a little downmarket. 'What about Florence?' he asked. 'There's lots to see there.'

'Nowhere I'd like better if Izzy and I go alone,' Seb said easily. 'But it's not suitable for children, not city sightseeing.'

'We'll be happy to sit in the sun with them,' Isobel said. 'Have you made any plans?'

'Not yet,' Tom said. 'I'm waiting for Flora to make up her mind.'

Flora felt she had to. Tom had brought home a number of brochures and almost every day he made new suggestions. Everybody seemed to think a two-week holiday in midsummer almost an essential. Tom would insist they went somewhere.

'Where d'you fancy, Mum?'

'Not Florence, Tom. It'll be hot walking about in a city like that. I'm inclined to say Lake Garda,' she said. 'Would you like that?'

He smiled. 'Of course, if you would. It will do us both good to have a break. Lake Garda would be nice. We can go to Florence another time.'

Feeling frustrated, Tom bit into another slice of walnut cake. He didn't fancy Lake Garda. He saw it as a Victorian resort, visited mainly by the elderly. He knew what to expect from holidays of Flora's choice. There would be boat trips round the lake, short walks round the towns and villages, visits to a tea room for a cup of tea. Hours would be spent on deckchairs in gardens.

A LABOUR OF LOVE

He wanted a holiday with a bit more go about it. He'd seen a camping trip across the Sahara advertised. Unfortunately, the days when Flora could be persuaded had gone. She had to be humoured now to keep her on course.

She was calling the tune more and more often. He was tired of dancing attendance on her and was finding it difficult to stay calm and loving towards her. She no longer responded to his hints and he was getting less and less out of their relationship. She used to be interested in sex, but trying to warm her up these days was like trying to pump life into a limp lettuce. She was an old woman and her body was a scraggy bag of bones. On some days she really got on his nerves, and he must never let her see that. Perhaps it was time to say goodbye?

If he could be sure of ending things with Flora as well as he had with Grace, he would, but he couldn't bank on having the same luck a second time. On the other hand, sooner might be better than later because she was growing more suspicious about everything, and therefore more difficult to cope with.

It was becoming more of an effort to hide his impatience and anger from her. Also, she was becoming quite miserly. She hadn't liked him treating himself to that cashmere pullover the other day.

He tried a slice of the excellent sponge cake and told himself he must keep an open mind and look for the right opportunity.

Flora walked home with Tom. It was a chilly evening so he lit the fire. She turned on the television set, but it was sport and didn't hold her attention. Tom was soon engrossed.

She found it hard to believe her romantic marriage was in any sort of trouble. Had she got it wrong? Was it all that bad? Perhaps she needed to try harder?

She'd tried to turn herself into the sort of wife Tom wanted; she made herself appear keen when he suggested going away for the weekend and pleased when he wanted to splash out on new carpets. She tried to prepare delicious meals for him to enjoy and never to argue, but she didn't always get it right.

It didn't help even if she did. She was beginning to think she'd be better off without him, but it was scary to think of being on her own at her age. Would she still be able to cope?

Flora was no longer sleeping well. She'd made such a mess of her life she felt she couldn't be trusted to make the right decisions. She knew she was becoming nerve-racked. Though she tried to appear her normal relaxed self with her family, she actually felt quite jittery.

The following week, Isobel came up after seeing Daisy into school. Flora was washing up the breakfast pots.

'Are you all right, Mum?' Isobel asked.

Flora was taken by surprise. She needed to talk about Tom but still didn't feel ready. Of what faults could she accuse him? Spending too much of her money? She'd tried that and it had made Izzy laugh. Her daughter thought they had more than enough and should enjoy it.

If Flora said she thought Tom had married her to get his hands on her money, it would sound as though she was having delusions. After all, they'd been together for more than eight years. She felt worn out and couldn't find the words to tell Isobel.

'Why?' was the best she could do.

'You seem on edge: not as happy as you were.' Isobel had picked up a tea towel and was drying the dishes for her. 'Is Tom all right?'

Izzy was hitting the sore spot. 'Yes,' Flora choked out.

'He's very good to you, squiring you round the way he does. Giving you a good time.'

All Flora's troubles were gathering on the edge of her tongue, ready to burst out, when there was a loud rat-a-tat on the front door.

Isobel said, 'I'll see who that is.'

Flora supported herself against the sink and took deep breaths. Izzy took Tom at face value. She wouldn't understand; she'd think Flora was making a fuss about nothing.

'It was the postman with a parcel he couldn't get through the letter box.' Isobel put it on the table.

'Books,' Flora said. 'Tom sends off for books to read.'

'Are you sure you're all right, Mum?' Isobel was frowning when she met her gaze. Flora couldn't stand any more.

'I haven't felt too well recently. My arthritis is playing up.' At her age there was always some frailty she could complain of. She sighed. Today she felt really old.

'Have you got painkillers?'

'Yes, love.' She kissed her daughter's cheek. Isobel had noticed so it must show. But what could Izzy do? 'I'm all right, really I am.'

'Your holiday should help. Not too long to wait now.'

'Yes. Nothing like getting warm sun on old bones.'

Flora hoped her holiday would settle her nerves and restore her relationship with Tom. She thought he was looking forward to it. He was certainly throwing himself into the preparations, buying a lot of new clothes for himself and

327

taking her round the shops and trying to persuade her to do the same. Tom had wanted to book the holiday himself rather than take a package deal.

'This way we can avoid travelling at night,' he'd said. 'And do things in our own time. We'll be able to see more of foreign parts.'

Tom could hear Flora moving about the kitchen. She was cooking their dinner – it was to be chicken pie. He sighed, and began fantasising about how he could end his relationship with Flora without giving up all the comforts it was providing for him. It must be a very different plan from the one he'd used to get rid of Grace.

That Flora was close to her family provided a problem he hadn't had with Grace. He didn't want her confiding her suspicions about him to one or other of her daughters, and she was always nipping off to see them or having them round here to drink tea. He needed to get on with it fairly quickly before she said anything to them. In the meantime, if she mentioned she was going to see them he made a point of going with her. But they lived close and often popped in without warning. So did Sophie, for that matter.

He could, of course, just stop putting himself out to placate her, let his impatience come gushing out. Tell her what he really thought of her. That would bring it to a natural end and have them heading for divorce or separation. He'd got his name on the deeds of this cottage, so he'd get his share of that, but not much else. Flora was really quite wealthy, but he'd not see much of her money if there was an acrimonious parting. No, better if he could end it in the way he had with Grace. Quicker too.

He was booking the holiday she wanted in the Italian lakes. At least it would get her right away from her family's prying eyes for the best part of three weeks. If only he could think of some foolproof plan to take care of her there . . .

He had brochures for several hotels at Lake Como. Mostly they were traditional guest houses that had been in business for more than half a century. Flora liked that sort of place, but there was one recently built hotel. It was said to have twelve floors and, although not exactly a sky scraper, it looked like one in the photographs. It was a luxury hotel of the first quality.

Tom decided to book a room on the top floor, with a balcony and a view of the lake. He had no firm plan in mind – he couldn't have when he hadn't seen the place – but it might give him a chance and he'd make sure he was ready for it.

The day Charlie and Gary had arranged to go to Sheffield came at last. They worked until half past two on Friday afternoon, when the lunch session finished. It took Charlie a while to take a shower and get ready. This time, they set off in high spirits, knowing they had full permission for the outing. It was almost eight o'clock when they got there.

Paul and the other three occupants of the flat gave them a great welcome. Roger had caught the sun on his bald patch, Frank had a new pair of rimless spectacles and Jim was growing his red hair and now wore it in a pony tail. Frank set off immediately to fetch an Indian takeaway for them all.

They had laid in a crate of beer to celebrate the occasion and were already in a party mood. When they'd eaten, Charlie brought out his large packet of dried cannabis and told them how he'd grown it in his father's garden centre. He'd found that snippets of information like that always enhanced his reputation.

'That's marvellous! You can grow all you want?'

'Yes, an unlimited supply. I'm practically farming it. I treat all my friends. Swop it for other things sometimes.'

Paul said, 'Don't give too much to our Gary. I don't want him hooked.'

'Give over,' Gary said. 'There's no harm in grass.'

'I've heard of students growing it in plant pots on window sills.' Paul laughed. 'But not farming it, not in this country.'

Charlie wondered if they'd call it farming if they could see his plants growing here and there round the copse. Perhaps he'd laid it on too thick?

'It's good stuff,' they told him. 'High class.'

But Charlie knew the grass that came from Afghanistan was in a different class altogether.

'Be careful with it,' Roger cautioned. 'You shouldn't be using it all the time.'

'Grass is all right,' Charlie said confidently. 'It's the strong stuff that gets you.'

'It's right to try it for the experience,' Paul agreed. 'But no need to go overboard with the stuff.'

'For me, it's an entertainment thing,' Roger said. 'Fine to have a bit of fun with it on special occasions. At the end of term and in the hols, but I wouldn't touch it in term time when I'm studying.'

It was late when they bedded down, but none of them cared. There would be time for a lie-in the next day. Gary commandeered the settee again so Charlie spread the remaining sleeping bag out on a mat and crawled in.

Late the next morning they had a real giggle as they donned their fancy dress outfits. Charlie helped Gary apply Sophie's foundation, mascara and lipstick. He looked a convincing girl when he'd finished, except for his feet. They were so big and wide he couldn't get them into women's shoes.

'Not exactly dainty and feminine,' Paul roared when he saw his robust black sandals.

'I've got to have something on my feet,' Gary protested. 'Do they look all right?'

All Charlie had to do was get into his cat suit and zip it up. It had a few bald patches in the fur and smelled of old age and damp, but it made him into a fine black cat.

Frank whirled round the living room wearing a top hat and tails. His striped trousers didn't fit very well. Once Moss Bros had hired them out for weddings, but they'd long since grown too shabby for that.

'Who are you supposed to be?' Charlie asked as he twirled a fancy walking stick.

'Guess?'

'A Victorian gentleman? Or is it Charlie Chaplin?'

'Champagne Charlie is my name,' Frank sang.

Paul was a pirate with a spotted red handkerchief tied round his head and large hoop earrings. Roger was a Red Indian chief with a headdress that was missing some of its feathers, and Jim was his squaw.

Charlie and Gary were given a supply of the rag mag to sell. They'd read out some of the verses and jokes the night before and thought them hilarious. In the bright light of morning, Charlie thought them less funny. He carried the tin into which the paying public would put the seventy-five pence for the magazine as a contribution to a charity for the homeless.

They were out on the streets in time to see the procession of lorries and floats that had been dressed to make still life scenes. There was even a boat full of students depicting a fishing scene. There were concert parties and glee clubs performing in the town parks and squares.

Everybody seemed to be having a good time, helped along by frequent stops in bars. Charlie thought it all good fun, though he found his cat suit rather hot on this warm summer day and it was a relief to slide his head out to have a pint.

He, Gary and Paul went in and out of shops selling the magazine and stopped everybody they could on the street. They did so well they had to fetch more copies from the students' union.

When the shops closed in the late afternoon, they made their way to the pub where Roger had suggested they should meet up. After a drink they went back to the students' union, where a room had been turned into an office and collecting tins were being handed in. A prize was being given to the team who collected the most and the atmosphere was electric as the contents were counted up.

Their group didn't win it. 'What a shame,' Roger said. 'No matter, I'm starving. Let's go and eat.'

Charlie felt very hungry as he fought his way out of the crush of bodies. Out in the town, every café and pub was crowded with students but they managed to get a table large enough for six in one and Charlie tucked into sausage, chips and beans, followed by Black Forest gateau. At closing time they staggered back to the flat.

'I've had a great day.' Charlie was full of beer, tired, and more in need of sleep than anything else, but as their hosts were settling down in the living room with more beer and a bottle of whisky, he and Gary had little choice but to join in.

'Have you got any of that homegrown left?' Frank asked, so Charlie got it out and rolled some joints. He felt better after a few drags. Jim started to play his favourite tapes to put them in a party mood. Gary looked terrible; his mascara had smeared. The Red Indian chief had lost more feathers from his headdress and the fake suntan both he and his squaw had put on their faces had smudged. By midnight they were all helpless with laughter.

Frank produced six tablets from a screw of tissue which he said he'd bought that afternoon and laid them out along the table, one in front of each person.

'What is it?' Charlie nudged his up an inch with his finger, which they all thought funny. Even funnier was Frank struggling to remember what he'd bought. That made them all offer outlandish answers – LSD, heroin, cocaine. Each new suggestion was greeted with hilarity and made them all double over with mirth. He watched Paul and Roger swallow their tablets and wash them down with whisky, but he slid the one meant for him into the pocket of his jeans. Some of them were high enough to think a double fix would be a good idea.

Charlie had heard Wally and his friends say they'd had some bad experiences on cocaine and heroin and he wasn't going to risk anything like that. He'd tried LSD and didn't like it. He'd had nasty side effects from that and it had made Gary sick.

The party in the living room was still going strong when he went to the bathroom. He felt dead beat and could hardly stay awake. Paul's bedroom door was open, and the beds looked inviting. The temptation was too strong. He slid under the eiderdown on Paul's bed, and heard another wave of raucous laughter as he drifted off to sleep.

'Hey, this is my bed,' Charlie felt Paul shaking him and tried to resist, but he was pushed unceremoniously on to the floor. Barely half awake he was aware of Frank stretching out on the other bed in the room, still mostly clothed.

He staggered to the living room, which was now in semi-darkness. Gary was already a mound on the settee. Charlie tripped over the sleeping bag intended for his use, rolled it out on the rug and pushed himself inside, two parts asleep almost before he'd zipped it up.

It seemed a long time later, well into the night, when he was disturbed by coughing from one of the bedrooms, followed by the sound of someone being sick. Gary was snoring softly on the settee above him and nobody came near the living room. After another shorter bout of choking and vomiting all was silent again. Charlie turned over and went back to sleep.

When next he woke, it was daylight and the sun was streaming in through the window. Gary was walking about in a state of undress and Frank was going through to the kitchen to put the kettle on. Jim was curled up in an armchair nursing his head.

Roger, fully dressed in a crisp clean shirt, looked bandbox fresh. 'How about egg and bacon this morning?' he asked. 'We've got sausages too. That should sort us out.'

Charlie wasn't sure. He sat up gingerly and felt for the clothes he'd thrown off last night. A white tablet rolled out of his jeans. He scooped it up with his things and half felt his way to the bathroom. Once there, he flushed the tablet down the loo, and decided a shower would wake him up and make him feel better. It didn't matter that the water was cold, in fact it was all the better. It pulled him round, made him feel almost normal. He'd brought clean clothes with him, and by the time he had them on the whole flat was permeated with the scent of frying eggs and bacon.

Back in the living room Gary was putting out knives and forks on the table. 'Where's our Paul?' he asked.

'The lazy swine.' Frank pulled a face. 'He's still in bed.'

He and Gary both made for the bedroom. Charlie followed more slowly and stood in the doorway.

'Come on, show a leg,' Gary roared. 'Rise and shine.'

'I hope you aren't expecting breakfast in bed,' Frank shouted, as he dragged the duvet off and flung it on the floor. 'Gary's starting to cook. Come on, get dressed.'

Charlie's attention was riveted on the half-clothed form on the bed. There was something odd about its position, head back rather than curled into a ball.

'Paul, what's the matter? Wake up.' Gary tried to shake him. It was then Charlie saw the stream of vomit over the bed. It wrenched at his stomach muscles. Gary's high-pitched scream split the silence.

The other two came rushing in. 'What's happened? What's the matter?'

'He's dead,' Frank said. 'Oh, God, he's dead!'

'No, no, he can't be,' Gary was wailing. 'Surely he's breathing?'

Charlie felt absolute panic ricochet round the room. 'He's got to be breathing.' He watched Paul's chest, but it didn't move.

'Get a doctor, quick.'

'No, get an ambulance. Get him to hospital.'

'How do we do artificial respiration?'

They were all crowding round the bed. Charlie was pushed back, but he could still smell that vomit. He felt his way to the settee in the living room and threw himself down. It came like a flash of light that he'd heard someone being sick in the night. Could that have been Paul? It must have been. It left him shaking with raw horror. He couldn't move. He felt sick with guilt.

Pandemonium broke out; nothing was real. He knew Roger was attempting to resuscitate his friend and that Frank had run out to phone for an ambulance.

Gary was crying and very distressed when the paramedic arrived. He started working on Paul but then said it looked as though he might have choked on his own vomit some hours earlier. He turned his attention to Gary, trying to calm him.

'What happened here? Did any of the rest of you vomit in the night?'

Charlie watched them all shake their heads. So it had been Paul he'd heard. Why hadn't he got up to help him? If he had, he might still be alive now. Instead, he'd let him choke and die alone.

'What had he eaten? Did you all eat the same?' They hadn't. They'd eaten in the pub and chosen different things from the menu.

'I think he had sausage and chips,' Roger said.

'Anybody else have that?'

Charlie said he had, but he hadn't felt sick at all. Not until he'd had a whiff of Paul's foul-smelling vomit this morning. He knew they'd all be dreading the next question.

'Were you taking drugs last night?'

'Yes.' Roger's voice was a whisper.

'What sort of drugs?'

'Paul had cannabis,' Charlie admitted.

'LSD too.'

The paramedic said, 'I'm afraid that means we'll have to call in the police right away.'

CHAPTER TWENTY-THREE

B Y THE TIME two policemen arrived, the paramedic had gone. The scent of fried eggs and bacon was still heavy in the air, although the food was now lying in pools of solidifying fat, cold and unappetising. Gary was lying on the settee with his eyes closed, while the three students stood around looking appalled.

Charlie's sense of horror mounted as he watched one of the police officers taking down all their names, home addresses, next of kin and telephone numbers. They asked about Paul. Charlie had to supply the answers. Gary was in a state of shock and completely switched off.

Then Charlie was asked to describe what had taken place yesterday evening. He didn't volunteer much and neither did the others, so it took them some time to get out the full story of the pub supper and the party they'd had in the flat. The questions kept coming, one after the other.

'Didn't any of you hear Paul being sick?' The police officer's gaze went round them all.

Charlie froze. He couldn't breathe. He couldn't admit he

had; they'd all blame him for letting Paul die. Nobody else admitted they'd heard him either.

'Who was sleeping here beside him?'

'I was,' Frank admitted, but he couldn't look at any of them.

A police surgeon arrived and was taken to the bedroom. He confirmed what the paramedic had told them, that Paul had died by choking on his own vomit at some time in the night and that once the police gave their permission, his body would be taken to the morgue.

Before going, he said that after a sudden death like Paul's there would have to be an inquest, at which they might be asked to give evidence.

One officer said, 'Next of kin will have to be informed. Do you want us to do that?'

Charlie hardly knew what to say. His skin crawled at the thought of telling his own parents, let alone Stella. But it would surely be a worse nightmare for her to be informed officially by the police.

'We'll do it,' he said. He made Gary sit up. 'We'll do it, won't we, Gary?'

Gary whispered, 'Yes.'

Then the questions about drugs started. Charlie had already thrown the packet that had contained his cannabis in the kitchen waste bin. He had to admit to it and one of the officers retrieved it, but he couldn't possibly say he'd grown the stuff. He could imagine his father's wrath if police officers went over his nursery beds inch by inch looking for it, flattening and ruining his crops. Charlie had boasted he'd grown it to the students here and Gary knew exactly where to find it. He was on tenterhooks in case they should drop a hint and alert the police.

Frank produced two tablets which he said were LSD and when pressed admitted he'd bought them on the street yesterday while the rag day carnival was at its height. He didn't know the name of the person who'd sold them.

Then Charlie's cannabis packet was pushed in front of him. 'I suppose you're going to say you obtained this in the same way?'

Charlie nodded, as he desperately searched for words. 'There were lots of pushers out on the streets yesterday.'

'I should warn you', the policeman's face was severe as he fixed his gaze on Frank, 'that you could be charged with possession.'

'Just for two tablets?'

'They're yours, aren't they? That could carry a penalty of up to seven years' imprisonment, or a fine, or both. For possession with intent to supply, it could be as much as life imprisonment and a fine.'

The colour was draining from Frank's face.

'You supplied your friends, didn't you?'

'I gave them a share. I didn't sell it to them.'

'Makes no difference in the eyes of the law, and the same applies to you.' He switched his eyes to Charlie.

'I've never sold any.'

'No, but as the law stands you could still get fourteen years' imprisonment for supplying your mates. That's what you did, isn't it? You brought it here and shared it round your friends? Supplying cannabis or marijuana carries somewhat lower penalties than LSD because the Dangerous Drugs Act classes it as less dangerous.'

As soon as Paul had been stretchered out, plain-clothed police detectives arrived and began searching the flat thoroughly. Charlie blessed the urge that had made him flush that tablet safely away.

When nothing else was found the occupants and their guests were taken to the police station. There they were fingerprinted and kept waiting for what seemed hours. Gary was still switched off but Charlie was in a state of panic and knew the others felt that way too.

'I wish I hadn't bought that LSD,' Frank whispered.

'I wish I hadn't brought the grass,' Charlie groaned. 'Thanks for not telling the rozzers that I was growing the stuff.'

'Better if you don't tell them too much. It can cause more trouble.'

'They said we might be charged', Jim said, 'for being in possession of drugs.'

'He was trying to frighten us,' Roger whispered.

'He succeeded,' Charlie said. 'He terrified me.'

Roger was frowning. 'Apart from those two LSD tablets and the empty packet that had contained cannabis, there was nothing else for them to find. I don't think any of us will be charged. Possession for one's own use isn't so bad, though they said we could still be arrested for it.'

'Have we been? Is this what being arrested means?' None of them knew.

Roger said, 'Those penalties are for the big pushers.'

'Or for growing it,' Charlie groaned.

Finally, they were led in front of a senior police office who gave them a sharp reprimand and a warning. He told them this would go on their records and if they were caught again they would end up in court. He listed the penalties they might then receive.

Once outside, Roger said, 'They must have decided it was

punishment enough that poor old Paul died after taking the stuff. At least, it won't be taken any further.'

Charlie had found it a very sobering experience. Gary had tears running down his face and they could all see how upset he was. 'Our Paul's dead,' he said. 'I can't get over that.'

'He was our friend too. To see him lose his life . . . just by being sick. It seems such a waste . . .'

By the time they returned to the flat it was after two o'clock. Charlie felt ravenous. He'd eaten nothing since yesterday evening and his stomach was rumbling.

'I'm starving,' Jim said, looking with distaste at the plates of cold egg and bacon. A sliced white loaf had been set out, still in its wrapper. He helped himself to a slice while Frank nibbled on a bit of limp bacon.

'I know,' Charlie said, looking at the two frying pans half filled with congealed fat on the stove. 'Egg and bacon sandwiches.'

He turned on the gas and started frying bread on one side. Then he warmed up the eggs and bacon and gave the first sandwich to Gary.

'I'm not hungry,' he said listlessly.

'Yes you are,' Charlie said firmly. 'You'll be fainting if you don't eat something. We all will.'

Once they'd eaten the others began to talk. 'I feel awful,' Frank said. 'I knew Paul was being sick. It woke me up, but I just couldn't move.'

'He woke me too,' Jim said.

'And me,' Roger admitted. 'He was making enough noise to wake the dead. Oh, God, I'm sorry, I didn't mean . . .'

'I just couldn't make myself get up,' Frank went on. 'Couldn't face cleaning up the mess of vomit. I thought it could wait till morning and I just slid back into sleep.'

'Paul's been sick before and come to no harm. Did you hear him, Gary?'

Gary shook his head, looking numb. 'Yeah, well, the living room's a bit further away, isn't it?'

Charlie was glad they hadn't asked him and that he wasn't the only one who could have gone to help Paul.

'How could it happen?' Frank wanted to know. 'I find it hard to believe.'

'He got stoned, didn't he?'

Jim said, 'I thank the Lord that our time here is over and we've sat our finals. It's too late for the dean to send us down in disgrace.'

Charlie gulped at his tea. The worst might be over for them but he felt a nervous wreck. The thought of telling Stella Ingram and his parents what had happened was worse than any nightmare, and they'd be expected back this afternoon. It was going to be the hardest thing he'd ever done and it was no use expecting Gary to be much help.

He collected his things together and got Gary in the car. Down the road, he pulled up by a phone box. He needed to warn them there'd been a disaster before he got home. He couldn't walk in and tell them from cold that Paul was dead. He'd have preferred to talk to his father, but if he rang the shop he was afraid Stella would answer and he couldn't risk that. It would be safer to ring the house and speak to his mother.

As he heard the phone ringing in the kitchen at home, he closed his eyes and tried to formulate the words to impart the terrible news.

'Hello.' It was Andy's voice. Charlie had forgotten it was Sunday and he might be there.

'Andy, I want to talk to Mum.'

'She's writing upstairs. You know she doesn't like being disturbed. Can't it wait till you get back?'

'No. I—'

'You won't be late, will you? I want the car to take Amy out tonight.'

'Andy, listen, will you? I want you to tell Mum that something terrible's happened. Paul is dead.'

'What? What was that?'

'Paul. Gary's brother.'

'I know who he is. What's the matter with him?'

'He's dead. Died in the night. Break it gently.'

'I'd better get Mum down.'

'It's too late now, I've no more change. Just tell her. Look, I'm still in Sheffield. We've been held up by the police. It'll take me three to three and a half hours to drive home from here. If that's too late for you, I'm sorry. Have you got that?'

'I don't understand. Did you have an accident?'

'It happened in the flat during the night. Gary and I are all right. Just tell her, OK?'

'But my God – dead did you say?'

'Yes.' The line went dead. Charlie dropped the receiver back as though it was red hot. At least he'd given them some warning. He got back into the driving seat and slammed the door.

Gary lifted a grief-stricken face. 'I'm never going to touch drugs again,' he said. 'Not any sort, not ever.'

Charlie took Gary home with him. As he drove through the gates and pulled up by the front door, it opened and his parents came out to meet him. He knew they'd been watching for him.

Their faces were grim. 'What's all this about?'

'Paul,' Charlie said. 'He died last night.' There was no easy way to say a thing like that. It started Gary's tears again.

'Come inside and tell us what happened,' his mother said, putting an arm round Gary's shoulders. Andy and Jamie came rushing out of the playroom. 'What's happened, Charlie?' they chorused. He almost burst into tears at that.

'Jamie, you go upstairs,' Ben said.

'Oh, Dad! I'm not a baby. Why shouldn't I know?'

Hilary said grimly, 'Let him stay. He's going to find out anyway.'

Once in the sitting room Ben said to Gary, 'I didn't know what to tell Stella – your mother. Without any details it was difficult. I've told her there's been an accident in Sheffield but not that Paul died. She went home when the shop closed and I told her we'd go over as soon as we had more news. So what happened, Charlie?'

Charlie pulled himself together and started to recount the tragic events of the weekend while Gary sniffed into his handkerchief. He didn't have to mention drugs. Mum suddenly straightened up and barked at him, 'Were you taking drugs?'

Charlie was guilt-stricken but had to say yes.

'All of you? What exactly did you take?' He could see her agonising. 'After all I've said to you about the risks. You don't know what you're buying. Street drugs are not sold in measured doses as they are from a chemist.'

Charlie admitted he'd provided their cannabis but not that he'd grown it himself. Neither did he mention there were forty or so healthy specimens of *Cannabis sativa* thriving a short distance from Dad's nursery beds, or that a large bundle of leaves was presently drying in Mum's airing cupboard. They were horrified and shocked enough as it was.

His father gasped, 'What you boys get up to!'

Charlie told them everything else: that they'd received an official police reprimand and a warning for possessing drugs. He had difficulty holding back his tears as he told them about the need for an inquest, that he might be called to give evidence and that it would be in Sheffield. He didn't want them to have any more nasty surprises.

Andy was sympathetic. He patted him on the back and murmured, 'You must have had a terrible time. Poor Paul.'

Charlie blamed himself. He'd helped to cause Paul's death by providing such a generous supply of cannabis. He felt gutted.

His father stood up. 'Right, well, we'd better take Gary home and break the terrible news to Stella.'

'Me too?' Charlie asked. He couldn't bear the thought of going through it all again.

'Yes, of course, you too.'

Ben felt sick. He knew he'd be expected to do this, but he didn't know how. He wanted to protect Stella, comfort her, not bring news of her son's death.

'D'you want me to come too?' Hilary asked. She was already chewing at her lip, which was a sign she was upset.

'I don't know.'

Really he didn't want her there. Under stress, Stella might seek the comfort of his arms, and he was afraid their relationship would be made clear. But Hilary was good at coping with disasters and Gary and Charlie would be there anyway.

'Yes, you better had. You'll be a help.'

It wasn't far but Ben felt too stretched to walk. He drove them there in the old car Charlie had left at the front door.

Stella looked shocked to see four of them on her doorstep. She was white-faced and shaky as she opened her arms to Gary. Ben knew she was expecting the worst as he followed her into the front room. He was glad to see Stella's mother was here. She saw everybody had a seat, but looked pale and anxious too.

'Can I make you a cup of tea?'

'No thank you,' Ben said, sitting as far away from Stella as he could. Gary was sitting beside her on the settee. She had one arm round his shoulders and pulled him closer now.

'I thought you were going to have a good time this weekend?'

Hilary was sitting on Stella's other side. She put out a comforting hand to her.

Ben cleared his throat. 'I'm afraid we have some very bad news for you.'

'About Paul? He's had an accident? He's hurt?'

'I'm very sorry, Stella. He's dead.'

She gave a little whimper of distress and stared at him, her mouth open in disbelief. 'Paul's dead?'

'He's dead?' his grandmother echoed, flooding with tears. 'But he was so well.'

'How?' Stella asked.

Ben said, 'Come on, Charlie, tell them what happened when you all got back to the flat last night.'

Charlie was fidgeting on the chair next to him. He felt agonised, his cheeks were crimson and he was staring down at his feet as he got the terrible story out.

It was Hilary who folded her arms round Stella and on whose shoulder she sobbed. Ben noticed that Charlie sobbed too and was glad to see him showing remorse.

Charlie would have liked to go straight to bed when he got home, but his mother made him join them for supper. It was fish pie, which was not his favourite dish, but none of them had any appetite tonight.

Charlie felt exhausted. He went upstairs as soon as the meal was over and set his alarm clock for six in the morning. He put it under his pillow so it wouldn't waken anyone else. It seemed hours before he got to sleep.

If only he'd got up last night to make sure Paul was all right – if only somebody had. Choking on his own vomit! He must have been as high as a kite, not to wake up when he was being sick. The doctor had said it would have been easy enough to save him if only one of them had been with him at the time.

When the alarm went off, Charlie got dressed quickly and went out to the airing cupboard on the landing. He removed all his drying cannabis leaves and took them out to Dad's compost heap. The nursery produced a good deal of waste green matter which was left till it turned to mulch, then dug into the soil again to enrich it.

It was a cool grey morning. There was nobody about; Rory and Gavin didn't start work till eight o'clock. Charlie crumbled his drying cannabis on top of the compost and pushed it down out of sight.

Then he walked round the football pitch and the shrubbery pulling up all his plants. He took them to the compost heap too and tore them to bits before mixing them in and making sure no fresh green leaves were visible. He was never going to take drugs again, or encourage other people to do so.

He wished he was more like Andy. Charlie felt he needed to change everything in his life. In particular, he needed to change his friends. He wanted no more to do with Wally. He'd give him his cat suit back, but he'd stop biking out to pubs to drink with that gang.

When he was satisfied he'd destroyed all his drugs and hidden the evidence, he went home and had a shower. He wasn't expected at the Dog and Gun until ten o'clock, but he'd have to be in a fit state to work by then.

It was days before Charlie's stomach stopped churning. Not only had he known Paul well, he was his best friend's brother. He even knew his family – his mother, for heaven's sake, had worked in their shop for years. Gary was walking round looking like a ghost.

Paul's death was like an explosion. The news and the horror spread in ever widening rings through the pupils past and present at Dryden Street School. The school had been proud of him, an able pupil who'd gone to university and was expected to do well in life. In the neighbourhood, the youth club and the garden centre, the name Paul Ingram was on everybody's lips. Many said it was unbelievable that he would touch drugs of any sort.

Charlie was ashamed and full of guilt. Everybody knew he'd been with Paul at the time; everybody knew he and Gary had taken drugs too.

CHAPTER TWENTY-FOUR

ISOBEL WAS shocked to hear of Paul Ingram's death. Before it had happened, she'd been itching to take revenge on Stella; she'd wanted to see her being thrown out of the job she clearly enjoyed, but the death of her son was so unexpected and so terrible it changed everything. The following evening, she went up to Oak Tree House with Sophie and Melissa.

She found Hilary cooking in the kitchen and said, 'I hope Charlie isn't taking it too hard.'

Moments later they heard Sophie's voice from the playroom. 'There was an article in our paper this morning about drug abuse in our universities. You've done it this time, Charlie.'

Charlie's groan was audible. 'Even worse, in the *Liverpool Echo* there's a report on Paul's death, and a whole lot more about us using drugs. It's really spreading the news, isn't it? Making sure everybody knows what we did. Everybody's talking about it.'

'It'll blow over, Charlie. Keep your head down for a while until the neighbours forget.'

'I'm never going to forget it,' he said with feeling. 'I don't know how any of us will get over this.'

Hilary said, 'Poor Stella. Ben says she's devastated by her son's death. He's had to give her time off.'

'What a shock it must have been for her.'

Isobel couldn't help but feel sympathy for Stella. She'd delivered an ultimatum to Ben about sacking her, but now the time she'd set had passed and she'd not carried out her threat to tell Hilly.

It seemed Stella was not working in the shop any more, but Isobel knew she lived nearby and gathered from Hilly that both she and Ben were keeping in close touch. She decided she'd wait to see what happened. If things looked like settling back into their old routine, she'd remind Ben they must not. She wasn't going to let him get away with it.

Isobel knew Saturdays were always busy in the garden centre. Almost a month later, she went up to the shop late one Saturday afternoon just before it closed. She took up a casserole and an apple pie, knowing that over the past month Hilary had had to put aside her writing in order to spend time in the shop.

'For your supper,' she said. 'Mum made them. We know how busy you are and want to help where we can.'

'You're both very kind. Tell Mum I'm grateful.' Hilary lifted the lid and sniffed at the casserole. 'Lamb. Smells lovely.'

'Mum says it just needs warming through.'

Earlier in the week, Isobel had cooked and shopped for Hilary too. She felt sorry for her sister, afraid she was about to be deserted by her husband. 'How are you?'

'Shattered,' Hilary said. 'It's hard being on my feet all day in the shop. It would be a real treat to sit at my desk again. I hope Stella comes back to work soon.'

Isobel had heard Ben ask the family to help Stella in any way they could. Charlie had taken time off work to drive her and Gary back to Sheffield on two occasions. Flora had suggested she and Isobel should help Stella and her mother cater for the funeral tea. Isobel had done so, feeling she had to forgive her for giving Ben lovers' kisses. Anyway, there was no way she could explain her reason for refusing help now.

Ben left Andy and Jamie to run the shop so the rest of the family could attend the funeral. It attracted an enormous crowd. The sombre sadness of such an unnecessary death caught in Isobel's throat. Paul had been so young and healthy, with so much of life in front of him. Hilary told her Charlie had taken it hard, but so had Ben.

'Of course, it gives Ben more work too. I can't manage the shop by myself as Stella did.'

This afternoon, Hilary was getting out the mop to run it over the shop floor and Ben had started to cash up when the shop doorbell pinged. Stella came in slowly.

Isobel thought she looked ill. She'd lost her vitality and the fresh bandbox look they'd all admired. 'How are you, Stella?' she asked.

Hilary said sympathetically, 'Come to the back, and I'll put the kettle on. We'll have a cup of tea.'

'No thanks, Hilly. I've just come to tell you', she was looking at Ben as though he was the only person there, 'that I want to give a month's notice.'

Isobel was riveted. It looked as though things would work out as she'd wanted after all.

'No, Stella.' There was no mistaking the intimacy between

them. 'No, don't do that. How will I manage without you?'

She shook her head again. 'I've put my house on the market. It's full of memories, good and bad, of Paul and Trevor, my ex-husband. I want to get away, right away, and start afresh somewhere else.'

'Don't be too hasty,' Hilary cautioned. 'Think it over first.'

Isobel wanted to wrap her arms round Hilary and say, *Don't stop her. Your world will be safer if she goes a long way away.*

'My mother's wanted to go back to live in Windermere for a long time. She was brought up there and still has family nearby – a sister she's very fond of. It's a beautiful place and there are plenty of hotels where Gary could find work.'

Isobel couldn't take her eyes off Ben. He turned and met her gaze. She saw his chin go up and he turned his back on her.

'I don't know what to say, Stella,' he said slowly. With an agonised gasp he added, 'You must do what you think is right for you.'

She said, 'I think it has to be this way.'

As soon as the shop door closed behind her, Hilary said softly, 'I feel so sorry for Stella. She seemed so settled in her job, said she enjoyed it. I'm sure the best thing for her would be to stay here amongst her friends and keep herself busy.'

Isobel sighed with relief and was glad she hadn't told her sister what she'd seen. Hilly didn't realise how lucky she was that Stella had decided to move on. It looked as though she intended to make a clean break with Ben. Much better that Hilly needn't know.

Hilary was worried as she and Ben walked across to the house after locking up the shop for the night.

'Who is going to run the place if Stella leaves?' she demanded. She was afraid she'd be doing it for quite a bit longer.

'We'll find somebody.' She knew Ben was trying to placate her.

'I could ring round the girls who used to come in part time, Sarah or Molly might like to come back,' Hilary suggested.

'Part-timers are no good now. I'll advertise in the local paper. We need a woman who's used to managing a shop on her own.'

Hilary was more bothered about the short term. 'The summer holidays are nearly here. Andrew and Jamie will be able to lend a hand then.'

She went straight to the kitchen to put the casserole in the oven to heat through. As she scraped some new potatoes to go with it, she thought about the book she'd written and had ready for publication. She'd pondered on it in the shop in quiet moments and found it took her mind off more pressing worries. Not that anybody in the book trade seemed interested in it.

Ben opened a bottle of wine to have with dinner. 'To cheer us up after a difficult day,' he said. He seemed even more fed up about losing his shop manager than she was.

Andy offered to give a hand in the shop without being asked. 'I can see Dad's a bit worried about having nobody,' he said.

Hilary sighed. 'Not as worried as I am. I'm his usual backstop.'

When Hilary had heard from four of the agents she'd picked out and none had wanted to read her book, she decided she'd type four more letters and send them all off at the same time.

It seemed unlikely she'd have four agents clamouring to represent her.

As she was coming to expect, the four stamped addressed envelopes started coming back. One came yesterday, and this morning she was heading upstairs to start writing when she saw another on the mat. She tore it open, expecting another printed slip. Instead, it contained a scribbled note asking her to send the first three chapters of her novel. The words *I'll be pleased to look at it* leaped off the page.

Hilary laughed out loud as she tried to decipher the name at the bottom. It was a jagged line followed by something vaguely like Mainwaring.

She dashed upstairs to her study. She'd prepared the chapters some time ago. All she needed to do was put them in a large envelope and type a covering letter. Then she ran through the garden centre to the village post office and had them in the post within an hour of receiving the note.

Now she had to wait again and wonder whether she'd get the first three chapters back or whether Ms Mainwaring would ask to see the rest of the book. In the hope that she would, she got it out and put it on top of her desk.

Then she tried to get on with the new book she'd started and to dismiss the buzz of hope she had every time she thought of *A Cliff to Climb*.

Four days later a postcard came, asking her to send the rest of her novel. It was signed Emilia Mainwaring. After that the buzz of hope became a roar, and she could think of little else. She was on tenterhooks about it for a week, and then while she was mopping the kitchen floor the phone rang.

'Emilia Mainwaring here. Is that Hilary Snow?'

Hilary's knees suddenly felt weak. 'Oh, yes. Hello.'

'I like your book *A Cliff to Climb* very much. I'm going to try to find a publisher for it.'

'Oh, thank you. Thank you.'

She asked if Hilary was writing another and how near completion it was. Hilary felt as if her brain had turned to porridge. All she could register was that an agent was actively seeking a publisher on her behalf. She didn't know how many times she said 'thank you'.

When she put the phone down, she went looking for Ben to tell him, but he had a rep with him and was discussing fertilisers. Then she tried to ring her mother but she and Tom were out, so she released all her excitement about it to Isobel.

It was only when she went into the kitchen to prepare a salad for lunch that she found the mop and bucket still standing there and the floor only half cleaned.

Isobel was now beginning to enjoy looking after Melissa, who was usually a happy and contented child. She was beginning to say a few words and was quite good company. On Wednesdays, Sophie had no lectures in the afternoon and was home in time to share a bite of lunch with her.

Charlie usually called for her after his lunchtime shift at the Dog and Gun. He was studying for two more O levels, biology and geography, this year and Sophie was helping him.

Through her kitchen window, Isobel saw Sophie swing herself on the back of Charlie's motor bike to roar off to Oak Tree House, and thought it was good for both of them.

She had a quiet afternoon, and then when Melissa woke up from her afternoon nap she took her out in the buggy for some fresh air. On the way back she met Daisy coming out of school. She was cutting chips for supper when Charlie dropped

Sophie off on his way back to work in the late afternoon.

'How are they all up at the garden centre?' Isobel asked.

'Still battling with the problem of finding a replacement for Stella.' Sophie went straight to Melissa and picked her up. 'It seems they can't find anyone to work every weekend as she did. Aunt Hilly's been round to ask Stella to fill in for the odd weekend.'

'Is she going to?' Isobel asked warily.

'Yes, until she leaves for the Lake District.'

'Really?' Isobel wasn't pleased.

'Ben's found a woman to work the five weekdays. He was showing her round, but he says he doubts she'll last long.'

'What's she like?'

'Quite old, forty something. Her name's Ruby and she used to work at B & Q. Stella's going to come in this Monday to show her what to do. Aunt Hilly hopes Ben will be able to manage without any more help from her.'

Isobel was anxious. 'But Stella coming back is only temporary, until she leaves?'

'Yes. They're going to advertise the weekend job again next week.'

Isobel told herself she had no need to worry. It still looked as though Stella would go soon. She had better things to think about.

'The tickets for the cross-Channel ferry came this morning,' she said.

'Great.' Sophie opened the envelope to see them. They had decided on a fortnight's family holiday in Brittany. Sebastian had booked a hotel and he wanted to drive over so they would have the use of his car. 'I hope I haven't forgotten all my French.'

'You won't have.'

Sophie and the children needed a holiday. When they returned, she and Sebastian would have another few days in Anglesey with Hilary and Ben.

Ben found it difficult to take holidays away because he never wanted to leave the business for long. This year, there was also the problem of keeping the shop open in his absence. Hilly had persuaded him to take a few days while Andy and Jamie were on their summer breaks. They should be able to cope with the help of the new woman. Anglesey was to be an adults only holiday, a complete rest. As Sophie would also be on her long summer vacation, Isobel and Seb were going to leave Daisy with her.

'Not long now before we all break up,' Sophie said.

'I'm looking forward to it.' Isobel stretched lazily. 'Not having to get up early to make breakfast for Dad and Daisy before they go to school.'

Two weeks later on Saturday morning, Sophie arrived at Oak Tree House to find an excited family uproar going on in the kitchen.

Aunt Hilly's cheeks were scarlet; she was ecstatic. 'My book has been accepted. I have a new publisher. They love *A Cliff to Climb* and want to know about my next one.'

Sophie joined in the chorus of congratulations. 'That's marvellous, Aunt Hilly. Well done!'

'I'm late.' Ben hurriedly kissed her cheek. 'I'll have to rush – the shop should be open by now. Shall we go out for dinner to celebrate? I'll book something.'

'Lovely,' Hilary sang out. 'I'm going up to work on my next book.'

The kitchen emptied. Charlie led the way out to the patio. 'I thought we might as well be out in the sun on such a lovely morning.' He already had his books open on the table. Sophie set about taking him through some written work he'd done earlier.

Gary was later than usual. When he arrived he took two gift-wrapped packages out of his bag.

'These are for you, Sophie,' he said. 'To thank you.'

'Prezzies when it isn't Christmas? Lovely.' She smiled at him. 'You didn't have to.'

'You've helped me a lot. Been very kind.'

'Chocs. A huge box, too. Thank you. You've put Melissa's name on this parcel, but I'm going to open it. I'll be consumed with curiosity if I don't.'

Charlie watched her take off the wrapping paper. It was a small soft toy, a pink rabbit.

'She'll love it, Gary.'

He said awkwardly, 'The label says it can go in the washing machine, so you can keep it clean for her.'

She nodded. 'Thank you.'

'If the teachers at school had treated me like you do, I reckon I'd have learned more.'

Sophie wanted to preen. He felt he'd learned from her! 'I've treated you and Charlie exactly the same – just as I'd want to be treated in your position.'

'That's what I mean,' he mumbled.

Charlie's heart was heavy. 'I suppose this is the last time you'll be coming, Gary?' Over the last weeks, he'd heard the Ingrams' house had been sold and they were packing everything up.

'We move to Windermere on Monday,' he said. 'The removal van will be at the door at eight in the morning.'

'Are you glad you're going?' Sophie asked.

'I think so. We're all missing Paul and it will be a new start for us.'

'I'm going to miss you,' Charlie said miserably. 'I wish you weren't going.'

He'd not had a night out with Wally and the gang since he'd come back from Sheffield, because he knew they'd be passing drugs round and he'd have to refuse. As it was, Wally came into the Dog and Gun and asked for him, wanting to buy some of the cannabis he'd been growing. He'd heard about Paul's death but still found it hard to believe Charlie had trashed the whole of his crop.

Now Charlie pushed his books away impatiently. 'I'm fed up to the back teeth. When you go, Gary, I'll have no friends left.'

Sophie put a hand on his arm. 'There's always me,' she said softly.

Charlie sighed. 'You're always going off with Ross Salter these days.'

'Shall I ask him if I can bring you too? We could make up a foursome with Judith.'

Charlie pulled a face. 'Andy said the same. He asked Amy to bring a friend along.'

'Did you have a good time?'

'We went to the pictures and then for a drink. I didn't like the girl Amy brought. I think she took against me.'

'Well, you know Judith.'

'Yes, since primary school. A bit toffee-nosed, d'you think?'

'You can't win them all, Charlie. It'll be a night out, anyway. Ross is talking about a show he wants to see at the Liverpool Empire. Are you up for it?'

'The way I feel, I'm up for anything. But as usual, it'll depend on whether I can get the night off.'

At lunch time, a few days later, Charlie was busy in the pub kitchen when a barman slipped in to tell him somebody was asking for him. He was afraid it might be Wally again so he took a peek round the door. Ross was sitting in the window seat with a glass in front of him. He went over. 'Hello.'

'Hi, Charlie. Sophie thinks you might like to come to the Liverpool Empire with us,' Ross said. 'It's a revival of a Terence Rattigan play, *The Winslow Boy*.'

Charlie was surprised. 'Thanks, I'd like to.'

'What nights will you be off next week?'

'Wednesday and Thursday.'

'I'll try to get tickets for Wednesday then. My sister's keen to come too. You know Judith?'

Charlie was pleased. 'Of course I do – from primary school and the youth club. Haven't seen her in yonks. Look, I'd like to stop and have a beer with you but I've got to get back, the lunch orders are coming in. Thank you for thinking of me. I could do with a night out.'

'I'll let Sophie know.'

As he went back to the stove, Charlie felt grateful to Sophie for organising things for him. She told him a day or so later that they had tickets for the stalls and the outing was definitely on.

He felt he should contribute something, and said, 'Shall I drive you all there? Andy has the car most nights, so he'll not mind my having it for once.'

Sophie was keen. 'That would be great.'

On Wednesday, Charlie had the day off. He got up late and

lazed around for most of the day, then spent ages having a bath and getting himself ready. He felt he desperately needed something new in his life. Something more than cooking in the pub and trying to improve his spelling.

He collected Sophie first and then drove on to the Salters' house. He'd seen something of Judith Salter in his childhood and early teens, but he'd never known her well. Now as she followed Ross out of their house, he looked her over. He'd noticed years go she'd lost the pigtails he used to pull, but not that her warm brown hair curled on her shoulders and bounced as she walked. He leaped out of the car to greet her. She was almost as tall as he was and wand slim.

'Hello, Charlie.' Her smile was radiant. If ever there was an ugly duckling that turned into a swan, it was Judith. He thought her an absolute cracker of a girl.

Ross got in to sit beside Sophie on the back seat. Charlie almost fell over himself as he rushed round to open the passenger door for Judith. She was friendly, asking him about his job at the Dog and Gun, and seemed to think it a fun place to work. He kept snatching glances at her as he drove.

She told him what she'd heard of the show they were going to see. Charlie felt lifted away from his mundane existence to her world which beckoned and glittered. It was the same in the theatre. He spent as much time looking at the pleasure reflected on Judith's face as he did watching the stage. Until, that is, the psychological intensity of the play gripped him and held him spellbound.

On the way home, the conversation became more general. Judith was impressed that Sophie was able to drive round in her own car. On most days, she left it at Hooton Station, but she could get back and forth from there.

'I'm taking driving lessons,' Judith said, 'but I'm not very good yet. Mum and Dad don't get much time to take me out to practise; they're always working late.'

'I'll take you,' Charlie offered quickly. It gave him a good reason to keep seeing her – heaven sent, in fact. She seemed pleased.

Ross suggested a nightcap. 'Let's go back to the Dog and Gun. By the time we get there we're near enough home. Charlie can leave the car there if he's no longer fit to drive.'

Charlie laughed. 'I don't propose to get drunk, but it's probably the wisest place to go.' It wasn't where he wanted to spend his time off, but it worked out well.

Later, when he pulled the car on to the Salters' drive to turn round, Ross said, 'I'll walk Sophie home from here.'

He was left alone with Judith, which was marvellous. He wondered if he'd dare kiss her.

She said, 'You've changed, Charlie. Suddenly, you seem grown up.'

'So do you.' He put his arm round her and pulled her closer, then kissed her full on the lips. 'Very grown up.'

Charlie drove home still fizzing with pleasure. He'd never had a real girlfriend. Yes, he'd taken the odd girl to the pictures, but he'd never met one he could really take to. He'd even felt envious of Andy because he'd attached himself to Amy. Now all that had changed. Judith Salter was the tops.

Charlie soon found that the hours he worked at the Dog and Gun made it difficult to see much of Judith. He'd always hated the split shifts, and working late meant he had only two evenings a week free. Once the summer holidays were over, he'd not be able to see her on his days off if they continued to be Wednesdays and Thursdays. It made him start looking round for a job with social hours. He wanted weekends off like everybody else.

He counted himself lucky when he was offered a job in a small factory making frozen cakes and desserts in Ellesmere Port. He needed his motor bike to get there, and was happy to go on it because it used less petrol than the car, but he made Andy promise he could have the latter in bad weather.

His life seemed to change overnight. He sat the two O levels Uncle Seb had entered him for, so for the time being there was no need for further tuition from Sophie. He found the new job more boring and the pay much the same, but he had every evening off as well as every weekend. He was made up because he could spend more time with Judith.

Judith's driving improved rapidly and he felt they were getting on like a house on fire. The Salters welcomed him at their house, even fed him if he happened to be there at mealtimes, and his parents had always been happy to do that for his friends.

Judith told him she'd never had a real boyfriend before, and that pleased him more than anything else.

CHAPTER TWENTY-FIVE

F LORA TOLD herself she must see her summer holiday as something she was going to enjoy. Isobel had been with her family to Brittany and said they'd had a marvellous time; that she'd come back feeling invigorated. The children had loved the beach, they'd taught Daisy to swim in the hotel pool, and they all looked the picture of health. Everybody else loved holidays. Flora told herself she must change her attitude.

Isobel encouraged her to buy a new dress and some comfortable sandals and presented her with a bottle of sunscreen to take with her. She and Tom travelled down to London by train and spent a night in a hotel in order to see Agatha Christie's *Mousetrap*. The next day they flew to Milan to spend two nights there.

Tom enjoyed visiting bustling cities. He loved the different food and the shops. Before setting out, he'd said, 'But we'll have only one full day there because you find cities so tiring.'

Flora had expected Milan to be baking hot at the end of June, but their visit coincided with a cooler spell and the weather was pleasant for walking round. It was just as well, because Tom had booked them on an evening train to Lake Como. When he'd arranged the trip, he'd persuaded her to stay four nights at Lake Como before going on to Lake Garda.

'We might as well see both while we're out there,' he'd said. 'I'm told the surrounding countryside is absolutely beautiful. To move round and have a different hotel will keep us interested.'

'I know I'll love it,' she said. 'When I was young I really fancied a holiday in the Italian lakes but it wasn't possible then.'

'Flora, when we get to Garda, Venice isn't all that much further. What about a couple of nights there before coming home?'

Flora had agreed, though it turned the holiday she'd envisaged into something quite different. The second day in Milan visiting museums and more shops kept her on her feet. She was tired by the time the taxi was taking them to the railway station.

'We'll have dinner on the train,' Tom said. 'It'll pass the time and I've heard the food is first class.'

Flora had a headache. As soon as she mentioned it, Tom was sympathetic. He ordered a gin and tonic for each of them and said it would lift her headache, and they'd go to the dining car early because food might help too. She thought an early night would have suited her better, but the train didn't get in until after midnight.

Tom was acting strangely tonight. He seemed tense and somehow anxious. He was talking more than usual and couldn't sit still. He ordered wine with their dinner and kept topping up her glass until she protested. Normally, he didn't press her to drink more than she wanted, but tonight he also tried to persuade her to have a brandy afterwards. She told him she didn't want it, but he had two.

By the time they were getting off the train, Flora felt a bit squiffy anyway, as though she'd drunk more wine than she should. Tom said she hadn't eaten enough and moved her and their luggage smoothly into a taxi.

'These lakes were a very popular holiday destination at the turn of the century,' he told her, 'and most of the hotels here were built in that era. But I've booked us into the five-star Palazzo del Lago. It's a new one, only opened last year.'

The street lamps cast a glow over everything, and at this time of night the town was quiet. As they approached, the taxi driver pointed out their hotel towering over all the other buildings.

Flora said, 'It's an enormous place.'

'It's beautifully positioned at the head of the lake,' Tom said.

They took the lift up to their room on the twelfth floor. He was inspecting it, and she knew he was impressed. 'Very spacious.'

'Vast,' Flora agreed. 'And there's a balcony.'

He unlocked the glass door and they went out into the balmy night air. She looked out over the lake shimmering like silver in the moonlight.

'It's beautiful,' she breathed. There were clusters of golden lights showing in the villages and little towns round the lake. The hills rose majestically into the darkness all round. Flora went forward to lean on the balustrade.

Tom followed. 'The view will be stunning in daylight.' She thought his voice sounded strangely taut.

'It is now.' Flora leaned over and looked down. A long way below a car was lighting up the ribbon of road with its headlights.

He was standing behind her. She felt his arms go round her and tighten against her hips. His breath was hot on the back of her neck. She felt him swinging her up. Why was he trying to lift her?

Her mind exploded and she screamed, 'What are you doing?' Panic hurtled through her.

'It's all right,' he said, but he was holding on to her. She fought till she burst out of his grasp, then shot back into the room in a cold sweat. Had he meant to topple her over the balustrade? She made for the bed. She had to lie down.

His face came close to hers. 'Flora love, whatever is the matter? Did something frighten you?'

She couldn't answer. Daren't answer. She was terrified. What would he do if she accused him of trying to throw her off the balcony to her death?

'It was so lovely out there and I was so pleased to be here with you, it was just a hug of joy. Did I hurt you?'

Her voice was a whisper. 'I felt dizzy. I thought I was going to fall.' Her heart was banging away, and she couldn't get her breath. 'It's such a long way down to the ground.'

'I wouldn't let you fall,' he said easily, and turned to lift his suitcase on to the stand provided.

Flora could feel herself shaking. She closed her eyes and the room eddied round her. She was terrified. What if he tried to do that again?

'It's getting late and you're tired after being on your feet all day. You're letting your mind play tricks on you.'

Flora stiffened. Had she imagined it? No, Tom had been different all evening, as though he was screwing himself up to do something dreadful.

'I shouldn't have let you get overtired like this.' He was oozing sympathy. It seemed genuine, but was it? 'I blame myself for not taking more care of you.'

Flora had been wary of him for some time, but now she was petrified. Had he really tried to kill her or had she imagined that moment on the balcony?

'You should have told me you didn't like heights,' he went on.

She'd been thinking of his first wife Grace. He'd told her she'd committed suicide, but what if . . . ?

Flora felt her blood run cold again. He'd told her that Grace had sealed up her garage to make it airtight and run the engine of her car until the carbon monoxide in the fumes killed her. Would it have been possible for Tom to fake that and make it look like suicide? Flora felt numb with fear.

He came to sit on the end of the bed, and she cringed away from him. Would he know what she was thinking? He was a big strong man and weighed almost twice what she did. Surely he wouldn't find it impossible to lift her over that balustrade? Had he really tried and failed?

'Poor pet, there's nothing to be frightened of. A dizzy turn like that when you're looking down from this height, it would be scary. Have a bath and get into bed,' he suggested. 'You'll feel better in the morning.'

The thought of spending the night lying next to him made her tremble more.

'Would you like a brandy to settle your nerves? We could get you one from the bar. It was still open when we came in.'

More alcohol was the last thing Flora wanted, but she said yes. 'Just what I need. Why don't we both go down?'

She shot off ahead of him to the lift. There was nobody in it but them as it descended. Flora held her breath and stayed as far away from him as the small space allowed. She needed other people round her before she could feel safe again. She was relieved to see there were two other couples still in the bar.

She sat down in a comfortable armchair and watched Tom like a hawk as he went up to the counter. He had to get a barman from somewhere behind and then his body shut off her view of what was happening. Moments later, he brought two glasses of brandy over and set one on the table in front of her. Flora eyed it nervously. The strong taste would hide any added flavour. How many crime books had she read where the victim had swallowed poison in her brandy? To be on the safe side, when Tom returned to the bar to get a light for his cigarette she swopped their glasses over and told herself she was becoming phobic.

She took tiny sips of her brandy. It seared her tongue and she didn't like it, but it gave her a chance to get a grip on her nerves. Tom drained his glass quickly, then tossed off what she couldn't finish. Twenty minutes later they went back upstairs.

What had happened had blown her mind. She'd never before imagined Tom might try to kill her. If he really had. Silently, they got undressed for bed. She mustn't give him the slightest hint of what was in her head in case it spurred him on to try again before she could voice her suspicions to anybody else. He'd never be able to pass it off as an accident if she'd told somebody he was trying to kill her.

Flora lay down beside him, ramrod stiff, every muscle tensed, keeping as far away from him as possible. She was a million miles away from sleep.

She relived that heart-stopping moment when she felt him lift her. Then, she'd been as sure as she'd ever be that he was trying to kill her. He'd chosen the right moment: they'd only just arrived at the hotel and most of their fellow guests would have already been asleep.

She felt sick. She wanted to go home, to be with her family and those she trusted. Their holiday had only just started; the days Tom had booked here stretched endlessly ahead. She couldn't face them.

The brandy helped Tom drop off but not her. Flora lay still, listening to his heavy breathing. While he slept she didn't have to pretend nothing had happened. She didn't have to hide her panic.

How she wished she'd confided in Isobel a month or so ago when she'd asked her if she was all right. She must explain her fears to her girls as soon as she got home. She couldn't go on like this.

Tom was snoring gently. Flora edged nearer the side of the bed and sat up slowly, praying she wouldn't disturb him. He'd insisted on leaving the door to the balcony open so they could get some air. It was full moon and light enough for her to eye the height of the balcony balustrade. It came about level with her waist; it wouldn't be possible to fall over it accidentally.

What was she to do?

She could confront him with her suspicions, but she knew exactly what would happen. His honey tongue would try to convince her he was totally innocent, that it was all in her head and possibly that she losing her marbles.

But worse, it would alert him to her state of mind. He'd know he had to act again quickly if he was to get away with it. He'd surely know that once she was home she'd tell Isobel and Hilary what he'd tried to do.

Or she could do what she'd been doing for years: grit her teeth and pretend nothing out of the ordinary had happened.

But she couldn't possibly stay here with him and watch him relish this holiday. She wouldn't dare step out on that balcony again and she'd be on tenterhooks the whole time. She'd be a nervous wreck before she got home. She couldn't cope with Tom after this. This evening, he'd been watching her as a cat watches a mouse. She knew she had to have help.

With a little snort, he stirred and rolled over on his back. Flora froze, but he resumed his deep regular breathing and, a moment later, his soft snoring. She couldn't possibly wait till morning. She couldn't face his anger and his objections. She'd have to go now if she was to get away.

Could she go home tomorrow by herself? She'd rarely gone anywhere alone and he had all the tickets and reservations in his bag. What were the essentials she'd have to take and where would she find them? She made a mental list.

The moonlight was bright enough for her to make out the outline of her handbag and the small overnight bag in which Tom carried essentials like tickets and passports. She had to have those, and also some more money.

It was always Tom who paid their hotel bills, and for their meals and drinks out. He'd changed their pounds into lire and as usual given her a few small notes to put in her own bag.

'In case we become separated and you need cash for a taxi or something.' She knew she'd need more than that if she was to get home by herself.

Now her eyes were accustomed to the half-light she slowly put her feet out on the mat. She'd brought a small torch to light her way to the loo if she should need to get up in the night in a strange bedroom. It was one of the problems of getting older and not one she wanted to draw Tom's attention to. He complained if she woke him in the night.

It was waiting ready on her bedside table. As she felt for it, her fingers touched her watch, and she strapped that on her wrist first. Her hand closed round the torch and, moving as softly as she could, she crept to the en suite, taking both Tom's bag and her handbag with her. She almost closed the door and turned her back on it before switching on the torch and opening his bag. She found her passport and her return train and air tickets. Stuffing these into her own handbag she helped herself generously from his wallet, which was bulging with sterling, but she'd need lire too and where were they?

She was shaking again. She spent a penny as silently as she could, but what was she thinking of? She couldn't leave in her nightdress. Very slowly, she pushed the bathroom door open again. It creaked, making her hold her breath, but his snores didn't falter. The clothes she'd taken off earlier were together on a chair. She scooped them up and retreated again to the bathroom to dress.

She could feel the sweat standing up on her forehead, but she was nearly ready now. Just her shoes, yes, and the lire. She put Tom's bag back where he'd left it. His other wallet was on the dressing table. She took most of the lire she found in it and stuffed them into the pocket of her slacks.

She straightened up. What if she'd got it wrong? What if Tom had just been giving her a hug as he'd said? What if it was all in her mind? She wished she knew for certain.

But she couldn't go on with this holiday as if nothing had happened. She scooped up her sandals and was on the way to the bedroom door when she noticed one of her suitcases at the foot of her bed that she hadn't yet opened. It contained all her new clothes. She snatched it up and took it with her.

Then, trying to get out, she found he'd double-locked the bedroom door. Holding her breath and watching the sleeping mound that was Tom, she slowly and silently turned the key in the lock. She had the door open and he hadn't moved. Once in the corridor, she closed the door just as gently. She'd escaped from Tom, and nothing, absolutely nothing, would ever persuade her to go back to him.

In the subdued light, Flora crept along the corridor, afraid now she might have disturbed him and he'd come after her. She found the lift but was worried about making it work. Tom always did that sort of thing. She headed for the stairs and was thankful they were carpeted and her feet made no sound. The staircases seemed endless, but at last she was in the ground floor foyer. It looked vast and eerie. She thought at first it was deserted but then she saw the night porter snoozing behind a desk with his mouth open. She stood in front of him and cleared her throat. He didn't stir.

'Excuse me,' she said, and then again more loudly. His mouth closed and he pulled himself upright on the chair.

'Excuse me,' Flora repeated. 'I'd like you to call a taxi for me.'

He spoke English with a strong Italian accent. 'A taxi? Now?'

His gaze went to the wall behind her, and her stomach turned over. Her first thought was that Tom had followed her down, but the man was looking at a large and ornate wall clock. The time it showed was twenty minutes to four.

'Yes please, now,' she told him. He lifted the telephone on his desk and spoke in fast Italian sentences she couldn't understand.

'Be here in about ten minutes,' he told her.

'Thank you.'

Flora didn't know what to do with herself. She couldn't sit down. Instead she pretended an interest in a stand displaying brochures that advertised visits to local beauty spots.

She felt suddenly sick, hot vomit rising in her throat. Looking round she saw a ladies' powder room and shot inside. She was just in time to throw up in the lavatory. She was hot and sweating and scared. She bent over a washbasin to gulp cold water and get the nasty taste out of her mouth. Then she rinsed her face and combed her hair. She was afraid to stay longer in case the porter hadn't seen her come in. Would he send the taxi away if she wasn't waiting for it?

Flora returned to the foyer, aware of the night porter's curiosity and that his eyes were following every movement she made. Her eyes kept going to the stairs. She was terrified Tom had woken up and missed her. She wanted to hide from him but stay where the porter could see her.

The heavy silence was broken only by the clock ticking away the minutes. Only seven had passed. She listened, filled with dread that she'd hear the whirr of the lift.

In front of another display stand, she suddenly realised she was staring at boat timetables for sailing trips on the lake. Would there be train timetables here? She wanted to be on the next one heading back to Milan. Yes, there were timetables for trains heading everywhere.

In her agitated state, it took an age to find the one she wanted, and even longer to pinpoint the information she needed. The trains ran every two hours during the day but not at night. The first would leave at six thirty this morning; she'd have more than enough time to catch it. Sixteen minutes had gone now. Would the taxi ever come?

At last, she saw the headlights outside. The porter got up and slowly unlocked the door for her. She picked up her suitcase and strode quickly out. Once inside the moving car she breathed a sigh of relief. She felt safer, but doubts crowded her mind. She'd chosen to rush away on an impression received in a split second. What if she'd got it wrong? She wished she knew for certain one way or the other.

She put her head back against the seat and closed her eyes, feeling bone weary. It seemed only moments before the taxi was pulling up outside the railway station.

The morning light was grey and cold, the ticket office closed. There was nobody about and no trains. There were very few lights on, but it didn't matter. The daylight was growing stronger, and she could see the empty platforms and the shiny rails stretching away into the distance.

CHAPTER TWENTY-SIX

TOM FELT fuzzy when he woke up. He lay still with his eyes closed, gradually recalling the events of the night before. He knew his plan had gone badly wrong. He should have achieved his goal by now, but instead he'd scared Flora. She'd been keeping her distance last night; he was going to have his work cut out to soothe her and get things back to normal. Still, here they were in the five-star Palazzo del Lago; he'd be able to indulge her, fuss round her. It might be easier here in the lap of luxury.

He turned over. The early sun was streaming into the room and he realised she wasn't in bed beside him.

'Flora?' The door to the en suite was closed. She'd be in there. 'Flora, dear.' He padded across and pushed the door open. It surprised him to find it empty. He stepped out on to the balcony. There were two chairs and a small table, but Flora wasn't using them. He looked at his watch. It was almost half past eight. She must have gone downstairs, perhaps out for a walk.

He swore and headed back to the bathroom. This wasn't like her; usually she stayed close to him. Had he frightened her more than he'd realised? She might have guessed at his intention out on the balcony last night, but she couldn't possibly know. He thought he'd calmed her and glossed over it quite well.

He'd shaved and dressed when he picked up his wallet to put in his pocket, and discovered there were very few lire left in it. Last night it had been bulging. He noticed, then, that her blue suitcase was missing and the small bag in which he kept important things like tickets, money and passports was gaping open. Surely Flora wouldn't . . . ? He searched through it furiously. It took him only moments to find that her passport and tickets and a good deal of the money had gone.

Tom felt the heat rush up into his face as fury surged through him. He flung the bag across the room and let out a string of oaths. Flora had walked out on him. She must have gone home!

'Damn Flora!' It must mean she'd rumbled him. What was he going to do now?

He went downstairs and ate a substantial breakfast, wondering what he should do next. He went back to sit on the balcony in the cool morning sun. His failure to push her over the rail had created a bigger problem than he'd realised. She knew exactly what he'd been trying to do. She'd run away from him. How could he have made such a bad mistake?

He'd thought it would work. Yes, it was daring, but it had to be. For weeks beforehand, he'd made a habit of lifting her in moments of passion. Of carrying her gently to a sofa or a bed and then being especially affectionate, so she wouldn't baulk at being lifted over this rail. But she had. Something must have alerted her.

He'd had to make his plans without seeing the hotel, but it

had provided exactly what he'd hoped for and the timing had been right: late at night and shortly after they got here. To tip Flora over the rail should have been well within his capabilities, but he'd failed to do it.

Her scream had unnerved him. She'd kicked out at him and he'd been afraid other guests might hear and report a struggle. He'd betrayed his intention and given up too easily. He had to take deep breaths to calm himself. He was furious with both himself and Flora.

It had taken him months to pick her out amongst the penniless widows of the bridge club, most of whom were running to fat and senility, and then he'd had to convince her of his eligibility. But he'd thought it had been worth it. He'd enjoyed a comfortable life since his marriage.

To start with, he'd found having sex with her surprisingly good. She used to be keen and that was the best aphrodisiac. For her age, she'd had a good body, too, though even then it had looked better dressed than undressed. Nowadays she was losing weight and becoming a bag of bones.

Worse, recently he'd felt Flora was less affectionate and less ready to fall in with his wishes than she had been. She'd taken to refusing him sex on occasions and he found that frustrating and demeaning. It really put his back up that she allowed him little input into what they would do and how they would spend their income. She was much less fun than she had been; they were no longer on the same wavelength.

Tom knew he'd grown bored with her and her family, and had wanted to bring it to an end. However, it was only sensible to take with him as many of the material comforts she'd provided as he could. Hence his plan.

After this shock, he needed to rethink his future. He'd have to go home immediately, and try to restore the status quo. He thought it might be possible to convince Flora she'd made a mistake, jolly her out of her fears and heal the breach. He'd lived on the state's largesse before, and knew it was worth trying hard to avoid returning to that.

Then, when he'd calmed Flora down, he might try again if he saw half a chance. He ought to start looking for another well-heeled widow straight away.

Flora felt exhausted as she tottered up the railway platform in the dawn. She shivered and wondered if there was a waiting room. She no longer felt safe. Tom would surely guess where she'd gone and follow her? She tried one or two doors that were locked, but one opened with ease. She'd found the waiting room.

'Oh!' She was surprised to find a family already inside. A young mother nodding over the baby in her arms, a toddler fast asleep, stretched out on the wooden seating that went round the four walls, a young father dozing in the corner.

'Sorry to disturb you,' Flora said, dragging in her suitcase and sitting down in the opposite corner. The man opened his eyes and nodded politely. The baby was struggling to free his arms from his blanket and began to mewl and fret. The mother cradled him closer. She looked near the end of her tether.

'I don't know who's disturbing whom,' she said apologetically.

Flora was relieved to hear she was English. There was a tear on her cheek she hadn't wiped away. The baby was crying more persistently.

Her husband took the child from her. 'Let me have him. You try to get some rest.'

'Thanks, Luigi.' His wife leaned back and closed her eyes but she kept one hand on the toddler to prevent him rolling off the seat.

'I'm sorry,' he said to Flora.

The baby's cries were reaching a climax. Even the toddler half woke and began to sob.

After several minutes, Flora said, 'Shall I try?' She'd done her share of looking after Daisy and Melissa and was confident she could. Luigi was more than willing to hand the baby over.

The child was struggling and kicking and quite an armful as she paced up and down with him, making soothing noises. Gradually, she felt him relax and his cries began to fade. Then she wrapped his blanket round him more tightly and laid him down in the corner of the seat, sitting in such a way that he wouldn't be able to roll off.

'Thank you,' his father murmured. She thought he was Italian – his wife had called him Luigi – but he spoke good English. 'I'm afraid he's overtired, we all are. We have to return to London in a hurry. A great hurry . . .'

'I'm in the same position,' Flora said.

'I hope not quite so bad . . . My wife's mother is asking for her.'

He told Flora that his mother-in-law had cancer and had taken a sudden turn for the worse. She understood he was desperate to get his family back before she died.

'Everything's on the spur of the moment and so disorganised.'

'I hope you reach London in time to see her. Things aren't quite that urgent for me.'

She had no intention of trying to explain, she didn't think

she could, but in soothing his baby she'd soothed herself too. It had taken her mind off Tom. Both children slept until their train was due.

Flora stayed close to the family when they boarded the train for Milan and was invited to share their taxi out to the airport. Her next problem was to change the ticket she had for the return flight to Manchester from a date two weeks hence to the next plane. Luigi pointed out the place to do it and she was relieved to find there was a seat available on the next flight. All she had to do was pay a small rearrangement fee.

Luigi went to phone a relative in London to ask him to meet their plane. It made Flora wonder how she'd get home from Manchester. Tom had arranged their return taxi and she didn't know the name of the firm.

But of course, if she asked Isobel to meet her, she'd be more than willing. Luigi gave her the code for England and she rang Isobel's number, but though she let it ring nobody lifted the phone. She tried Hilary's number with the same result.

She could ring the garden centre shop. That would be open now, so she'd get somebody, possibly Ben, but she'd be here at the airport for hours yet and could try Isobel's number again later. On the off chance, she redialled it now.

She was flustered when the phone was immediately lifted, but the line wasn't clear. 'Isobel, is that you?'

'It's Sophie. Are you all right, Nana?'

'Is your mother there? I need to speak to her.'

'No, she and Dad have just left for Anglesey.'

'Oh, dear. Could you ask Hilary if she'd meet me in Manchester? I'm coming home this afternoon.'

'Aunt Hilly's gone too, Nana, and Ben. They've gone for a few days' holiday. Didn't Mum tell you?'

'Oh, yes! Goodness, I'd forgotten. How am I going to get home from the airport?'

'Don't worry, I'll see somebody's there to pick you up. What time is your flight due?'

Flora told her.

'Why are you coming home? You've only just gone. Has something happened?'

'Yes. I'll explain when I see you. It's a long story.'

'You're coming by yourself? Not Tom?'

'That's right. You won't forget?'

'No, Nana, of course not. Either I'll come myself or Andy will.'

'Thank you, dear.'

Flora put the phone down feeling relieved but light-headed. She hardly knew what she was doing. She was sorry Luigi's little family were going to Gatwick and their plane left before hers. She had another four hours to wait. She had a meal and some coffee, though she was beyond feeling hungry.

She ached with fatigue. She went through the formalities and settled down to wait for her flight to be called. The seat was comfortable, and she fell heavily asleep sitting upright, only waking up when the other passengers were boarding. She'd be all right now. Tom couldn't catch her up.

That morning, Sophie had set her alarm clock so she could get up to see her parents off on their short break. She'd dressed and taken Melissa down to their flat and taken Daisy under her wing. She'd helped cook their egg and bacon breakfast and eaten with them.

She intended to have a few lazy days while her parents were away. With Daisy to look after as well as Melissa, she wouldn't have much time to do her own thing. Before he set off, Dad had suggested she take Daisy out to distract her. He was afraid she'd miss her mother.

Sophie turned washing up into a game, though Daisy seemed happy enough, and then, as it was drizzling, got out the children's wet weather equipment. The best she could think of was a walk down to the local shop for a few necessities, and then perhaps a trip to Raby Mere. Daisy loved feeding the ducks and if the rain held off it could be a pleasant way to pass an hour.

This afternoon, one of Daisy's school friends was having her birthday party. Isobel had left Daisy's party frock hanging ready, with a wrapped gift to take. That should keep her happy through the first day.

Tomorrow, Sophie decided, she'd get up late and take the kids to Chester Zoo. The next, perhaps she'd take them into Birkenhead and give them lunch at McDonald's.

She'd slammed her mother's front door and was pushing the buggy down the path when she heard the phone ring. She shared the number with her parents and thought it might be Ross. Sometimes he rang from work. By the time she'd let herself in again, the phone had stopped. She stood waiting.

'Let's go.' Daisy was jigging about impatiently. 'I want to buy a paint book. Mummy gave me some pennies.'

'All right,' Sophie said.

'One of those that only needs water and the colours come by magic.'

Sophie was retracing her steps to the door when the phone

rang again. She turned round and pounced on it. It was Nana, not Ross.

After she'd put the phone down, Sophie sank down on the seat in the hall and tried to think. Daisy's party was from three until six. It would take her about an hour to get to the airport, and if she was to be there by six thirty to meet Nana's plane, she'd need help.

Sophie groaned. She had a family that provided willing help with child care, but at the moment they were almost all away.

Not Andy, though. He was on his long summer holiday just as she was. Perhaps he'd collect Daisy from her party. She was dialling the garden shop number when Daisy pleaded, 'Come on, Sophie, I want to go.'

'I won't be a minute. I just want a word with Andy.'

It was Ruby who answered. 'We're busy, I'm afraid. He's serving.'

'Couldn't you relieve him? I won't keep him more than a minute.'

Sophie heard the shop bell ting and Ruby said, 'Oh, there's more customers coming in, and a delivery of something. Here's Jamie. Can you talk to him?'

'Hi, Sophie. What is it?'

'I want Andy to fetch Daisy from a birthday party at six o'clock tonight and look after her for an hour or so. Ask him and tell him to ring me.'

'It's Amy's birthday and he's taking her out,' Jamie said. 'He's got tickets for some show in Chester.'

'Oh, damn.'

'Can I collect her for you?'

'No, Jamie, thanks. You'd need a car and to be able to drive. I'll try Charlie.'

385

'Sophie, come on,' Daisy wheedled.

'I want to ring Charlie first.'

'No,' Daisy protested.

Sophie had never needed to ring Charlie at work, but she felt it was worth a try. It took her an age to find the number and even longer to have him brought to the phone. She had to ignore the fuss the children were making by then.

At last Charlie's voice asked half jokingly, 'Is this an emergency? The boss says it had better be.'

'It could be,' Sophie told him. 'Nana's flying home alone this afternoon. Something bad must have happened. I need to meet her at the airport.'

'I'll come with you.'

She explained about Daisy's party. 'Otherwise I'll have to cancel that and take her with me.'

'OK, I'll see to Daisy. I'll be home about five thirty. I'll come straight down to your place to tie things up.'

The Milan plane was late; Sophie had to wait. It had been anything but the lazy day she'd expected. Melissa was getting grumpy; it would soon be her bedtime and she was tired. There was a steady stream of passengers coming out now, and Sophie examined their faces while she hitched Melissa higher in her arms. When her grandmother came, she almost didn't recognise her, she looked so ill and frail. Sophie kissed her and tried to take her case.

'No, no, you've got the baby.'

'Nana, you're shaking like a leaf. Whatever is the matter?'

'I'm all right now I'm with you.'

'Let's get you to the car, then, and you can tell me what's happened.'

Sophie had to concentrate on getting out of the car park and back on the motorway. When she was gathering speed, she asked, 'So what's made you come home early, Nana? You'd booked for two weeks or more.'

'Sixteen days.'

'Didn't you like the Italian lakes?'

Without any preliminaries, Nana let her worries come out. Her voice was flat, and she sounded dead-dog tired. 'I'm frightened of Tom. He scares me to death.'

It was the last thing Sophie expected. 'But why? I thought you were happy together. Mum said you were.'

'He tried to kill me.'

That took Sophie's breath away. 'No, Nana, surely not?'

There was no answer. One glance at her grandmother's face told her she was deadly serious.

'What did he do?'

'Our hotel room was on the twelfth floor.' She shivered. 'I felt he was about to throw me over.' She talked of the lake shimmering silver in the moonlight and the car headlights lighting up the tree-lined road far below.

Sophie thought it sounded like something out of a novel. She found it hard to believe. 'This isn't just a story, Nana? You aren't imagining it?'

'No!'

Sophie had never liked Tom but this sounded far-fetched. She couldn't see him doing anything like that.

Flora said, 'Please believe me. I need help. He wants to be rid of me.'

'He wants a divorce?' Sophie had a sense of mounting shock.

'No, not that. A divorce is what I want, but he doesn't.

He'll drive me out of my mind if he doesn't find some way to kill me first.'

'Kill you! Nana, Tom wouldn't do such a thing! Are you sure?'

Again, the long silence. 'I think so, but no, I'm not absolutely certain. That's the worst part. I've had a gut feeling for some time that he's putting on an act. It's growing and I'm scared of him. But is it all in my head?'

Sophie was inclined to think it might be, but how could she tell her nana her mind had blown? She wished Dad was at home. He'd know what to do.

She knew by her breathing that Melissa was asleep. The next time she glanced at Nana, her chin had sunk to her chest and she seemed to be sleeping too. Sophie drove slowly into the village and drew up outside her grandmother's cottage.

'You're home, Nana. Time to wake up.' Sophie was out of the car and reaching to get her suitcase from the back seat.

'No!' An icy hand gripped her arm. 'No, I can't come here.'

Sophie was perplexed. 'You left everything shipshape. I came up this morning to make sure, and I bought a fresh loaf for you and a pint of milk. Everything's fine.'

'No.' The grip on her arm tightened. 'Don't you see, this is the first place Tom will look for me, and then . . .'

'Look for you? But he knows you've come home?'

'No. I crept out in the night while he was asleep. I had to escape from him.'

'But won't he be worried? When he finds you've gone?'

'Not as worried as I was about staying with him.'

Sophie swallowed hard. 'Nana, this is your home. You've lived here for years. You love this place.'

'But Tom has a key. He could walk in on me at any time. I wouldn't dare go to sleep.'

'Oh. Where d'you want to go?'

'Sophie, I'm at my wits' end. I don't know where to go or what to do. I don't want Tom anywhere near me. Not after I've run away from him like this . . . I've been thinking about it so long . . .'

Sophie was alarmed. 'I'd better take you to my place.'

As she drove home through the village, she was afraid she couldn't handle Nana in this state.

'Who's here? Whose car is that?' her grandmother demanded when she pulled up beside it on the drive. It made her even more worried about Nana's state of mind. She couldn't believe she hadn't recognised it. Aunt Hilary had been driving it round for years.

'It's all right, it's Charlie's. He's looking after Daisy.' Sophie lifted Melissa out of her car seat. That woke her up and made her cry, which made them all more edgy.

'Nana, come in and sit down.'

'I should give you a hand.'

Sophie's carpet was strewn with newspaper darts, Charlie's idea of keeping Daisy entertained. She looked sleepy too; it was well past her bedtime. Sophie wondered where best to start, but Melissa was howling now, sounding very distressed. She'd have to give her priority.

Charlie's head came round the bedroom door. 'What d'you want me to do?'

'Put Daisy to bed.'

'I've tried, but she wants you to do it.'

'OK. I'm hungry, are you?'

'Starving.'

'Could you start cooking, Charlie, please? There's lamb chops in the fridge. Ross is coming for his supper.'

'Great. For Nana too?'

'There's enough if she wants some.'

It took Sophie only minutes to undress Melissa, change her nappy and put her nightdress on. She wiped her face and hands with a damp flannel and popped her in her cot. Once she was lying down her sobs subsided. Daisy was cuddling up against Nana who seemed to be nodding off too.

'Bedtime,' Sophie told her, lifting her to her feet.

'Don't want to go to bed.'

Sophie insisted and had her tucked up on the camp bed in Melissa's room in no time. Her mother and Aunt Hilly were firm believers in bedtime routine, baths and stories, but tonight Sophie was too worried about Nana to bother with stuff like that.

Charlie had made a pot of tea. Nana had a little colour in her cheeks now. Sophie refilled her cup and poured one for herself. The time for explanations had arrived.

CHAPTER TWENTY-SEVEN

FLORA FOUND herself on the settee with Sophie beside her. 'What cold hands you have, Nana,' her granddaughter said, trying to rub some warmth back into them. There were appetising scents coming from the kitchen. Charlie was hovering in the doorway, keeping one eye on his cooking and the other on his grandmother.

'Why have you come home by yourself, Nana?' he asked.

Sophie said, 'Now I've put the babies to bed, I want you to tell us what went wrong, Nana. Charlie and I need to be clear about what's happened, then the three of us can think about what we should do.'

Flora knew she must pull herself together. What she told them must make sense. Sophie was finding it hard to believe Tom had tried to kill her. She gulped at her third cup of tea before starting.

'Tom has always been a total parasite.'

'My mother says that,' Charlie told her. 'But she says you knew he would be before you married him.'

Flora winced. So the family talked about her and Tom.

Sophie said gently, 'But you're rich. Does that matter?'

'He married me for my money and that matters.'

'You don't know that.'

'I do. When we were first married, he persuaded me to change my bank accounts to joint ones. I made a new will in his favour too. I suppose I was seeing him through rose-tinted glasses. It took me a long time to realise what he was up to.'

Flora saw that Charlie's eyes were almost popping out with shock. 'Heavens, he does look after his own interests.'

'He lied to me from the beginning; deliberately lied about his age. Recently, I found out he's twenty-one years younger than me, not the ten years he said.' She shook her head, deep in misery. 'I was a romantic idiot to believe he was in love with me. An old trout twenty-one years older than him.'

'Nana, you're not an old trout.' Sophie looked sympathetic.

'If I get cross with him he puts his arms round me and says he's sorry and he loves me too much to fight. You never heard such sweet talk. He can make me believe it's all my fault.'

'Sweet talk throws us all off course. Even us young ones.'

'Yes, well . . . I know nothing about him, Sophie. In eight years of marriage, he's never introduced any friends or relatives to me, not one. There's nobody who knew him before I did. That bothers me.'

'Why didn't you say something before now? You've bottled it all up; worried yourself sick.'

'Pride, I suppose. It's hard to admit we make mistakes like that. I was taken in.'

'Don't I know!' Sophie was smiling wanly. 'I've been there too.'

Flora let out her pent-up breath. 'He told me his first wife committed suicide and I worry now that he drove her to it or

392

perhaps murdered her and covered things so well it was taken to be suicide.'

'Nana! This is absolutely awful!'

'And even worse, I think Tom's fed up with me and wants to be rid of me. You see, if I die, Tom will get everything. If it's divorce, he'll only get half. And if he's done it before and got away with it . . .'

Sophie put an arm round her shoulders and pulled her close. 'What does Tom say about all this?'

'How can I talk to him about it?'

'Couldn't you just spill your worries on his shoulder? It might settle your mind.'

'Tell him I think he's trying to kill me? That my guess is he'll make it look like an accident?' Flora was aghast. 'If I died in an accident, he'd have everyone's sympathy. He'd be seen as a kind and loving husband, sadly bereaved. Everybody would believe his story. No, I can't tell him. I'm too scared.'

Sophie and Charlie were staring transfixed. Together they said, 'Nana, I don't think . . .'

Flora could see they didn't believe her. 'I don't want Tom to know I'm saying these things about him. You think it's me going gaga, don't you?'

'No,' Charlie said, but she was afraid it wasn't the truth.

'You say you've never told Tom how you feel,' Sophie said. 'You've pretended there's nothing wrong?'

'That's right. If he thinks I've seen through him, goodness knows what he'll do.'

Sophie saw Charlie swallow hard before he said, 'Sophie, have you got anything to drink? Supper will be ready in fifteen minutes.'

'There's beer in the fridge.'

'Nana doesn't like beer. What about sherry?'

'No, but Mum will have some. Run down and fetch the bottle. She won't mind if it's for Nana.'

Moments later Charlie put a brimming glass in Flora's hand. She let a mouthful roll round her tongue.

The doorbell shrilled.

'You're not expecting visitors?' Flora shrank back quaking at the thought.

Sophie smiled. 'It'll be Ross. He pops over most evenings.'

'No, no . . .' She couldn't face Sophie's friends now.

'I'm sorry. I asked him for supper tonight. I thought there'd be just the two of us.'

'Oh, dear . . .'

'Look, Nana, I want you to talk to him. Ross is a solicitor. He'll help you.'

Ross came in looking as though he'd just got out of the shower. Flora was surprised to see him sweep Sophie up in an affectionate bear hug.

'Good evening, Mrs Waite,' he said. He looked a serious and capable young man.

Sophie said, 'I'm going to tell Ross about your difficulties. He'll be able to advise you.' Flora felt a little embarrassed at that but Sophie was taking matters out of her hands.

'Time to eat,' Charlie said, bringing plates to the table. 'Come on, let's sit up.'

Flora hadn't eaten much all day but she didn't feel hungry. The youngsters were telling Charlie how nice the dinner was but they were all picking at their food. It seemed they were as worried as she was.

Sophie looked up and said, 'Tell us, Nana, how long have you been arguing with Tom?'

'It isn't like that.' Flora found it hard to explain but knew she must try. 'We never argue, never have. We both, for different reasons, want to preserve domestic harmony. In the beginning, I suppose I wanted married bliss. I wanted us both to be happy.'

'Then how long before you realised Tom wasn't . . .'

'Wasn't what I'd supposed? I think I had his measure within four years. He kept asking me for money.'

Sophie said, 'But Mum reckons you're tight with it.'

Flora knew she must have winced, because Ross said quietly, 'Let's say thrifty, shall we?'

Charlie said, 'Is Tom just open-handed? Because if so, you can afford to indulge him and you probably need encouragement to spend. Think of Aunt Mavis.'

Flora was indignant. 'I'm not like Mavis. I'm not a miser. You don't understand.'

Sophie leaned over to top up her sherry glass. 'But we thought you were happy with Tom. Aunt Hilly's positively envious of the way he takes you out and about.'

'It's not like that at all,' Flora said. She felt close to tears. 'He wants a good time for himself. He's aiming to get it and enjoy the best of everything. I've been scared stiff since he tried to throw me over that balcony railing.'

'What did he do to make you think he was going to do that?' Sophie asked.

'He stood behind me with his arms round me and seemed to be lifting me. I screamed and kicked at him until he let me go.'

'Did he admit he meant to throw you over?' Ross asked.

'No. He said he meant it as a hug of joy.'

'He's denied it, then, and you have no proof?'

'That's Tom's way.' Flora gulped at her sherry. 'But I felt so sure at the time.' She didn't know how to convince them. 'I've done some very silly things. He wanted me to put his name on the deeds of the cottage.'

'And you did?' Ross asked.

'Yes. He could talk me into anything.'

'If you've given him half your home, I'm afraid, Mrs Waite, you won't be able to take it back now.'

'I know that.' She sucked ruefully on her lip. 'I've been very foolish. I don't know what can be done about any of it.'

'What else did he persuade you to do?' Ross asked gently.

'When we got married, I made a will in his favour.'

'No problem there. You can make a new will. That will make the present one null and void and you can leave your money to whomever you want. What else?'

'My bank accounts, both current and deposit accounts, I made them joint so he could draw on them, his signature or mine. He's bleeding me dry.'

'You can stop paying money into those accounts. Go to a different bank and open new accounts in your own name, just yours. Then transfer the balances.'

'I can do that?'

'Yes, why not?'

'Tom'll be furious with me.'

'Well, before you do it then, you'd better decide whether you want a divorce or not.'

'I've already made up my mind. I've got to have a divorce.'

'Then I'd start proceedings before he finds out you've moved your money.'

Flora felt ready to make a start. She asked, 'Do you handle divorce cases?'

'I do.' Ross paused to think. 'But for you, I'd recommend my mother. She's the senior partner and I think you'd be more comfortable with someone older than me.'

'Right.'

'There's one thing, Mrs Waite. You should occupy your cottage. If it's empty, Tom could come back and take possession, and then you'd be homeless. You might have difficulty getting him out.'

Flora's fingers pulled at the neckline of her blouse. 'I can't . . .'

Sophie was watching her. 'Melissa and I could come and stay with you, Nana. You'd feel safe if we were there, wouldn't you?'

'No, no. I wouldn't want to put you and the baby at risk.'

'Oh!' Sophie put down her knife and fork. 'Don't worry, we'll find you a bed where you'll feel safe for a few nights.'

'You don't have a guest room here, do you?'

'No. I could strip Daisy's bed downstairs and make it up clean for you, but she'll want to sleep there as soon as Mum comes home. I was wondering about Prue. Would you be happy with her?'

'Isn't Andy living with her?'

Charlie said, 'Actually he's back at home again now. Mum and Dad are away and Jamie's off school, so Andy's come home to look after the business and keep an eye on the kid. He and Amy have joined a cycling club and they're going youth hostelling with them when Dad comes back. They're going to Wales for a fortnight, so you've got a choice. You could move into our guest room or stay with Aunt Prue.'

'Ben and Aunt Hilly work hard.' Sophie was shaking her head. 'You'd be on your own a lot. Wouldn't you be better off with Aunt Prue? Shall I give her a ring and ask if you can come?'

Flora didn't need to think about it. It would be better. She watched Sophie go to the phone. She couldn't hear what was said, but she heard her say, 'Nana, Prue wants a word.'

She got up feeling stiff in every muscle.

'Don't worry,' Sophie added, 'she's more than pleased to have you.'

Prue's rather quavering voice said, 'Flora, you'll be more than welcome. I'll be glad to have your company. Come as soon as you like.'

Flora was comforted. 'I'll be along in a little while,' she said. She went back to the table, but she'd eaten all she could. What she really wanted to do was go to bed.

'I'll run you down to Prue's flat,' Charlie offered. 'Now the babies are in bed, Sophie won't want to go out, and I've got the car outside.'

'Thank you.'

It was only down the road, but Flora was glad not to have to walk. She asked, 'Would you mind taking me home first? I need to get my things.'

'Don't you have enough stuff in that suitcase for tonight?'

'No, it's full of dressy stuff. My new go-out-to-dinner outfits. I want my comfy slippers and some warmer clothes.'

Charlie drove her up to her cottage. Once inside, it was so comfortingly familiar it pulled at her heartstrings. She thought she might even find the strength to stay here, but now Prue was expecting her at her flat.

He carried her suitcase and her bag into Prue's spare bedroom. 'You'll be all right here for a few days, Nana,' he comforted her. 'Don't you worry about Tom.'

*

Sophie and Ross were still sitting over the remains of their meal when Charlie came back with the loaf and the bottle of milk. 'Nana thought I should bring these back to you. They'd only go off if they were left there.'

Ross pushed his chair back. 'Shall I make some coffee?'

'Yes please,' Sophie said. She was still worried about her grandmother. 'Charlie, what d'you reckon to Nana's story? Do you think it's possible that Tom tried to kill her?'

'I've been wondering about that. I don't know. Somehow, I can't see Tom in that light.'

'She's terrified of him. He must have done something . . . unless it's all in her mind.'

'She seemed pretty clear about everything else,' Charlie said. 'Quite calm and rational on the way to Prue's.'

'She wasn't on the way home from the airport. I wish Mum and Dad hadn't gone away. They'd know what to do. Should I tell them?'

'Ring them up, you mean?'

'Dad said he'd ring me every evening. To make sure everything was OK and to have a word with Daisy.'

'He's left it a bit late for that. Unless he rang while you were out.'

'He must have done.'

'Nana will be fine with Prue for a few days. I don't think you should worry my mum and dad. They need these few days' holiday – they don't get much. Don't bring them home early because of Nana. A day or two won't make much difference, will it?'

'No. A few restful days with Prue might be the best thing for her. But what if Tom comes home too?'

399

'That could prove difficult.'

'Very difficult.' Sophie frowned. 'How would she cope with him?'

'Tom's fond of his holidays, isn't he? Perhaps he'll stay on in Italy on his own.'

'I hope so,' she said fervently.

Sophie was cleaning her teeth before going to bed when the phone rang again. She scooted into the living room in her nightdress, thinking it must be her father. She recognised Tom's voice immediately, and it made her heart bounce in her chest.

He said, 'Is that you, Isobel?'

'No, it's Sophie. Mum's away for a few days.'

'Oh! Is Flora with you, Sophie?'

She took a deep breath. How was she to handle this? 'Yes,' she said cautiously. 'She came home this afternoon.'

'Thank goodness. That's a real weight off my mind. She was with me at the hotel last night but she'd gone by the time I woke up. I've been worried stiff. I've had a search gang out looking for her. The Italian police too. I rang your number and Hilary's earlier, twice each, but I couldn't get any reply.'

'I went to Manchester to meet her. She's home safe and sound, Tom.'

'Is she all right?'

Sophie hesitated, 'Yes, but I don't think she's very well. She's not herself.'

'She was a bit like that last night. A bit confused.'

'She'll be better now she's back in familiar surroundings. Don't you worry, Tom.' Sophie wanted to say, *Don't bother coming back early*, but would that be laying it on too thick?

'I can't help worrying,' he said. 'She's never done such a thing before. Going home on her own like that without a word to me.'

'Was it too hot for her there?'

'She didn't say so. It wasn't too sticky. It's almost as though she was desperate about something. I really didn't think she'd be able to manage it, changing her ticket and all that.'

'I wouldn't worry, Tom. She'll be fine now. Really she will.'

Sophie was glad to put the phone down. Tom had sounded genuinely worried, really upset that Nana had left him like that. It seemed a normal reaction for any husband, but what would he do now he knew she was here safe and sound?

She hoped he'd stay and finish the holiday he'd booked, but is that what a normal loving husband would do?

Tom had hung around long enough in Milan airport to work out how he must appear to Flora and her family. He'd be the loving husband almost out of his mind with worry; upset and confused as to why Flora had left him so suddenly.

With that in mind, he tried to phone Isobel and then Hilary to set the right tone, but nobody lifted either phone. He was angry and frustrated on the journey home and had to wait until he reached Manchester before he could try again. He thought he'd played it just right with Sophie.

He'd had too much luggage to think of using public transport to get home from Manchester, so he'd waited a long time for a hire car.

Tom had expected to find Flora at home. Sophie had certainly given him that impression, but nothing had been disturbed in the cottage since Flora had tidied it up before leaving. He was pleased to see his car parked outside exactly where he'd left it. Flora had come home, but clearly she didn't feel like driving yet. Sophie could be ferrying her around.

He'd have liked a cup of tea but there was no milk. He'd have liked an egg and bacon breakfast; there were a few eggs in the fridge but no bacon and no bread. He drove down to the village shop, which opened very early to sell newspapers. He bought one together with some bread, milk and bacon, then went back to the cottage to cook, calm down and think.

Flora seemed to spend more time with Isobel than she did with Hilary, but both her daughters were away. Sophie hadn't said she was staying with her, and now he thought about it they didn't have a spare bedroom to put her up. Hilary did, but then there was old Aunt Prue. She and Flora were pretty close, so probably that's where he'd find her. He hoped Flora wasn't saying too much about what he'd done on that hotel balcony.

Having eaten, he set off to see her. He mustn't hang around too long, had to seem impatient to find out what had happened. He ran his car up the short drive to Prue's front door and pulled on the handbrake.

'Damn Flora.' He was angry with himself for failing to tip her over the balcony. He hadn't expected to make a hash of that, but he was even angrier with Flora for screaming and kicking out at him. He had a terrible bruise on his shin. But he was anxious too, afraid he might have ruined everything. She couldn't possibly know what he'd intended but he must have made her suspicious. What other reason was there for her headlong rush home?

He'd have his work cut out now to settle her down and convince her that he loved her and wouldn't harm a hair on her head. It was not easy to show affection when what he felt was bordering on hate. He must hide his real feelings at any cost, if he was to recover his position. He rang the bell and assumed a suitable expression. He must show regret that he'd hurt her feelings without knowing how, but at the same time she had to understand he was upset too.

Prue answered his knock and took an involuntary step back when she saw him. 'Oh!'

'Prue, can I come in?'

She hesitated, and it gave him the chance to step straight into the hall. 'Is Flora with you? I'm afraid I might have upset her.'

He saw Flora hovering in the kitchen doorway. He strode down the hall with outstretched arms, ready to wrap them round her in a forgiving hug. 'You poor dear, whatever is the matter?'

She took a step back and tried to brush him away. He had to stop this. He threw his arms round her and gave her a loving kiss.

'I was so worried about you. Thank God you're safe and well.'

Sophie had a restless night which gave her plenty of time to think over what her grandmother had told her. She felt oppressed and couldn't decide whether Tom really had tried to kill her or whether it was all in Nana's mind. She wished she knew.

The next morning, Daisy woke her by climbing into bed with her. The sun was already streaming in between the curtains: it was going to be another hot day. Melissa was standing up in her cot and clamouring to be lifted out to join them.

Sophie knew she'd have no peace until she obliged. She threw back the curtains and got back into bed, taking the baby with her, fondling her firm chubby limbs. Melissa had a pretty face with deep green eyes and butter-coloured curls like most of her family. Everybody told her she was a lovely baby. Sophie meant to have a lazy morning and stay there as long as the children would allow.

At twenty-one months Melissa could speak in simple sentences, was playful and good company. She and Daisy rarely left each other alone. Daisy was slim and leggy and moved like quicksilver. They looked very much like sisters.

With the children giggling and climbing all over her, Sophie had soon had enough. She got up and ran the bath, then put them in together with a motley selection of Melissa's plastic toys. For the best part of half an hour they splashed happily, getting Sophie almost as wet as they were. It was a painless way of bathing them and they enjoyed it.

She lifted Daisy out, wrapped her in a towel and was drying her when the phone rang.

She said, 'Just a minute, love,' and turned to Melissa. She couldn't leave her in the bath while she wasn't in the room. She grabbed another towel, plucked her daughter out of the water and ran to the phone with her. It was Prue.

'Help, Sophie, come quick. Tom's here.' She could hear her grandmother's agonised voice in the background. 'Flora's terrified.'

Sophie felt herself buckling at the knees. She didn't feel capable of intervening between Nana and Tom. Until now, their affairs had been none of her business and she didn't really understand the sudden rift between them. But she'd have to go. The two old ladies were frightened of him, and they were asking for her support. If only Dad were here . . .

'I'll be as quick as I can,' she said. 'Daisy, put your slippers on. I want you to come with me.'

'Like this? Where are we going?'

'Aunt Prue's.'

She had to slot Melissa into her car seat; it was a tug of war, because the towel was wrapped too tightly round her legs, but eventually she managed it.

'In here, Daisy.' She lifted her in and dumped her unceremoniously beside the baby.

Sophie threw herself into the driving seat, thankful she was dressed. She set off, throwing up a shower of gravel from the drive. It was only a couple of hundred yards down the road, but already she could see Nana's car parked on Prue's drive. Sophie's tyres screamed as she turned in and drew up alongside. On this hot morning, Tom had left the windows fully open and she saw the keys dangling from the ignition.

'Stay there, Daisy. Be a good girl and look after Melissa for me. I won't be long.'

The front door was open, she shot inside. They were standing in the hall. Prue was wringing her hands while Nana was cringing back beside the grandfather clock. Tom appeared calm and rational.

He said, 'Flora love, what have I done to upset you?'

'I don't want you here,' she spat at him. 'Frightening me and Prue.'

'We can sort this out, Flora. Look, we need to sit down and talk it through.' He tried to steer her into the sitting room but she stood her ground and wouldn't let him near her.

Sophie didn't know what to do, but put her arm round her

grandmother's shoulders to show her support. She could feel her trembling.

'She's scared, Tom. Perhaps if we leave this till later?' At that moment she felt Nana's fear was unfounded. Tom looked every inch the worried husband who was doing his best to help. 'Until she feels better.'

'I don't understand,' Tom said.

'You do,' Flora said. 'This is all an act.'

Sophie felt she wasn't helping much, but she tried to explain to Tom, 'Nana's taken against you. She doesn't want you near her right now. I think you should leave things as they are for a few days until she's feeling better. Prue and I will look after her.' She wondered if they should take her to the doctor.

Tom said, 'Sophie, stay out of this. It has nothing to do with you.'

'Well, I think it has. Nana needs time . . .' She was a frail old lady and so was Prue. They needed help and there was nobody here to give it but herself.

Tom stood his ground. 'Flora . . .'

'Tom.' Sophie drew herself up to her full height. 'I don't think you realise how far this has gone; how strongly Nana feels. She's talking about divorce. Wouldn't it be better if—'

At that moment, Sophie saw Daisy getting out of the car and trying to carry Melissa, who had no shoes on, over the gravel drive. She was too heavy for Daisy and slipping lower at every step. Both had shrugged off their towels and were stark naked. Sophie ran to save her daughter.

CHAPTER TWENTY-EIGHT

TOM COULD feel himself getting hot under the collar. He barked at Flora, 'What's this about divorce? You're not serious?'

'Yes. I am.'

He was getting angry and he mustn't if he was to retrieve his position. He must try again. 'Flora! Not divorce, please. We have a good marriage, over eight years of happiness. I want it to go on. You mean everything to me.'

Sophie was back, straddling one brat on her hip and holding the other by the hand. Both were wrapped in their towels.

Flora said vehemently, 'You tried to throw me off that balcony. You scared the living daylights out of me.'

Tom was shocked. So she'd understood what he was trying to do! Had he made it that obvious? And now Flora was accusing him to his face. He hadn't expected her to have the guts for that.

'Throw you off the balcony? Don't be silly, darling. You know I love you.'

He'd seen her back off many times, lose her nerve when it

came to a confrontation. He'd thought he could rely on her always doing that. But this morning she kept looking at Sophie and seemed to be drawing strength from her. She was standing up ramrod straight, severe and determined. 'No, I don't think you love me. I don't think you ever have. I think you see me as a meal ticket.'

'Darling Flora . . . !'

'I think you're so greedy you'd actually kill me in order to inherit all I've got. You want everything, don't you? If you agreed to a divorce you'd get less.'

Sophie's mouth had dropped open. 'It's true, isn't it? You did try to kill her.'

'No! I'd never hurt her. How can you say such things? How can you think such things of me?' Tom began to think he was wasting his time. 'Sophie, perhaps you're right. Flora isn't well, she isn't thinking straight. We should let things be. When she feels better and comes back . . .'

'I won't be coming back to you,' Flora said. 'I've told you, I want a divorce.'

He felt a sudden rush of anger. 'On what grounds? I've been a good husband to you.'

Sophie's voice wobbled. 'Unreasonable behaviour.' He wished she'd stop putting her oar in.

Flora added, 'I want you to see a solicitor so we can get on with it.'

He shook his head. 'I'm shocked. It's all too sudden. We both need time. You need to rest, and perhaps talk to a counsellor.'

'A counsellor! I understand only too well what you're doing to me and I'm sure it's deliberate. I can't speak to you; can't question anything you do, can't reason or argue. You just throw your arms round me in a huge pretence of affection.

You aim to keep me quiet and get your own way with everything. I'm not having any more of it.' She took a deep breath. 'I don't trust you and I'm too old to cope with you. I want to be left in peace.'

Tom could feel his mask of appeasement falling away. He made a final effort and said between clenched teeth, 'Please come home so we can sort this out.'

'I would like to return to my home but I'm not going to while you're there. I'd like you to pack your things and find somewhere else to live.'

The bitch! Tom knew the bubble he'd blown up round them had finally burst. 'No way,' he burst out. 'The cottage is half mine and you know it. You made it over to me. I've as much right to live there as you have.'

As he turned to go, he almost knocked Sophie off her feet. She was standing behind him looking incredulous.

'You can leave Nana's car here,' she had the cheek to say. 'She'll want to use it when she feels better.'

'I want to use it now,' he said belligerently.

'It's my car,' Flora protested. 'I paid for it.'

Sophie shook herself free from Daisy and took off like the she-devil she was. He saw her rush out to the car, put an arm through the open window and snatch the keys from the ignition.

He could take no more. 'What do you think you're doing? Give me those keys.' He made a grab for them. He meant to get them.

Despite being hampered by Melissa she eluded him. Stepping back, she hurled the keys as hard as she could across Prue's garden. They hit the dividing fence and dropped into the flower border out of sight.

'You bitch!' He leaped at her and swept the baby out of her arms before Sophie realised his intention. The towel fell to the ground.

'Mama! Mama!' Melissa yelled. 'Want to get down. Don't like you. Want my mama.' She was screaming and kicking at him and struggling to get down.

'Don't play silly buggers with me, Sophie. Get those keys this instant. You'll not get your snotty-nosed bastard back until you do.'

Sophie struggled to get the words out. 'I'll call the police.'

'For your information,' Tom said, 'I am the legal owner of this car. I took the precaution of registering it in my name when I took delivery, so you don't have a leg to stand on. You're far too trusting, Flora, you're up on cloud nine. And I'll tell the police I took this little horror away from you, Sophie, because I was worried for her safety. Look at her, stark naked. Now get me those keys, you silly little cow.' He advanced on Sophie. 'If I have to start walking she's coming with me.' Melissa's screams were going through him, and he aimed a slap on her bottom. It made her scream louder and kick even more.

Prue and Daisy were parting the clumps of dahlias. It was Daisy who found the keys and came running back to throw them at his feet. As he bent down, he felt Melissa sink her sharp little teeth deeply into his arm. It almost made him drop her, but she was going to pay for that first.

He bent her over his arm with her chubby pink bottom uppermost. This time he used a heavy hand to give her a good spanking and she squealed like a stuck pig.

'You bully,' Sophie was yelling at him, tugging at her baby and fighting off his blows. Suddenly, he dropped Melissa and

tepped back. She fell on the grass and screamed louder than
ver. Sophie scooped her up and hugged her.

'How dare you? A defenceless baby. You're a bully and a
ouse, and I hope you rot in hell.' She'd lost her rag because
ae'd hit her baby. There was a lot more but her voice was
eing drowned out by Melissa's cries.

With his head held high, Tom got into Flora's car, turned
he key and drove off without another word.

'Come inside and sit down,' Prue said. 'I'll make some tea.
Ve all need it after that.'

Melissa's sobs were racking her body, and tears were
louding Sophie's eyes. She couldn't comfort her baby.

'Oh, Nana,' she wept. 'I've been a fool. I should have
elieved what you told me about Tom. I should have been on
ny guard, not let him anywhere near Lissa.'

'Poor pet.' Flora caressed her blonde curls. 'That was
hild abuse. Tom's a con man, Sophie. Nobody believes he's
vil.'

'I do now.'

'Melissa will be all right. She's quietening down.
'ortunately, she's got a well-cushioned little bottom. He didn't
eally hurt her.'

'He might easily have done.' Sophie hugged her baby
nore closely.

Flora said, 'You were very brave, Sophie. To stand up to
im like that.' She helped Daisy climb up on her knee.

'So were you.'

'I've never stood up to him before, but when I saw you, I
new I mustn't be a coward.'

When Aunt Prue brought the tray of tea into the sitting

room, Sophie said, 'I think I ought to ring Mum and Dad and let them know what's happened.'

'Do it now,' Prue said. 'Use my phone.'

'Dad wrote the hotel number down for me, but I'll have to go home for it.'

'Look it up in the directory,' Prue suggested. 'You know the name of their hotel, don't you?'

It took them ten minutes to get Isobel on the phone and considerably longer to explain what had gone on.

'I'm sorry to interrupt your holiday like this,' Sophie said, 'but Nana's upset and I thought you'd want to know.'

'We do. Dad and I will come home and talk to Nana,' Isobel said. 'It won't take us all that long – there's a good road now. We can be back here in time for dinner tonight.'

'Right,' Sophie said, 'but don't ring off for a moment, Daisy wants a word with you.'

Afterwards, she drove home to dress her charges, feeling a little better. It was early afternoon when Prue rang her to say her parents had arrived and would she come down. By then, the children were neatly dressed and she decided to walk them there.

Sebastian let them in and kissed them all.

'Ben and Hilary wanted to come with us,' he told Sophie, 'but I persuaded them to have a lazy day on the beach. They're leaving this to us, though from what Flora says you already had it sorted.'

That made Sophie feel fully grown up at last.

'Come into the sitting room. We're having a little talk to your nana.'

*

Flora felt calmer and more herself. She was glad she'd had it out with Tom and he'd shown his true colours. Now her family could understand what she was up against.

Isobel was saying, 'Tom's been a con man all along. I had my doubts about him, but he convinced us all that you were happy together.'

'And all the time', Sophie said, 'he was fleecing what he could from you and then tried to kill you. He's a criminal.'

'We should tell the police,' Isobel added.

Flora sighed. 'Would they believe me? A silly old woman, they'd think. Falls for a fellow twenty-one years younger. In return for marriage she lets him share her money, but when the romance fades she regrets it. Now she's looking for revenge and accuses him of trying to kill her.'

'Nana.' Sophie was sympathetic. 'For you, it wasn't like that at all. You believed in him.'

'I've no proof he ever did anything to harm me. It would be his word against mine and you know how good his version is likely to be.'

'All the same,' Seb said, 'we should keep track of him in case he tries to do the same thing with some other poor woman.'

'Yes. I don't think I was the first.'

Flora had been pondering on divorce for some time but to take the first step towards it had seemed a huge leap into the unknown. It had frightened her, but now she knew she couldn't go on living with Tom.

Isobel asked, 'You're happy to have Maureen Salter handle things for you?'

'Yes. I've used her services before. She put Tom's name on my house deeds and drew up my last will.'

'She'll understand why you want to change it when you say you want a divorce too.'

'I want to get on with it as soon as I can. The sooner the better.'

'Maureen might be home this afternoon. Shall I give her a ring? See how soon she can fit you in?'

Flora was glad to let Isobel take over. She spoke on the phone for a few minutes. 'Maureen says why don't you come over now and talk about it over a cup of tea.'

Flora felt a sudden shaft of panic. In her eyes marriage was an indissoluble state. 'I'd like you to come with me.'

She could see Isobel would prefer not to. She was looking at Sebastian.

'Will I do, Nana?' Sophie asked. 'Mum and Dad want to get back to Anglesey.'

Flora wasn't quite sure. Sophie was really very young.

'She managed Tom well enough this morning, didn't she?' Sebastian was smiling at her.

'Of course.'

'It's just that we don't know how long this will take, Mum.' Isobel was apologetic.

'You can leave the babies with me, Sophie,' Prue said. 'I'll look after them while you're away.'

'Melissa's dozed off,' Sophie said, laying her down in the corner of the settee. 'So it's just Daisy to amuse. Right, Nana, let's walk over then.'

Flora said as they crossed the road, 'You know Mrs Salter well, don't you?'

Sophie smiled. 'Very well. She's Mum's friend and Ross' mother. She's very kind, Nana.'

Maureen Salter greeted them at her front door. She said

I thought we could do this over tea in the garden. Come through this way.'

She was dressed in sandals and a cotton print dress. Even so, there was an air of efficiency about her. She said, 'I've brought a pen and pad with me, so I can jot essential facts down.' She seated them at a wooden table on a shady part of the patio.

Sophie said, 'Your garden looks lovely. Cool and inviting on a hot day like this.'

Flora was not at ease. She had to force herself to go through the story of her marriage to Tom again.

'It is a divorce you want rather than a legal separation?' she was asked.

'A divorce,' Flora confirmed without hesitation. With the error she'd felt on that balcony still fresh in her mind, she wanted the break to be complete.

'Right, a divorce then.' Mrs Salter was scribbling on the pad.

'And a new will,' Flora said. 'I want Tom cut out but I haven't decided who should inherit what I have left.' Perhaps Sophie? She was trying to help her and she had a daughter to bring up. But what about Charlie and Andy? And there was Jamie to think of, and little Daisy.

'Think about it and come and see me in my office next week,' Maureen suggested.

'I had Tom's name put on the deeds of my cottage,' Flora said.

'I'm afraid . . .'

'You did warn me about that at the time, but', she sighed, 'it seemed the right thing to do then.'

Maureen said, 'If you don't quite believe how his wife died, have you ever thought of checking the records?'

'No. Is that possible?'

'It might be if you can give me her full name, date of birth and of death. I'll need her address too.'

Flora had seen a Liverpool address on some of Tom's documents. It had also been on his passport and driving licence, and though he'd had it altered to his lodging and later her cottage, she was able to remember it. But Grace's date of birth defeated her. She thought Tom had said Grace had been fifty-one and that she'd died in 1974.

'I'll also check whether your husband has a criminal record. It might be relevant to find that out.'

To Flora, it felt as though she was admitting publicly that she'd been a complete fool. It was comforting to have Sophie sitting beside her putting in an occasional helpful comment.

Mrs Salter confirmed that she'd have to pay over to Tom one half of the value of her cottage, or alternatively it could be put up for sale and the proceeds divided.

'Or', 'she said, 'he could buy the other half from you and continue to live there.'

'He wouldn't be able to,' Flora said.

'Well, no need to make a decision here and now, but you should think about it and get an estate agent to put a value on it. Be sure to tell him it's a divorce case not a straight sale.'

When Sophie walked her back to Prue's house, Flora was relieved to have started proceedings. She smiled. 'So much easier to do it with a friend that way.' Really, all she wanted was to live the rest of her life in peace.

The shock of Tom's duplicity and knowing how bad Nana's marriage had been hit Sophie again that night. She lay awake remembering how he'd used Melissa to force them to give up the keys of Nana's car. It had gone through her to see him wallop her daughter's bottom and brought home to her that she and Nana had both made the same mistake. They'd loved a man who wasn't worthy of their devotion and had been badly let down.

Everybody was telling her how strong she'd been but Tom still had the upper hand. He'd taken Nana's car and was living in her house. The next morning, she telephoned Ross, who told her Tom had the legal right to do both those things and nothing could be done about it.

When the garden shop closed the next day, Sophie strolled up with the children to see Charlie and Andy. They both needed to understand what had been going on. Nana was going to need a lot of help to get through her divorce.

On Friday morning, Nana telephoned Sophie. 'Now Tom's come home and looks as though he's going to stay, I need to get my clothes and personal things from the cottage. Would you come with me?'

'Of course,' Sophie said, but her stomach churned at the thought.

'I'm sorry to involve you again, but I can't go alone and I'll need a car to bring everything back to Prue's flat. She's offered to look after the children. You won't want to take them near Tom again.'

'Shall I come now?'

'Yes please.'

Sophie drove down and handed the children over to Prue. She was following Nana down the hall when she hesitated. 'Had we better let Tom know we're coming and why?' she asked. Her grandmother looked tense.

'Yes,' Prue said.

Sophie went to the phone. She could hear it ringing and ringing in the cottage but he didn't pick it up. 'I think he could be out,' she said. 'Come on, we'll go anyway. You've got your keys?'

When they could see the Mercedes wasn't parked outside, Sophie heard her nana's sigh of relief. 'He's definitely out.'

Sophie parked her Mini as near the gate as she could get it and opened the boot. 'Let's take everything that's yours, Nana. You mightn't get another chance.' She guessed Nana would never have dared take her box of jewellery and her best Doulton tea service if Tom had been watching her.

Ross often invited Sophie to cinema and theatre shows or to have a meal out, and with willing resident babysitters she loved to go. She repaid him by asking him to her flat for meals. Occasionally on a Saturday evening, she'd invite Charlie and Judith too to make up a foursome.

With all the older members of the family away on holiday Sophie couldn't go out, so at the beginning of the week she'd asked the three of them round tonight. She found looking after two children left her little time for cooking and it was a struggle to get everything ready.

She had prepared coq au vin and appetising scents had been coming from her oven all afternoon. A rich gooey dessert was setting in the fridge.

Nana had said, 'Sophie, you're growing more like me and Hilary. We've always loved cooking for our friends and family.'

By seven o'clock, Sophie had put Melissa down for the night and Daisy was bathed and in her dressing gown. She'd

418

given her a duster and got her to help straighten up the living room. They were setting the table when the doorbell rang. Daisy ran to answer it.

Charlie was slouching on the doorstep. 'Am I too early? I need to take refuge from Andy.'

'Come in,' Sophie told him. 'You're always welcome here, but you'll have to help. Daisy's promised to be a good girl and go straight to sleep if you'll read her some of *Sinbad the Sailor*.'

'OK. Come on, flower, get yourself into bed first.'

It gave Sophie time to change her dress and put on a bit of make-up.

When Charlie came creeping out of the children's room, she asked, 'You've not had a row with Andy?'

'More a difference of opinion. He thinks I should be running the garden shop.'

'I thought you were doing that?'

'I have today and I do at weekends, but he means permanently. He's nagging just like Dad. Ruby didn't turn up for work yesterday and said she won't be coming in on Monday, so Andy had to spend all his time in the shop and didn't get round to doing other things.'

'He has Jamie to help, though? '

'Yes, but he says Fridays can be busy. Ruby isn't much good anyway; she isn't pulling her weight. I'll be there tomorrow and I can't see why he can't manage on Monday. All I did was complain about my frozen cakes job and he had a real go at me, said I should join Dad in the business and settle down.'

'Charlie, you change jobs too often. You're not looking for another?'

'No, the job's a bore but I like the hours. Every weekend off. I wouldn't get that if I worked for Dad.'

'You'd benefit in other ways and you'd find it more interesting.'

'Don't you start, Sophie. Whose side are you on?'

'Yours.'

'Doesn't sound like it. You know how I've worked at getting these O levels. I've got four that are halfway decent. Your dad says if I get another two I'd maybe be able to train for something better, a career. You made me promise to stick at it, didn't you? Well I have, so why should I give up now and go into Dad's business?'

'Charlie, you don't have to give up studying, but you need to know what you're aiming for.'

'Not Dad's business. Andy doesn't want to work in it, not permanently. He's aiming to be an engineer. He and Amy have got it all sorted. They're going to get married as soon as they're earning enough.'

'You're jealous.'

'Yes, I am. Andy's got everything going for him.'

'It's going to take him years to achieve it.'

'But he's got it all planned. He sticks to his plans until they work out.' Charlie looked angry and frustrated.

'Do you and Judith want to get married?'

'I can't afford it, can I?' Charlie sounded disgruntled. 'That's the other problem with my job, it doesn't pay enough. Yes, I'd love to get married if I could.'

Sophie was setting out wine glasses on the table.

'By the way,' he said. 'I've brought some wine. What's to eat?'

'Chicken.'

'Oh, dear. I've brought red.'

'That's great, Charlie, it's coq au vin. Open it, and let's have a glass now. You sound as though you need it.'

A few minutes later Sophie swirled the wine round her glass. 'I suppose you're going to tell me Judith earns more than you do.'

'Not yet, but she will. She's got her plans laid out and she'll stick to them.'

'Charlie, you're your own worst enemy.'

'Why?'

'You've got terrible hang-ups.'

'I haven't.'

'Charlie, you won't consider working for your father, yet you've always been interested in horticulture, ever since you were a boy.'

'I've got to stick to—'

'You've never been keen on schoolwork but you love growing things. You're really into roses. Somebody needs to talk sense into you.'

'And you're going to do that? You can talk. You've got hang-ups too.'

'Bollocks. If you joined the family business your problems would be over. Why are you scared of working for your dad?'

He was shaking his head. 'I'm not.'

'What's stopping you then? Judith and Ross work in their family business. You spend most of your time off in the garden centre; you're not bored when you're there, are you?'

'Nobody wants to work in the shop at weekends. I do it for the extra cash Dad gives me.'

'Sure you do, but your dad would love you to take some responsibility. He really wants you there full time helping to run the business, not just doing the jobs he can't find anybody else to do.'

'I know. He's been on my back about it for years.'

'There you are then. Why not?'

He shrugged. 'I don't know. Once I was in, there'd be no escape, and I suppose I feel I might let him down, that he'd be disappointed in me yet again.'

'For heaven's sake, Charlie! You didn't let them down at the Dog and Gun, did you? They loved your cooking and wanted you to stay. You know far more about growing things and you're interested in gardening and all that. Your dad needs your help. His business has grown and grown. Get your head straight, Charlie. Make up your mind what you really want.'

Sophie's dining room overlooked the front drive. 'Here's Ross and Judith coming now.' She got up to let them in.

Charlie caught at her hand as she passed him. 'OK, you're right, but I'm right about you having hang-ups too.'

'Don't be daft.'

'Why don't you marry Ross then? He's dying to tie all the knots he can. For heaven's sake, you must know you can trust him.'

Sophie's guests were replete and sitting round her table drinking coffee. She looked across at Ross. His handsome face was animated as he talked about growing peaches to Charlie. He sensed her gaze and looked up to give her a warm smile.

'It's time we went.' Judith prodded Charlie towards the sink. 'Let's wash up. We can't leave it all to Sophie. She's already cooked for us.'

The four of them cleared away and washed up together. Sophie had enjoyed the evening. Charlie took Judith away first and she saw them out.

Ross was stretched out on her settee when she went back

to her living room. He patted the cushions beside him and when she sat down he put an arm round her shoulders and murmured, 'Am I invited to stay the night again?'

'Of course – while Dad's still away.'

He came over on many nights but was always up and away at dawn before the household woke up.

Ross said, 'When your parents are here and I have to creep in and out I feel like a criminal. I know your father doesn't approve of my being here at night.' He sighed. 'I'd like to get married and make it all open and above board. I want us to share a home. I want to be with you all the time.'

Sophie could feel his warm breath on her neck. She did love him. He was making her tingle with longing.

'I've promised I'll wait, and I will,' he whispered, lifting her up and carrying her into her bedroom. 'But I keep hoping you'll change your mind.'

CHAPTER TWENTY-NINE

BEN HAD ENJOYED his few days' holiday on Anglesey. Both he and Hilary looked suntanned and rested. It had whetted their appetite to have a full two weeks somewhere abroad – he hoped that would be possible in the future. He could afford it and they really needed a longer rest, but he had nobody willing and able to run the business for that length of time.

Still, the short break had done Hilly good. They'd had a good time and done everything together. He hadn't allowed himself to think of his business; instead he'd concentrated on her. He felt they were closer as a result.

His garden centre was not doing so well at the minute, but five days away wasn't going to send it down the drain. The shop would be fine over the weekend under Charlie's management. Andy and Jamie would do their best on the weekdays, but Ruby wasn't going to be much help. He'd have to look for somebody else to run the shop. She was never going to be any good.

At Sebastian's suggestion, they had a good lunch at a pub on the way home.

'So the girls won't have to turn round and cook this evening,' he'd said.

Isobel had laughed. 'We'll be all right. Sophie's offered to cook a meal for us tonight.'

'I don't know what to expect,' Hilary said. 'But the boys will have to be fed. Perhaps, Ben, we should take them out for a meal as a reward for standing in for you?'

They didn't rush home, but stopped for an hour or so to look round the marble church at Bodelwyddan and then drove up the hill to the castle. It seemed sensible to make the most of their short holiday.

Ben was pleased to find Charlie cooking chicken marengo for their supper. One of the frozen cakes from his factory was thawing out on the kitchen table.

'For afters,' he said. 'It's a bit lopsided, as you can see. They sell them off as seconds in the staff shop, but it'll taste the same.'

'Are they any good?' Hilary asked. Ben knew she and her mother believed homemade cake was the only sort worth eating.

'They have to be.' Charlie was indignant. 'They wouldn't sell otherwise, would they? You'll love it.'

Ben saw that cake, coated with lush cream, as the reason Charlie wouldn't work for him. He wasn't prepared to like it.

'I'll go over to the shop and see how they're getting on,' he said. 'Is everything all right?'

'Sit down and have this cup of tea I've made,' Charlie said. 'Andy and Jamie will be over as soon as they've locked up. You can hear all about it then.'

'Has something happened?' Possible disasters were already running through his mind.

'Well, you know the worst. Nana wants a divorce. She's very upset.'

'Yes, of course.' They'd talked about nothing else since Isobel and Seb had come home to see her. Charlie wanted to bring his mother up to date on that, while Ben expected to be brought up to speed on how his business had fared.

Andy and Jamie came in, but apart from telling him the sum of today's takings at the shop, they too went on talking about Tom and Nana.

Ben decided he'd walk round the garden centre after supper, which Charlie was about ready to dish up. Working in restaurants had taught him how to serve a meal. He'd organised wine and a starter of prawns.

Ben thought the chicken marengo was excellent, as good as anything they'd had in the hotel while they were away. Hilary too was full of praise. 'To what do we owe so much effort on your part?' she asked.

'There's something I want,' he said, suddenly serious.

'What?' Ben was guessing he wanted help to buy a car. He'd talked about getting one of his own recently.

'I want to come and work for you, Dad. Join the family firm. Is the job still on offer?'

Ben couldn't believe his ears. He gave a nervous laugh. 'Of course. Nothing I want more.'

Hilly was beaming at them both. 'I thought you didn't want to.'

'I'm getting nowhere on my own. I'm being stupid,' Charlie said. 'I know I am. I always manage to do the wrong thing.'

'Not always,' Ben said. 'I really need you. The business is getting a bit much for me. I'd given up hope that you'd come in. I'm made up, Charlie, I really am.' He leaped to his feet to give Charlie a hug.

'I could never understand', Hilly was all smiles, 'why you didn't jump at the chance when you first left school.'

'Neither could I.' Ben felt as though a load had been lifted off his back. 'You were always about the place, asking questions, and I knew you were interested in what I was doing. Still, you'll come in now, and that's what matters.'

Flora felt guilty because by the time Andy and Amy came back from their cycling holiday she was well established in his room at Prue's house. 'I'm so sorry,' she said.

'Don't worry, Nana. Mum was expecting me back home. I stayed at Aunt Prue's so she wouldn't be on her own, but you can be with her all day. You can be real company for her.'

Flora was glad, because she felt settled with Prue. They seemed to need each other. As Tom was hanging on to her car, she was glad of Andy's offer to take them to the supermarket on Saturdays and for a little run out in his car on Sunday afternoons.

'He's a lovely lad.' Prue was loud in his praise.

Because she didn't want to come face to face with Tom, Flora didn't go to play bridge in the church hall that first week. Prue went and reported that Tom wasn't there either and persuaded Flora to go with her the following week. It helped to make her life seem more normal.

She felt able to keep further appointments with Maureen at her office in Chester. They were arranged for first thing in the morning so that Ross could drive her in. Flora found the Salter family deeply sympathetic and ready to help in every way they could. Maureen told her what she'd found out about Tom.

'He's had three convictions for obtaining money by false pretences: the first in 1964, the second in 1969 and a third in 1975, for which he was sentenced to six months in prison. What he did was to visit areas where the property was owner-occupied. He'd knock on the doors of elderly women and tell them that he'd been repairing a roof in the same road and could see slates slipping on theirs. He'd offer to do a quick repair before rain started to leak through.'

'Even when there was nothing the matter with their roofs?' Flora found that shocking.

'There didn't need to be anything the matter. He'd put a ladder in position and spend a few minutes up it admiring the view. Then he'd ring their doorbell again and present a hefty bill.'

'That's exactly the sort of thing I could see him doing. Getting others to give him money . . .'

'That's what he did to you, Flora.'

Flora could feel her head spinning. 'If he was sentenced to six months in prison in 1975, he must have been released shortly before I met him.' She'd told Maureen the full story. 'He'd had time to think of other ways to prey on elderly women.' Flora took in a jagged breath. 'By then he wanted one silly old fool he could batten on permanently. There's no fool like an old one, is there?'

'Don't be hard on yourself. You weren't the first to fall for his silver tongue. He's a con man.'

'Don't I know it? He's perfected the art. Did you find out how his first wife died?'

'Yes.' Mrs Salter looked through her file. 'Yes, here we are.

Ross did the searches into this. Her age was not what you supposed.'

She started to read. '"On 5 March 1974, Mrs Grace Mary Waite was found to have committed suicide by means of carbon monoxide poisoning." That's breathing in engine fumes from a car.'

Flora said, 'He did tell me that.'

'Did he tell you she was fifty-nine years of age?'

'Oh my goodness, no! What would that make him? About twenty years younger?'

'Seventeen, I think.'

Flora felt sick. 'Then she was definitely a meal ticket too?'

'It looks like it.'

'I feel I've had a lucky escape.' Flora swallowed hard.

'It's better if you look at it like that. I'm afraid Tom won't vacate your cottage until you buy back what you gave him.'

'Will he be able to claim more from me?' Flora was afraid he might.

'We'll fight that,' Maureen said. 'After all, he has served a prison sentence for battening on women.'

Thinking over what she'd heard gave Flora more sleepless nights. She'd expected divorce to be an unpleasant experience and it was. She told herself that at her age she should have had more sense than to marry Tom.

Sophie kept telling herself she was more than content with her lot in life. She was enjoying her course and the new friends she'd made at university. Bringing up Melissa was giving her great satisfaction, and most of all she loved Ross.

As the months went on, they were spending more and more time together, and she began to see she'd made a mistake. Having a lover wasn't enough. She wanted Ross here with her all the time, and she wanted to know he always would be.

One night when she was lying in his arms, she whispered, 'I'm having second thoughts. About waiting to get married. I mean, there's no point, is there?'

A smile lit up Ross's face. 'None at all. I'm delighted to hear you say that.'

'Let's do it then.'

'Yes, let's. When?'

'The way I feel now, the sooner the better.'

Ross laughed. 'How long will you need to get everything ready? And what sort of wedding do you want? A big one with all the trimmings?'

'No,' Sophie said. 'The simpler the better.'

'Good, that's what I'd like. In church, though. My mother would be dead against the register office.'

'So would my nana. Could we be ready by the long summer break so we can fit in a honeymoon?'

'We could try. Where are we going to live? Shall we look for that cottage we talked about?'

'No, Ross, we need to stay here. That's one reason I wanted to put it off. Mum looks after Melissa. We need her close at hand while I'm at uni.'

'Of course. What am I thinking of? Anyway, if all I have to do is to move in here, it makes it easy.'

Both their families were delighted at the news. Aunt Hilly offered to put on the wedding breakfast at her house. Ross's parents suggested they put up a marquee in their garden and have it there.

The following Sunday, Sophie and Ross were having lunch

with her parents when her father asked, 'Would you like us to book a hotel?'

Sophie shook her head and said, 'Ross and I . . . well, we've talked it over and we don't want any fuss. Would it be possible to have it here at home? It needn't be too much work for you, Mum, if we got caterers in.'

'We'll both help,' Ross added.

'It depends how many guests you're going to have,' Isobel said cautiously. 'But possibly . . .'

'Just our two families and one or two people from the office.'

'I'd like to ask two girls I know at university.'

'Rory and Mrs Grant,' her father added.

'You've got lovely big rooms here. The sitting room . . .'

Isobel said, 'If it's a fine day, we could use the patio and the garden so there'd be plenty of room, but if it's raining . . .'

'We can open up the main stairs and use my flat too.' Sophie was getting excited. 'That would give us more than enough space.'

'Let's walk down to the vicarage after lunch,' Ross said, 'and see when the vicar can marry us. We need to fix that first.'

They found the church was booked for weddings on every weekend throughout the summer and autumn, but a weekday would suit them just as well. They fixed on eleven o'clock on 1 August.

Sophie felt she was being swept off her feet in a joyous rush to make the arrangements. The following day, she went down into town between lectures and found a dress she really liked. It was ballerina length in her favourite green and of soft filmy material. She was torn between a hat of green straw and a hair ornament of laurel leaves and small daisies. She decided to wear her long hair up and twist the laurel leaves and daisies round the bun on top of her head.

She'd meant Melissa to be her only attendant, but as Daisy wheedled to be a bridesmaid she gave in. The following Saturday, her mother took her and the two little girls into town. They chose matching cream dresses trimmed with green for them.

The next time Sophie saw Charlie, he told her Ross had asked him to be his best man. 'I was right,' he said, 'you did have a hang-up about getting married.'

She frowned. 'It's a big decision.'

'Sophie, you and Ross have been as good as married for the last year or so. It's just a question of tying the knot.'

'OK.' She laughed. 'I was as bad as you, but I'm straightened out now.'

Sophie's wedding day came in the middle of a settled spell of hot weather. The guest list had grown and was still growing. Two days beforehand, Sebastian felt confident enough to order twelve small white tables and forty-eight matching chairs to put up on the back lawn.

Ross and Judith carried down some flowering pot plants from their own house, and Charlie brought many more from the garden centre. The Broadbent house and garden were a riot of flowers.

Sophie elected to walk down to the church on Sebastian's arm. Her mother had taken the two children earlier and was waiting for them in the church porch. Ross was standing ramrod straight in his smart grey suit at the front of the church and turned to smile at her as she walked down the aisle towards him. She had no doubt at all that marriage to him was what she wanted.

A LABOUR OF LOVE

Most of their guests strolled back to the house after the wedding photographs had been taken. A waiter, provided by the caterers, was serving glasses of sherry at the door. The buffet set out on the dining table looked luxurious and tasted delicious. Sophie wanted to remember for ever the sunlit lawn, the banks of flowers and the pleasure of having all her family and friends around her.

At five o'clock in the afternoon, Ross's father brought his car to their door. He was going to drive them to Manchester airport to catch the plane for their honeymoon in the Algarve. Charlie and Andy just had time to tie an old boot and some tin cans and balloons to the rear bumper, and chalk *Just Married* on the polished paintwork.

Sitting beside Sophie on the back seat, Ross felt for her hand, while she cuddled Melissa on her other side. She felt she had everything in the world she wanted.

EPILOGUE

SOPHIE ACHIEVED her degree a year later. When she started her teaching practice, she knew she'd chosen the right career and thought long and hard about what sort of school she would like to teach in.

Once she was qualified, she accepted a post teaching English language and literature at Rydal Street Comprehensive.

It came as something of a shock to find she was responsible for teaching several children struggling with dyslexia. Having seen at first hand the difficulties Charlie and his brothers had faced, she felt great empathy for them. She turned to her father for advice.

'Dad,' she said, 'how best can I help them? There's a remedial class in the school but no extra resources for those with dyslexia.'

He smiled. 'Didn't they tell you it was now called Specific Learning Difficulty?'

'Yes, but that's such a mouthful, who's going to call it that? Is it easier for them now than it was for Charlie and Andy?'

'No, Sophie, in many ways it's harder. In those years any help they got was largely up to the parents. You and Isobel taught them, so it cost Ben and Aunt Hilly nothing.'

'They gave us very generous gifts for Christmas and birthdays.'

'Yes, but nowadays, for parents who have to pay for special lessons, it's become very expensive.'

'But surely great strides have been made on how best to teach these children? Bring me up to date on that. Dyslexia didn't get much of a mention in my training.'

'It didn't get any at all in mine, and it's teachers of my generation who are running the schools now.'

'Go on, Dad. What if the child really needs specialist teaching?'

'Well, the school budget can't be stretched to cover everything. The problem is, if you or the remedial teacher can't provide the teaching that's needed, it doesn't come automatically. Getting specialist teaching boils down to getting money allotted to each individual child. First the child must be diagnosed as dyslexic and his educational needs assessed. If they can't be met in the school, a statement must be applied for. That has money attached to it for bespoke help. The child may be given a special needs placement at a fee-paying school. Even a boarding school.'

Sophie frowned. 'That must cost a lot.'

'A statement can be for as much as twelve to fifteen thousand pounds a year. Is there any wonder lots of parents are agitating to get their dyslexic children assessed and then statemented? Some Local Education Authorities do a lot and others virtually nothing. Unfortunately, they're all perennially strapped for cash and reluctant to grant statements. They resist giving them for as long as possible. Rarely does a child in my school get one until he's about to move to secondary school.'

'Who applies for these assessments and statements? The school or the parents?'

'Either can, but if the school applies then the Education Authority pays for it. Sometimes they're refused. Once so many children are statemented, it becomes almost impossible to get more. For parents seeking help for their children, it's a horrendous situation and you'll have lots of them coming in pleading for your help.'

'I already have.'

'And you'll know how badly help is needed, but unless we all keep pushing for it, the child may get nothing extra.'

Sophie thought sadly of how hard Andy and Charlie had struggled even with extra tuition. 'There's a girl in my form called Heather Groves. She's twelve but undersized for her age and severely dyslexic. She's had remedial lessons but no special help up to now. I could weep when I think of her.'

She heard her father's heavy sigh. 'What's really needed is an automatic test to pick out the children who are likely to have reading problems when they're coming into primary school. They're tested for all sorts of other difficulties, so it ought to be possible to add that. Early identification and intervention are crucial. Think of Jamie.'

'But what can I do to help them now?' Sophie asked. 'Some are in desperate need.'

'For those still awaiting their statements, the best thing to do is to divide the dyslexics from the others, and give them the sort of tuition you gave Charlie. That's what I do in my school. You've just got to do the best you can for them, love.'

Flora felt Tom deliberately kept her waiting for her divorce. He was slow to find himself a solicitor and dragged the process out for more than two years. Being without a home of her own, Flora felt like a refugee. Prue made her welcome, and without her company and the help of her daughters and their families she didn't know how she'd have got through those years.

As it was, her nerves were shot to pieces and she was losing weight after years of trying to keep it down. She felt mentally and physically under par. She hated having a chance encounter with Tom in the village, and did her best to avoid him.

Tom seemed happy to live alone in the comfort of her cottage. Not only did he refuse to move until she'd bought back the half share she'd given him, but he demanded maintenance from her too. Flora found Maureen Salter provided the professional support she needed. She was trying to reduce the amount he was asking for but negotiating with him was proving difficult.

Most people in the village took against Tom, but it didn't seem to bother him. He ate most of his meals at the Dog and Gun and bought his newspapers and other supplies from the village shop.

One by one her family tried to persuade her to pay Tom off to get him out of her house. Hilary and Isobel first offered and then insisted on contributing towards the expense.

'I don't want you to feel short of money,' Isobel told her, 'not when you were so generous to me with the money Aunt Mavis left you.'

For Flora, to give Tom more money really went against the grain. It was Sophie and Ross who convinced her she had no alternative and the sooner she did it the sooner she'd be able to move back into her cottage.

When he moved out, Tom left the place in a mess. Flora

had to have the damage repaired, and then she had it painted and decorated throughout. She wanted to get rid of everything that reminded her of Tom, and changed her double bed for a single divan. Isobel and Sophie helped her spring clean and choose some new carpets.

Flora was glad to move back in and delighted when at Christmas her family clubbed together to buy her a red Mini like Sophie's so she could get about. At the court hearing Tom's request for maintenance was not granted as he was still of working age while she was not. When at last her divorce came through, Flora felt only utter relief that it was all over.

She was free, but it took her a long time to get herself together again. She made an effort to go out and about more, but felt a little lonely. She'd grown used to having a permanent companion and didn't find living alone suited her.

Ben was concerned that Prue was getting too old to cope on her own, and had asked her to move in with him and Hilary. Flora often walked down to Prue's flat to have a cup of tea with her and pass the time of day. She took her shopping and occasionally to the cinema, but Prue could no longer walk up to her cottage though she was still good company and able to play a skilful hand of bridge.

Flora thought about it for some time before she said, 'Prue, I certainly won't want to get married again, and it can be a little lonely on my own. Would you like to move in with me?'

Prue had to be persuaded. 'I'm getting too old to do very much. I'm afraid I'll be a burden to you.'

'No,' Flora said. 'I'd love to have you with me. I like looking after people. I always have, and I want to have somebody to cook for and eat with.'

'Then I'd be very grateful. Everything in this flat reminds

me of Primmy. I won't sell it. Perhaps I should offer it to Andy?'

One morning, Hilary was basting a joint of beef for a big family Sunday lunch when Andy came in with Amy, who looked somewhat embarrassed.

'We're bringing our wedding plans forward,' Andy told her. 'We're going to get married next month.'

Hilary had understood their wedding was still two years off, and she was so used to seeing Andy planning for the years ahead and patiently plodding on until he'd achieved his goal that it came as a shock.

She slid the joint back in the oven and shut the door. 'Two years does seem a long time to wait,' she said. 'What's made you change your minds?'

A pink flush was running up Amy's cheeks. 'I find myself unexpectedly pregnant,' she said.

'Oh!' Hilary hardly knew what to say. Her generation still saw that as a misfortune, but the 1960s, the pill and modern thinking had changed that. They were doing the right thing.

Andy said, 'Our wedding plans will have to be scaled down too.'

'We've decided it'll be in the register office,' Amy added.

'And Mum, would it be possible for us to have the reception here at home?'

'Well, yes,' Hilary agreed. 'Probably that would be best, but not too many guests. It'll be October so we'll have to hold it indoors.'

'Thanks, Mum. And will you help us tell the family?'

'Of course.' She smiled. 'They won't have long to get used to the idea. We'll do it at lunch today.'

Hilary knew her family would rally round the young couple. They gave surprised but eager congratulations. Charlie offered to make the wedding cake and Prue undertook to provide the champagne.

Hilary thought the wedding went off very well, with no sense of rush. They all had a lovely day to remember. The bridal pair took a package holiday to Crete for their honeymoon and were both thrilled to be able to rent Prue's flat when they returned and have a home of their own.

Charlie's wedding took eighteen months in the planning. It was to take place four years after Sophie's and almost three years after Andy's. The Salters wanted a big wedding for their only daughter.

Charlie and Judith took out a joint mortgage and chose their first home, an eighteenth-century cottage behind the church. Much of the furniture and household equipment they'd need was given as wedding presents. The sale was completed three weeks before the wedding, which gave them time to get everything ready to live there as soon as they came back from their honeymoon.

Maureen took Judith shopping for the wedding dress and Charlie was told to hire a morning suit. The Salters worked on their large garden in the preceding weeks and it looked manicured on the big day. A marquee was erected there, though they hoped for, and got, a warm summer's day.

A horse and carriage had been arranged to take the bride and her father to the church and bring her and her groom home, though they lived even nearer than the Broadbents.

On the day itself, Sophie saw a very smart landau pulled by a pair of matched grey horses waiting at her in-laws' front door as she and her family walked past to the church in their finery.

Inside it felt cool, and there was an air of expectancy. Charlie, waiting at the front of the church, kept looking round anxiously. He made a polished and handsome bridegroom.

Dearest Charlie. He'd always been her good friend. Judith could be as proud of him as she was. Andy, his best man, looked distinguished in his morning dress, as all the men did. He was now the proud father of a two-year-old toddler. She could hear Peter's piping voice as he spoke to Amy, who was expecting her second child next month.

Sophie had been delighted when Andy had achieved his degree and started his career with the county council as a civil engineer. He'd beaten his dyslexia by working at his difficulties with dogged determination. Charlie had suffered most: he was the one who'd under-achieved from an early age. He had changed jobs too often, never finding one which satisfied him until he went in with his father.

That had proved to be the making of him. Not only did he hold his head higher, but his shoulders had broadened. Ben was delighted with the way he threw himself into the business and took on more than his fair share of the work. Charlie had found a special interest in roses and had added to the varieties they grew for sale. With his energy and enthusiasm, the business had become more profitable than it had ever been.

Jamie was sitting in front of her. He'd been much luckier, because as a result of his older brothers' problems he'd had extra help from the age of five. He was now nineteen years old and following in Andy's footsteps working for an engineering degree.

She appraised the back view of Aunt Hilly's new straw hat.

She was sitting very close to Ben. Mum had said she was glad to see Hilly looking so much happier, but why shouldn't she be? She'd now written a whole string of novels and was quite well known.

Sophie felt the congregation stir as the bride arrived at the church door. She turned to take a peep as the cadence of the music changed. Judith was coming down the aisle on her father's arm looking stunningly beautiful in her frothy white gown. She was attended by four child bridesmaids dressed in identical dresses of lavender silk: two small Salter cousins, together with Daisy and Melissa. Melissa smiled at her as she came past holding up Judith's train. She was growing up, and at six and a half all her baby chubbiness had gone.

Ross had been cradling Sophie's hand in his, and now he squeezed it gently. 'She's a beautiful child,' he whispered. 'I shall be well pleased if the next one turns out half as well.'

Sophie was now three months pregnant and couldn't be happier about it. She was really looking forward to having Ross's baby. She was still teaching at Rydal Street school and finding it fulfilling in a way she knew her mother and grandmother never had.

It had become almost her mission to help the dyslexic children in any way she could. There were days when it broke her heart to see them gritting their teeth and struggling to do what she asked of them. She couldn't give it up just yet, and she wanted to return to it after her maternity leave.

Sophie felt the tears start to her eyes. Weddings were emotional occasions. It was lovely to have an extravagant day of feast and celebration like this, but she hoped Charlie and Judith would have something more. That they'd have the ultimate blessing: a long and happy life together.